PRAISE FOR NEODYMIUM EXODUS

"The fascinating characters matched with inventive biological details makes this an adventure that's sure to enthrall."

—*Publisher's Weekly*

NEODYMIUM EXODUS

The Neodymium Chronicles

JEN FINELLI, MD

WFP
WordFire Press

EBook ISBN: 978-1-68057-186-8
Trade Paperback ISBN: 978-1-68057-185-1
Hardcover ISBN: 978-1-68057-187-5
Casebind ISBN: 978-1-68057-288-9
Library of Congress Control Number: 2021937822

Cover design by Janet McDonald
Cover artwork images by Adobe Stock
Kevin J. Anderson, Art Director
Published by
WordFire Press, LLC
PO Box 1840
Monument CO 80132
Kevin J. Anderson & Rebecca Moesta, Publishers
WordFire Press eBook Edition 2021
WordFire Press Trade Paperback Edition 2021
WordFire Press Hardcover Edition 2021
Printed in the USA

Join our WordFire Press Readers Group for
sneak previews, updates, new projects, and giveaways.
Sign up at wordfirepress.com

DEDICATION

Dedicated to Hashem Rapha.
Thank you for never letting go.

CHAPTER ONE

Lem

EVERYONE IN THE ICE CREAM PARLOR FROZE WHEN LEM BENZARAN grinned.

Everyone except the meat-man: the literal lizard in a suit, consummate businessman who dealt in favors and pounds of flesh —he didn't notice. His ruby-scaled claw left a streak of something like sweat on the plastic parlor table as he leaned over and cooed at Lem's little sister. Lem stirred the dregs of her milkshake, her eyes never leaving her glass: in its reflection she watched the string of drool drip down onto the monster's business suit. Lem was listening … listening to his heavy breathing.

"She ain't for sale, Skins," Lem said. She said it for everyone in the ice cream parlor to hear. She wasn't a big fan of warnings herself, but the people who ran her life required them.

The businessman's green hair puffed in offense; his slit eyes gleamed in the sunlight filtering through the wide storefront windows. "Mind yourself, *witch*," he sneered.

Witch, huh? Lucky for him he didn't call her crazy.

A loud slurp silenced the whole parlor as Lem finished off her shake, savoring the cool sweet cream on her bitter tongue.

Four seconds later Lem had chopped down the businessman like an overgrown holly bush. No one interrupted. No one helped, either. The space-lemur policeman in the corner stared at the phone in his paws, ears perked as he pretended not to see; the Wonderfrog server behind the counter tapped his bulging fingertips on his skull as if truly worried about dessert.

Lem tightened her grip on the meat-man's wrist, spitting through her teeth as she ground his face harder into the plastic table. "Whatever I am, everyone in here knows you're selling little girls to the grays, and one day I'll prove it and get Officer Scritch there off his duff for a change." Her voice dropped to a husky whisper. "But the day you talk to my sister again? Officer Scritch won't be lookin' for you. Won't *be* a you to find."

Meat-man grunted. He got it. A'ight. Lem straightened, wiping her brow on the sleeve of her rough brown civvies. She yanked the guy to his feet. He wheezed hard—she whacked him on the back. "Go, get outta here. See a healer about that asthma."

The ruby-scaled businessman stumbled between the cafe tables and out the wooden door, huffing and crying. Lem smirked after him—man, if only all problems could get solved like this. If they'd just let her off her leash, she'd turn the entire town upside down.

Lem's wristband lit up with an incoming message; she groaned. See, this, this was exactly the problem! *I didn't violate any treaties this time, man, just roughed him up a little.* How'd Captain Rana catch her so fast anyway?

"When rules matter more than people," Lem grumbled. She waved at her little sister: "Hey, Juju. We gotta go."

Juju slid out from the booth, eyes wide in her mahogany face as she licked the purple lechichi fruit topping her frothy cream-shake. Her hair, strangely blondish for its tight, kinked texture, stuck out like a halo as she trotted head down, mouth shut and eyes open while Lem guided her, hand on this warm, bony little shoulder, out of the cool shadows of the parlor into the tropical heat of the Luna-Guetala sun. Good little girl. Pretty little girl—exactly what the meat-markets wanted alive and the grays wanted dead.

Lem's stomach knotted as she glanced at the message on her

wristband again, then scanned the crowded black-earth street for someone on their phone or transmission screen. Who'd reported her? Man, she was always in trouble, but this was record time from beating up the perv to the "in-my-office-now."

The civilians stared back. Lem slowed her swagger to pretend she didn't care, shoulders back and chest out. Her military issue "civilian clothes" looked like she'd raided a tablecloth factory, and people liked to pretend there wasn't a war on.

That wasn't why they were staring, though.

Witch.

It stung, you know. When people you protected feared you for the one thing that made life sweet.

Lem counted her tense paces along the blistering street, and took a deep breath of relief when she and her sister finally slipped into the shade of the jungle beyond the town. This, the soft velum of the leaves against her skin, the playful vines tugging at her ankles, the gentle give of the earth under her soles, this was home. Her toes longed to sprout claws and clamber up the bark of the nearest trees to hide from it all.

But she was human, and she had a human family now. Gone were the days of freedom in the treetops, hunting peacock-feathered guinea pigs and wrestling with her space-lemur brother. Lem set her jaw and unchained her sparrow-shaped air-rider from its roost, checking the camouflage engine for sabotage, small explosives, tracking devices …

"Why'd he call you a witch?" little Juju asked, shifting from one foot to another with a little ice cream slurp as Lem knelt to check the air-rider's undercarriage.

"Because I talk to an invisible guy," Lem said. "Same reason the grays want me dead."

"Well I noticed something," Juju said. Lem's fingers dug into a groove under her seat, tapping the gritty metal as she felt …

"What'd you notice, sweetie?"

"Lieutenant Seria and Dr. Patty—they don't talk to invisible people. But the Growen still want them dead, too."

Lem grinned. "Yeah, the grays kill anyone who don't like to be told what to do." She didn't bother to tell her sister that sometimes the other freedom fighters struggled to keep "witch" off their tongues, too. Juju didn't need politics yet. Lem hefted her up over the swooped wings onto the long bike-seat of the air-rider and swung herself up behind her.

"I wish we could go north to the city next time," Juju sighed. "I heard they got pretty birds, and glass airships like gems."

"You know that's Growen territory. We'd get shot."

"Still. I still *wish*."

Lem laughed gently. "Quit tryin' to get me in trouble with your wishing." She revved up the engine—

Whoosh! Lem's stomach jumped backwards and Juju squealed as the air-rider zipped off into the woods. Lem leaned into the wind, *oh*, she delighted in the speed, the chill on her cheeks, the warmth of the little back pressed against her chest, the pure unfiltered joy—!

"I don't care if they say you're crazy!" Juju yelled into the wind. "You're not!"

"I know!" Lem called back, laughing as the air-rider soared towards the treetops and then dove again—oh, a smile, in the ripples of air around her! Invisible fingertips brushed her forehead. "Njande, where are you?" Lem whispered.

Me? Her invisible friend's laughter tickled in the wind and flapping jungle leaves, and something like words, but not quite, flooded Lem from her spine to her fingertips. *Me?* said the something. *I Am Now. Where are you?*

"I'm here on the double-planet, in the woods," Lem whispered back. "You know that, right? You mean, where in time, or something?" She didn't catch his answer. "Man, I can't hear you. Hey, what if I could race into your dimension? Go so fast I just bust through this thin reality, open a barrier in space time ..."

I love your thoughts, Njandejara said. *Look! I got you a surprise. Left, as you come around this bangla tree.*

Lem hurtled around the trunk and looked—and leaned waaay

4

back to slow the air-rider down hard. "Whoa!" she mouthed. She tapped her sister's shoulder in lit-eyed excitement, pointed left, and then let that finger dart to her lips to signal silence.

They'd have missed it if they hadn't been looking for it. A grove of thin trees rose like a fence between the sisters and a sunlit clearing, and in that clearing grazed an enormous, long-necked beast as long as a small skyship. Live butterflies covered every inch of its hide; if you knew what you were looking at, you could squint between the butterflies' wings and just barely make out green and yellow flowers growing from the creature's nose to its long tail. It was a reptile, a Behemoth—the tree-trunk-limbed giraffe-like jungle monster, sparkling like living gold with all those dainty wings.

The girls watched for a few minutes before the thing slunk off into a darker grove.

"Wow, I never saw one of those before!" Juju clapped as they started off again.

"They're shy," Lem smiled, crossing her arms across her chest. "Even when I lived out here I only saw one or two. Cool, huh?" To Njande, she mouthed: "*Thank you*—I wouldn't have seen that."

I know! I saw you coming, and checked in the Back Then, and there I set up an airfield that pushed Tomorrow's storm south, so it broke early and drove the Behemoth up here!

"Wait … you saying you went back in time just to set up a view for me?"

Well, and a sister moment. She'll remember this one for a while.

"No, that's not the part I'm fuzzy on—it's the 'back then' stuff."

Don't worry about Back Then. I Am Now, remember? Where are you?

"Now, too, I guess."

Drink it in.

Yeah.

Yeah, this Now, racing through the cool purple, red, green canopy with her sister, no bombs, no screams, no one shooting at her—this was as good as it got. Screw command, and the other soldiers, and the explanations and standing at attention that made her so nervous she got straight up *silly*—screw them all. This was the Now she was fighting to defend: her planet, her sister, her invisible best friend.

Maybe she could talk Captain Rana down to just two weeks scrubbing the slop chute after meals.

CHAPTER TWO

Cadet Commander Jei Bereens

I DIDN'T MEAN TO BE A JERK. I JUST SEE TOO MUCH DEATH TO TAKE any chances. When Captain Rana called me to his office, I figured that long overdue promotion was coming—finally time to toss the cadet commander bars and start enjoying lieutenant stripes a full year ahead of the other cadets my age.

I was training when my wristband lit up. My boots impacted hard earth as I leapt from the tree, slamming my mace down in front of me. I tasted blood in my sweat. One, two—another shove of polarized charge down towards the earth, and I leapt again, flipping towards the forest canopy. Okay, three, four, spin, smack my mace there, there, hit targets five and six painted on the side of the tree—just two more reps, and I'd fix the tactical weakness that had cost me one of my rescuees last week.

I switched hands; two more targets on the way down met two bulls-eyes from my pistol, and I landed again, this time light as a leaf, tapping my bitten lip with my finger to check the blood as I squinted through the salt in my eyes. The jungle here was as humid as the inside of a Burburan worm's mouth.

I knew from experience.

The birds and day-lizards sung and squawked in the hidden crevasses of the trunks above; the sunlight seemed to poke holes in the leaves far, far away up there. The burnt marks and strikes on my makeshift training ground confirmed that I'd fixed my error, but I needed at least thirty more reps to solidify that change.

Shouts of anger put all my hair on end.

I ran towards the sound of children, sorting their voices out from the jungle chitters, the tap-crunch of my light step weaving around the trees, and the distant hum of motors from the nearby fort. I floated up a trunk at the edge of the clearing by the fort's white wall, forcing my heart rate to slow its foolish panic.

No danger, just stupid kids. Four preteens in our typical Frelsi fighter uniform circled a smaller boy, who hugged himself, cringing as they yelled and pointed. One of the larger boys walked around the periphery with a large rod, whacking the earth over and over as he snarled at the terrified kid in the middle. He reminded me of someone. Not in a good way.

I landed beside them. They scared easily and all drew the small regulation pistols they'd been assigned—until they recognized me.

Then they jumped to attention.

"What did he do?" I asked, leaning on my staff without acknowledging their respect. I nodded towards the kid they'd trapped in the middle.

"Uh, sir," the big kid with the stick turned a bit red. "It's nothing, sir."

"Not nothing!" a squirrely looking human snapped, pointing an accusing finger into the circle. "He's why the grays killed my parents. They must have sensed him because he's Contaminated, and the whole group got caught!"

Contaminated—someone who speaks to an invisible interdimensional energy being. Usually one in particular, since our universe only had contact with a few and most of them hated matter-creatures like us. It was a common rumor that some of the Growen commanders could "sense" Contaminated people.

I broke a cinna-coke twig off the neighboring tree and put it in my mouth. "Were you there?" I asked the accuser as I chewed.

"No, but he just admitted he's Contaminated!"

"That's a gray term. Don't use it." I didn't bother to yell. They'd seen me throw adults ten meters with just my finger. "Who or what Shrimpy here talks to makes no difference to your parents now. The Growen did it. Blame them."

The sharp flavors of the bark tingled the roof of my mouth as I turned away from the clenched teeth of the orphan to gaze at the trembling "Contaminated" kid. I didn't ask about what had happened to him "last year," about the people killed in front of him, about the lie that when something happens *to* you it's *because* of you, and I knew he hadn't answered all the pestering questions of his grieving, angry classmates. You can't, not for a long time. He had a future full of nightmares and sweaty memories ahead of him.

I knew that from experience, too.

"You're all wearing Frelsi uniform. You'll be soldiers when you're regulation fighting age." They had no choice; the Growen would slaughter kids, too, if we didn't learn to fight back. "Act like soldiers, not slobbering rabid dogs. You," I nodded at the poor Contaminated kid. "Walk with me."

He trotted after me in silence. I laid my hand on the seamless pearl wall of the fort, and it recognized my DNA, and then the kid's, and slurped us in.

The dam on the kid's snot and tears nearly broke. I listened to his heavy breathing as he tried to choke everything down. "They're jerks," he said finally.

"When your parents die, you'll look for someone to blame, too," I said.

He said nothing then. I looked at my watch again. Five minutes. I had ten to get to Rana's office. I didn't stop to change—the bioactive compound in my undershirt had wicked away all the sweat and grossness while I walked. It cost more, but some sentient species communicated by smell, and I preferred not to make my presence known on stealth missions.

"It was Stygge Diebol," the boy whispered.

I stiffened. My skin crawled, and my mouth dried. "I'm listening."

"It was seconds. He killed everyone like you could blink, and—everyone was burnt and crushed," he swallowed, and his gaze grew distant. "There was blood and somebody's arm and this crunchy sound and—"

I knelt down and stopped him with my hand on his chest. He was breathing fast, his heart fluttering against my palm and his pupils constricted in terror. "Stop," I said.

"I can't," he whispered.

"Think of the color green," I said. "What kinds of things are green?"

"Leaves, sometimes," he said.

"What else?"

"That's—that's all the green, I can't, I—"

"Some birds are green, right?"

"Yes. And some singing lizards." His breathing slowed down. "The big ones."

"Right. You like singing lizards?"

He nodded. An uncertain smile flickered on the edge of his lip. "Njande made the lizards for me, I think," he whispered.

I tried to smile back. I didn't talk about interdimensionals. It was too personal, painful, even, something that brought back *once upon a time* with excruciating happiness and confusing pain, because back in the wooden cage, guarded by Growen soldiers under the command of Bricandor himself, I too had a secret friend.

"Okay," I said. I patted the kid's back awkwardly as I stood. Panic attack over. Kid needed to leave; I never reported late, and wouldn't now. I nudged him toward the secret entrance to the children's barracks with my palm. He trotted, then paused:

"Should I report them?" he asked.

"Up to you. If they bother you again send them to me," I said, then slipped myself through the silvery wall of the neighboring command building.

Alright. Promotion. With a grown man's rank at only seventeen years old I'd finally have the leverage to make a difference around here. I checked the crease in my pants, sharpened the folds of my sleeves over my biceps, and walked in to give my Wonderfrog captain a crisp salute and even crisper smile.

Captain Rana's return salute was more like he was batting away annoying flies, and Wonderfrogs never bat away flies. He pointed a ball-tipped blue-green finger behind me.

I turned to see another uniformed Frelsi cadet, an Enforcer one rank below me. My smile evaporated like the mists back home.

It was troublemaker Lem Benzaran.

"I don't think I know her, sir," I lied.

"Yeah, look, Captain, whatever it is, I didn't do it," she said.

"Right?" I said; I could see why she'd think she was in trouble. "Muddy uniform, half-jacked salute—" Her elbow knocked a glass of water off the shelf. I caught it in mid-air. "Are we even in the same military?"

"I dunno, I'm in a military, you talkin' like you're in a fashion show."

"Be quiet, be quiet, be quiet," Rana grumbled. He rose on all fours off the large cushion by the compuwall, dropped his lion-sized girth right between us, and snatched the glass out of my hand to splash on his face. "You! And you. Especially you," he pointed at each of us twice. "You need to work together, together, together now."

I opened my mouth to protes—

"With all due respect," she jumped in ahead of me, suddenly polite as a princess. "Sir, you assigned me to my first human trafficking case this morning, remember, to help return that little boy to his family, right, and I really got a good thing going, I think I know the perp, I promise, just gimme a little—"

Rana gurgled. Both Benzaran and I tightened our stances. "Lem-Lem, I'm aware," Rana said, referring to her by doubling her first name for some reason. "Aware, see? We're small and spread thin, thin and small. Don't have the luxury of always doing one thing at a time. Seria will work the case till you get back. It's still yours yours yours." He paused, his large, wide-mouthed face inches from her chin. "Have you ever heard of a Stygge?" he asked.

Diebol. My breath boiled in my throat; I had to force it down.

"Stygge—that the new drink they got down on the town?" Benzaran joked. "Think I spilled that on my civvies this morning."

"I know them, sir," I growled, interrupting her shenanigans.

"A buzz about them within the Growen," Rana went on. "A buzz like flies. They do things … things like you two. Electrics. Magnetics. Fires. From their fingertips. Fingertips!" He leaned back on his haunches and flexed his webbed forefingers.

"Like Bricandor's Twelve?" Lem narrowed her eyes. "I thought those were just rumors Growen soldiers tell to make their commanders sound badass."

Rumors? My left hand clenched over the old burn in my palm; I repressed a bitter grin.

"One Stygge can destroy your whole unit," Rana went on. "A swipe of the hand, all gone. One swipe. Except maybe you and Bereens here because, well. Fancy fingers. Fancy fancy!" Rana extended claws from his own webbed ball-tips as he talked. "But almost nonexistent, yes?" He turned back to his cushion, undulating across the floor on all fours like a sidewinder, and tapped the compuwall. "Until now."

Pictures flickered across the wall beside us, images of the large rec center in the middle of our barracks area. A shadowy figure poised atop it, orbs levitating around its head.

"There was an attempted bombing last week at the edge of the fort," Rana said. "Surveillance caught these images before he ripped out the cameras with an electromagnetic pull."

"Was that the 'training accident' we all know wasn't training?" Benzaran scowled. "Where Colonel Win got hurt?"

"Reported and stopped by your little brothers, actually," Rana nodded at her; her eyebrows lifted. "A story for later. The attacker left a fur sample on the roof of the recreation center. Computer says Bichank land-walrus, walrus, Bichank: the boys say Stygge powers, powers, powers. We have no idea why he went for the rec center, instead of a more tactical area."

"That's where the moon refugees are staying!" Lem declared. "The Biouk space-lemurs who came in last week? My cousins."

I rolled my eyes and said nothing at this other human calling space-lemurs family. I only had a glancing acquaintance with her, but I'd overheard her in the mess hall multiple times talking about how much she missed space-lemur life. I always wanted to tell her to suck it up—we all missed something or someone the Growen had taken.

"Perhaps the moon refugees are the target of the bombing. Perhaps not. More concerning, concerning concerning …" Rana's long tongue flickered out across his eyeball. "It sounds like there are more like him, more reports of electromagnetic people than ever before, across the Growen ranks and attacks in all our bases in the Contested Zone. This is the first time we've caught one on camera. You track him—" Rana wiggled his fingers. "You find him—" He did it again. "You find out how the Growen suddenly have so many Stygges."

Yes. This made me so hungry. There was no way my old cell-mate wasn't involved here, and I wanted back at him like I wanted a world that allowed cinnamon pie for breakfast every day. "When do we leave, sir?" I asked.

"Immediately, right away, go," he said, stomping his big, webbed hind-foot with a *plat* on the floor suddenly. "You'll find your mission leads uploaded to your wristbands. Dismissed. Dismissed! Goodbye." Two webbed hands platted on Lem's back and shoved her out the wall. I didn't need a push. My old Stygge friend had a thing or two coming. My wristband beeped, and I was already reading mission details as I stalked down the hallway. I was known for this, for knowing—I stole and devoured Growen tech read-outs with the same hunger some people my age memorized Burburan soap operas on the lightchannels.

"I'll see you at the air-rider station in twenty," I shot to Benzaran without looking up from my reading. "Bring your mace."

She stumbled after me with a scowl. "Excuse me, Mr. Orders, but—"

"Oh, and Lem-Lem?" Rana called after us, shoving his face through the polymerwall.

"Sir?" Lem turned back. I paused, too.

Rana's big eyes blinked with another twinkle of amusement. "Two weeks scrubbing out the slop chute when you get back."

"Yes sir." Benzaran laughed with a sigh of relief, as if punishment was an inside joke.

I shook my head and left. Whatever she'd done, it wasn't my business, and I didn't care.

But she had better not screw up this mission. We had a galaxy to save.

Early is on time, on time is late, and late is unacceptable.

Lem Benzaran was late. She came *strolling* towards the air-rider station surrounded by kids. I stood back, arms crossed, resisting the urge to tap my foot on the stone floor. The big parking station hummed with technicians chattering, engine parts clattering, and air-riders taking off through the huge garage door that opened towards the jungle. Kids' voices weren't uncommon here, but these were little kids, not even old enough to break a man's finger. Thirteen is regulation fighting age when you live in a world where adults will kill you for sneezing at them wrong ... maybe *one* of these kids was thirteen.

"Bye JE, bye Jake—Juju, Joseph, J'miah, Jaynes, and," Lem stopped to kiss the head of a little baby carried in the arms of the maybe thirteen-year-old boy. "Bye Jackie. Love you."

She swung herself up on the air-rider beside mine. "You coming?" she asked—as if she'd been waiting on *me*—and took off, out of the garage and into the jungle.

"Whoa, hey!" I zipped after her as we plunged into the hot air outside. "Let up just a second!"

I didn't know then that she wasn't one to "let up."

CHAPTER THREE

Lem Benzaran

CADET COMMANDER BEREENS YELLED SOMETHING; LEM YANKED her air-rider to a halt, leaning way, way back to hear.

The change in balance stopped Lem's air-rider so suddenly Bereens zipped past her. The guy only had two expressions: the "you kick puppies" disgust, and the chewing-his-lip concentration. He had the former on now as he flew his bike back around.

"What?" Lem asked.

"Why were you late?" he asked.

"I had to make a stop first," she said. She'd gone to make sure the lieutenant taking over her human trafficking case knew everything she knew about the missing little boy—they had to get him home safe. And then she'd gone to say goodbye to the new refugees from the moon: the Biouk space-lemurs who'd lost their villages last week. She didn't know which reason to tell Bereens, or how much detail to give before he'd get annoyed.

He didn't seem to care about the actual reason anyway. "We need to see what we're working with," he snapped. "They say you have electromagnetic abilities. I haven't seen them."

He hopped off his air-rider, and then threw up his hand. His air-rider slid away from him as if pushed by an invisible force.

"Em-push," he said.

Lem sighed. She knew *what* he was doing: thinking *out*, channeling the negative chlorine charges in minuscule loops in his neurons to repulse like-polarities like an electromagnet. She just didn't know *how* he was doing it, and it frustrated her to no end because she had tried over and over on her own, any time she could get the gym alone.

But Lem covered up the embarrassed anxiety with a wide, goofy grin. "I'd rather 'em-hance,'" she cooed.

"Stop making up words," he said.

"It's accurate! My inner magnet *enhances* my strikes, speeds up my moves—you know, gets me an extra push to jump higher, things like that." She refrained from shrinking inside her tunic.

"Yes, I'm sure *jumping* will be useful against a Stygge who can read your mind, or blow up rocks with his face."

"Yeah, well, my special power is not being a jerk." She stuck her tongue out at him and pushed her palms onto her smooth compuscreen to speed up her air-rider; she swiped *up* to zoom up over Bereens's head, and then swiped down again to cut down in front of him, taking the lead.

Lem felt weird about this one, this mission—it struck too close to home. She'd seen refugees come to Fort Jehu from all over the galaxy, including humans from Alpino like Bereens, but when her cousins from the moon fled here last week, it felt … different. She didn't know everything about the moon-Biouks, but she remembered planet-Biouk life fondly, with hidden woven orb-huts in the trees, and raw fish, and roasted root-bread, and fruit-flavored meats, and innocent furry cuddles in the community beds … and she remembered visiting the moon with her adopted family as a child, and making codes with her cousins' accents, and playing with her cousins' wooden carvings. Biouk life was safe. Sacred. The Growen hadn't targeted Biouks before—but now, they'd wiped out their home on the moon, and then what—sent someone to bomb the last refugees, at the rec center? Would they come for all Biouks? For … Cinta?

"Enough," Lem growled, gritting her teeth. Maybe grumpy-face's powers could work for something. "Hey, can't you track people?" she yelled back.

"No!"

"Why not?"

"I can't."

"Why, though?" Lem pressed, getting annoyed now. She hated it when people refused to explain themselves, like you had to take them on faith or something. "Hellooo—"

He caught up to her with an exasperated whoosh of hot air. "Em-tracking requires not only transmitting electromagnetic pulses, which I can do, but also receiving them back into the forebrain with extreme precision. It's like echolocation, but with sodium channels. I just don't have that ability."

"Maybe with both of us, then," Lem shrugged. "One could be like the receiver, and the other the transmitter."

"Or we could use our brains like normal people and add up what we know."

"*Psh*, what do you know about tracking forest people?" Lem laughed.

"Enough."

"How?"

"Well, I found and rescued the moon refugees," he said.

Lem stared at him. Really? *He* was the teenager who'd brought the moon tribe here? Her belly warmed a bit, like on the day her human mom complimented her Biouk-style meat stew. "That's cool, man."

Bereens didn't respond to the compliment. Lem took gentle, almost shy advantage of the pause: "Well, maybe we could try em-tracking together, for like … the future," she said.

Bereens gave her the puppy-kicking face and rode off.

Lem grumbled wordlessly as she hunched into herself and followed him. Shrinking, shrinking, shrinking … she wanted to shrink away and disappear. *Njande …*

I don't want you to disappear, little one, he smiled, tickling her neurons. She sighed as the soft tingle, like the rumble of a cat's purr, rolled over her scalp and almost made her giggle.

You make me happy, she said to him. *But* ... With her next breath, her chest constricted. She found herself driving her knuckles in clenched fists into the compuscreen in front of her, leaning forward and speeding up. She couldn't get over this jerk's stupid —*Everyone says impossible too early. Impossible is more important to his kind of people than saving my kind. Njande, don't you*—

He interrupted her internal rant with the flicker of a dew-drop rolling over her screen, glittering like a jewel.

I delight in you, he said.

Lem's chest relaxed. Njande made all the stupid worth it.

BEREENS

The parrots screamed overhead like the nagging in the back of my mind as I leaned into the wind, ducking my head down against the leathery purple leaves smacking me. Agh, I felt guilty. I wanted this way too much.

Lem's air-rider pulled up beside mine as I slowed my breathing to clear my head. *Focus. Just catch a bomber.*

An extraordinary, Stygge-like bomber.

No big deal.

I glanced back to see the enormous translucent wall around our base shrink in the distance, disappearing into the forest like a pearl in a kelp-patch. I'd seen a pearl once, in a seaweed garden on Burbura, before my mother died.

The Bichank settlement lay about an hour's ride to the south. Lem and I drove in relative quiet, if you can describe anyone or anything on Luna-Guetala as quiet. Some bird or singing lizard was always saying something, and every now and then Lem would speculate about how we'd manage em-tracking. I didn't answer much. The damn air-rider didn't go fast enough.

Like Rana said, this sounded bigger than just one Bichank bomber with powers. The increase in Growen soldiers with electromagnetic abilities had to be intentional—like an experiment, or a series of gifted kidnappings. Maybe hunting this bomber would lead us to an army of Stygge super-soldiers. If we did find such a "special force," I had a private bet we'd find my old prison-pal.

Jared Diebol.

He was such a lonely kid back then, during my captivity—we were both freaks. Hyperactive sodium channels that somehow didn't give us seizures, weirdly-shaped action potentials that sent skyrocketing signals through the prison doctor's EEG: we could use our heads like radios and our limbs like magnets. *You're like me!* That's all you need to form a friendship when you're eight.

"Whoa!" Lem leaned back suddenly, trying to stop her air-rider too quickly. It careened sideways towards me, her bike's rusty wing jutting towards my chest like a sword—

I slid my hands *up* across my windshield, jerking my air-rider toward the tree-tops to dodge.

I stabilized a few feet above her head; she slid to a stop centimeters from a wide, drooping, many-trunked bangla tree. My heartbeat punched through my temples and my older model air-rider sputtered like it wanted to stall.

"What the bloodseas was that?!" I roared down at her.

"Look over there!" She laughed. She was laughing. Laughing! Like almost running me over was nothing more than a silly-looking misstep in a video game or something. "Look!"

"There's nothing over there! What the bloodseas is up with your driving?!"

"Look, I'm sorry about your heart attack, old man," she said. "What are you, seventeen? Your life expectancy's only like twenty-three in Growen territory anyway."

"All the more reason not to drive like an idiot and die early!"

"Nah, you gotta live it up while you can. Look, that's the entrance to the Bichank settlement." She pointed into what looked to me like a thicker tangle of forest expanding into nowhere.

I narrowed my eyes at the landscape, then glared back at her.

"You gotta start from the skyline and look down," she said. "I been trying for like two years to get into a Bichank grove. You better bet I know it when I see it."

I sighed, and like she said I looked at the flickering distant blue sky above the trees, and then traced my gaze down …

It was dizzying. For a moment I saw through the illusion to a tree-high hedge of jagged poisonous thorns, posts for a gate, the entrance to a maze—but then I blinked and saw only forest, with tree trunks stretching into nowhere.

"Come on! We might have to fight the gatekeepers to get in." Her teeth flashed in the afternoon sun as she spoke; her eyes sparkled as she tied her air-rider to the Bangla tree she'd almost hit. This was fun to her!

With a wordless grumble I dismounted, swinging off my bike seat to leap the two-story distance to the ground; I softened my landing with a levitative em-push. Leaves exploded around me in a wet shower as my boots hit earth. I left my air-rider floating—with the engine complaining like that after the stall, I feared if I shut it off it wouldn't start again.

I wanted to scold her still. But Lem Benzaran was quiet now, dark eyes wide and ready, hand on her belt where her neodymium mace hung compacted like a short bamboo staff, and now was not the time for scolding.

She took casual but halting steps, zigzagging into the shadows of what seemed like an ordinary orchard of thin, short fruit trees. We paused in front of a half-fallen lechichi tree resting its trunk on an enormous weed with soft, emerald bark. Lem stepped under the arch of the angled trunk; I followed.

The color change was startling. No more bright Luna-Guetala hues, the purples and reds and violent jades I'd gotten so used to during my sojourn here—suddenly two high walls of stark grey-brown wicker blocked us on all sides. I looked behind us, expecting to see through the archway into the jungle again, but saw only subdued browns, maples, and cold ivories. Rock, and thorn.

"I don't understand what I'm seeing," I murmured.

"I know, isn't it wild?" Lem inspected the four walls around us, her head angling and darting like a curious parrot looking itself in the mirror. "Bichanks see ultraviolet light, so this shyte looks way less confusing to them. There's shadows, patterns, edges we're missing to see the entrance in the wall."

Ultraviolet? I swiped the surface of my wristband to change its light settings to the dark-light. I'd installed it to study ship design manuals for species with different eyesight than my own.

"Move over," I said. She stepped aside with a smirk—she didn't like my tone, I guess, but well, now was not the time. I held up the dark-light in my wristband and waved it across the wall of thorns.

"Ah." Lem pointed. Perspective, depth, it was all off. Half of the left wall wasn't a wall at all, but a tunnel whose sides converged in the far back to form another weird illusion. You wouldn't know without touching—and, you know, poisoning yourself on the jagged spikes.

"I don't understand how this is put together," I said, stepping into the tunnel now illuminated with new perspective from my UV light. "This is so—other. In a way where … I want more, somehow."

"Yeah? That's what talking to an interdimensional feels like," Lem hinted, glancing over her shoulder for my reaction.

I gave none. I remembered the cage, and my invisible friend. It wasn't dissociation: I was still there, in my body, awake while they screamed at me to tell them my parents' location, or how to bypass the newest Frelsi bunker doors, or a hundred other things I didn't know. But whenever anyone *hurt* me a still, small voice from another dimension would lead me into these anesthetized pockets in my mind, playrooms full of stories, pictures, and colorful lights. He showed me a green button on the wall of the innermost playroom, and if I pressed it, sudden euphoria erased all pain. Dr. Pattie believes I somehow consciously triggered my pituitary to flood my veins with enkephalins, the human body's home-made super-morphine. I don't know. I've often tried to find that button again on my own, and never could—maybe Njande knows I'd never leave it if I did.

I licked my lips, focused on the color green, and blinked away the memories. Here and now, guided by the shadows from the UV light, we wove through the thorn tunnel without a single prick to our soft human skin … and finally stepped through the other side of the defense system into light, clarity, and a wide open street under towering crystalline rock structures. Petrified trees towered like skyscrapers; ragged pale-pink stone homes evoked Behemoth limbs; everywhere bathed in the beiges and greys you expect only in the highest mountain ranges. Cool air washed the sweat off our faces.

The street was barren.

Lem darted ahead of me from house to house, peering through the translucent stone walls and open doorways. I followed, my breath bated, as if sound would summon the ghosts the town had lost.

No signs of struggle. Heavy stone cups, lacquer plates, oak utensils, all lay out on the tables waiting for their bygone families to sit down and eat. Warm rock baths carved into the floors of the homes and sides of the streets lay dry, or stagnant. Nests in bedroom corners were neat and tidy, lined with coarse furs that once sheltered tired Bichank couples after marital spats and tough days at work and troubling in-laws … the nests held no one now.

My ears rang. No birds chattered. No stupid lizards sang. Even Lem bit her lip, wide-eyed and silent. All was silent except for the creak of a few old rocking beds under an awning on the far street corner.

There, four elderly Bichank land-walruses rested their thick legs and polished their trunks, heads held high and heavy jaws set under their grey and tan muzzles as they stared into empty space. Noble? Resigned? Despairing?

Lem and I trotted over to them. My hands hovered by my belt for my mace on the right, and my flayer-gun on the left.

They stared at us with tired eyes. Their long, furry dinosaur-tails drooped by their sides, and their paunches—normally firm, round and proud on a healthy Bichank—sagged.

They had seen paradise lost.

I couldn't shake the eerie dead feeling of the Bichank settlement, even after we'd left and the lively lizard-songs and purple leaves bathed my senses in vibrant cacophony again.

Guetala Bichanks would never leave their elderly behind. Never. Lem's whisper repeated in my head.

The space-lemur language Lem spoke was similar enough to Bichank that we'd gotten a decent lead. But it was an odd one, and a bit disturbing. When we showed the old Bichanks our brief video feed of the bomber, and explained the description the boys gave of him, they scowled, or cringed, or in some form or another demanded we put him away. Okl, they called him: one of their own who could levitate, who wanted to unite them, he'd said, break their civilization out of antiquity into a globalized, no, *galacticized* new age.

The elderly Bichank said that last bit with sneers. *He seduced everyone with his witchcraft power, and everyone wanted to go*, they said. Over the span of a month, they said, Bichanks began developing electromagnetic powers suddenly, and during that time, Okl pushed negotiations with the Growen.

And then the Growen arrived, and Bricandor took the entire town away in the span of a single afternoon.

Wait, Bricandor, the leader over the entire Growen forces? And wait—the entire town suddenly gained electromagnetic abilities ... and left?

But the elders would answer no more questions, and clarify nothing. Couldn't we see it was over, they growled? They were discarded. They didn't want our help— not Frelsi help, not Growen help, not anyone's help. They never wanted to see another outsider again. Okl and Bricandor had robbed them of their culture, their people, without shedding a single drop of blood.

So as the elders wished, we left, and left them alone with their lost world. We scanned some DNA off this Okl guy's old hunting bag, and it matched the hair sample from the rooftop of the attempted bombing site. Armed with that, we left the ghost-town behind, venturing back out of the cooled, thorn-protected complex in to the wet, hot jungle—Lem, with many halting steps backwards, as if drawn to stay in the frozen moments of silent conquest; as for me, I couldn't wait to leave the silence.

Back in the chaos, colors, and heat, Lem's air-rider was already sliding to another stop ahead of me. "Got another buncha hair here," she said, letting her air-rider float down onto a wide tangle of branches.

I pursed my lips, looking at the bag of samples we'd already collected. Since leaving the Bichank settlement it seemed like suddenly the entire jungle was covered in traces of Okl.

Lem stepped off her air-rider onto the tree branch, and crouched, running her wristband along the bark. "Genetic scanner says it matches the sample from the settlement, and from the rec center back home. Claw-marks in the branch fit the height, and maybe the size of the guy in our mission files. Fits the boys' description of the attacker on the rec center." She looked away, and down at me. "You really think Stygge *Bricandor*'s involved?"

I rode up next to her and crouched on the seat of my air-rider to see the sample. I gnawed on my lip. I would've said Bricandor was too important for some forgotten Bichank cove—he was busy hobnobbing on the giant gas planets, stealing the strategic alliances that could win wars.

Something *smelled* like him, though.

"I don't know," I answered finally.

Lem scampered to another side of the tree to look for more clues, strolling along the black-barked verdant limbs as confidently as if she wasn't twelve meters above the ground. Like the acrobats I once saw dancing on the glass airships up north at Retrack city, before the Growen took it … I'd always wanted to see the design plan for one of those gems. My home planet's foggy, volcano-strewn plains never looked the same after those colors. Maybe because Dad brought me to that festival. Back when he could hear invisible people.

I got captured a few weeks after that festival.

"Stop looking at me like that," Lem said. "Stop judging me."

I realized I'd been staring at her. I didn't turn away. "I'm not thrilled with how easily we're finding clues," I said.

"Nothing makes you happy, does it?"

"It takes a lot."

She crouched, close to me again. "So … you think we're hunting a trap?" she asked.

Yeah. I did.

Because suddenly a red dot appeared on her forehead.

I leapt between her and the bullet before the word *sniper* formed in my brain—it's instinct to save your crew, *idiot* you don't always think clearly in the split second and I knocked her down and we fell out of the tree as the shot whizzed into the trunk above us and three more brightly-colored cartridges lit up the air around us and I tried to roll so my body would hit the ground first to save her, maybe I could cushion the fall with an em-push and—

But something stung my neck before we hit the net below. I remembered the old whip, syringes, wooden cage; I lost consciousness in a convulsion of light.

Beep … beep … beep …

Another syringe.

Medical facility?

Stars outside the window … medical spaceship?

No. Too much gray. Frelsi don't wear gray. Two Growen blitzers, child-killers stand over the bed with guns. Talking. Relaxed. Think the prisoner's asleep …

"Look, Banks, I don't know what your double-planet recruiter told you, but unity ain't about economic power." The blitzer's gruff voice doesn't help the headache.

"Well, that's why I joined up ..."

"No. Lemme tell you what this is about. It's about ending war. All war, forever." Gruff jams his finger into Banks's chest-plate. "Unity means more than a strong government with an organized trade code. Unity means we all share one culture. One set of goals. We take the best of every culture, every belief system, every planet, and we engineer a society where no one hates anyone because they can't. Ain't no hate speech with no differences to hate."

But different is beautiful ...

Vision fades.

Blink, more gray, and a girl's slurring voice: "Bereens, I think we can roll over and hide in the supply closet."

The words seem so heavy, lips ... fat ... "That's stupid. They'll ... find us."

There's no escaping the inevitable.

CHAPTER FOUR

Lem

ENTER THE TROUBLEMAKERS.

With the aftereffects of the K-O still rattling through her brain Lem saw the world like she was outside her body. The cavernous main hall of the spacecraft echoed with cries of hundreds of electromagnetic prisoners from every genus; soldiers pushed through the captive mob, dragging with them a teenage girl and a teenage boy. A long, thin gash traced the girl's chestnut cheek; a dark splotch of blood soaked the roots of the young man's flaxen hair.

The girl needed to snap back to reality. She was a freedom-fighter, for shyte's sake, she'd taken plenty of classes on "When They Capture You."

But now that it was happening, as the gray soldier's rubbery glove tightened on the back of her neck, she thought she recognized the old man in silver at the head of the room—

No way.

It was sensory overload. Her nostrils flared with the sweaty musk of so many aliens crammed into one place; the hum of the engine vibrating below the brass floor tickled through the soft soles of her boots; the crowd's reflection danced, twisted and distorted in the silver orbed helmets of the soldiers, like a surrealist painting from a nightmare. *Wake up!*

"You're not going to wake up, little one," said the old man. "And you're not a freedom-fighter. You're a terrorist." His soft blue eyes glowed under dark, weathered wrinkles as he searched her face, then sneered to his soldiers, his blitzers: "I can smell the Cont-amination on these two from a mile away. Drop them both out the airlock."

Lem couldn't process. She couldn't freak out. There just wasn't time. Wow, old Counselor Bricandor really could read her mind.

But the airlock—would she feel it, exploding in space? Or freezing solid—what happened first again? "Not a freedom-fighter my ass," was what she said. "I s'pose you're not a dictator, then, either."

"Not yet." That was the last time Counselor Bricandor spoke to her. He left the room out one door, and the blitzers dragged Lem through another. She glimpsed the old man's silver robe fanning out like wings—

A'ight, think. Lem scanned the tiled bronze hallway as the door to the giant room closed behind them. *Find a loophole.* Well, this spacecraft was a little older, since it still had more doors than poly-merwalls. No phasing through piezoelectric liquid ceramic from room to room meant no DNA checks at entrances. Nice. *Okay, what else?*

Well, the blitzer on Lem's left was really digging his fingers into her triceps.

Forget that. Okay, what else? Observe! Arms bound with wrist-chains. Legs slowed by a glowing stasis field. Five blitzers, two here with her, three with Bereens up ahead, and hallways just wide enough for four humans to walk abreast.

And?

Observing Cadet Commander Bereens, he looked pretty pissed off. He was still bucking his shoulder now and then like a horse shaking water off his back, almost more out of revulsion for their touch, it seemed, than an attempt to loosen their grip. *Okay.* The guy on Bereens's right seemed like a real hard-ass—he barked marching orders to the others, his voice quasi-electronic and rumbly through his helmet's distortion as he clipped along the hallway like he had a deadline; service personnel plastered themselves against the wall to let his troupe rush past.

Okay, none of this was useful! Shyte and thunderstorms, this was the worst possible time to die! It was Juju's birthday in two weeks. Lem had promised not to miss this one. And her missing person's case—now who'd bring that little boy home? Seria? No. No no no—

"You're muttering," Bereens growled.

"And you're stupid," said Lem. *"'Oh no, I don't like Lem's idea of hiding in the supply closet, I'd rather get dumped out the air-lock, 'cuz in space no one can hear me punk out.'"*

"He'd have found us anyway. You were delaying the inevitable."

"The inevitable?" Lem laughed. "What, like he can read minds through walls."

"Sometimes he can."

"Sometimes! Well that's not so inevitable, now, is it." But Bereens and his guards disappeared around the corner ahead. Lem turned to the guard on her left. "Hey, look, can we reschedule for next Tuesday?"

"Tuesday?" The blitzer asked.

"Banks, shut up," said another blitzer.

"The whole airlock thing, that don't fit my schedule right now," Lem said. "But I'm good for next Tuesday, if you're down."

Banks chuckled. His laugh loosened his grip a tiny bit ...

And that was her opening. Lem yanked her arm out of his relaxed hand, slamming herself against the blitzer on her right. Mr. Right knocked against the wall, armor clanging like an iron bell. He fell, grabbing for Lem with flailing fingers to drag her down with him—she squirmed away as he hit the deck and lost his grip.

Banks dove for Lem as she scrambled on her belly across the warm bronze floor. Lem pivoted to swing her boots up hard into his faceplate; he stumbled back with a grunt of pain. Mr. Right rolled over to try to grab her—she mounted his back, hooked her feet in around his knees, and looped her wrist-chain around his neck. He choked—the edges of the manacles cut against her wrists—his thrashing body-weight crushed her as he threw himself against the floor, slamming her on her back but she held her embrace for dear life as she heard his breath fading—

A couple of the blitzers up ahead came running back to help. *Dammit no no no*—Lem kicked and cursed as they peeled her arms and legs off the choking blitzer. A guard on each limb, rough gloved fingers squeezing into her flesh—*Let go!* They spread her out like laundry as the remaining blitzers dragged Bereens back around the corner with them, his scowl quizzical now.

One of Bereens's handlers, the leader, slung his flayer rifle off his back.

"You know what, kid? I'm sick of you already," he said. He stepped over Lem, his legs straddling her supine form, and aimed the gun at her chest. A point away from point blank. Lem's reflection stared back at her from his mirrored orb-mask with eerie stillness, chest heaving centimeters from the rifle's service end. "And the Commander didn't *specify* what *condition* you needed to be in to leave the airlock."

Lem managed a smile. "C'mon," she said. "Can't expect me not to try, right? I mean, you're tryin' to throw me out into space, here. That's kind of a one-way trip! If us Frelsi caught you, and you tried to escape, we wouldn't hold it against you …"

The blitzer flicked his thumb against the rifle. Safety off. His forefinger slid across the trigger …

Lem bit her breath.

The rifle *swerved* to the side before it fired!

The shot went wild, into the blitzer holding Lem's right arm. He fell backwards with an anguished cry, clutching his shoulder—his armor sizzled.

There was a split second of inaction where everyone tried to figure out what had happened—how on earth the blitzer had *missed* at point-blank.

But Lem knew. *That* was an em-push from Bereens. *They*

shouldn't have brought him back around the corner. She shot the boy a grateful grin—he nodded—and then before anyone else could move she hooked her now-free right arm around the trigger-happy leader's left ankle and yanked. He fell—the rifle flew from his hands to clonk the guy on Lem's legs right in the face. Lem elbowed, kicked, and scrambled free.

Now the leader's loose, fallen rifle spun and floated in the air on its own—under Bereens's control, firing at the other blitzers. More blitzers ran from all directions to join the fray; two of them pinned Bereens against the wall, screaming: "Put your guns away, you idiots, Bricandor said airlock for a reason! They're both gifted! Stygge-like!"

"Get her hands in stasis so she can't do that!"

"It's not her, it's the boy, stupid!"

"Banks, I am going to shoot you myself if you don't get his wrists in stasis now!"

Lem saw the hallway to the emergency lifeboats, and made a break for it—

Her world became blunt force trauma as she was clothes-lined on someone's outstretched arm, and fell soundly to the deck.

In the end, the whole thing only bought them three more minutes. Lem found herself shivering in the airlock—and maybe it took twelve blitzers to put her there, but she was there all the same, and time was so unfair. She blew hair out of her eyes and tried not to think as the knot formed in her stomach.

It would be over fast. It would.

"Sorry I didn't save us," she said to Bereens.

"You just ruined my shot at a dignified death, that's all," he smirked.

"Sorry. Also—" She remembered Bricandor's words with a smile. "I didn't know *you* were Contaminated, too."

"Don't use their language, it's degrading. Yes, I talk to Njandejara."

"We should get in touch with him. Ask him to jam the doors."

"He's an interdimensional being, not your robot-slave, you can't just tell him to—"

"Save my life? Sure, I can *ask*." Lem closed her eyes. "Njande, don't let us die yet. I need to get that little boy home. Heck, I'm still trying to learn to pronounce his name! And my sis's birthday—"

A click. Lem opened her eyes. That would be the latch for the outside door. It would open into space, and she'd see an infinity of stars before she froze—

No. It was the inside door, behind them.

Bereens's eyes widened. Lem grinned. "Told ya."

They both turned. A young man, maybe about four years older than they were, stepped into the airlock with them. Pockets decked his loose black pants and ebony jacket; spiked gauntlets covered his wrists and knuckles, and beside his holster dangled a short bamboo staff. Lem wanted to ask if it was *her* neodymium mace he had, hanging there in compacted form, but something about the way this guy walked, the way Bereens stiffened when he stepped in, the way the stranger's green eyes glittered as they met hers—she kept her mouth shut.

"Thought you could get away from me," the stranger said.

"Looked like it, yeah," Bereens said. "What are you doing here?"

"I cut a deal with Bricandor. I'm fairly certain I can cure you from the Contagion."

"I'm fairly certain you can't."

"Well, we'll find out." The stranger grinned a winning, dominating smile that made Lem's belly writhe. *Cure us? That's new.* She shuddered.

The stranger waved his fingers outside the door. Four people stepped into the room: two humans and two Bichanks, all dressed like the stranger, only in gray.

"Escort these two to solitary cells," said the stranger. "Keep them separate from the other trainees. We don't want any *infections*."

"Wow, thanks for that," Bereens scowled.

"You're welcome. I'm just trying to protect everyone."

"I was being sarcastic, Diebol."

"I know." The young man bowed and exited the room, leaving them with the four oddly-dressed guards.

Diebol? Lem wanted to ask. But it seemed like something you *don't* ask. She really didn't *know* Cadet Commander Bereens, and you can't just bring up people's rumored past. But she was pretty sure he'd spent almost six months in captivity as an eight-year-old because of that guy. So … why'd they seem so … chill?

Bereens wasn't chill the moment Diebol left. Lem saw his teeth grind, eyes burn. He breathed hard, like he'd just used up his last fleck of restraint—

Bereens leapt, kicked two guards in the head, and vaulted over them out the door after Diebol. All four guards shouted and threw their hands forward. Lem felt the air tingling, a magnetic pulse, as the polarities of every molecule in her body shifted just a tad, drawing her near the four—

Bereens was frozen just outside the doorway by the guards' em-pull. He cursed.

"Of course you're all Stygges," he spat.

They didn't answer. Lem did.

"I mean, we're both gifted, and everyone in that huge holding room back there was practically pissing electronegative pulses. Looks like the Stygge elite's real, and like, they used the bomber to lure *us* here to join 'em. So mission kind of accomplished? We found several hundred secret super-soldiers in training?"

Bereens only scowled at her in response as the four guards escorted them down the hallway. Lem wished he'd say something: the silence was heavy enough with the guards glaring like she'd done something to them personally. The cold way they held her at arm's length, the constant tingle they kept in the air, so ready to activate their abilities—it hung on her shoulders like a yoke, and she wanted to fight it. *I'm sorry for making you hate me*, she wanted to say to them. *I'm sorry for talking to dangerous sprites.*

But every time she opened her mouth, it was like a tomb waited to swallow her words. Because she wasn't sorry.

CHAPTER FIVE

Bereens

*C*LICK, CLICK, CLICK ...

Blitzer heels outside the door, against the copper floor. On their way to lunch, maybe?

Those two, always arguing.

"Eliminate differences, eliminate war. Ain't no hate speech with no differences to hate."

"And—and I'm not arguing with that, b-but I think that's a very long-term goal that most independent planets aren't ready to pursue," the moderate pleaded. "I think our political wing should focus more on the economic advantages of unified government, and once that's in place, and everyone's prospering, then we go into social engineering. We agree democratically between all the member planets on what is the best mandatory uniform culture, and we implement that together. I think a lot of Frelsi wouldn't be opposed to that."

Scoffing: "You kidding me? You ain't gonna sell the Frelsi on economic advantages when the unification code requires ditching backwards practices. The Frelsi think they're sticking up for each other, they love that shyte. You got one guy who talks to imaginary sparklies, and this other guy don't, but sane guy fights so crazy guy can keep dreaming. You got migratory insectoids gettin' up every mornin' freaking out about zoning laws; Bichank Alliances that won't let no one but a Bichank tell 'em what to do; and that bug-brain's willing to die to protect that furry's arrogance as long as the feeling's mutual."

Nervous shifting ... "But isn't that the right feeling after all? We want people groups to care about each other's rights, we can leverage that! It's just a matter of adjusting the unification code until that bug, and that Bichanks, want to join us."

But we won't join you ... because we want to be free.

I was getting flashbacks like crazy. They sat us down in a processing room to enter us into their computer system. Name? Frelsi ID number? They charted height, weight, scars, brought out the familiar form 1082—that got me. The stasis field now slowly paralyzing our necks, hands, and feet, I could handle. It meant they feared us. But helping them fill in the check-boxes like a good little schoolboy while they sorted and labeled us like warehouse crates under those flickering fluorescent lights—that brought back unwanted memories.

I tried to calm myself by observing my surroundings, thinking through the tech read-outs I'd memorized about Growen freighters like this. Know your enemy: I knew mine. I—

Lem's thick black braid squished against me as she backed up, stumbling from a Stygge push; they sat us down on the warm floor in the middle of a pack of blitzers with the barrels of their flayer rifles centimeters from our heads. I caught her glancing at her reflection in the bronze wall, fingering the scratch on her cheek and the tan-line on her right hand where her wristband used to be, a pale latte against the rest of her agate skin. Frelsi cadets never remove our wristbands. They're lifelines, monitoring our vitals and location for our Frelsi teammates: the blitzers had confiscated ours and turned them off back on Luna-Guetala.

"It means someone's looking for us," Lem whispered to me with a smile.

Sure. As soon as the wristbands left our skin, alarms lit up at our duty-station. That didn't mean they'd *find* us, out in space, though. I covered the blank spot on my left wrist with my hand.

"Since we're capture-buddies now, Cadet Commander Bereens," Lem tried again. "What's your first name?"

"Cadet Commander," I said. I didn't mean to be an ass. Well, I sort of did—but as they dragged me to my feet, and shoved me into a cold, plastic seat in the middle of the room, I was busy wondering if I'd gotten us captured in the first place.

Did I maybe give something away to Diebol during our last game? Somehow let him know I was stationed on Luna-Guetala? My stomach pitted.

No, I couldn't have: Diebol and I didn't … *talk* per se. We just sent brain waves back and forth. We literally closed our eyes, wherever we were, walked into the mental simulation we shared, and sat down to play the same game we'd played for the past ten years—and creating that virtual room using only our neural electricity wasn't like mind-reading, as paradoxical as that sounded. Unlike mind reading, it took *effort* to transmit information; it was like a radio that only two people in the entire universe had. We'd formed it when Bricandor locked Diebol in the wooden cage with me … when he forced him to endure everything I did.

Children play. It's what they do. Lionesses teach their cubs to kill by giving them live antelope babies as playmates, and that was the only reason I wasn't gassed with the other fifty kids the Growen rounded up that day. I was special. Bricandor taught Diebol to care, let go, and betray—using me.

We still played now. We'd open this mind-channel we made and step into the wooden cage of our past, with the same squares scratched out on the floor, the same twigs for playing pieces. Maybe it was a pathetic grasping at a universe where we could be friends, or maybe we did it because that's what we'd always done, and humans are sick creatures of habit. I didn't know. I couldn't not play.

Still, when they dragged Lem away, and she shot me one last quizzical, narrow-eyed glance in the doorway …

Well, Lem Benzaran, welcome to our game.

"It's strange seeing you in person, Bereens," Diebol said.

The cold plastic seat creaked under me as I swiveled. He'd slipped through the soft polymerwall behind me without a sound; the wall hardened behind him now as he walked over to the blitzer manning the chest-high compuwall about a meter in front of me.

"How did you find us?" I asked.

"How do you think? You took the bait. I sent you an electromagnetic bomber, and the Frelsi sent their electromagnetic hunters after him, right back to me." Diebol leaned over the blitzer's shoulder and tapped the compuwall. "Evaluations are in," he said to the blitzer. "You need to execute this one, that one, and … this one. They're all faking Stygge abilities, so you can just shoot them. These twelve have abilities"—he drew his finger in a circle—"but they're all too mentally deficient to handle training. You'll need to throw them out the airlock. That'll free up a room for our special Frelsi patient, here." He smiled back up at me as if I hadn't just seen him order disabled civilians killed. My chest constricted like I'd inhaled syrup. The compuwall chimed a pleasant "ba-da-ling!" as the order went through. Easy text message. I couldn't even move—I could do literally *nothing* to save those people.

"You don't even know them," Diebol said, watching my face. "And we're on a freighter in the middle of the void. You must understand mentally deficient individuals with *electromagnetic powers* endanger us all."

"Funny, coming from someone who wants to cure everyone," I muttered.

His face darkened for a moment.

Then, with pursed lips, he stepped over to me, unsheathed an imaging pen, and drew a game board in the air between us. He scribbled a few twigs on my side, and a few on his side, replicating the game we'd played in our minds for years. We'd invented it while in captivity together; the goal was to capture grid squares, and your opponent's sticks, by surrounding them on all sides with your own sticks. I was currently in the lead.

Diebol took a deep breath, and drew a twig by one of my existing sticks. "*You'll* be alright," he said. "We can fix you. And then you'll become a Stygge legend."

"I think I liked it better when you wanted me dead," I said. "You remember. My lifestyle is violence to you. That." I glared at him; he handed me his pen, and I blocked his move by placing my own twig to the right of my existing one, surrounding his stick on two sides.

"Oh, it absolutely is," he said, taking his turn. "If you allow the Contamination in your brain to spread, you destroy other people's ability to think freely. I can think of no greater violence."

"I can think of some. Mostly special violence just for you."

"Strong words for someone who's lost the last three rounds." Diebol smiled. He erased the board and patted me on the shoulder. "It'll be alright." I tried to buck him off, but the field kept me still; he left the room whistling.

I closed my eyes, heart heavy. Bloodseas, I was literally waiting for people to die before I could be transferred to my cell. Me, thirteen blitzers, four Stygges, all waiting for the okay that meant a bunch of poor confused wide-eyed souls had collided head-on with the universe outside …

What did I have to work with, here? A compuwall anchored to the floor in the middle of the room, probably a desk chair behind that. Two plastic chairs shaped vaguely like headless women. Four bronze, reflective polymerwalls hemming us all in …

I didn't know how much good escaping would do on a moving spacecraft, but it was my duty to try whether or not I wanted to. That's what they teach you in the Frelsi Corps: the longer you're in captivity, the more time the enemy have to extract data from you that puts others in danger. That creed made me miserable as a little boy in an unbreakable cage. I wondered if our guardians taught us this so we'd get killed instead of tortured; so we'd cost our captors so much effort we forced them to end our misery. I searched for details in the room now out of tired mechanical routine.

I wish they'd shut up over there, it's hard enough to think already. The Stygge trainees stood silent, but two of the blitzers in the corner kept arguing …

"It's just a matter of adjusting the unification code until that bug, and that Bichank, want to join us," said the guy they called Banks.

"Changing the code for one people group screws it up for the others," said the gruff lead blitzer who'd tried to shoot Lem in the hallway. "You let the insectoids jus' flit around wherever they want, you make 'em difficult to monitor. That's dangerous. You want those giant bugs goin' unchecked? They got physical advantages!"

"Physical advantages? S-so what are you going to do about that, then, just genetically engineer everyone into one species?"

"Eventually. But that's real long-term. We end differences, end war, we move all sapience to one evolution'ry pinnacle of peaceful perfection."

Banks stepped away from his companion, arms crossed, and muttered something I couldn't catch. *You and me both, buddy*, I sighed. But the other blitzer wasn't having it.

"Oh, so what do *you* propose then, Banks?" Gruff got up in his companion's face. "We just sit on our asses waving a petition for everyone to get along? Why not just leave the independent planets alone, then, to rot in their violent filth? You're stupid."

"N-no, that's not what I said. I—"

"Then what?! *Why are you even here, Banks?*"

"I-I-I'm here because we need a unified galaxy to protect us from the interdimensional threat, that's why I'm here!" Banks squealed.

Gruff fell silent for a moment. "Shyte, you really believe they exist."

"They do! They get in your head and trap you into this insane dedication, and then you become just this channel, this channel for them to enter our dimension and control us all, and then they consume you! It's why we gotta kill those kids, and quarantine people's thoughts, and all this other horrible stuff—it's a disease, a horrible undead disease!"

Gruff sighed, shaking his head. "Banks, Banks, Banks. Banks, with all due respect to the boss, interdimensionals aren't real. They're made up. A weepy sympathy story to put zeal into something that's all about money. The weapons-dealers running the Frelsi don't want war to end—they profit from it!"

Yeah ... I'm profiting so much right now.

"Not to interrupt this absolutely fascinating conversation, gentlemen, but ah—is there a latrine I might use?" I raised my eyebrows for the friendliest smile I could muster. This room had too many hostiles—I might have a better shot in something smaller.

CHAPTER SIX

Jei Bereens

IT REALLY IS ALL ABOUT THE LITTLE THINGS. THAT EXTRA SIX centimeters those stasis fields leave you around the ankles to trip people. The slight vulnerable shift of bodyweight as your guard rocks on his heels, impatient and uncomfortable in a teeny bathroom with another male. The tiny soft spot where the helmet meets the armor's neck, a perfect place to drop your full bodyweight on your elbow to blood-choke your guard who's tripped by the toilet for "some reason."

I'd just knocked my guard out cold when a glowing red neodymium mace smashed through the bathroom's polymerwall and suddenly Lem was burning open my stasis field collar with the mace's laser-edged handle and now she was whisper-shouting at me to hurry—

As if whispering would counteract the whole smashing-the-door thing.

"What the bloodseas?! This is the men's bathroom!" I hissed.

"That's your first reaction?" she chuckled as I chased her and her tattered tunic down the hallway, stepping over the bodies of ten blitzers who'd apparently had their helmets smashed in by a girl wielding three pounds of crystalline magnetic metal. Everyone was there but the lead blitzer. "It's not like you were actually using it."

"Where the bloodseas did you find your mace?" I asked.

"I knew it was mine Diebol had," she said.

"Wait, *you* robbed Diebol? *How?*"

Lem leapt around the corner, out of sight—I followed, thinking that—I don't know what I was thinking, but I wasn't thinking she'd be fully engaged in slamming skulls and breaking knees. It became a full-on five-person brawl *with armed Stygges* in the middle of the copper hallway. Screams, shots, someone pulled an alarm—

"Go, go!" Lem shouted, waving me down the hall. I knew the layout from my studies: we were a few hallways down from the transmission tower. "I've got my mace, you're unarmed, I'll catch up!"

"You'll catch up?" I couldn't just leave the girl to—

"Call home!"

One of the Bichank Stygges broke free from the pack and charged me, hand outstretched to freeze me in my place. I ducked and slid across the hallway, dropping as close to the metal as possible, using the sea of electrons in the bronze floor to weaken the accuracy of his em-pull. I could move, I wasn't frozen, but still I felt dragged backwards—

Lem's mace flew toward the back of the Bichank's head. He released me to whirl and stop it midair with an em-push, and by the time he turned around I was already out of range, down the hall.

This is all kinds of wrong. Like it or not, I'd left her behind. I was running for the transmission tower with my jaw grinding, face heated, throat tightening. Why the bloodseas had she done it this way? This was clearly a modified tanker ship. It had at least two lifeboats, escape pods. So why the bloodseas hadn't we headed towards the lifeboats, and *why in the galaxy* did she smash the door open with a loud *mace?*

The Bichank's tree-trunk-sized legs thudded on the metal behind me, his breath rising into a growl. The hair rose on the back of my neck, and the air became heavy like I was running through honey. He was pulling again.

This time I whirled and leapt at him. His pull yanked my sidekick into his own snout. His paws wrapped around my ankle; he slammed me against the ground. I repulsed the metal floor, cushioning the blow; I transferred the energy and snatched at his foot. He slid off balance and released my leg. I pushed off the floor, into his head, to slam his skull back against the wall.

It should've knocked him out. But before I'd turned two corners I heard the bass drum crescendo of his heavy footsteps again.

I glanced around the hallway. A small door lay just ahead to the left—supply closet. I ducked inside. A ventilation grate hung above my head. Darkness beckoned through its slats: an escape route!

The closet was narrow enough for me to place one boot on each wall. I climbed up to the grate, wedging myself between the hanging mops; my fingers slipped on the grate's screws, I clenched my teeth, I cursed under my breath …

"Come on, come on—"

My fingernails scraped rust. One more sloppy half-turn and the grate fell open with a corroded creak.

I held the grate with one hand; with the other I gripped the edge of the entrance and pulled myself up. I squirmed inside, pushed the screws back into their holes—backwards, since I could no longer reach the outside. I hoped no one would notice that.

My eyes squinted, adjusting to the darkness in the square metal tunnel. Sweat broke out on my face; the floor began to burn my hands as I crawled. I dropped to my belly and snaked forward. The heat suffocated me. I wheezed. *Look for the next left.*

I could do this. A fuel-tanker's ventilation system is almost always the same—mostly because there's an optimal layout to prevent the ship's precarious cargo from overheating and exploding —and even if the Growen bothered to change, I'd spent the last two years stealing ship maps and tech specs. They'd have to rebuild *right now today* if they wanted to lose me. I found the comms center without much difficulty.

But as I stared through the grate at the glowing blue office cubicles sprawling beneath me, my shoulders sagged. Any confidence I'd had melted in the stifling heat as the polymerwall at the far end of the room wobbled, bubbled, and then burst open for sixteen more blitzers in full body armor, gray orb-helmets gleaming under the fluorescent lights. Six Stygge trainees followed: two humans, two Bichanks, and two Wonderfrogs, all wearing the same gray, multi-pocketed vests and pants as the first four guards in the air-lock.

"Everyone remain at your stations," said Gruff again, waving his hand like he'd granted the cubicle-mice some kind of wish. *Looks like Lem missed one when she was playing whack-a-mole outside the men's bathroom.* "One of the escapees will be heading this way shortly."

What to do? Out-wait them? I glared down at the technician below me, envying him his workstation. It stood about his height, with compuscreens covering all four cubicle walls from floor to top. He hummed—he was a pleasant guy, I guess—as he slid images around the four walls with his fingertips, flicking the screens with his bare elbows to swish back and forth between sets of blueprints.

Wait. I recognized the layouts on those blueprints. With six rows of barracks spread around the hospital like wings—

That was Fort Jehu. Lem's home base on the Luna-Guetala double-planet. I'd been stationed there for the past two years; it was unmistakable.

I squinted and sucked in my breath. Bloodseas, this looked like an attack plan. The technician brought up another blueprint with arrows and unit names on it.

Shyte, go back to the map, I was reading that!

Okay, now he was opening a roster. It looked like this guy was double-checking the background info on the individuals posted at different attack points, maybe to make sure personnel were placed in the most effective positions for their skillsets ... no, now he was checking training status.

Stop flipping screens, would you!

Shyte, a thousand Stygges: a thousand super-soldiers. That's what this was: the first battle plan for an army of mini-gods.

But where the bloodseas did Bricandor find so many people with electromagnetic abilities?

Forget that, I have to get this intel home. How many seconds would it take, I wondered, to jump down on the technician, open the transmitter, and forward all the files he had open? Or better question: how many burning holes could my body take from the sixteen blitzers in the doorway before I keeled over dead? Because that would probably happen before I finished keying in a transmission address.

Maybe if I waited 'til the technician opened his email or something. I could send from there; that'd probably shave off a second or so. He had to slack off at some point.

Right?

A bead of sweat dribbled down my nose and plunked against the metal grate; I wiped it with my sleeve before it could slip down onto the technician below me.

I scowled. I wished I had a knife or something to push out these screws. I couldn't bust out this grate without a lot of force and noise, and that *bang* would give them at least another second to put at least another flayer shot in my ribs.

There's gotta be another way down there. I closed my eyes. I found the color green in my mind and gripped it close to my chest, pulling up the blueprints in my head. Any other access points to the comms center?

Got it. Another supply closet. I titled my head to the side to try to see—yes. I'd need to keep going forward and take another left to double back, and that'd put me down in the closet just two computers in front of this guy. That would be quieter.

But then a mace smashed through the polymerwall and everyone was screaming.

Are you kidding me?! Lem and three Stygge trainees tumbled through the wall, crashing at the feet of my sixteen blitzers.

While she busted heads, my old Bichank pursuer appeared through the gap she'd made, screaming. I couldn't understand his words, but I saw him point at the air vent, the supply closet, and the air vent again. Lem was making a hell of a fuss but in about two seconds someone would listen to that Bichank and find me.

Bloodseas, why did she do shyte like this?

"Just keep being distracting, woman," I muttered as I sat up and swiveled. I kicked through the vent grate and rocketed down atop the poor humming technician's head, into his cubicle. I swiped my hand across his screen and pulled up his email. I punched Rana's numerical address into the wall—swiped the other screen back to drag the first blueprint into the email—and slammed my palm into the corner of the screen to send it.

Sent. Done.

"Ooh, very nice. Too bad I just disabled all outgoing communication on that frequency."

I groaned as I turned around.

Diebol leaned against the cubicle wall behind me. The screen behind him flashed and flickered under the pressure of his shoulder. Lighting up around him, and above his head, clinked an error message for my email.

"Denied."

CHAPTER SEVEN

Diebol

DIEBOL THOUGHT ABOUT LETTING BEREENS GET IN A PUNCH OR two, just to screw with him that little bit, but in seconds three of his Stygge trainees had already wrestled the escapee to the floor. Bereens breathed hard, staring coldly straight ahead, jaw clenched as a Wonderfrog's reverse knee pinned his temple and ground his cheek into the bronze floor. They had his arms pulled back just slightly too far; his steeled face twitched as they snapped another stasis collar around his neck. But Bereens had had worse days. He'd be alright. Diebol left his Stygges to their work.

This Lem Benzaran, on the other hand, she needed sedatives or something. Diebol crossed the maze of cubicles and watched as she went down kicking, screaming, biting, and everything-the-hell else. Even after they got the collar on her, her eyes dashed around the room, across the faces of her captors, out the cubbyhole ceiling window to the stars outside—and back to Diebol's face. For a moment he felt searched—and then her gaze darted on for another escape route. She would not be contained.

Well, she had to be. Unless Diebol decided she was not worth curing, and threw her out the airlock, which was, at this point, a real possibility.

Oh, hello, here was the blitzer captain who'd left ten subordinates knocked out by the latrine. Diebol smiled. It wasn't a nice smile. "Get two of mine, and twelve of yours, to escort her to my office," he said. "Mind telling me how she got out of her cell in the first place?"

The captain stood there dumbly.

"Sir, you'll want to see for yourself," a deep voice behind him interrupted—a blind, deaf, and noseless gray Bichank, Okl, the bait that had captured Jei. One of Diebol's best. "Would you mind accompanying me?"

Diebol nodded, eyes still on the blitzer captain. "Get her moving."

The man scurried away with a scowl at the prisoner, as if blaming her for his own incompetence.

Diebol followed his companion in silence—he trusted his Stygge not to waste his time with something he could have just told him.

Faith well placed.

The bronze door to Lem's cell wasn't on its hinges. It lay across the hall, bent in the middle like crumpled paper. Burn marks and blood streaked the walls as if an explosion had gone off in the doorway.

"Whose blood?" he asked.

"Hers. I believe only the wound on her face and a few old scars reopened, but I did not have much opportunity to examine her as we fought."

"She exploded?"

"She may be electrogenic. Energenic, even."

Diebol's eyes lit up. For a human, that would be a first.

"She did not attempt to use the ability during combat," Okl said. "I do not think she knows how it works."

Diebol narrowed his eyes. So she attempted to break down the door based on, what, pure spunk and glory? He stepped into the room, fingering the torn hinges.

Scuff marks, from her boots in the far corner, marked her running start. Diebol placed his boots in her muddy steps. That placement crouched him down like a runner, and forced his hands to drop to the floor beside him so he could look straight ahead at where the door had been.

There, in her spot, in her starting pose, he understood her.

This wasn't some manic fool flailing around the room, hurling herself at the door until she randomly triggered a superpower she didn't know she had—this was the kneel, the determined gaze forward, the focused aim of a sniper. She did not see that door. She saw only, like he did now, the other side where she needed to be. She knew the other side could be reached. She took one shot at it with everything she had.

And she made it.

He stood up with a deep sigh as the spell broke around him. It was not normal sanity, certainly. But in its hopelessly hopeful way, it was beautiful.

"I can work with this," he whispered. "I can set her free."

When Diebol entered his dimly-lit office he found a blitzer missing his helmet and gushing blood from his nose and mouth as he ground Lem Benzaran's face against the desk, roaring at her and kicking her shin. Another blitzer stood a few feet off clutching his hand, cursing his broken finger and the "deformed gutter-prostitute" who'd snapped it.

Diebol cleared his throat.

The bloody, helmet-less blitzer jumped to a semblance of attention, still holding Lem bent over the desk. This was *again* the same high-speed blitzer captain who somehow came out unscathed when his crewmates ended up unconscious. Diebol was fairly certain Lem hadn't *ripped the man's helmet off his face*—when you design something to breathe in space you don't make it for easy removal. And the torn shoulder on her jumpsuit didn't happen without the blitzer grabbing at something that wasn't his.

Degenerate fool.

Diebol unhooked his flayer gun and, in rushed strides, closed the distance between himself and the captain. Without ceremony he thrust the barrel into the man's mouth.

Oh, it seemed said mouth wasn't open at the moment of entry—the weapon had perhaps broken a tooth or two in the process. The captain's garbled yell indicated as much.

"I hope you're appreciating the unique sensation of someone thrusting something into your body uninvited," Diebol said. "Is this pleasant?"

"Gnoo suhh!"

"I couldn't quite make that out. It didn't seem as if you were really trying to answer my question. That's insubordination, no?" Diebol yanked back the slide bolt on the weapon; the flayer hummed to life as a glowing redox cartridge dropped into the chamber, and the blitzer's eyes widened almost enough to dwarf his bloody mouth still puckered around the barrel. "It seems like you're still clinging to the ways of your *old* unit. You'd best tell me *my* stance on unauthorized assault, and make it clear enough to record as a service announcement."

"Zee. Hro. Tah. Lo. Hrents." The blitzer's mouth moved like molasses to ensure each syllable survived the trip around the flayer barrel.

"Very good. I hope you'll remember that when you're eating mashed lechichi this month." Diebol's forefinger clicked the side of the flayer's frame, right next to the safety, to switch the weapon to stun—and fired.

The blitzer jolted, once, and fell to the floor unconscious. No taser-style shuddering, unfortunately. These new nano-engineered shocks were much less entertaining now that the wave-particles targeted the brain's GABA-A and NMDA receptors directly.

Diebol holstered his weapon. "Banks, is it?"

The other blitzer snapped to attention, broken pinky suddenly forgotten. His fear was hilarious, but Diebol wasn't laughing. He'd grown tired of this. This was how they all were, political gun-monkeys who joined up believing interdimensionals didn't exist, believing they somehow knew better than their enemies, believing they'd unify a galaxy by force and then keep it that way with kumbayas. Shyte-faced agnostics. They did not know fear. Fear was when you looked a spirit-being in the face and realized it wanted you, and that you might have to torch the universe to escape it. That was fear.

"Well, Banks," Diebol smiled with all his teeth at the remaining trembling blitzer. "You're dismissed." The blitzer dashed to the door — "You're just going to leave your crew-mate?"

"No—no sir!" The blitzer dashed back, apologizing and stuttering some nonsense, and grabbed the unconscious man by the arm. He yanked. The man's hand flopped. His armor screeched across the floor. Lem and Diebol stared at the stumbling, waddling blitzer the whole way out the door. Step. By step. *Screeeeeeeeeeeeeech.* "Sorry—sorry sir!"

"Helmets *on* when dealing with prisoners," Diebol said, closing the door behind him. He turned with a sigh, leaning against the iron frame for a moment while the Benzaran girl righted herself, blowing hair out of her face.

"I must apologize for that," Diebol said.

"He got nothing," she said. "You think it's *my* blood all over my forehead?"

At that, Diebol grinned. The girl couldn't more than shuffle in the full-body stasis field: the rays inhibiting sarcoplasmic calcium release in her muscles made it hard for her to even stand. Yet *still* she would not sit in his presence; she leaned her hip against the desk, glaring at him, tufts of her black braid sticking out while other bits of hair clung to the sweat on her face. Blood dribbled to the corner of her lip from the gash in her cheek.

Diebol loved this. Her heated stare, the pouted lips, the *spirit* in her face that superseded the mess they'd made of her composure— he loved it. Thinking of some interdimensional sundering that soul … Diebol could vomit.

"You're not getting any kisses either, brother," Lem snarled. "So quit staring."

"Again, I apologize. It's been a long day for us both." Diebol approached and reached for the collar around her neck that generated the yellow immobilizing field. "I'm going to turn off the stasis, and I'm going to ask you to have a seat in that chair. Alright?"

"Go ahead," she challenged. Her eyes sparkled; her body tensed.

Diebol rolled his eyes and withdrew his hand. "I suppose I have to tell you the bad news first, then," he said, "since it's clear you're just going to bolt again, and then I'm going to have to thrash you, and then I'll have to tell you the bad news while we're both nursing bruises. So here it is. Are you ready?"

"Hit me. But not literally."

Diebol took a breath. "If you don't behave yourself, I'm going to send a mercenary to kill your family."

Her eyes didn't widen. Her forehead didn't crease. She didn't look shocked in the least. "You—do know you guys are *always* trying to kill my family, right? That's kinda your job."

"You misunderstand, Frelsi. I'm not sending soldiers who get paid the same wage whether or not they find your family, hunting the latest faceless mission and the next body-count record, unconcerned if those bodies belong to you or someone else. No, I'm sending a mercenary whose entire time under my employ will be focused on turning every *body* that shares your blood into a room temperature *soup*. I'm hiring the Ebon Shadow."

That, thank goodness, did get a reaction. Everyone knew the mercenary's record. An eyebrow raised, her eyes narrowed, and her lips parted.

"Why."

"You've cost six thousand drachma in medical bills for my men in one day. You're very difficult to keep alive, since your entire combat style revolves around throwing yourself at people's weapons. And your little escape attempt almost compromised the location of something much, much more important than your lonely life." Diebol sat and thunked his boots up on the desk beside her hip, crossing his shins. "Connect the dots."

"The dots say you'll do anything to control me for this experiment. S'not like anything's changed. You're just outsourcing." She paused, as if waiting for him to argue, and then argued at him further. "It's gonna take forever. I'll be dead by the time you even reach my family."

But when Diebol clicked off the stasis field and removed the collar, Lem didn't bolt. She sat in the chair across from him and ran her fingers through her braid, pushing little strands back into place. "So what's *behaving,* then?" she asked. "What do you want?"

"I know it's difficult for you, but I want you to keep an open mind and try to cooperate with our cure. We have medications and —what are you doing?" Diebol stiffened.

Her eyes glittered. Her fingers kept moving through that braid. "Nothing. Keep talking."

Really.

He grabbed her wrist. She twisted away, hand back to her hair, and bolted for the other corner of the office. He slid onto his desk and pounced off it, drawing a knife from his shoulder pocket as he cleared the air between them. He swiped her legs out from under her with a floor kick, yanked her hair back as she fell, and sliced it off as she hit the deck.

And in his palm, hidden in her thick black braid, he found her Frelsi wristband.

Private civilian frequency, read the interface. *Message sent.*

Oh shyte.

CHAPTER EIGHT

Diebol

LEM SCRAMBLED TO HER FEET WITH A WRY GRIN, FISTS RAISED AND eyes bright. "Gotcha," she said. "You only blocked outgoing military frequencies, huh? So focused on your old buddy, you totally missed *this* magic flying in *right* under your radar."

She certainly looked proud of herself. It wasn't endearing. Diebol threw out his hand and em-pulled her close, dropping the wristband to grip her ragged collar and hold the knife blade to her throat. She moved her hands to meet his—

"No," he growled, pressing the edge into her skin. "Hold your arms out. Now."

He let her think about it for a second. The blade bit. She raised her hands with a smirk.

"Sit," he said, backing her up.

She did, still gloating. Her eyes sparkled at—oh, shyte, the drawer *right next* to where the blitzer captain had bent her over the desk. "So you got your wristband back while I was berating my soldier about you," Diebol muttered.

"It was pretty tough. That stasis field ain't made for easy moving," she said graciously. "You were such a sweet little white knight, I almost feel bad."

"How did you know it was *there*?"

"Eh ... read your mind," she said, suddenly avoiding eye contact. Her face wore guilt like a color. Oh-ho, she'd done something she didn't like. Diebol leaned closer.

"Look at me," he said.

She glanced down at the knife first, as if to make sure she actually had to obey, before looking back at him. His eyes flickered back and forth, watching the forced stare in her deep browns ...

Her gaze wavered. She was justifying something in there. Someone *deserved* it.

"You beat it out of one of my men, didn't you," Diebol grinned.

"Woman, actually," she muttered.

"The supply S4 you got your staff back from."

"Maybe she shouldn't have joined an army of child-killers."

"But you regret it." Diebol straightened, triumphant.

Her hand flashed to the knife-handle; her eyes blazed. Standing up had weakened his stance, his grip on the knife—her fingers slipped under his as she twisted his wrist, popped back his elbow—

"No," he snapped. He clenched his fingers, untwisted himself—an em-push slammed her back against the wall, tipping over her chair with a clatter. He kept the knife.

But he was getting fed up with this. She'd barely hit the wall when he leapt over the fallen chair to pin her there, slamming his palm like a collar over her throat. He sheathed the knife, whipped his imaging pen out of another shoulder-pocket, and in four jerky, angry strokes drew a square on the wall beside her.

"You see this?" He smiled through clenched teeth, yanking her chin towards the projection as a blurry, dark image formed within the square. "This is my new friend, the Ebon Shadow. Shadow, meet Lem."

"A pleasure." The image clarified; a night sky twinkled in the background, dominated by a huge, full, greenish-white circle. Diebol knew Lem recognized Luna, the sky-orb twin to her Guetala homeworld, the softer sister in the Luna-Guetala double-planet pair.

The silhouette of a man cut into the ivory orb. His mask, shaped like a human face without eyes or mouth, gleamed in the Guetala twilight. He seemed made of liquid onyx; his armor had no seams.

He was not exactly blindingly professional. "Oh hey, she's a cutie," he said.

"Compared to someone so ugly he gotta hide his whole body in one mask, yeah, anyone's cute," Lem spat.

Diebol pursed his lips. She was truly wearing away his patience. "Why don't you tell us where you are, Shadow?" he asked tersely.

"As a matter of fact, I'm inside the Frelsi Luna-Guetala Head-quarters. Fort Jehu."

"That's impossible, he's lying." Lem jerked her chin out of Diebol's hand, away from the image, to glare him straight in the face.

Diebol understood her skepticism. He'd studied that fort's defenses in detail: two layers of sentries, a six-meter-thick DNA-sensing double polymerwall, and an iris-scanner blocked entry to the private barracks.

"Unless he farts nukes, and everybody's dead, your boy's lying," Lem repeated.

"When you're invisible, sentries don't notice you," said the Shadow, taunting her like a child—and clearly quoting something he'd said before: "When you can sequence someone's DNA by touching them, everyone you meet is a polymerwall key."

Diebol struggled not to roll his eyes at the braggart's buffoonery. What nincompoop revealed their tech to the enemy like that? But Lem gripped the edge of his jacket; her need to argue intrigued him. "Okay, the cloaking technology he's talking about? That's still in development," she snapped up at him, struggling to prove some-thing. "And DNA-sequencing? So what he can read someone's DNA, he can't get through polymerwall without wearing it!"

"That's what molecule-modeling armor is for," chuckled the Shadow.

"That doesn't exist!" Lem cried, eyes still locked with Diebol's. Hm. Would wonders never cease. This idiot was scaring her.

"It does exist. It's just not readily available," said the Shadow. His helmet swiveled mechanically, like a security camera, to look over his hulking shoulder. "I'll have to get back to you on this, though, cutie. I've got a job to do."

Diebol clicked the pen's eraser to eliminate the image and rose, yanking Lem to her feet and righting the chair he'd knocked over.

"It's not gonna happen," she said. She was gripping the back of the chair so hard her knuckles were turning ashen. "The fort's a city, and even if he *finds* it the children's bunker is impenetrable." She closed her eyes and swallowed hard. "It's not gonna happen."

This girl. Diebol kicked her bruising shin.

"Ow! Shyte in a pig-ass-sandwich, what was that for?"

Diebol leaned his face inches from hers and sharpened his gaze. "Enough," he growled. "I need your attention, now. We're landing in half an hour. And you will run obstacle courses, take classes, and attend therapy just like any other student. Or your family will die."

"You haven't even caught them yet!"

"You can listen to me and live, or you can argue with me and die."

"But you're going to kill us all anyway!"

"Only with that attitude," Diebol snarled, gripping the edge of the table. "Look, I'm trying to *help* you here, and not just you! If we can make this work, we can prove to Bricandor and all the Growen Forces that you are curable, and we may be able to end the child slaughter. You help me, and we make warfare saner for everyone! Gas chambers will make way for re-education camps! You may indeed end up saving not just your family, but thousands of others."

"And we all dance under the stars and hold hands forever, I get it." Behind her sarcasm trembled a voice heavy with something like remorse. Wet, sad eyes held his as she whispered: "But the stars will have no meaning because you'll take away the diversity that gives them poetry, and the hands we hold will belong to empty husks, all the same, all thinking the same things and doing the same things, and I'm not sure the life we'll have is worth living."

There, he saw it there. The infection, gripping her throat, fluttering across fervent lips under haunted eyes—"Damn," he muttered. "I long to set you free."

Lem turned away. "Yeah, when you say it like that, sounds like we both want the same thing," she grumbled.

"Yet your version of freedom infringes upon my every right to it."

"Says the guy who had me in a stasis field." The lips fluttered no more. The crossed arms raised an inch, and Lem became one big smirk. "Me talking to Njande's not going to hurt you."

"There you couldn't be more wrong. He's planning an interdimensional invasion that will destroy the very fabric of our reality. But you won't believe that now." Diebol stood to end the conversation. "Nevertheless, very soon, you will choose between *him* and a real flesh-and-blood person who loves you. I hope you choose wisely."

Lem rose, too, stepping up to him, both fists clenched on the chair like she might beat him with it. "I won't choose," she spat.

"You'll have to."

She tightened her lips, nostrils flaring. He saw her throat move as she swallowed. But she did not throw that chair.

"It will be alright," Diebol said softly. "Come. I'll accompany you to your room, if you'd like to walk."

"I'll walk. But don't try to hold my hand or anything."

"I'll try not to."

Diebol smiled.

Through the doors, down the bronze hallway, their footsteps reverberating in low harmony together with every step, his just slightly lower pitched than hers … they made it all the way back to her cell without a fight.

The instant the cell door closed behind her, his smile evaporated. His wristband was shimmering with two missed messages—bloodseas, he was in an enormous heap of shyte. Bricandor wanted to see him in his council chamber, and Diebol knew exactly why. Damn that was fast. He'd hoped to have at least a few minutes before the "in my office now" to manufacture a good excuse.

Hopefully he could talk Bricandor down to a few more weeks.

CHAPTER NINE

Lem

As soon as the door to the small copper cell closed behind her Lem collapsed against it with her eyes squeezed shut. She hurt. Her face contorted without her permission, her teeth clenched, one hand gripped her shoulder ... the other clawed at her stomach.

It wasn't just slamming through the door, or getting kicked in the guts by people who wore freakin' armor, or straining against the stasis fields 'til her neurons screamed at her to stop. None of that mattered. Shyte, he couldn't have her family—not a single one of them. Lem couldn't afford to fail anymore on these escape attempts. Now she had a time limit. One shot. *Shyte* ... she exhaled, eyes still squeezed shut, and slid to the floor.

"Are you okay?"

Gah! Lem's eyes fluttered open; Bereens was crouching across from her, elbows on his knees, leaning against the opposite wall of the small copper cell.

She nodded, forcibly slowing her breathing to prove it. He rose, and knelt beside her to check her vitals. Yup, that was this guy, true to protocol, all reaching for her throat to check her pulse. Lem pushed his hand away. She could still hear Dr. Pattie Loylan's squeaky bird-like voice in basic battle first aid: *"No, the human carotid is here, silly" … "Always look out for each other, cadets. No one else will."*

"You need to answer me, cadet," Bereens said.

"Yeah, yeah, gimme a sec, I'll be fine," Lem said, squinting up at him. "Is it Fernando?"

"What?" He straightened, away from her, as if the name physically repulsed him. "Excuse me?"

"Is your first name Fernando," she repeated, stifling a giggle.

"No my name's not Fernando," he scowled. "You gonna tell me what happened back there? What got you the idea you could just start a battle in the middle of the hallway and send me off to make phone calls?"

"Sorry, I'm used to being in charge."

"So am I."

"Guess we'll have to rock-paper-scissors next time then."

"I don't know how to get this through your head, but I'm not joking," he snapped. "We should've headed to the escape pods."

"And gotten blown to bits when they see them floating away?" Lem raised a laughing eyebrow. "What messed-up science fiction you watchin', man? You got something against living?"

"Fair enough. Maybe if we took them quietly no one would have noticed. But with the way you monstered down the door, and then started pounding random people in the hallway, it's a miracle we didn't have *every blitzer in the tanker* on us."

"I'm sorry, did you want me to knock first?" Lem asked. "Maybe dig you out with a spoon made of feathers? I didn't have a 'quiet' way to get out of my cell—moment I broke loose the clock was ticking, so I was in *just a little hurry* to get stuff done."

"What stuff? Did you know about the attack?"

She stiffened. "What attack?"

Bereens sat back against the door beside her, running a hand through his hair and exhaling stress. "Strike force of a thousand Stygges," he said. "Scheduled to demolish Fort Jehu next month. They've got blueprints of the entire base, somehow."

"The Shadow!" Lem leaned forward, a hand on her forehead. "Shyte, did you see the children's complex on there?"

"No. You know that's never documented. Why?"

Lem dropped back against the door. "They got the Ebon Shadow hunting my family."

"You think he got them the blueprints?" Bereens asked. "That makes sense. He costs way too much for them to hire him just to get to some no-name cadet."

Some no-name cadet—gah, what an a-hole. Lem rose to the bait. "Why are you like this?" she asked. He stared at her like he wondered if she really wanted an answer. "Scratch that, everyone knows why you're like this," she groaned, rubbing her hands over her eyes. "Look, I'm sorry, I can see that Diebol—"

"We're not going to talk about that."

Lem sighed, leaning her head back against the wall and staring at her reflection on the ceiling. "A'ight. You know what we should talk about, though. How we're gonna get the news of the attack back home. I got a message through on a civilian freq while you were tangling with your boy back there, but I didn't know about the attack when I sent it."

"Who did you send it to?"

"My buddy Cinta."

"You mean the civilian space-lemur you hang around?"

"Yeah. We kinda grew up together. His family took me in the two years my parents were in—you know. When the Growen had them." She let her head fall to the side to look at him, make sure he knew what she meant. He nodded—actually made eye contact for a second. Hey, progress. She went on. "It might be too late for the fort by the time Cinta gets someone to come pick us up, and it'll definitely be too late for my siblings. So we've gotta figure something out."

"You mean *if* he gets someone to come pick us up," Bereens grimaced. "You did good work, but you sent your message from a point in outer space. We'll have landed somewhere by the time anyone back home even takes off."

"He'll figure it out. Biouks are master-trackers."

"It's not like his nose is going to do much good in *space*."

Lem scowled. "I'm not talking about his biology—he's a person, not a dog or something coming to sniff me out. It's just that Biouks are usually smarter about hunting."

"That's speciesist."

"No, it's not. I said *usually*, and usually means usually. I'm not saying all other species universally suck, I'm saying—"

Bereens dragged his palms over his face in exasperation; he might as well have told her to shut up. Lem wanted to punch him.

"What is wrong with you?" they both exclaimed at the same time.

Bereens huffed and looked away; Lem ran her fingers through her now much-shorter hair and chuckled: "Okay, you first. What's wrong with me?"

Bereens messed with the hem of his pants leg instead of looking at her when he spoke. "Look, I really don't mean to be a jerk. We want the same thing here. But—bloodseas, what world do you even think you're living in? Everything's funny to you, in your mind everyone's coming to rescue you—first Njandejara, now your friend —and that's not how this universe functions! Life's not a video game: these levels aren't somehow designed with a way out!"

"That's when I make a way out," Lem grinned. "Bust a hole in the wall."

"No! That's—"

"Okay, my turn now."

"You don't get a turn," he said.

Lem punched his arm. Damn, his shoulder was hard. "Yes, I do. You admitted you're Contaminated. That means you routinely talk to an invisible dude from another dimension. So how come you're so incredibly hopeless? You need to chill out. Or at least, quit trying to throw your soggy attitude on me, 'cuz I don't need to mope about dying tomorrow when I still got today. Also, something's *really* not right with you and that Diebol guy. And also—what? What's funny?"

Bereens smiled. "Guess I'm not the only one with a list."

"Oh, you had more? Let's hear it." Lem folded her arms.

He laughed. "What is this, group therapy?"

"Maybe. You sure need it," Lem said. He didn't answer for a second, and she almost took it back. Maybe you didn't joke about group therapy to a guy with trauma issues …

Bereens glanced at her momentarily, eyes twinkling, and lay back on the floor with his hands folded behind his head. "Alright, here's my therapy couch," he said. "And you? You're going to listen now."

"Okay."

He sighed and looked at the ceiling for a moment. When he turned his head to look up at Lem, straight in the eye, the seriousness was back in full force.

"Lem," he said. "I don't mean to act like I don't think Njandejara cares. I'm sure he's got good reasons for when he shows up and when he doesn't. That's part of my issue with you, actually: don't you think he's got bigger things to do? In his own dimension, with his own wars against all the other interdimensionals who hate him for talking to us—isn't it a bit arrogant to act like he revolves around you? Like things are always going to go well because he's always going to be there?"

Lem hugged her knees. Wow, he was kind of intense. "I do think he's always here," she said quietly.

"So what happens when he's not?"

"That's not a real thing."

Bereens sat up suddenly, his gaze sharpening. "Yes, it is," he said. "There are moments when you'll find yourself completely, utterly alone, no backup, no ride home, no phone call. Moments when you live day to day in hell, and you make every choice for survival *on your own*. And that's real life. That's where we are."

She stared back at him for a second. Shyte, he was talking about his past. Lem balked a moment before answering. "He's—he's invisible, dude. 'Course you're gonna think you're alone. But you're not."

Bereens turned away from her to scowl at the hem of his pants again. "Well, if you were right, he'd be an extremely horrible friend for standing there and doing nothing."

"Mebbe he is doing things, and you can't see it. He's invisible."

"Well in that case, what *difference does it make* if he stands there and does things I can't see, or if he's far away and visits once in a while? It all amounts to the same reality: you're steeped in false hope, and it's not just annoying, you make bad tactical decisions because of it. We don't fight because we're guaranteed to win, we fight because it's the right thing to do!"

"Screw the right thing to do," Lem snapped. "I fight 'cuz I like him, and I like him here with me. So you can keep your good tactical decisions and your tragic honor or whatever, but I'll keep smashing things 'til they let me go. Screw you all!"

Bereens threw his hands over his face again. "Do you even hear yourself talking? Keep smashing things?"

"I know a face I'd kinda like to smash right now, actually."

"Whoa, hey." Bereens raised his palms. "Easy now."

Lem hugged her knees tighter and stared straight ahead. She wanted out of this conversation. Away from this loser who thought she was crazy. Cinta believed in her. Where the hell was he?

"Look," Bereens said. "All I'm saying is, I'll be eternally grateful if you'd lay low until we landed, because you're *this* close to getting us executed."

"I gotta get out before they make me choose between my family and Njande!" she hissed. "'Sides, you didn't seem to have a problem with getting executed before. Something change when your boy showed up?"

"What? No! I absolutely did have a problem with being executed! But now the game's different. They don't want any information out of us: they want to turn us into them. And we may be the only living sapients outside of the Growen army that know about the Stygge attack. We've got to play along, maximize our chance of survival." He lowered his voice. "Build a better escape plan later."

Lem looked around the room. "You just talking for the cameras?"

"Does it matter?"

Lem crossed her arms. "I don't wanna pretend, and I'm not gonna pretend to pretend. They don't have the right to control how I act."

"Yes, fantastic, and shoot everyone else in the face with your freedom, please." With that the pleasantness was gone. In three strides Bereens crossed the room and lay down with his back to her. "Good night."

"It's not night."

"Yes, thank you, good-insert-time-of-day-here, then."

So silence fell. At least she had someone else's breathing to listen to instead of just her own. Dammit, she wished she had better words, words that didn't sound so simplistic and naïve. She longed to draw back the curtain, the thick veil of mist and shadow that bound her to this limited, boring dimension of threes, and show him Njande in a different way ...

But she couldn't, because she was stuck inside a human experience as limited as his. A huge empty room with no way out.

"I will make a way out," she muttered. But her heart whispered: *Cinta ... please hurry up and save me.*

CHAPTER TEN

Cinta

WHEN A SISTER IS TAKEN, A BROTHER IS LOST.

So said the proverb. It meant, in an old-fashioned manner, that Biouk space-lemur women were hunters and brothers as worthy as Biouk males. Now Cinta saw it differently. His sister Jaika—Lem, the humans called her—she was gone, and he felt lost.

When Cinta first received word of Jaika's disappearance, he tried to trust her paramilitary group would handle it. He was a scientist, not a soldier. He did not enjoy this, this trusting them. He hated it. Yet he found himself helpless to believe anything else, for no matter how long he scoured the same spot in the forest, pawing the earthy leaves for her footprint, dredging the air for her scent—

"Those who live by the sword, die by the sword," his grandmother would say.

"Leave it to the professionals," Jaika's commanding officer had said.

Yet in this new text message, Jaika had not asked for the professionals.

She had asked for Cinta.

Cinta took to the trees to answer. Long, oval leaves streaked with green and purple soothed Cinta's furred skin with their cool velum, and a sweet, acidic tendril of scent called to him as he passed: fresh bunches of violet lechichi fruit hung plump nearby, sensually veiled by scant vines, begging for a touch, a taste.

But the summons went unheeded; Cinta's gallop through the treetops did not slow. Leathery Biouk paws wrapped around the folds and nicks of the tree bark; Cinta's foreclaws retracted as he ran, then extended as he reached the end of the branch and leapt stretched out like a flying squirrel—

He latched onto the next tree, his heart thudding in his thin chest like a war drum. Almost there. He smelled bleaches and wet, aromatic engine fumes, and the sharp plastic undertone of melted polymerwall long before he saw the Frelsi base, its crystal walls glistening in the sunlight, a giant dewdrop among the forest leaves.

Cinta scampered on all fours down to the mossy soil, ears the size of his face standing erect and alert on his bullet-shaped head, flickering to this side, then that. He broke out of the underbrush onto the walking path beside the main road. His reflection in a mud puddle scolded him: *Your fangs do not even show outside your mouth yet. You are a child, not yet thirty. What are you doing here?*

Cinta drew back his upper lip and snarled. He would show them his fangs.

The clear walls towered above Cinta's head, at least the height of two full-grown trees stacked end to end atop one another, and as thick as three trunks. Sparse traffic from the main road—a few sparrow-like metal air-riders and a camouflaged land-car turned left to follow the wall toward the vehicle gate; Cinta continued straight ahead on foot.

The four military police at the walking gate greeted Cinta's approach with rifles ready, feet planted and shoulders squared: one purple reptilian, one mantis-like bipedal insectoid, a Biouk like Cinta—sand-colored, instead of rich chestnut—and an olive-skinned female human. They did not relax their stance, but the human greeted him with a gentle smile and spoke in Biouk, Cinta's mother-tongue.

"We haven't heard anything new about her, Cinta," she said.

"No, but I have," he said. "I need to see her commanding officer."

"I'm afraid he's not—"

"She sent me a message!" Cinta cried, yanking the little square transmission screen from the pouch in his midsection and shoving it towards her like an entry badge. "I need your help to track it!"

The tan colored Biouk policeman flicked his paws into some signal Cinta couldn't quite catch, and the taller guards backed off. The Biouk dodged around their legs to approach Cinta. "Patience, my son," he said. "I'm requesting entrance for you now. Have a seat in the shade."

Cinta nodded in respect to the stranger, retreating a few paces to plant himself under a hibiscus bush. He watched as the tan gentleman fiddled with his wristband, and wondered if the policeman came from the moon: his muzzle seemed too narrow to belong to a planet-bound family like Cinta's. The policeman's incisors jutted almost to his chest, and his bulky, thick musculature belied a Biouk at least fifty years old. He wasn't any taller than Cinta—still less than three feet, including his giant round ears—but his waist was at least twice Cinta's slender form. *He is old enough to know better.*

"Forgive my impertinence, uncle," Cinta asked. "But what is a neighbor of your wisdom and age doing with a *military* group?"

"Helping you find your friend, my son," the gentleman replied.

Cinta rubbed his muzzle with his paws, embarrassed. Best not to insult people you'd just asked for help. "Forgive me—I meant it as an honest question."

"And I gave an honest answer." The gentleman looked off in the distance for a moment, and then back at Cinta with one ear twitched to the side. "Tell me, young son, what do you do?"

"I'm studying biomedical science, uncle. To become a healer or a researcher."

"Mm." The gentleman grunted; Cinta expected him to tell a lesson, perhaps a pithy quote about how knowledge would not end tyranny, but the gentleman's wristband lit up; his ears perked, and he waved his forepaw at Cinta with a grin. "Come, scientist. Let me check your pawprint and pat you down, and then I shall escort you inside."

DIEBOL

The cool scent of minty incense pricked Diebol's senses, as if waking him from sleep. He blinked, eyes stinging a bit as the polymerwall to his master's chambers gelled shut behind him.

His master was seated on the floor of the empty room, legs crossed and eyes closed. Various communication devices lay around him, shut off for a few precious moments; the master spent most of his time negotiating with the myriad known planets. It worked because he looked like someone's loving grandfather, but had the tenacity of the most powerful corporate leaders in the galaxy. Bricandor's words could kill and create.

The master's eyes opened as Diebol knelt in front of him. Bricandor wasted no time: "We have poured enough money to conquer an entire planet into the coffers of these assassins, and you're using one of them for your personal games?"

"It's another way to build the Stygge army, father," Diebol blurted. Bricandor narrowed his eyes; Diebol had better slow this speech to show control. "The Ebon Shadow is hunting a family the campaign would capture anyway, sir. The relatives of an electromagnetic likely have the gene, too."

"We're killing their electromagnetics, not capturing them," Bricandor muttered, rising now to fasten the various devices around his belt.

"Unless I can cure them, you said, remember, sir," Diebol reminded him. "There are many ways to build a monopoly on power."

"Mm, I did say that." Bricandor had begun texting someone— but then looked up, and tilted his head, as if listening …

"Don't kill the family. Bring in her sister," he said finally.

Her sister. Alright. Diebol nodded: Bricandor's unusual insights had caught many a Contaminated intruder, and saved many a failing mission. The man almost had the power of an interdimensional himself.

"I will bring in her sister," he repeated. Bricandor had drilled the TEAMSTEPPS rules into his head: when given a command, you repeated it back to avoid miscommunication.

Bricandor lifted another device, and began texting there. The lack of eye contact didn't really bother Diebol—he'd seen Bricandor woo and destroy an enemy, and it always involved a great deal of eye contact and copious friendly body language. Being semi-ignored was a comfort. Diebol refrained from coughing in the uncomfortable silence—to show he could handle it—and then spoke again. "Bricandor, I greatly appreciate the chance you've given me. I know you will find Jei Bereens an incredible asset once he's cured."

"Mm." Bricandor continued texting. "It's a pity we could not enlist that old Bont lizard in our assassin's crew—Lark Scrita, was it? I believe she's killed for us before."

"I don't recall, sir," Diebol said.

"That tentacled gentleman does well, anyway. These assassins have extended our reach far beyond this Contested versus Undecided Zone foolishness." Bricandor masked his disdain for the Spaces Treaties in public, but in private, both the Growen and the Frelsi leaders detested the interplanetary agreements that restricted conflict to the Contested Zones, away from the independent planets. Both Frelsi and Growen leadership found it difficult to protect the independent planets from the others' invasions when they couldn't approach them; this new string of mercenary contracts, secured with funding from new technology sales, would now allow the Growen to circumvent these rules and promote independent regimes in favor of the Unification cause.

Bricandor looked up abruptly: eye contact. Diebol bit his lip. "But you've taken the best assassin for yourself," Bricandor said.

"His kill count is almost double that of the others put together," Diebol felt his insubordinate mouth fire off before he had time to breathe. "His signature is killing two targets on two different planets at once. My request will not slow him down."

Bricandor stared at him.

Diebol rose before the master could say anything, his heart racing suddenly. He had no more to say. He backed towards the door. *Breathe*, he told himself. Relax his body. Trust the master. Diebol needed that assassin, and he clung to the hope that the master would understand that as the stare grew harder and tighter and reminded him more and more of cages, whips, and a little boy who clung to the color green …

The master resumed texting on one device, and began a voice call on another.

Diebol let out a deep breath, and left to prove he could cure Jei Bereens.

CINTA

Cinta clenched his paws over his muzzle, cringing by the entrance to a plant-filled, slime-covered office, his back against the polymer-wall. Lem's commanding officer was throwing a fit.

The Wonderfrog slammed his wide, glistening face against the compuwall, leaving a wet streak in his wake. Cinta's little square transmission screen hung embedded in the wall, displaying Lem's message, and above it flashed a series of numbers Captain Rana apparently did not like. The amphibian's wide lips drooped as he groaned.

"That's so far out of the Contested Zone—so far out! Near a whole mess of undecided planets, a whole mess. Something like fifty treaties—fifty, maybe more!—keep us away from there. Growen aren't even supposed to be there. 'Course they can break all the rules and get away with it any day, any day. We get caught there and the terrorist claims come a'flying. Flying like flies. To our dead carcasses!"

The Wonderfrog collapsed on the floor beside the wall, his hind legs splayed and his front legs sticking out to the sides like the arms of a melting snowman. Cinta waited for a moment—perhaps the theatrics had worn him out? Cinta did not know many Wonderfrogs outside of Lem's Frelsi companions, and the over-the-top emotional body language in most sapient amphibian cultures took some getting used to.

Perhaps—maybe he was thinking?

A little water spray-hose came out of the floor to moisten the Captain's face.

Still there he sat, eyes closed.

Cinta checked his grammar in the common trade language, Grenblenian, and cleared his throat. "You cannot just give up!" he said.

The Wonderfrog whirled. His sharp, bulging eyes glistened. Cinta gulped.

"I say something about giving up, furry?" barked Captain Rana. "No. No Frelsi military presence, no sir, no sir. Bam. What we need's a good lie. A liar. I knew a liar once. I'll hire that liar."

Captain Rana began to scribble orders across the compuwall with his webbed hind-leg. It made a splat sound every time he pressed send, or lifted his foot to switch to another screen. Cinta tilted his head. *Does he know I am still here?* He raised his forepaw. "With respect, Captain, I am Biouk. We are—good for finding things."

"See now, I'm not speciesist. Not speciesist. Not assuming non-biological abilities based on your species. Also, happen to know you're underage. Too young."

Cinta folded his forepaws across his chest. "I am four years from thirty, older than most of your unit!"

"Ha! Again, not speciesist. I know Biouks. I know you're not adults 'til fifty revolutions around your sun. I don't see fangs on you. No fangs. No fangs, no adult, no job."

"That is—no, we are different. Emotions adult at thirty. Sex-u-al adult at fifty." Cinta stumbled over the pronunciation.

"Don't hire folks who haven't hit puberty yet. Puberty first, job later."

"But that is silly! I am best in my class, for research—for finding things, bi-oh-medical—and best hunter in my tribe. Why it matters if I can make babies or not? This job is not about making babies!"

The side of the Captain's mouth twisted, and the top of his muzzle flashed red for a second. The Wonderfrog equivalent of laughter—Cinta did not like it.

The Captain turned back to the wall and continued his plat-splat-scribbling. "I said, don't hire folks who haven't hit puberty yet. Legal liability. But twenty-six-year-old Biouks in my *unit* who finish their training—*finish* their training—I trust them. Don't hire, but do assign missions. See? You see."

Cinta flattened his big ears against his scalp and narrowed his eyes. He saw where this was going. "I will not join your war. Live by the sword, die by the sword."

"Eh, some things are worth sword-dying for," the Captain's wet eyes twinkled. "Benzaran told me you'd make a good soldier. Great soldier. But wanna be a doctor, huh? Doctor. Don't even like visiting this place. Anti-war?"

"Yes. Killing is evil."

"Am I evil, then, I wonder? I wonder." The Captain sidled over to Cinta, his back legs swimming across the floor and his torso undulating like a sidewinder's. His wet breath clung to Cinta's fur like fog, and Cinta became keenly aware he could fit in the Captain's wide mouth with room to spare. "I wonder." The Captain licked his lips.

Cinta puffed out his chest. His fur stood on end. His foreclaws extended.

"Hold on, now, don't be angry." The Captain sidled away, back to the compuwall. "I'm just being an amphibian, you're just being a mammal. Just being us. If you took cultural sensitivity training you'd know, you'd know. You'd know."

Cinta's face heated and his chest flared in anger. Cultural sensitivity? His forepaws stiffened like knives. "You do not understand," he growled, struggling to steady his voice. "I am not afraid of you. I am not angry at you. Your face is strange to me, but that is not my problem. I want my friend, and you stand in my way."

"You're not a soldier, furry. Not a soldier. Can't send civilians on dangerous missions. You die, then what? Then what." The Captain's muzzle flashed blue this time, and his big wet eyes sloped —sadness? "You better leave now. I must find my soldier. My soldier."

The Captain pulled Cinta's little transmission screen off the wall and held it out to Cinta in the palm of his webbed back foot. Cinta glared at it.

In freighter en route to training center for Stygge army. Pantota mika sifta, watch out for my si—

The abrupt ending gave Cinta little comfort. But *Pantota mika sifta*—Cinta, to me, arrive like the wind, written in the Biouk moon language instead of in the standard planetary all their friends and family used. Written in their private code …

Cinta lowered his head, a slow burn rising from the embers in his eyes. "You find her first, I join your fight. I find her first, you quit. No more killing for you."

"Cultural sensitivity training said you'd say something like that. Something like that—ultimatums, bets of honor, very Biouk, Biouk, Biouk." The wet hind-leg flopped across Cinta's shoulder in a pat. "I'll see you at training. But I told you not to go. I told you not to go. I told you not to go."

Repetition meant importance in many amphibious cultures. But in the Captain's thick, warbly accent, deep and guttural, reminiscent of isolated paths through foggy, tangled swamps filled with eerie sounds and watching eyes—all glistening wet orbs with slit irises, glowing in the musty darkness—the warning sounded like a threat.

CHAPTER ELEVEN

Lark Scrita

BOUNTY HUNTER LARK SCRITA POPPED ANOTHER STICK OF VANILLA ChewDat in her mouth as she read from the compupad mounted on the treadmill. She kept an eye out for the late-night gym security guard who had perhaps possibly realized she did not in fact have a membership here, and she kept her free hand swinging her fire-whip. Must build that wrist strength.

I know what you are.

I do not, in the strictest sense, know what you are physically. Bont lizard is what you want us to think—wide-snouted, heavy-set, scaled tan reptilian biped with that breathing mask for high-oxygen environments. But you and I both know what you really are.

And that is a liar.

This Frelsi bloke, Captain Rana, had Lark's attention with the insult. And it looked like she had his, too, after her brilliant pro bono rescue of Zhirskahm Frland. Cute little lizard-boy kidnapped by a meat-marketer just outside of Retrack City—home safe now, undamaged, but scared silly, poor lad. Apparently the lass originally assigned to Zhirskahm's case went missing a few days ago. These Frelsi nutters just couldn't keep their people at home.

Belt up! Lark almost spat on her compupad. They wanted her because she could move in the Undecided Zone and they couldn't—

but they wanted her to bring a recording device with them? What was she, a glorified guide? No. No no no no. Lark Scrita did consulting, not guide-work. It said that on her business cards, and those were embossed and everything. She'd had to kidnap the print company manager to print those business cards. Couldn't the croaker read?

I am sure you're aware of the politics surrounding these coordinates; if my two electromagnetics are being held on an Undecided planet we'll need to know. Just find them, and I'll handle any diplomatic developments.

Lark Scrita smirked and deleted the transmission. She'd accept the mission, but dancing to a rhythm from someone hundreds of planets away? Beans no, no waiting around for diplomatic support, no thank you, never in a million years. If she had to finagle a rescue that didn't look Frelsi, and didn't look hers, either, she'd need bloody room to *breathe*, thanks. The tough part? Getting the Frelsi to feel like heroes without actually letting them *do* anything.

Lark vaulted over the side of the treadmill and pranced to the locker room, grinning as the lit hallway mirrors lied back to her, shimmering with the reflection of a wealthy woman who might have a gym membership here. Bright red insectoid carapace; full painted purple lips on a long stalk proboscis; diamond chains draped around her long, grasshopper-like abdomen, thin wrists, and elegant spiked arms; and a model slim waist and flat thorax free of the natural fat-pad build-up these odd sapients struggled against.

"Odd sapients"—*ack no*, Lark corrected her own thoughts. What affluent Vibrant-class Insectoid thought of herself as odd? "Oh beans, I really ought to be classified as a reptile, or a mammal, or something else, because I breathe through nutty lung-gills, not holes in my arse like a cockroach." No! She wouldn't give a spiky toenail over it. Sure, she might get twitchy antennae squishing a grasshopper because it looked like a fairy to her—but she didn't think of *herself* as a bug.

Lark altered her thoughts further, diving full-method into her role. She wasn't odd, unclassified, or even discriminated against.

She was on her own planet, a high-society aristocrat, a company owner, the most eligible bachelorette in town. Lark tilted her chin a little higher, swaggered a little wider … and slipped into the men's locker room.

"Hey!" The security guard burst through the door. "You can't go in here, this is—"

"Eh? Why can't I go in here?" The patron growled back at him.

The security guard stammered, for now the bathroom mirrors told a different lie. Gone was Lark's feminine red exoskeleton, the soft swollen abdomen ripe with eggs; say 'ello to a thin, short, hard rear with poisonous spikes, jasper-colored wings folded across a long, proud thorax, and mottled brown built-in armor. A male Vibrant. A rather intimidating male Vibrant, clicking together large black mandibles in irritation. "A li'l privacy, eh?"

"Eh, for sure, for sure, sir. Excuse me."

Lark grinned as the guard hustled away muttering about "where that suspicious little wench got to." Liar? Yes she was. And a bloody good one, too. She'd haul up Lem Benzaran and Jei Bereens faster than a singing day-lizard could swallow a peacock-pig.

Lark tapped the film on her shoulder, altering her DNA projection to fade out of the insectoid and into her standard lizard identity; then she buckled her utility belt under her leather jacket, slung her holster to her hip, tied her whip over her belt, and slipped on her heavy, broad-muzzled helmet. She yanked black leather gloves over her claws and swung her flayer cannon onto her back.

Time to lie.

CHAPTER TWELVE

Lem

THE STARS TWINKLED WITH GENTLE LAUGHTER AS LEM STOKED THE fire with a smooth stick she'd found in the woods, snuggling her arm closer to Cinta's warm fur as his crusty voice started to tell her …

"Hey. Wake up and strap yourself in."

Lem grumbled. The dream evaporated and the groggy reality of a shaking copper prison punched her in the eyes. "Didn't even get to hear what he was gonna say," she muttered.

"What?" Bereens asked.

"Nuthin'." The floor's gentle vibrations had disappeared under a wild clattering, rocking, shudder, like a giant baby'd found their cell in a box and wanted to know what was in it. Shake shake shake! Lem crawled to the wall, reached for the vinyl straps hanging there, and belted herself in against the copper. "Looks like we're landing, huh."

Bereens adjusted his buckles, settling in by her side. His knuckles paled as he gripped the straps. Lem watched his nervousness for a second—no way was this guy afraid of atmospheric re-entry. So what was …

Ah. He was grimacing at the door. He wasn't worried about

exploding mid-air or crash-landing as the hulking freighter set down. He was worried about what came after they landed.

"It's easier to escape on a planet than in space," she offered reassuringly.

He huffed and didn't answer. Oh, right, back to this grumpy silence. She paused for a moment, tilting her head to the side. "Is it Carlitos?" she asked.

"Are we *still* on my name? Is there a reason you keep picking names from one particular extinct language?"

"You kinda fit a genetic profile, that's all. It's not a bad thing."

"Wow."

"Okay, fine," she snapped. "How about Richtensteinhind, is that a better guess, ass-face?"

The side of his mouth twitched upward. Uh-huh. "Good luck holding in that laugh, Cadet Commander Tighty," Lem said. "Careful you don't bust a blood vessel."

"You're ridiculous," he grumbled. But he was smiling, and as he leaned his head back against the wall to look at the ceiling his shoulders relaxed. "You don't give up, do you?"

"Never."

He licked his lips, still staring at the trembling ceiling. "So how'd you get out of your stasis field back there?" he asked.

"They took it off me when they put me in my cell. Then I busted the door down."

His eyes narrowed. "You busted the door down."

"I mean, you can ask Diebol if you don't believe me."

"No, sorry, I don't disbelieve you, I just—I wasn't aware your abilities were that … functional."

Lem let herself glow just a tiny bit with the compliment-insult. "I just tried harder," she shrugged. "That's how it works with everything: you try harder, 'til you see lights and it hurts, and you push through that hurt, and things happen."

"Why not?"

"Took a class on epilepsy. With Dr. Pattie, right? She said epilepsy happens when you get over-firing, over-stimulation of neurons—too much of a thing called glutamate—and sometimes you'll hallucinate lights and stuff before a seizure. So now I'm kind of scared of going too far."

"So you think the sparks you saw aren't real." His inquisitive stare was uncomfortable for her, and she tried to inch away from him a bit. "You think you were hallucinating lights."

"I'm not crazy," she muttered. "'Course I know they weren't real."

"You should do it again," he said. "Not bust down the door, because that's obnoxious, but make sparks again."

"What, and kill myself?" Lem dropped a nervous laugh. Bereens waited and said nothing. "Wait, you're serious," Lem realized. "You think I can make electricity."

"Well. Eels on the human homeworld could."

"Dunno if you noticed, but I'm not an eel."

He didn't rise to that—he leaned in with earnest excitement in his sober eyes, like he had a secret. "Okay, Lem, you know how the nerve connection to your muscles works, right? From Dr. Pattie's class?"

"Yeah." Dr. Pattie always went out of her way to teach far more science than a teen soldier actually ever needs to know. Lem figured the woman was lonely and needed someone to listen. "Nerves drop a chemical, ACh—uh, acetylcholine—that releases the calcium burst that make your muscles move."

"Right. So in electric eels it's like that, but instead of synapsing with a muscle, this nerve synapses with a group of specialized cells lined up as electric plates. When acetylcholine hits these plates, it opens sodium channels in them."

"A'ight." Lem followed. But … "Why would that make a spark? I mean, that sounds like how normal nerves work. Sodium channels open, positive ions get into the cell, that changes the charge of the cell, that charge-energy-stuff leaves as an action potential. Like a thought. A signal along the wire. What's different?"

"Because these specialized eel cells aren't arranged like a wire, but in five thousand plates parallel to each other, like thousands of tiny capacitors. Now that energy doesn't have a wire to travel. So you're stuck with five thousand plates all adding up to a huge charge difference compared to what's around them. That electricity has to go somewhere, so …"

"So it discharges in a spark," Lem realized. "A shock?"

"Roger that." He grinned.

Lem pursed her lips. She didn't exactly have a reason to disbelieve him, but eels that could fire electricity did seem a little crazy. "Why don't they shock themselves?" she asked.

"I have no idea." He shrugged.

"So you think I can shock people? Like an electric eel?"

"I don't know. It'd be a pretty exciting find if you can. I don't know how else you broke a solid door and still can't em-push to save your life." He smirked. "Literally, you can't em-push to save your life."

Lem groaned, slumping back against the wall. "Oh gosh, you seriously getting on my case about the hallway, by the airlock? When that guy had his rifle in my face?"

"Yup."

"So, fine, I have a weakness, okay? Guns are my weakness. So shoot me."

He laughed. "I think they're everyone's—"

A deep grinding sound interrupted them—then, a sudden thump. Lem looked to Bereens, her eyes wide; he bit his lip, and stillness overtook them. The shakes stopped; the vibrations of the engines ceased; all was dead, lukewarm metal. After a few seconds the walls hissed, and a whooshing blast of pine-scented air filled the cell.

They'd landed.

Lem looked at the door as she unbuckled her wall harness, suddenly jittery. Now came the opportunities for escape.

The opportunities she couldn't mess up anymore.

BEREENS

No one came to get us for a while. I'd transported prisoners of my own before, so I could literally walk through the minutes, envisioning when they'd set up a security perimeter, when they'd unload what equipment, when they'd unpack everyone else, and when they'd come get their troublemakers. Focusing on the process was supposed to keep me calm.

It actually just made everything feel inescapable, as inevitable as the march of time.

Lem, on the other hand, was either not stressed at all, or dealing with her stress by saying dumb stuff. I couldn't decide which. "So," she asked, "we gonna make a bet to see who can cost them more money during our escape?"

"No, we are not. That will get us killed."

"Nah, a little sabotage is fun! We—"

I turned to face her squarely. "You need to do two things. One, you need to come to terms with the fact that we might die."

"Done."

"No, seriously."

"Yeah."

"Okay, forget it. Two—" I glanced at the walls and leaned in. My hands hid my lips by her ear so their cameras couldn't catch the flickers of more gradual escape coalescing in my mind. I whispered—

Diebol fanfared his way through the door, clapping, flanked by six Stygge trainees carrying two stasis fields. "Oh, I'm sorry, were you plotting?" he sneered. "Or were those sweet nothings you were planting in her ear? My, it appears you're moving in on my damsel."

Lem snarled—and bolted.

But not for the door. She was on Diebol's throat, screaming in his face, her knee jammed between his legs, fist pounding again and again at his jaw, fingernails tearing at his neck—

He threw her off him with a hoarse cry and drew his mace. Six other maces lit up: the Stygge trainees pounced, snapped the stasis field around her neck, and one of them raised his mace over her head—

Diebol held up his hand, coughing as he rose to his feet. His face mirrored my shock; eyes wide, mouth open, and everything tensed as he panted, stooped over in pain, wiping his mouth. I think he didn't kick her back because he was, for a brief moment, terrified.

"What the hell was that?" he gasped.

"I'm not yours. I don't belong to anyone." She snarled in almost the eerie double-voice of a threatened cat. Her eyes blazed. "And if you forget it again I'll tear out your throat."

Diebol looked at me with a nervous laugh. I didn't know what to say. I didn't think it was funny.

CHAPTER THIRTEEN

Lem

LEM'S CHEST WAS STILL HEAVING WHEN THEY STEPPED OFF THE gangplank into the sunlight. The scent of cedar wafted toward her; she blinked against the oranges and pinks in the sky, trying to orient herself and slow her breathing. Wow. She'd blown it. Shyte, that was the worst ever, maybe worse than a year ago. She'd been doing so well.

But she wasn't his! She didn't belong to anyone! She wasn't—

Calm the hell down, she told herself. *Calm the hell down, or you're going to get everyone killed.*

Bloodseas, she needed Cinta. He'd have stopped her—he could almost smell it before she flipped out. He'd catch the flicker in her eyes or something. What'd he always say?

Njandejara showed me the trees. Be the tree. A tree knows peace.

There were plenty of trees here to tap. Conifer needles rustled in a chilly breeze that somehow didn't carry much air; Lem inhaled a long draught, her face tingling as the sweat evaporated and the altitude shocked her system. A delightful jolt. Behind her, the freighter was parked on a cliffside overlooking miles of pine, and in the far distance jutted mountains and cliffs—but mountains of stranger shape than she'd ever imagined, another piece in her surrealist dream. *I'm lighter here.* Less gravity meant spiraling rock clawed like fingers reaching for the sky, scraping the heavens against a pink sunset as if they'd made it bleed. The rocks twisted like ghouls frozen in beautiful screams.

I'd totally put my re-education center here, too.

"Looks like we're on Revelon," Lem heard Bereens mutter to Diebol. "This is Undecided Space."

"Is it? I wouldn't know," Diebol smiled.

A Growen center illegally hidden in civilian territory?

The Bichank on Lem's left pushed her, and she shuffled on yellow rock away from the tanker and the view. They entered the shade of the forest and gradually traversed a dry, powdery soil uphill. Lem wanted to take her boots off and run through the pine needles. *Cinta would love this place.* Cool, regal, stern ... peaceful.

Everything she wasn't. Dammit, what an awful lapse. How many synapses had she burned this time? How many fits 'til she drove herself insane, or gave herself a seizure, or

Gah, but none of that mattered. Her connection to Njande mattered. Rage, cruelty, unfaithfulness, greed, lust—lots of things killed it. Anger wasn't evil any more than desire was, but those sudden, violent fits burned out the synaptic patterns in her mind that let her *sense* him. She shivered. If this got worse, he'd be there, but she'd never know, never hear him again, as if he didn't exist; she'd be like the woman with her spinal cord nicked, the injured mother who can't feel her lover's touch on her skin or tell hot from cold or sense her child's wet kiss on her hand. Lem would keep all that. But she'd lose her sense of *him*, those rare moments when the weight of the stars, the scent of the earth, a tingle in the air, everything became more than it was, and brushing beneath her fingertips, soft like full fur and sharp like ice water, she touched pure happiness; when she glimpsed him for a moment, and her every neuron grew overwhelmed with—

What would Njande say when he found out she'd singed more synapses? He probably knew already. Her cheeks burned. She glanced at Bereens out the corner of her eye, trying *not* to guess what *he* was thinking. He probably knew about the synapse thing, too. All Contaminated people did.

In an instant they'd stepped out of the forest. A white spire rose from the cliff-top before them, its shape a parody of the mountains Lem had seen behind the landing pad: a crayon imitation to a master's *magnum opus.*

"Welcome to the Stygge Training Center," Diebol smiled, waving his hand. The wind played with his hair and vest. "You won't be receiving orientation with your fellow students because you're Contaminated—and apparently also have rabies"—he glared at Lem—"but don't worry! We'll get right to work."

Blablabla … Lem eyed the side of the cliff, below the white spire, where a sewage pipe shot out over a deep, rushing river. The hill narrowed as they approached the steep incline leading up to the spire; soon they walked only three abreast, with a cliff on either side. On their left the drop ended in stones and spear-like cedar trees; on the right the river settled into a sandy-banked pool. Lem began to wheeze in the thin atmosphere.

That sewage pipe, though. Escape route for sure.

Giant white wall, right in front of them. Holy *shyte* did the Center look taller up close. Lem watched Diebol as the Stygges stopped; he waved his palm over the creamy surface, and the entire wall retracted, slurping up into an archway, to let them pass.

So Diebol's DNA was the masterkey: security was so tight they had to peel up the polymerwall to let anyone get in. That meant not even the guards' DNA would let them phase through.

Inside, under the cool shadow of the doorway, Lem immediately began counting hallways to memorize her escape route—

"Blindfolds, please," Diebol smiled.

"Shyte," Lem spat.

Diebol chuckled.

She'd seen three arched, ivory hallways branching off from the entrance. But without any other identifying markers, and no clear doorway separating the polymerwall from the rest of the wall, now she had no way to remember where the entrance *was*. She tried to keep count of the left and right turns they took …

It soon felt like they were going in circles.

No wait—because they *were* going in circles? Wait, why were they spinning her?

"This is stupid," she grumbled.

"Roger that," she heard Bereens growl. "First reasonable thing you've said all day."

"Alright, new rule." Diebol's voice sounded like lechichi fruit left to spoil out in the sun—sweet on the surface, full of angry writhing bugs underneath. "You two will not be speaking to each other except during training exercises. If you do, you will lose food privileges. Understood?"

"Go rot in the sun," Lem muttered.

"Understood," Bereens said. Man, screw his compliance.

"I want you to contemplate your new rooms," said Diebol. "They mean something. They are here to teach you. To break down your faulty understanding of reality."

Lem started to retort. "I'll break down *your*—" But someone shoved her, spun her around, yanked the stasis field collar off her neck, whipped the blindfold off, and slammed a door. She stumbled backwards—she blinked—she stretched out her arms and caught her balance.

The cell's dimensions caught her off guard. The back wall seemed so far away, like they'd left her in a dim, empty, monochrome silver hallway—

But now she was touching the back wall.

That wasn't right.

Lem whirled to check the distance back to the door.

The door was gone.

Huh. So they did have polymerwall installed here.

But—wait, hadn't she come in through a door? Polymerwalls didn't slam. They might hum as the sensors detected your genome, and they slurped as the wall softened to let you through. But no slamming. She'd heard a door slam?

No. I'm not *hearing things.*

Wait, there was the door. On her left. But shouldn't it be behind her? Or in front of her, actually, since she'd just turned around —hadn't she?

Oookay, time to sit down.

But the floor felt sloped, and it was uncomfortable to sit sliding forward. So she stood to lean on the wall. And the floor was flat again. And she was leaning on the door?

"What the bloodseas is this supposed to be?" Lem shouted. "Hey, you people—I know you got a camera in here—hey this's a weird way to get your funsies!"

No answer. Like the silent guards in the hallway. Like the dead Bichank settlement.

"You people suck," Lem said. She lay down. She could see her reflection on the ceiling, with that scratch on her cheek and the cinnamon tan-line on her right wrist …

Ah yes, her wristband. She had one thing going for her: she'd gotten that message home to Cinta. He would find her. A deep exhale flowed past her lips as her heart rate calmed.

Maybe she'd even make it back in time for Juju's birthday.

That was a good thought. She closed her eyes for a moment, trying to meditate on that thought. *Someone's looking for us.* In her mind she formed a water droplet and let it fall into a stream, and as she reached into the stream she whispered his name. *Njandejara.*

Was that his brush against her face, or a draft? Did he sparkle in the corners of the room, in the metallic gleam on the walls? But no. It wasn't like in the woods where he danced under the shadow of every leaf. The shades here stood motionless, dead and gray.

But maybe he whispered in her ear, urging her into the space between their dimensions—or that was only her own breath and her ears ringing.

Lem closed her eyes and groaned, rubbing her hands over her face. When would she hear him again? How bad was the damage? Was it her, or was he just not in here?

Find me, he'd said, that first time she met him by a mossy, pebbly stream back home on Luna-Guetala. She'd stood knee-deep in the crystal clear water when suddenly the evening sunlight reflecting off the bubbling surface took on a different form—a presence materialized besides her like solidified wind. *"Who's there?"* she'd asked.

"We've met," he said in Biouk.

We've met. Those two words changed everything. They welcomed her as warmly as if Njande had already lived out their entire friendship before that moment: Lem suddenly had a sense of being utterly "inside" and familiar, like listening to a mother greeting her newborn, but *more* than that. He *knew* her, said that greeting, and to be known, really truly known and understood, satiated a lonely hunger she didn't even know she had. No one else *knew* her.

Njande was quiet for a moment, flickering in the riverbed as Lem tried to digest the form she saw and didn't see hidden behind the light. The fullness and warmth of the quiet amazed her. It was like she'd been on a long journey and just now come home. How did he do that? He didn't have to say much at all. One word conjured a thousand thoughts.

Lem's heart raced; the air was super-charged. *"Cinta told me about you,"* she blurted. *"He said to come looking for you out here ... I guess you know that already?"* She blushed. *"What are you?"*

"I am a still voice and a Dragon-hunter. What are you?"

The absurdity of her own question tickled her. *"I'm a human. And a girl? People call me Lem."*

"Jerusha-Lem."

"Yeah." Lem fidgeted.

A flash of youth and energy and excitement about life, like the toothy grin of a six-year-old prankster, reverberated through the stones lining the stream bank. *"Let's play hide and seek,"* Njande said. *"Let's play hide and seek forever."*

Lem opened her eyes and sighed, conscious of her prison cell yet again.

He had to be in here somewhere. Maybe not in the room itself—maybe in the situation. He was an interdimensional; he could hide in abstracts. She'd found him in the corners of Biouk refuge nests, under the bunk bed in her barracks after some jerk in her training squad belittled her, even in the margins of her science textbook. She'd once glimpsed him in the blood-red dawn over a battlefield, when blitzers came to burn down the civilian homes outside Fort Jehu.

She'd always wondered what he was doing there that day.

But right here, right now, she heard nothing. Or maybe she heard something and didn't know it? She hugged herself, shivering. *I haven't broken too many synapses, I haven't ...*

A tingle shot through the air. Lem opened her eyes. The ceiling above her—

Shyte, where'd her reflection go? The silver was a dull gray now.

Lem scowled. This room was jacked up. Time to escape.

She marched to the back wall. She could shove off it, fly through the air, smash through the door, just like before. She crouched like a runner—

But the back wall moved behind her several feet. The door spun into the ceiling.

Lem whirled at the wall, her face heated—wait, was she about to yell at it to stand still? She kept her mouth shut. *Not crazy.*

But with her mouth shut, her imagination babbled and her ears buzzed. Silence was the moment in the woods when the birds held their breath before an apex predator struck. Silence was death. Silence was filled with muttering ghosts.

Movement in her left peripheral—Lem lifted her hands to strike!

A wide-eyed two-dimensional girl, her chest heaving as she crouched in terror, did the same.

"My reflection's back," Lem coughed, lowering her hands, breathing hard. "Just my reflection."

On the right, and above her, and all around. It was dizzying. Lem's colors replaced the silver in all directions, always and forever. A million pairs of soft black boots; a million tan-brown tunics splattered with blood, torn to reveal a million black jumpsuits underneath; a million scratched cheeks; and two million wide eyes watched her every move.

Lem folded her arms and sneered. These circus tricks had nothing on her.

But they folded their arms, too, daring her to judge them, accusing her with upturned chins—each of them knew everything she'd ever done.

Lem turned her head to lock them out, to look away from them in disdain.

But there on the floor, on the ceiling, everywhere she turned she saw them from every angle, her disgust amplified back on her. She whirled to hide now, and now they stretched out their hands to keep balance, eyes darting to each other, to the ceiling, to the floor, searching for the door. Their parted lips threatened a collective whimper as they breathed hard, mocking her weakness.

She hated them. Look at them, their hair crumpled everywhere, skin mottled with bruises, that scared "help-me" pose with palms out to say "don't hurt me please"—

"Suck it up," she snapped.

"Shyte, don't start talking to yourself now," she muttered. She sat on the floor and covered her eyes. But she could hear them, looming over her …"No, they're sitting now."

"Shut up!"

… a whimper of frustration …

"Oh gosh oh gosh Cinta please come through soon."

CHAPTER FOURTEEN

Cinta

CINTA CLAWED HIS WAY UP THE LONE TREE BY FORT JEHU'S REC center, swishing past draping lechichi vines to settle on a sunlit limb swaying under dancing butterflies. *Flowing around the mountain, slipping past it, and eroding it away, water beats rock. I am water. I am peaceful.*

I will find my sister.

The sun glinting off the roof of the rec center forced Cinta to narrow his eyes as he pulled his transmission pad from his stomach-pouch. He checked the strength of the transmission signal and opened his sister's message again. *Jaika …*

Cinta had not bet against Captain Rana out of naivete. Hunting wolves bare-handed, stealing eggs from dens of two-headed reptile-bears—yes, they were not the same as penetrating a Growen facility, but a hunt was a hunt.

Following a bomber, Jaika and her partner left Fort Jehu, sent by their Captain, who lost them just beyond a Bichank settlement …

The Frelsi adults would tell him no more, but Cinta had spoken to Jaika's human brothers; he called her family every day to inquire about the health of the children, about JE, Jake, Juju, Jaynes, J'miah, Jose, and the baby. They told him during the initial bombing attempt, JE and Jake had seen the Bichank over the rec center *destroy cameras with his mind.*

That did not seem routine.

Moreover, the Frelsi sent two *electromagnetics* after the bomber, one of them known for uncovering new Growen weapons and memorizing Growen tech readouts—Jaika had complained about him once or twice. It seemed … special to send him.

It also seemed … special … to bomb the rec center, instead of something else. Even more special to send a Stygge for something so small, to put him at risk, and then not kill his hunters.

Special, then, this capture.

Cinta hopped from the tree to the roof; his claws scraped and slipped, but the pads of all four feet stuck on the warm surface, and the powerful smell of Bichank musk struck his nose immediately. It smelled injured or ill? A gentle rot, or the memory exposed blood, tickled the inside of Cinta's muzzle but—tainted, with some other chemical? No, not … hm. Cinta's left ear dropped, and his right ear twitched. *Something so strange, this.* He would not earn his healer credentials for decades yet, but even in this early training he could always smell diagnoses. Yet *this* smell remained … mysterious.

Cinta scampered along the edge of the domed roof, and then up to its apex, sniffing. The meaty, fruity scents of a male and a female Biouk met him in the air, and on the other side of the dome, on the downslope, sat two moon-Biouks, one a tan, slender youth with a slavery collar, and the other a long-furred, almost black beauty Cinta recognized by the glimmers of her nearly purple highlights. The wind kept their argument from reaching Cinta's ears; he heard a snarl from the girl, but before he could approach the slave collar lit up, and the tan male fled.

Cinta slid down to perch beside the female. "The sun is high, Con-trol," he said to his cousin.

"Ah, the sun's up, Cinta," she grumbled in an amalgam of planetary and moon dialect, waving her forepaw. "Well, not really. I miss the moon. I come up here on the roof to be alone, and this guy keeps bothering me."

Cinta's ears stiffened.

"Nah, it's not like that," Con-trol said. "He wouldn't try anything, he's—you know, like you, like your tribe. You all, that only talk to the one outer-being, think all the others are ba-eaters, and such."

"They are," Cinta said, sniffing into the wind again as his fur bristled. Before either speaker could fall into another argument, like last summer, he asked: "Does your tribe have a feud with any of the planetary Bichanks here?"

"Yeah, no, the Frelsi asked the same thing—but the bomber was Growen, wasn't he?" Con-trol sighed and dropped her back paws out flat behind her, like a human on its belly. "That's what this crazy slave wants me to do, tell the Frelsi there's some force between our healer and the Growen leader, feeding them new soldiers with Stygge powers." She enunciated the last words with a mocking grunt. "Crazy talk."

Cinta's ears twitched back—not flat, not threateningly, but just enough to express displeasure. "You know slavery's illegal in Frelsi territory, yes?"

Con-trol smirked, baring her left fang. "Right, sorry. The healer's … *helper*."

Cinta's ears remained flicked back. "Why would he come to you?"

"I'm all that'll let him talk to me. He's not allowed far from the healer's side, or he'll get a shock. *Ratschica*, what a life." She cursed, and chuckled with another smirk. "And of course, selling the Frelsi some magical story about his 'evil master' has *nothing* to do with escaping his indentured servitude, right?"

Cinta blinked at her cynical face for a few seconds. False reports of interdimensional beings and strange forces happened all the time across the universe for less. "Can you blame him?" he asked.

She shrugged. "All suffering happens for a reason, Cinta," she said, looking away now towards the jungle just beyond the pearl-like wall. "Whether in a past life or now, he's a—*helper*—because he deserves it. Doesn't have enough *sprach.*" Faith, confidence, spunk, nobility, all somehow expressed in that word, *sprach.*

"Is that why your tribe is homeless, too?" Cinta retorted. "Not enough *sprach?*"

Her fur bristled. "That's different."

"I am sorry for the pain." Cinta semi-apologized and dropped his head. He knew her, and would not argue with her further.

As Cinta wished his cousin a good day and left, however, one of his paws danced into his pouch for his transmission pad ... and before he'd left the base, he'd already sent a text message to the Frelsi gate guard about the slavery situation in the rec center, and formed a reasonable new hypothesis on Lem's whereabouts.

Not long, now, Jaika.

Cinta's *sprach* had faded somewhat by late afternoon. He sat in the family's tree-home, in the nest of feathers and furs he and Jaika used to share; scientific papers and notes he'd gathered meticulously over the years lay scattered and wrinkled around him like fallen leaves after the late season monsoons. He had asked the rest of the family to leave him alone to his studies, but he heard some of them returning now, chattering through the treetops.

He groaned, and lay back in the nest—still with no certain location.

The slave's conspiracy theory had sparked Cinta's mind-fire. Cinta remembered rumors of super-soldiers among the Growen. Now, the Frelsi had sent two *electromagnetics* after the gifted bomber considering for some *important reason* that whoever confronted him might need special abilities and known recon experience; in answer, for likely the same *important reason*, the Growen had not killed them. Cinta had already visited the southern Bichank settlement, following the leaf-litter trail from the air-riders, and the scents the two humans left behind. He'd found the place almost abandoned, marred by the same odd scent as on the rec center roof.

Cinta believed Jaika and her partner had stumbled upon a secret Stygge army—and their kidnappers had taken them to join.

The problem now was discovering what planet within range of Jaika's transmission could tolerate a Growen installation large enough to train a Stygge army. It was in the Undecided Zone, according to Rana, so Cinta had space maps pulled up on his transmission pad, and in his biomedical papers Cinta was cross-referencing different atmospheric conditions required for different species. Every known sapient species had at least one historical specimen with electromagnetic abilities, but the training center likely existed on a planet that worked best for Bichanks, humans—and perhaps Wonderfrogs?

Cinta groaned, and ran his paws over his snout. The shadows were long now, and the light through the thatched walls split in speckles … and he felt no confidence in his thoughts. Luna-Guetala and Alpino, right here, far from Jaika's coordinates, would sustain Bichank and human life best—and of course any good training center could incorporate some habitat modifications, so perhaps atmosphere did not matter. Anyway, he had no guarantee about the Wonderfrogs: they had a higher incidence of electromagnetism historically, but that didn't mean the Growen necessarily recruited from their number. Really, the ichthian and insectoid sapients had the most electromagnetics of them all, so should the Growen not build that army around them?

But the three sapient insectoid species were nomadic, and the twelve ichthian species all lived on Burbura, several solar systems away from Lem's coordinates.

So nothing. Assuming nothing, and getting nowhere.

Cinta slipped his compupad back into his stomach-pouch and climbed up the woven wall, out the roof-hole, and further up the tree, until he had broken the jungle canopy. Here, under the sky, he heard no signs of sapient life—only the rustling leaves, tittering insects, and singing day-lizards. His ears sagged on his head; his muzzle dropped onto his knees as he crouched on the branch alone, staring far, far down at the webbed tree-roots sprawling below.

This tree was so big.

He glanced up.

The sky was so big.

The universe was huge, and he did not even know if the Growen *stopped* near Lem's space-coordinates. Yes, a stop in the Undecided Zone would make a strategic location to hide from the Frelsi. But perhaps they kept going. Maybe they took her to a Growen world.

Maybe they killed her after all.

Cinta's ears flattened against his scalp and a whine rose in his throat. He could not help it. His claws dug tighter into the bark; his chest ached and fluttered as something heavy settled in his stomach. He wanted the thought gone, but his grandmother's favorite phrase nagged at him like an infected splinter in the crease of his paw: *Live by the sword, die by the sword.* Lem's ire argued back: *"We're defending ourselves, Cinta. We can't keep running forever! There's nowhere to go!"* He squeezed his eyes shut. She was not dead. The sword would get her one day, but not yet, not now!

"Njandejara, please," he whispered. "Come talk to me for a moment. Or—I know you're always talking to me. Let me hear."

Can you hear me now?

Cinta opened his eyes. A smile etched into the tree-bark if he looked at the right angle; something stroked his muzzle, like a brush of butterfly's wings; a thin flicker of light, a beam at a strange angle, as if it ignored light sources and refraction to float there, independent of anything else, not perpendicular to the planet, not parallel to anything at all—

The sun still shone, but it seemed pale now. A soft shiver covered Cinta; every muscle in his body relaxed, and he sighed.

Hello, said Njandejara. *I am here with you, and I am on my way to you.*

The paradoxical statement did not register to Cinta as anything more than an otherworldly greeting. But Njande's form—

"Are you—translucent today?" Cinta asked. "I had believed you were solid."

I am, but you are mist, and if I touch you, or breathe, or coalesce too close to you, you will disperse into particulate.

"Did you not touch me before, that time you healed me?"

A little, yes. Carefully. Njande smiled. His words sunk as deep into Cinta's head as if the Biouk had thought them himself—but Cinta's ears tingled as if the message floated on the wind.

"Being near you makes me glad," Cinta sighed. "But Friend, I need you to break a rule for me. I know you are not imperialist. I understand you do not want to meddle in our dimension and conquer us. But I need you to interfere."

Dear One, I am always interfering.

"But you said before—but—forgive me, but if that is true, why is Lem gone? Why do you not go get her?"

Why don't you? It seemed cruel—if any other voice had said it, Cinta would have drawn his claws. But when Njande asked, it meant something gentler. It was not an accusation, or a retort. It was as if Njande really wanted Cinta's answer, as if Cinta was more than he thought he was.

But Cinta was sure he was no miracle-worker, and he did not have time for introspection. It made much more sense to him for the infinite space-traveling energy beam to save the day than to send a Biouk who had not yet grown his fangs.

"Because … I cannot find her," he said. "Please, I am so much smaller than you. I do not understand why you'd make *me* do this—please, Njande! Help me understand."

The light changed; chill overtook the breeze. The butterflies retreated, and Cinta's fur rustled as his eye caught gathering storm clouds far, far off, over the edge of the jungle.

"Did you make that storm?" Cinta asked into the quiet.

Two days ago a butterfly flicked its wings thirty kilometers from here, Njande said. *Winds from other parts of this world joined its stroke; mountains formed eons ago broke the air streams; but the butterfly's wings sent a puff of air in the right direction, at the right time. Did the butterfly make the storm? Did the mountains? Did I?*

"Am I the butterfly?"

Njande emitted a wet sadness that drooped over Cinta like soaked moss. *There are players here you have not begun to consider*, Njande said. *Every move you make, every move your sister makes, every little thing we change has ramifications, good and bad. That is why you must move.*

"Are you afraid of breaking everything if you touch it?"

The sadness dissipated in a burst of heat. *I am not afraid*, said the interdimensional. *I know what I'm doing.*

"But what *is* that?" Cinta cried. "Why do you not tell me?"

Something twinkled in the air around them—not frustration, but something just as volatile, perhaps humor. *Cinta, how old are you?* Njande asked.

"Twenty-six."

I am older than your planet. Why don't soldiers tell children vital war secrets?

"Because they spill them ..." Cinta grumbled.

Or because children make bad decisions with the information, and knowing too much can destroy a childhood. That is what I am worried about.

"But you are sending a child to rescue Lem?"

We all have our parts to play.

"Maybe you should play the entire part! Forgive me—" Cinta put his paws over his muzzle and chewed his tongue. "But I thought you loved her!"

I love her more than life. But I also love you, and the universe she is slated to destroy.

What?! Njande drew a finger, or a tendril, or a laser, across the bark besides Cinta, tracing a burnt line in his wake. He continued speaking as if he hadn't just dropped an explosive into the conversation. *Did you know time is a place for me? I am more extra-dimensional than the other interdimensionals. They are interdimensional for space, but I can step outside of time as well. And there is a time I have seen, a time I am looking at right now, where your Jaika brings your universe to heat death.*

Cinta gripped his ears, pulling them down over his face in

confusion. What did that even mean? How could she—and wait, Njande walked outside of time? His little human sister would destroy—the whole universe?

"It is too much," Cinta muttered. "I am crazy. I am making this up." He shoved his muzzle between his knees. "I am not hearing this."

His ear twitched. He heard a hiss. He peeped over his knee as Njande drew another burning line in the bark. It was real. It was a real burning line. Cinta could touch it, and its heat radiated through his palm. Njande drew the Biouk character for *Jaika*—little white bird, Lem's adopted name, and Cinta could not plead insanity to escape this trial. This was real. Terribly real. How—what—he could not even imagine what to think right now. What could he even do about—?

No. Stop. He breathed. He reached out his paws and held them over the warm mark, inhaling with his eyes closed as the rain began to fall. "I am so confused right now, Njande," he whispered. "But I trust you, my friend. I trust you know what you are doing."

A last breeze tickled Cinta's nose as thunder hummed in the distance. The pressure in Cinta's chest, the new burden, did not relax, but Njande's warmth spilled around him, and that was enough.

One last thing, Cinta, Njande said. *When you find Jaika, tell her only that* if she stays connected with me, she can save the universe from heat death. *Do not tell her she is to destroy it. Do not preemptively damn her.*

"Sir—*when* I find her?"

About that. If you pride yourself on being different *from the Frelsi, why are you trying to solve your problem the same way? You cannot beat them at their own game.*

"Njande, they have tried *everything*. Except maybe asking," Cinta sighed.

Njandejara waited. Cinta's ears flicked to the side, one ear up and one ear down. "Truly?" he chuckled, wide-eyed. "The Frelsi will not approve."

But his heart lifted. He knew what to do now. He scampered across the limb, back to the tree trunk, jaw set and heartbeat steady.

This may not turn out at all like you expect, or intend, Njande whispered.

"I know. Promise me you'll go with me?"

Always.

"Is there a limit on that?"

When you can take no more. Then I will step in.

The storm fell full-force. It soaked Cinta's fur.

CHAPTER FIFTEEN

Lark

SMOKE FIZZLED AROUND THE DARK BOOTH IN THE CORNER OF THE bar, its sweet, drug-scented thickness disguising the sharp undertone of urine and alcohol permeating the damp air. Trashy plastic cushion creaked as bounty hunter Lark Scrita leaned forward over her portable compuscreen, her scaly jade claws tightening around a dull-pink glass of beer.

This little Biouk was *nutty*. Beans, the furry was either smoking everything she was smelling right now, piss included, or he had the bollocks of a full-grown land-walrus. Rana's report described him hopping from Growen base to Growen base, literally asking the blitzers at the gates how to find a Stygge army to join. He'd got nothing so far—still no one admitted an electromagnetic elite existed—but Lark liked his gumption. Twelve forts in the past three days—and that was only the buzz Frelsi database trolls dug up searching the forums for mysterious Stygges. If they searched particularly for "wild space-lemur," perhaps they'd find more.

"D'you get a picture of this bloke, Rana?" Lark smirked.

The warbling amphibian sounded like singing through her helmet. "No, no. But pretty sure I know who it is. Pretty sure, pretty sure. Sent that note about him to warn you, warn you. Considering what I should do? What should I do, what should I—"

"It's alright, croaker. He's not Frelsi, right?"

"No, no, but he wants to find my trainee, might get in the way, in the way, in the—"

The repetition annoyed her. "Sir, please stop. I did hear you the first time. And please, don't do anything. You're giving me room to work, ay? Just let me work. And let that fellow work, too."

Rana's surprise sounded like a burp. "Let him? Let him? Are you working with him?"

Lark laughed out loud. "Of course not, you think I'm crazy, mate? I say if he *is* the same furry you know, and there's a Stygge army out there, he'll be dead in a week. If he's not, and he really wants to join up, he'll join up. Either way, he'll disappear somewhere, and *that* is where our trail begins. So let him alone." Lark paused.

The radio fell silent for a moment. Lark leaned back against the cool, sticky booth, biting her lip. Oh dear. She'd interrupted her client, said too much, essentially just told him to belt up—not good. *Include him, include him!* "Thanks for the warning, though—please do keep them coming!"

Alright, now that sounded condescending. Beans, she needed this job! "I don't mean to offend, Captain. I'm not telling you to clear off, just want you to know you don't have to worry. I can do this."

"Wouldn't have hired you if I didn't think that already." No repetition. Each word slow and crisp. The line cut.

Lark's face heated in her helmet, and her shoulders slumped as she released her breath in a huff. Maybe it was an amphibian speech pattern. Now she'd sounded bloody speciesist, and worse, she'd sounded as insecure as the teenage human girl she tried not to be.

I hate talking to clients who care.

She drew her glass towards herself, adjusting the straw for the gap in her breathing mask as she sipped her alter ego's favorite fragrant *rosa* beer.

The long, grey, ridged muzzle of her mask—built for a wide,

reptilian snout—reflected over her beer's surface, reminding her who she *said* she was. Who she'd invented. Who she needed to be.

That person wasn't terrified of this case. That person wasn't a fifteen-year-old orphaned human with a falsified employment record. And most importantly, that person wasn't struggling for leads, she didn't need the blasted Frelsi, and she had plenty of behind-the-counter specials to mix up the drink in this investigation.

Come on, now, buck up! She was Lark Scrita! The sexy sixty-year-old Bont lizard who'd rescued Zhirskahm Frland. Who single-handedly took down the entire Gnash drug ring. It said that on her business cards. She'd kidnapped a woman to make those.

And—Lark released her breath, relaxing at last—soon she'd be the Bont lizard who got rich snatching two heavily-guarded electromagnetics out from under Growen noses. A nice addition to the resume.

This Biouk. *What've you found, little man?* Lark tapped around her screen for a few hours ... the empty glasses piled up beside her, and the sunlight changed through the stained glass windows of the bar, angling and glinting into Lark's eyes, and then passing beyond her gaze again as she followed side trails. Different forums ... security cameras from various sides, Growen and Frelsi and planetary governments and corporations ...

Hm. Looked like the Frelsi had bigger problems than two missing electromagnetic nutters: besides the normal skirmishes and battles, a string of targeted assassinations was going down. In the Undecided Zone, too, not just the Contested Zone. Buncha Frelsi bigwigs murdered in safe places by big name hunters: Ebon Shadow, that tentacled guy everyone hated, and ...

Wait, this list of killers seemed bloody familiar.

Oh, jipes, that's because she'd been offered that job. Lark pulled up the solicitation she'd received last week—and yup, the list of bounty hunters and targets matched. Of course, the list she had was much longer, since it included all the targets that hadn't been hit yet. Bloodseas, she'd almost forgotten about that! This wasn't some coincidental crime spree: the *Growen* paid these assassins! Smart way to operate in the Undecided Zone with pretty pink impunity, but sure to backfire politically if they got caught. Warcrime, and all.

Should she share this information with the Frelsi … ?

Lark quickly closed those screens and deleted both lists—no, beans, thank you, no, she didn't want anything to do with that mess. No politics, not since Sector Alpha.

Back to work. She struggled again through the original Growen sentry logs the Frelsi hackers had downloaded about the Biouk. Anything strange about his meetings, any patterns he'd found? Patterns broken?

You could just ask him?

Lark leaned back with a huff and crossed her arms, growling to herself as she watched the barkeeps stalk by her table shouting dish-names and brawling with drunkards about their orders. She sighed, shutting the job out of her head for a moment to just eavesdrop. She imagined backstories, elaborate lies for the conversations she heard —perhaps the tall, blue reptilian maid got that order of Wurms wrong because she wanted to send a secret message to the customer, and his original order didn't work for passing notes. It was quite soggy. Or perhaps it was poisoned, but the waitress couldn't let anyone know she knew …

The gabber died down. A tall human form slipped through the polymerwall, slinking around the bar in the center of the room to a dark corner booth. His head-to-toe black armor gleamed in the flickering light of the incense candles and kerosene lamps. He faded out of Lark's sight behind a long table packed with rowdy young Bichanks celebrating a birthday; as he disappeared behind the mountains of fur and tusks a damp coolness washed over Lark's skin.

Beans, what was the Ebon Shadow doing here?

She'd lost five jobs to him. That, she told herself, was why the side of her lip rose in a snarl as he crept past. That, and the way he disturbed her thoughts every time he entered them …

It wasn't like that. It was just unfair how everything he touched turned to golden drachmas for him and death for someone else, and

Lark found herself comparing his every move to hers—the way his left glove always hovered by his belt, how he faded into the shadows with that over-priced armor, the continuous, slow, calm swivel of his helmet, like a cannon tripod scanning for motion to fire on—what did he have that she didn't? They said he was cursed, his soul split, ever two places at once—

But he probably started the rumor himself, Lark grumbled.

Lark raised her hand, flexing her claws to summon the blue reptilian waitress. She drew a slip of paper and a palm-sized, square plastic baggy of white powder from her leather jacket as the woman pranced over to the table, bouncing on her backwards-bending legs like a velociraptor. "Can I help you?"

Lark slid the paper across the table, making sure the waitress could see the URL written on it with a 600-drachma spending limit underneath. A bribe.

"My friend over there, in the black," Lark grunted. "He ordered a drink, right?"

"The same *rosa* beer you're having. Why?" The spined sail on the waitress' back stiffened.

"This," Lark waved the baggy "is his favorite flavor. Bloody fantastic with *rosa*."

The waitress' clear third eyelid washed over her cat-like iris a few times as she stared at the obviously poisonous white powder in the baggy. Her sail stood straight out, as taut and stiff as starched leather. Lark waited as the waitress squirmed. It was a lot of money, and *everyone* knew what the Shadow did.

"You Frelsi or something?" the waitress asked.

"You're stalling," Lark said, adjusting the whip on her belt quite deliberately.

"Come on," the waitress breathed. "I'm not crazy."

Lark sighed.

Neither was she. That was the problem.

Lark withdrew the money and tucked the poison back into her belt, her chest heavy and her back suddenly sore, as if for that instant of possible murder a weight had lifted and now, as the weight claimed its place on her shoulders once again, everything hurt.

The waitress' spine-sail folded up and rested back against her skin in relief; her long, thin head drooped like a swan's in shame. "You think a Frelsi'll do it one day?" she whispered.

"Never. They're bloody useless. We can only hope he'll piss off a Growen client somehow."

The waitress took Lark's glass; her third eyelid flickered unhappily a few more times as she turned to go. She paused, glaring over her slender shoulder with slit-eye blazing:

"They're not useless," she gulped. "A Frelsi soldier saved my life when the Growen invaded my planet last year."

"The Growen wouldn't be invading anyone if the Frelsi had nuked Sector A ten years ago like they were supposed to, mate."

The waitress opened her snout to speak—then stopped, ducked her head down again, and scurried away, sail flared.

Lark's breath rushed through her mouth and her heart pounded; if Lark really had been the broad-snouted sail-less Bont she pretended to be, her fingers would have lit bright red. Anger, relief, frustration—and terror—at what she'd tried to do.

She couldn't pull off an assassination now, and she hadn't pulled off a rescue then.

I'm sorry, Mum ... Dad. I'm still sorry. Sorry did nothing. She was impotent. If only she'd reached the alert system when the Growen came for them. If only the Frelsi could've gotten there in time. If only someone had nuked Sector A so the Growen *didn't exist.*

If only ifs could reverse the sordid human history Lark erased under a beautiful romance of reptilian lies; if only she was actually the Bont with the business card, and not the fifteen-year-old human kid who'd created the persona to escape getting her hand chopped off for stealing three years ago.

Lark Scrita didn't have the *guts* to feed revenge. She was left grasping at little rescues, trying to make the universe "better" for this little family or that, and in the grand scheme of things it meant nothing as long as gravity worked. Because the universe was tilted towards down and inward. It was easy to fall, and hard to get up. Life could be ended, but death could not.

Lark huddled over her compupad and sighed. *I'm not getting any work done like this.* She packed to go, hugging her elbows against the chill that would not leave. In the smoke around her hung the presence, the ghost her Contaminated parents had died for and left to haunt her; she said nothing to him, as usual, and he floated about her in silence, warming her skin. Sometimes in the corners of her eyes she saw him, a shadow like her father, but she didn't bother turning to look anymore. She never saw anything if she looked. He never did anything. He was just there—like the Frelsi, like the starlight, like herself, moving through every day without change, ever one step closer to death and never an inch closer to life. Held down by gravity.

Useless.

A glass bottle clinked against her beer-mug. Lark stiffened. Her eyes trailed the huge fist attached to the glass bottle, up the shining, seamless armor to the blank, ghost-like face-mask … of the Ebon Shadow.

"Cheers," he said.

"Cheers," she grunted. Beans, was it always this cold in here? She huddled tighter around her beer mug, wondering how fast she could get her whip off her waist—he had a lead on her, with his glove resting on his holster like that.

Beans, wait, he had *three* holsters on each hip, down each thigh, all smoothly integrated into the sides of his muscled armor so you couldn't quite see what make of gun he carried. Six guns? Was that truly necessary?

"You trying to compensate for something, sirrah?" she asked.

He said nothing. He set his beer down beside hers, and nudged it towards her. He crossed his arms and waited.

"Sorry mate, you're going to have to say something," Lark said. "I'm not telepathic."

"Rosa."

Uh-oh. Did little miss sail-fin snitch, now? After all that talk about Frelsi-goodness, she squealed? Three possible falsehoods spun into Lark's mouth—she settled on playing dumb. "You've got the worst way of asking to buy a lass a drink," she said.

"I know the name of every person who ever thinks about killing me," he said. "You each get one free pass. But next time I see you, I will kill you." The Shadow left his glass on the table and simply walked away. Awful, non-dramatic exit, quiet and innocuous—Lark almost laughed out loud at his awkward, stilted phrasing.

No wait, she did laugh out loud, and made sure to let him hear it. He couldn't threaten her! He couldn't just drop an atom bomb into the conversation anywhere he wanted, no explanations, no transitions, no finesse, just bam, "I will kill you"! Lark made a nasty face mimicking his words to herself as she rose, sucking out the last draught of *rosa* from her glass mug as she eyed his path out the door. He could keep his "free pass."

Lark slipped her business card under her glass and stalked out the door into the cool, mildewed shadows of the Retrack City alleyway, fuming. "Next time" he saw her? Drop that, there was no next time, he didn't get to decide when times began and ended. This beat-down was happening now. He wouldn't even see it coming.

CHAPTER SIXTEEN

Bereens

W<small>HEN</small> <small>THEY</small> <small>PEELED</small> <small>ME</small> <small>OFF</small> <small>THE</small> <small>SILVER</small> <small>FLOOR</small> <small>IN</small> <small>THE</small> <small>MORNING</small>, Diebol had the gall to ask me how I was doing.

"Dizzy," I said, blinking as they dragged me out of my gray cell into the bright, white-walled hallway. Was it morning? The walls glowed, but nowhere in the gleaming, sculpted hallway was there so much as a peephole for a window.

"What did you think?" he asked.

What did he want me to think? I kept my scowl to myself—I'd spent the night sleeping, thank you very much: the minute I saw one wall move I was out, eyes closed. I didn't intend to put up with his shenanigans.

But he needed to see cooperation from me if I wanted him to let his guard down, so I sucked up my disdain and pretended I'd paid attention to the crazy-walls. "That was … psychedelic," I said. "What does it all mean?"

And just like that, he launched into a lesson and I had him off my back. I'd learned during the annoying post-rescue therapy as a kid that asking questions is a fantastic way to keep someone from asking *you* questions.

We sloshed through a polymerwall into a small mess hall—or mess room, I guess, since it only had one plastic table with two benches, and nothing else on the tiled floor. At the other end of the room two glass doors looked out over a huge training gymnasium without a floor, a multi-story void with a slew of platforms floating in the air, all carrying exercise equipment or running tracks or sparring rings.

A Stygge trainee set two bowls of orange nutrient mush on the table.

"Yay, The Orange Stuff," Lem's voice laughed behind me. I turned to see her escorted by three Stygges and wearing a stasis field. I smiled: I agree, when you're limited to nutrient sludge The Orange Stuff is pretty much the best.

"Medications first, then you have five minutes to eat in silence before training," Diebol said. "You're allowed to talk to each other during the training exercise."

"Oh, thank you for allowing us that *basic human liberty*, Great One," Lem spat. "If you think I'm knowingly taking drugs from you, you're insane."

Yeah, I didn't know why he didn't just slip them into our food. Her lips sealed shut—they had two Vibrants trying to pry her mouth open while she thrashed, and then they got bit, and then someone accidentally clicked the button off on her stasis field and now she was kicking and thrashing and throwing people and now when the Bichank got her in a headlock she wouldn't—or couldn't —swallow ...

Diebol rolled his eyes and handed me two pills. I popped them in my mouth, tucked them under my tongue, swallowed spit while he watched my Adam's apple like a creeper—and when Lem kicked one of the nutrient sludge bowls into Diebol's head I spat the pills out, behind his back, into the orange slop pooling on the floor.

Lem saw that. I know she saw, because she started to laugh, cough, and then choke as she swallowed her pills and tried not to. I winced, and sat down for my bowl of nutrient goop. This was an odd partnership we had, here, and in an uncomfortable way I began to realize it worked to my advantage. Without her distractions I'd never have discovered the Stygge army, and, well, I'd have to take pills.

Alright, now this was getting disturbing. She hacked, holding her throat as they dropped her to the floor, and gasped for breath as sweat or tears or something gleamed on her cheeks. I wanted to tell her to stop now, to stop trying to hurl or whatever, to just let it go for now, but if I talked she wouldn't get a chance to eat. So I sat in silence, biting my lip, just hoping she'd please stop and sit up and let this battle go for now. Please!

Her eyes burned at Diebol as she pushed herself up on her hands and knees. "Remember what you said about shoving things into people's bodies they didn't ask for," she coughed.

He stiffened—my eyes widened. Bloodseas, I had no idea what she was talking about, but good for her for making it personal. He left the room without another word.

Lem didn't get anything to eat before the remaining trainees shoved us into the gym.

"What is this place?" she coughed.

We stood on a small entrance platform made of wide, black metal tiles; we'd come in through a glass or perhaps plexiglass set of doors, now closed behind us, leaving us alone. Before us, and around us, hung an enormous void, extending deep into the core of the mountain below the education center. Platforms floated all around us, and small tiles in the stone wall hid some kind of machinery—perhaps weapons, or observation ports, I thought.

A platform carrying a running track lit up and sailed through the air towards us.

"Step aboard the track and start running," boomed a mechanical voice.

"I like running," Lem shrugged, stepping over the gap into the floating platform with a face more of curiosity than compliance. I hesitated for a second, wondering what kind of enforcing power they had in an empty—

Ooph, okay, rubber training round to the thigh. I stumbled forward onto the floating track, my teeth clenched to stifle my shout

—that was going to leave a nice bruise. I squinted to see where the bullet came from, to see if I could em-push and crush the gun turrets ...

An electric fence shot up around the track; more rubber bullets followed, and I couldn't em-push through an electric field, and agh those bullets stung—!

So, prodded forward like eating-frogs at a Burburan salt race, we ran, with strikes to the heels and thighs if we slowed down. No purpose, no questions, no torture, just an assumption that we were already training for their cause. This was humiliating. Even Lem didn't want to talk.

After about three laps around the track she began to stumble—and even kind of step in the wrong direction, like she couldn't coordinate her movement. I glanced over, keeping my pace, and saw her lips fluttering, ashen, as she blinked and pursed her forehead like something in there hurt. She gripped her stomach.

Oh man, poor ...

She tripped; I stopped in a hailstorm of stinging rubber to help her up. "Leave me alone—ow!" she snapped, slapping her arm after another round *thwingk*'d against her skin. "I got this!"

"I'm not trying to help you because I think you can't do it," I yelled, yanking her to her feet—yelling because I'd just taken another training round to the shoulder. "I'm trying to help you because I think the meds are kicking in and making you nauseous!"

"Whatever, Schmidt."

"Still not my name!"

She steadied on her feet and pushed me away from her. And we ran.

But she worsened through the day. They'd randomly switch our activities—oh, now it's time to lift weights like normal people for a few minutes, wait, no, sprint until you vomit—no, actually, now you have to hang upside-down forever and listen to stringed instruments warbling over whispered propaganda. To me, it was just a bunch of stupid random shyte, but watching Lem I could see it was entirely different when you were drugged. She'd blink, and breathe hard, or react suddenly like she saw something; when we were upside down she held her ears as if they hurt.

"It's like *in my head*," she whispered to me, her eyes wide as I looked over at her. The electronic voices in the room began to scream at her to drop her hands, and rubber pellets pelted her back, but she squeezed harder, and man, I wished I could do something to help her! What, so if I threw a fit next time, then maybe *she* could spit out her drugs?

I didn't know. This was so dumb. The platform holding up our ankle cuffs rotated slowly; I couldn't see the ground in the dark depths of the multi-story room below me, and the blood rushing to my head pounded my temples. The room wasn't spinning, but it began to feel like that as I dizzied, and the pounding became pain, and the whispers needled into my eardrums ... *You are alone in the universe ... You are alone ...*

The whole time hearing her struggle beside me I knew it would get worse if I got pills. Bloodseas, I got lucky today, but what about the next day? They could inject me, or drop it in my food, and then what could I do? Starve? Maybe! It was my head, they couldn't have it! I'd talk to or not talk to whomever I pleased. Leave me alone!

"Please don't yell, it makes my headache worse," she muttered.

"Wait, did I yell?"

"No, but you're about to," she said.

She was delirious, but she was probably right—as the sounds grew louder, and the pounding in my head fiercer, more heavy, more full and solid, and the whispering faster and faster—

I was almost glad the moment something shot me—not the punch-sting of a rubber bullet, but the sharp stab of a stun cartridge —and I fell unconscious.

"You work for us now. You'll start by pretending, but little by little we become what we pretend to be. That's how children grow up, my friend."

They warn you about the nightmares, in weapons training—the unwelcome side effect of the shock-free, "cruelty-free" stun cartridges that work globally on NMDA and GABA instead of direct calcium release. Hey, sure beats electrocution, right? They don't tell you what you'll see in your nightmares, though, or that some psychopath plans to use your nightmares to talk to your subconscious mind.

"You think the whip's in your past. But don't you know you're enslaved now? Your fear of the future enslaves you. You can't think beyond war, can you? You don't want to imagine a universe at peace and you don't want to listen to someone else construct that universe for you because you're afraid of letting go. Afraid of what you don't know. You never dream about the future, do you?"

When I awoke, I found myself alone.

I sat up back in my silver cell, suddenly jarred by the change in scenery. Lem was gone, the gym-abyss gone, and not a hair or a single fingerprint proved anyone else ever existed. I checked. I caught myself inspecting the floor, the walls, looking for some evidence I'd ever left this room. No prints. Not even my own—as if I'd spontaneously appeared in this cell, full-grown, at the beginning of time, and never moved.

Huh. The cell had cleaned itself after they took me out this morning. Or afternoon. Or whatever time of day they decided to make it feeding-time. Everything gleamed. I touched the cool silver floor: it seemed damp, but without clear droplets—perhaps recently damp and then freshly air-dried. There was a slight incline to the room now, and I now saw a crack between the floor and the wall at the bottom of the incline. Whatever machinery moved the walls and tilted the floor apparently could also tilt the floor far enough to open up that crack so the room could wash away waste.

I crouched by the crack, looking through it to the gears and— sure enough, a waste chute hidden on the other side of the wall.

Guess Diebol thought having any kind of latrine *inside* the cell would ruin the whole dramatic effect of pure nothingness; I scowled. I wondered … could I pull the crack open, and squeeze out through the waste chute … ?

No, not a chance. I'd have to be space-lemur size.

Suddenly, the crack closed completely, almost taking my finger with it. I moved back, and shrugged—it meant nothing, anyway.

I lay on the cool floor to think, trying to gather my flustered brain that suddenly cared so much about fingerprints and waste. So. Today. Running in circles on a floating platform? Or battling Diebol in a lighted arena? I thought I knew which one really happened, and which one came from the stun-cartridge-induced dream …

Hold on, in fact, I more than thought I knew, I *knew*. Bloodseas, Diebol couldn't make me question what I *knew*! I imagined him listening in on me, smirking at my bewilderment. In my mind's eye the corner of his mouth twisted as he dropped another twig on our makeshift childhood gameboard; he flicked it sideways into my territory, right in the midst of all my sticks poised to attack it. *Why are you doing that?* He never answered; he'd only grin while I puzzled myself over the aggressive, stupid move, until I turned around a few moves later and found out he'd won the area.

But he wasn't winning now. "Your weird mind-games don't prove I'm insane, Diebol," I said to the cameras. "I'm not the one who spends his time coming up with this shyte."

He didn't have to respond, though. *They were in here while I was sleeping.* That was comeback enough. I shivered. I still remembered awakening in the cage back *then* with injection sites on my triceps, never knowing what they'd put into me or why. I sat down now, rolled up my tunic sleeves and pants, and checked for pits, marks, something …

The hair rose on the back of my neck, and I clenched my teeth. *Paranoid freak they've turned me into. Battle buddy's disappeared and I'm freaking out about imaginary drugs.*

What had they done to Lem now?

They'd drugged her, that's what they'd done, and knowing

that was enough. I checked for injection sites under my shirt, along my neck—bloodseas, how did I even sleep with all this paranoia? Did I have a concussion or something? I checked the raw spot on my forehead where they'd struck me when they first captured us. No lump. No depression. Just a tangle of dried blood. But I'd known a human who got struck in the head just like that in a construction accident, insisted he was fine because he wasn't bleeding, flat-out refused treatment, and a few hours after the injury fell into a deep sleep he never woke up from. "Epidural hemorrhage," they said.

And he died.

I scowled and cut the obsessions out of my head. I could just do that. I could think about nothing.

But with nothing to think about, the glint of the room on my eyes, the ringing in my ears, my reflection spinning a hundred times into further and further space—

I needed to touch the wall again. I craved it. My eyesight was lying—I could see only myself, in different sizes, gleaming off into reflective infinitum. I was alone on that infinite plane the physicists talk about, alone with myself everywhere. A horizontal abyss.

I crept forward on my fingertips. Just to tap my finger against the wall. Just to confirm it was there …

I stretched and my fingers whooshed through air.

I stood and walked.

And walked.

What the bloodseas?

I held my breath and closed my eyes. *Don't run. Don't run— then they'll let you hit it, and you'll be a break-time joke for the camera-jockies.*

I walked. Treadmill under my feet, perhaps? Move the floor back instead of stretching the wall out? I stared at the floor as I took another step—

Dizziness struck me. Below me, I was standing on my own feet, but around him, around my reflection hung a nothingness, a great silver height that contained only repeated, shrunken me. The image changed to something I couldn't process as the floor sloped—I fell towards the nothing—

I hit the floor. *Thank goodness for the floor, I love the floor, the floor's real.* I lay on my back, staring up at my infinite self, gasping hard. The ceiling angle shifted every moment, just a bit, and the perspective brought me nausea. My fevered mind insisted it had to mean something. *Don't fear yourself.* Diebol wanted to say, maybe. *Enjoy infinite you.*

I wanted to break his jaw. My vision swirled; I closed my eyes; the world tilted and on the back of my eyelids I saw infinity still.

I sat up. Pinned my eyes closed. Sealed my hands over my ears so I couldn't hear myself breathing. But my panting was as loud as a chainsaw.

Sweat steamed on my chest. My fingers tingled. Tingled. Bloodseas, I was em-pulling with them, using my abilities as a reflex, trying to drag the wall back to me without even thinking about it. *Stop. Stop, calm down!* My head ached. My stomach gurgled. *They say we kill ourselves by giving ourselves seizures*, Lem had said. I could see it happening, right now. Right here. Bloodseas, where was she?

The floor rocked. I opened my eyes for a moment and swill leapt up my esophagus. Acid burned my throat—I struggled to swallow. *No, no, he can't see me vomit!*

Why not?

What do you mean, why not, Njandejara, I'm showing enough weakness as it is!

Why are you so afraid of weakness?

My delirious mind felt his whisper—the message crossed the infinite distance between us to implant on the inside of my ear, and I heard him say *I am still strong.*

What do I care if you're strong? You're in another dimension, for shyte's sake. I'm the one they're watching.

Looking for me.

Damn "cure." I planned to hide my connection to him until they let me out—to become the unreadable wall, whatever that meant.

You can hide an invisible person, smother him in your own cold personality.

But showing him, letting the signs, the symptoms of contagion bleed out of me—perhaps I could infect them with him. I'd heard of it happening—

No, Njandejara. I don't want Diebol to 'get' you. I want to pay him back until he begs for mercy. Until he screams for you, and you're nowhere to be found.

That's messed up, little brother, Njandejara replied.

I'm having trouble being sorry.

The floor rocked again. Vile taste plunged across my tongue, bursting against the sides of my mouth—

Oh, forget it.

I let it out. My face burned as I wretched; the floor tilted, and a hard spray hose shot out over me to wash the vomit down the hill, into the waste crack that re-appeared between the wall and the floor. I was bathed like a dog, pawing at the crack again to see if I could fit through it and escape, but weak and too large, I collapsed in my own watery filth as the wall escaped me.

Weakness is strength, read the interdimensional's message. *Do not fear it. My strength will permeate your weakness. It is a Paradox you must learn.*

It was an oxymoron that made no sense, that's what it was, but I repeated it to myself once, spitting acrid saliva as far from me as I could, wiping my sweating face on my tunic sleeve. "Weakness is strength."

Its silliness calmed me, and in my weary wretchedness, it let me breathe.

CHAPTER SEVENTEEN

Bereens

I'D STARTED COUNTING. A RECOMMENDED TECHNIQUE FOR maintaining sanity during torture, I'd never used it for something as stupid as this, but after I found my fingers clawing each other I broke down and allowed myself the luxury of numbers. I counted until the water-jet arrived from nowhere to wash the vomit off the floor, off me—that spray, the fact that I could count to 12,032 and it would arrive exactly on 12,033—that spray kept me from crying, or screaming, or rising to my feet to run manically at the wall I couldn't find.

It comforted me most each time I counted 1,314, when the floor tilted to open up that space below the wall, and I glimpsed again the troughs and pipes that collected all the swill washing out of the self-cleaning room. Thank goodness. The wall wasn't infinite. Something else existed. Too bad I couldn't fit in there to escape through the sewage system. It would be nice to escape. Oh gosh my head ... I closed my eyes. 1,400 ... 1,401 ...

The cell door opened, and Lem stumbled inside. *Thank everything. Thank you thank you thank you.* No magic, no smoke and mirrors, just an open door and she was here. Unbound. Unbound?

"What'd they do, tame you?" I smirked.

"What is *with* you and Diebol?"

"Well hello to you, too." I closed my eyes, licking my lips. So glad I hadn't vomited yet this cycle. Instead of seeing me covered in stomach contents she could see me sweaty and wet like a newborn, clinging to the floor like it was my mother. *How are you today, soldier?* My drill sergeant roared in my memory. *Outstanding, sir.*

I opened my eyes. She stood rubbing her forehead, biting her lip, her eyes narrowed as she stared confused into the distance—at the place where her reflection wasn't.

Shyte, she didn't have a reflection. Dammit, I was talking to a— I'd invented her. Invented her to be a stark *difference* from the homogeneity of my own infinity. And shyte, my imaginary Lem was asking about Diebol? Really?

"I don't want to talk to you about this." I closed my eyes and ducked my face into my knees. "I'm not even sure you're real right now. Lem Benzaran wouldn't be in here *not* throwing a fit."

"Man, they've really done a number on you," she said. Her words slurred a little. Her soft boots tapped—a tap I wouldn't have been able to hear before, but seemed so loud now after the time alone—tap, tap, tap, over to me. She sat beside me, close enough for me to feel her warmth.

"Permission to hug you?" she asked. "I *am* real."

"I'm all wet."

"I see that." She wrapped an arm around my shoulders. I could still have invented this. Where was my feverish head going—

"Don't get weird or anything," she said. "I need to hug some-one. It's super weird that you've got like a million reflections and I've got none. It's freaking me out. How do they do that? What am I —holy shyte!" She squeaked. Her fingers clawed into my shoulder. My eyelids flashed open.

"What?"

She swallowed. She cleared her throat and lowered her voice. Her squeak seemed to embarrass her; she overcompensated, and I almost laughed when she started talking in a deep growl. "Ahem. Nothing. Just saw my reflection for a second. Appeared and disap-peared. Stupid shyte." She shook her head and shuddered a little.

"Heh, I'm a total waffle. All bark, no bite, scared o' my shadow. Damn."

She withdrew her arm and hugged her own knees instead, ducking her face into her kneecaps.

I scooted closer and bumped my shoulder against hers. "Hey," I grumbled. "I've been in here hyperventilating and vomiting all night. So I'm not judging if you get jumpy."

"Thanks. I'm sorry they suck."

"Me too."

"Are you—" Her voice, muffled against her kneecaps, paused. She lifted her face to turn towards me. "Is there like an actual *thing* going on between you and Diebol?"

"Don't worry," I grinned. "I'm sure he thinks you're prettier."

"Oh great, okay, never mind." Lem laughed, rubbing her hands over her face. "Please don't think I'm fraternizing with the enemy or any shyte like that. I didn't mean—it's just—"

"We confuse you. Sorry. He's always been a creep about freeing my mind. It's like his passion, a romanticized obsession, and now he's finally got a chance to take his shot." I closed my eyes and rubbed my fingertips across my temples. My jaw tightened. "Damn, it makes me mad. You know what, can we …"

"Not talk about it. Okay. Sorry." Lem pursed her lips, staring at where her reflection wasn't. One eye scrunched; the other widened. So quizzical! I shook my head.

"You're so readable," I said. "You know that, right?"

"And you're not as impenetrable as you think, Cadet Commander Secret-Name," she smiled. "Is it Roz?"

"That's a girl's name."

"It's totally not! I know like, three dudes named Roz." She sulked. "I had such a good feeling about that name, too. I bet it was your name in an alternate universe or something."

I smirked. I was contemplating giving her a hint, actually, when the door slammed open.

Lem leapt to her feet. Diebol shoved her to the floor again and crouched beside her, drawing a pen out of his pocket with a snarl.

"They told me what you did to your new cell. I don't suppose I've made this clear enough. *Your sister is in danger.*"

"It's not my fault!" She still spoke with a bit of a slur. "If you hadn't given me so much drug-shyte I wouldn't've misfired and blown up your precious cell. I thought I saw a dragon! You try sitting pretty when you see dragons!"

"Just goes to show someone doesn't have a very good grip on reality," Diebol sneered, drawing a circle on the wall with his imaging pen.

I struggled to rise to my knees. I'd get that pen and shove it through his eye.

He didn't even turn to look at me. Whoosh, a soft em-push, and I collapsed onto my stomach again. My face heated; Lem winced and looked away from me. "Her grip on reality is only *shaky* because you *drugged* her, you idiot," I grumbled through wet, weak lips.

"Ah, but now she knows she can be made to see the unreal," he said. "*Everything* you see is just a chemical dream. And it's the same with her imaginary friend. I can make you see and un-see anything I like."

"Man, you can't—"

"Be quiet," Diebol said. He held out his hand, and dammit now I couldn't move my mouth. Or anything, actually. He kept the full-body em-push going, keeping me stiff against the floor, as he activated the video on the circle he'd drawn on the wall. "Do you see this?"

Lem sat up, narrowing her eyes as she peered into the dark image. A shadow moved in a world of shades, and it was difficult to see anything. A faceless man put a finger to his lips.

"Ebon Shadow," Lem growled.

"He has us muted, my dear, he can't hear you," said Diebol. "Wouldn't want to wake the children."

The camera swiveled to a little girl asleep on a pile of pillows and tablecloths on the floor. Anyone would recognize Juju Benzaran with her full bush of kinked blonde hair against dark skin like Lem's. The mercenary's shadow fell over her. The camera shut off.

I sucked in my breath.

Diebol smiled, and with a flair of his hand released me from his hold. He knew I didn't have anything to say. I resented that. I was bracing for Lem's storm.

But her hyper-readable face was strangely cold. She pressed her palms flat against the floor. "The poster on the wall is from a band my sister hates," she said. "It's a fake video feed. You created it on the computer."

I gaped. Seriously? Lem was *that* much in denial?

"I know what you're gonna say," she kept going, as if she *needed* to convince him. "That even though no adult recruit knows where the children's bunker is, I know, because I just graduated from it, and maybe Bricandor read my mind or something, and told the Shadow, or some shyte like that. But you're wrong. They change the polymerwalls every time someone graduates. So you can't find the entrances. And even if he did, even with his fancy morph armor, he'd need her DNA to get in. And he doesn't have that."

Diebol smiled at her as he clicked the erase button on the end of his pen, and rose to his feet. There were a lot of ways to get DNA samples, actually, but I didn't say that. Any time they went out to the town, a dirty glass, a scratch on a thorn, anything was a DNA sample.

"He didn't get in," she said. "He didn't follow her to the doors, because her trainer would see him following them. He didn't kill her trainer, because he can't."

"Why can't he?" Diebol asked, his smile widening.

"Lem, you should stop talking," I said.

"Because he can't! He just can't!" Thank goodness, she wasn't revealing information, just freaking out. Her knuckles were becoming red-purple as she pushed her hands harder against the floor. "You just said yourself we can be made to see anything.

That's all this is—you making me see more things so you can take away reality from me. Get out!"

She rose to her feet now. Diebol raised his eyebrows. Bloodseas, could his smile get any more condescending? He stepped away from her with a salute, and left the room with a laugh. "She'll be here soon," he said as he closed the door. "You can watch her die, if you like."

Lem collapsed against the wall. It moved back away from her, and she fell down on her butt. I looked away from her, and she looked away from me, both pretending we didn't see each other put in our places by Diebol.

"I gotta get out of here," she whispered.

"You've got to stop egging him on," I muttered back. "You're only making things worse for yourself. And … you've got to decide what you're going to do when your sister arrives."

"That's not going to happen!" she shouted. "Njande's going to rescue us! Cinta's sending somebody! I *will* be out before she's caught!"

I glanced up at her. Still, she had no reflection.

What a sad hallucination, I thought as I turned away.

I didn't tell her, but unless the video was real I didn't think she'd see her sister again. I knew Bricandor didn't like Diebol's cure idea. He'd always said the only way to save us was to kill us. And I didn't think Diebol could prove him wrong before Bricandor found out how much damage Lem had done and had her gassed or poisoned. So either Diebol got Lem's sister and forced a decision, or he didn't, he ran out of time, and she died.

Bloodseas, I had to convince her to play cured.

CHAPTER EIGHTEEN

Lark

LARK'S TUNIC BALLOONED OUT BEHIND HER LIKE A FOREST-GREEN cape as she leapt through the air above the alleyway and strapped her climber claws to her hands—in mid-air, no less, like the bloody *professional* she was. She stretched all four limbs, like a lizard, towards the next slippery sloped roof—*ow!*

Lark landed with a jolt and sucked in a painful breath. The blasted claw-straps rug-burned her wrists.

Above Lark towered higher roofs, balconies, sky-scrapers and glass buildings a hundred hues of azure grey, and above them floated cloth balloons, transport kites, and crystalline shuttles filled with colorful people.

Below her the Ebon Shadow marched through Retrack City's crowded backstreets. People, rats, strays, and trash-bots scattered before him, and anything that didn't scatter seemed to disappear around him as if he pushed through it like an arrow through fog. He slipped in and out of shades of visibility as if nothing around him existed.

Lark kept eyes on him with the primitive heat signature tracker in her mask. Heat. Blast it all, this *planet's* unnatural nutty heat was getting to her, and it made her grumpy. She wished she had a cartridge that could penetrate that armor. Bully, she'd shoot him from right here. Serve him right for leading her on a pointless chase.

Eh, who was she joshing, anyway? She should be working. His threat had made her so mad, though. She dreamed of just waltzing off with something of his, leaving a business card, letting him stew in defeat shaking his fist while she … cackled maniacally or something? This had sounded so classy in her head, but now that she'd followed the bloke for half an hour the whole kerfuffle sounded like something only a dimwitted hot-head did to get shot six times in the thighs.

In the thighs, because Bont lizards kept their primary brain centers there. That was another reason Lark wished she could actually shape-shift into a Bont instead of just pretending: you could cut off a Bont's head, and she could still run around and live, maybe even grow a new head. Breathing, heartbeat, all that control-stuff necessary for life was beautifully integrated into those powerful naturally-armored legs, with only memories, personality, and highest thought reserved for the head-brain. Back on the Bont homeworld this caused a bully-butt-load of ethical debates—if you cut off a head, and it grew back, was this still the same person, with the same rights? When was a person really dead?

Lark sighed. *This* person would be "really dead" the minute the Ebon Shadow looked up. Blast it all, they'd already gotten as far as the spaceport in the Southern end of the city, and it was becoming quite dark—Lark could see the orb of the twin planet in the sky. What would anyone want behind a fancy private port, anyhow? Hurrah for the *least*-seedy area of town.

The cobblestone street was deserted except for a few aquamarine trash-bots humming through the alleys, slurping up whatever dirt they could find into their tube-bodies; every now and then the lids on top of the tubes would jitter and tinkle as the trash-bots rolled over bumps, but otherwise, all was quiet. The windows of the stores along the street closed, all at once, with soft, quaint chimes; the streetlights faded into a gentle pink glow. The only imperfection marring the peaceful neighborhood was one trash-bot, apparently broken, leaning against a shop wall.

Eh … this place wasn't worth the time it took to rob a jewelry store. The Ebon Shadow was just standing by the broken trash-bot looking at his wristband. Lark turned to go. She glanced back over her shoulder once with a frustrated sigh—

"Hey there, lovely."

Lark almost vomited up her heart. The Ebon Shadow lounged beside her, languid limbs draped across the rooftop and mask inches from her face, squeaky-clean armor reflecting the rosy setting sun.

Lark snatched for her belt—

His grip pinned her wrist to the roof, his sharp knee pinched down her other arm as he practically mounted her, and he placed a finger to where his lips would be.

"Shhh, wouldn't want to alert my brother now, would we, beautiful?"

Stammering flabbergasts and bouncing bun-beans, there were two of them! Lark looked down over her shoulder at the Ebon Shadow she'd tailed here, the stiff, cold, silent killer standing by the broken trash-bot, and then at this comfortable would-be charmer almost chest to chest with her.

He nodded and she thought she *felt* his smile, on the other side of the mask, as he slowly let go of her.

"Good," he whispered, hands open towards her like he was calming a wild horse. "Now I know you want a date with my brother as badly as I do, but you're really not his type, what with the claws and the snout. You're certainly mine, though—"

A *click* by her wrist, and she was handcuffed to the roof.

"And now he won't shoot you when you romantically come to my rescue." He chuckled as if they knew each other, and Lark still had no idea what to say. This bloke talked more than a teenage girl!

Still talking, he unholstered two of his six guns, twirling them around his wrists. "I'd normally have to kill you since you know our secret. But you're such a cutie … I guess I'll just have to kill him instead."

He leapt off the roof in a showy swan dive complete with two perfect and perfectly unnecessary front-flips. The other Ebon whirled and fired; classy mouth-man spun mid-air and released his own swarm of flayer shots. The men tumbled into each other, and Lark could no longer tell who was who.

Well, no bloody time to stay here tied to the roof. Lark unsheathed her laser knife and began sawing at the metal. The skirmish below took seconds—and when one man rose victorious, she didn't like the result.

"I think your girlfriend's going to kill you, brother mine," coughed the charmer, lying on his back with his twin's boot on his chest.

The stilted ice-man didn't bother to answer. He fired point-blank, and the body below him jolted back against the cobblestones with a buzzing crunch, and then faded into invisibility.

WHAT.

The colder Shadow rose stiffly. He didn't even seem human—bloody *robotic*, Lark sneered. The handcuffs melted away and she sheathed her knife, pressing her belly tighter against the rooftop. Now he was taking the broken trash-bot away, eh? She'd forgotten about it in the scuffle.

Rather odd heat signature on that trash-bot. Lark adjusted her mask lens.

A little kid! Where the trash-bot's machinery and computing should have been, there drooped a human child, curled up with her —seemed to be a "her," aye?—with her head lolling to the side, clearly unconscious. Human trafficking, behind the posh jewelry store.

Well this was the most unexpected thing Lark had ever seen. Was that an age-old sibling rivalry that'd just ended right there, then, as unceremoniously as—well, as a man taking out his trash? One man kidnapped a girl, and just like that, his brother murdered him and stole his job without so much as a goodbye? That was *it*?

This certainly explained how the Ebon Shadow managed to become such a prolific hunter: with two hunters sharing one identity you doubled your kill count *and* built that "two places at once" reputation.

But it was over now. An era no one but Lark even knew *existed* ended right here. And Lark knew which nameless evil twin she liked the best. It was not the one who didn't even bother saying anything when he shot his double. Sure, the dead bloke had his horrible sins—human trafficker and all—but what with that smooth voice, those laughed last words, Lark already had an entire tragic backstory spawning in her head. Regret. Limited options. That feeling that he knew this line of work would kill him, that he deserved to die, but never expected it like this. *Brother mine*, he said, with all the sarcasm of betrayal. Aye, that fellow had panache.

Or, had *had* panache before his *brother* shot him.

Lark scrambled in closer. The Ebon Shadow paused—

Lark ducked behind a faux-chimney. Was he looking up? He didn't hear her, did he?

She heard him stop the rolling trash-bot. Then footsteps, back towards her, and the dead man she'd join if he saw her …

The footsteps stopped again.

Soft clicks and scratches. Was he messing with his armor? Blast it all, she wanted to peep around the chimney. She didn't want him leaping up *behind* her on those rocket-boots—! *No, hold still! Don't look!*

"The game's changed," said the Shadow. What? Lark gripped her whip, ready to whirl around and face her death like a lizard—

"I only correspond with the person who's paying me. You tell me who that is. Then you and I will never talk again."

Lark's shoulders relaxed. He was talking to a client. She pressed her back against the chimney and slowly edged her face around the corner …

The Shadow knelt over the body that flickered in and out of visibility as he tore some machinery from the man's wrist. *Must be a video camera, there, the way he's holding it and talking to it.*

"Is Diebol the one paying me? No? Then I won't talk to him."

Diebol? The Growen second-in-command? This was getting

good. Lark opened her mouth to hear better—a sciencey friend of hers once told her humans hear better with open mouths—and strained, leaning over as far as she could without falling onto the street.

"Put me through to Bricandor, then. Silver Knight Six."

Silver Knight Six? Growen code-name for the dictator? Good to remember.

"Silver Knight Six, this is Ebon Shadow."

"I remember you," crackled the radio.

"My current deadline is unacceptable," said the Shadow.

The radio laughed a gentle, tinkling, chuckle. For an evil dictator-wanna-be, Bricandor sure sounded like a kind old grandfather. "Commander Diebol established that deadline," he said. "I would be glad to change it. In fact, I will pay you a small bonus if you promise *not* to arrive before his deadline—we have a harmless wager of sorts going, and at any rate I have my own plans for the girl. I just don't have the heart to tell my boy, you see."

"I don't need to hear any of this," said the Shadow. "Please stop. I'll arrive after the deadline. But don't expect any more video logs from me. This isn't a spectator sport."

The Shadow dropped the camera on the street and crushed it under foot. It faded into invisibility as he carted his trash-bot off towards the spaceport.

Lark slumped against the chimney for a second, her eyes wide. Well bloody blasted bean-fricassee, this was a find! She'd never heard Counselor Bricandor speak. He sounded so harmless and rambling that she almost wondered for a moment what was wrong with his opponents. Clearly the man had the kindest intentions, poor old talker.

Except that was a load of ninny shyte. Lark shook herself off and crossed the roof on all fours towards the space-port after the Shadow. Bricandor had *plans* for some little girl? Plans so personal he didn't want his second-in-command knowing about them? Old men would pay a lot for a number of things, and Lark's imagination went dark places quickly.

Lark felt her compupad vibrate in her vest—ay, that'd be Rana's men trying to get in touch with her. Well, they and their resume-building electromagnetics could hold on. They didn't need to know about her detour any more than they'd needed to know about her association with the killing list—she still felt a little weird about that, a little nutty knowing the Growen had the coffers to send assassins after Frelsi allies even in the Undecided Zones, but she figured that was big picture politics, and not her business.

With a little girl on the line, everything else could wait.

CHAPTER NINETEEN

Diebol

LEM BENZARAN WAS GOING TO DIE.

Diebol leaned over the sink like a drunk man retching, his fists clenched on the dull aluminum rim. Three weeks at this game and almost no progress with her left him worried about his own sanity. Now his bounty hunter had cut off contact with him for some reason, and he had no way of knowing when the idiot would even show. Bricandor's deadline loomed *next week*. That meant the gas chamber for her? After all this?

"Damn you, Lem," he muttered.

A beep from the vest strewn across his bed told him his imaging pen was sounding its five-minute warning. He splashed cold water across his face and bare chest. He had to get it together. He had another session with her.

Diebol drew a square on his palm to check his messages as he slipped into his jumpsuit and threw his vest over top. Oh stars, the physician again. This woman had a morbid obsession with surgeries, and she would *not stop contacting him*.

"No, Cindy, you can't have 'just a little nick' in Bereens's hippocampus," Diebol grumbled, dictating to his palm as he started down the hall. "I don't care if you think that's where the interdimensional infection is, I like the progress we're making with him as is."

Oh no, she was online. She replied via voice-chat. "Commander, the entire basis of his relationship with the Njandejara Contamination is a past kindness during his first incarceration. He barely talks to the thing anymore. If we eliminate those past feelings and he forgets what the creature did for him, he's stuck in the present—and yours to reason with!"

"That's not what I want. I want him to want the change," Diebol said. "The infection is in his *will*."

"The will is in the basal ganglia. I have a surgery for that."

"Not a risk-free one, you don't," Diebol said. "You haven't even produced a complete neuronal map for yourself yet—you expect me to believe you have one for my captives?"

"That's why it's experimental, Commander. We have to start somewhere."

"These are people, dammit, not lab cats. I don't want brain-dead lobotomized soldiers, I want loyal, free *friends of our cause*."

"Oooh, speaking of lobotomy," Cindy cooed. "You're still having personality problems with the female, right? I can actually just take a slice out of her pre-frontal cortex, and she'll be as docile as a—"

"If you speak to me about this again, you will find *yourself* the subject of experimental surgery." Diebol knew she could see his vicious smile on the video feed, and he knew it had the desired effect. Her terrified silence made him laugh.

"Oh come now, Cindy, you know I'm teasing, right?" He made sure his tone suggested he wasn't. Shocking these people was one of his few everyday pleasures. "Don't lose hope."

He clicked the erase button and slipped his pen back into his pocket.

Here it was. Ugh. The polymerwall to the electric therapy room. Diebol's gut twisted. "Who knows, I might come to you about that lobotomy after all," he muttered.

Deep breath. He entered.

Lem was barefoot in an orange tank-top and black tunic pants, and the prison clothes flattered her far more than the second-rate armored jumpsuit they'd captured her in. Her long fingers clenched the faux-wood handles of her chair; the muscular tone of her arms pressed against the tight, thin restraints, as if at any moment she might tear the wires and flee into the abstract mural on the walls ...

Hold steady, he thought, to himself more than to her. He reviewed her schedule in his head as he crossed the shimmering onyx floor under her glare to sit in a simple wooden chair across from her. She seemed about as pissed as usual. She hadn't eaten or slept in twenty-four hours, and she'd spent twelve hours in forced reading, so she should have elevated cortisol levels, decreased cognitive defenses, and perhaps even a few new concepts learned. A reasonable cause for pissyness, from her perspective.

Diebol caressed the black marble button on his chair's armrest as the light formed rainbow reflections in its bubbled surface. It was a comforting button, connecting him to her, through the wires— connecting them through the empty room they both hated. "Well, you know the game, so we'll jump right in," he said. "I look forward to a productive session today."

Positive psychology. He wasn't feeling it at all, but one had to stay positive.

"'I am powerful, and I belong to no one,'" he said. He liked to start with that, since she seemed to have some phobia of "belonging." "Repeat?"

Lem rolled her eyes, but the wires on her chair weren't for show, and after fifty sessions she knew that well enough. "I am powerful, and I belong to no one," she said, with exactly the same sincerity, tone, and rhythm.

In this, they'd made progress. The first day he'd spent two hours just trying to get her to drop the sarcasm.

"Very good," he said.

She bared her teeth. She hated his positive reinforcement, and he knew it, but he couldn't help teasing her a little. At low levels her anger was adorable. "I do not belong to the Frelsi," he said.

"I do not belong to the Frelsi." This one had taken about a week.

"I do not belong to any one way of life—homogeneity is beautiful, and diversity is death. Differences cause war. I do not owe my allegiance to protecting them," he said.

She repeated perfectly, her eyes beacons of rage. This one had taken two weeks.

He took a deep breath. Time to dive right in. "I do not belong to Njandejara."

Her shoulders drooped.

Yes, he knew. He knew she'd hoped he wouldn't bring this one up yet. Her mouth opened weakly as she eyed the round button under his hand, and for a second he thought she'd say something— but she was only sucking in her breath.

He waited for her, his hand steady, his eyes on hers. *Come on. You can do this.*

She trembled.

Come on!

"Will you just do it already?" she shouted.

He did. He pressed the marble and steeled himself, his eyes on hers as the mild electric charge shot through her bare soles and she ground her teeth and fought to hold back the cry gurgling in her outstretched throat. He wanted to look away. He knew by now, after this many sessions, she'd become hyper-sensitized to the mild shock, and it hurt more than it harmed. "I do not belong to Njandejara," he said again, softly … patiently.

"It's not like that!" she shouted. "I can't say that because I don't want to overwrite my brain synapses and mess up our connection and it's not like that because it's mutual and—gah!" He pressed the button again. Repeated the phrase again.

And again. *Stay strong.*

And again. *Please …*

For thirty more minutes. She yelled, she pleaded, she struggled: he sucked in his breath and shut out her excuses. He couldn't afford to become contaminated himself. He had the patience for this, he had the strength, he could save her, hold on, please, he could! *Just block her out! Focus!*

But her face alone spoke volumes, and it said she was so right and he was so wrong and she was sweating and crying and so tired and he was only hurting her and—dammit, *Bricandor was going to kill her!*

He lost it. "I'm trying to help you!" Diebol leapt to his feet, gripped her shoulders, roared in her face: "Please stop it and let me help you! Please please please! Don't you understand—you're going to *die* if you don't let this go!"

"I'm going to die anyway!" she screamed back, her spit and sweat splashing his cheeks. "One day or another your people are gonna kill me or some sickness will get me or I'll crash into a moon so leave me alone and let me have what I love while I'm alive!"

"What you love is poison!"

"You think I don't know that?!"

Her words took the both of them aback.

Diebol staggered backwards, wiping his brow as he waited for an explanation.

She stammered, breathing hard.

"So you know the truth, somewhere in there," Diebol hissed. He would grin, but he couldn't. "You know it, now *repeat after me*."

She only burst into angry tears, screaming, and he fled the room with a curse.

Diebol squeezed his eyes shut and leaned against the wall outside, wrist on his forehead. Dammit. Dammit! He really shouldn't care, at this point. He really shouldn't. But she wasn't just the only electrogenic mammal he'd found, *ever*, or even the final proof he needed to bring about peace—she was *herself*. And dammit, she was …

He coughed on his own breath, sweating. He couldn't do it. He just couldn't. It was worth a lobotomy to save her life. Maybe she'd still be herself. If not, at least she'd be like a control group for Jei. Something along those lines. He didn't know the methodology terms well, but like Cindy said, he could figure out which cure style was most effective.

Cow-shyte, he wanted none of that. He wanted her as her! He

wanted to die. She made him want to die. He was a horrible person for doing this. He—

Let go, my son! Let go of your attachments.

Diebol groaned and forced his muscles to relax. Thank goodness, his training still existed somewhere. Yes. He was suffering because he was attached. Attached to his plan, his dreams, his desires, his thoughts of right and wrong—he clenched his fists for a moment, thought of the color green, and let go.

Diebol inhaled. Closed his eyes. *Release.* Wrapped emerald thoughts around his mind as he drew his pen to send the message authorizing the surgery.

"Captain, Captain! Excuse me, Captain!"

Diebol's hand dashed to his holster as he whirled on the blitzer running at him from the left. He snarled. "What do you think you're—"

The blitzer snapped to attention and thrust a compupad in front of himself like a shield.

That picture solved everything.

A little chestnut-skinned human, about twelve, cuddled in the shade of a lechichi fruit tree, leaning back into its shadows against sprawling tree roots. A patchwork of small animal pelts covered her. Her head rested on the rich chocolate fur of a Biouk's chest. His paw tangled in her hair and his muzzle rested against her cheek; their eyes shone as if together nothing could ever hurt them. Like brother and sister. A distinctive black triangular blaze trailed from the Biouk's ears down his forehead, and Diebol recognized him.

This was the same Biouk peddling questions at the gates of all the Luna-Guetala forts, asking about a Stygge army. The common troops didn't know anything about the Stygge elite yet, for fear of compromising the training center and the debut attack, and interfering with the Biouk's fruitless rambling would only lend him legitimacy. So Diebol's team left the Biouk alone in his Sisyphean search.

But he'd never mentioned *Lem.*

The corner of Diebol's mouth rose. His shoulders lifted; he

laughed. Finally! *Finally* he had her. "Pick him up at the next fort he visits …

"Bring him here alive."

LEM

She staggered into lunch almost crying.

They'd made her run four kilometers in the damn floaty-spaces abyss gym, as always—but this time *after* the Diebol-session. She wrapped her arms around herself, as if that'd offset the pain in her calves, the sensitivity in her soles, the—just—defeat—and slumped into her chair. She did 10ks no problem back home all the time, but after the—and all the things she had to say—She couldn't plan escape, or look Bereens in the eye, or even deal with Njande's stupid absence right now. She just wanted to melt under the gray-speckled plastic table in a puddle of dead.

A long *scriiitch* lifted Lem's eyes away from her plate of soggy green nutrient straws. Bereens was pushing aside his full dish. Lem looked up at him. They both knew what happened if they talked, and you couldn't afford to go without eating when no one knew when they'd feed you next.

But Bereens laid down his chopsticks.

"Whatever they're doing to you," he said, eyes blazing behind the veil of hair falling across his face, "you can handle it. Someone believes in you, cadet."

Webbed paws as wide and flat as flippers snatched his plate. The Bichank guards jerked him to his feet.

"Weakness is strength," Bereens said.

So he would rather say that to her than eat today.

And because of that, as the glass doors to the gym closed behind her prison-partner, Lem's soul rested for a moment, and the painful weariness settled into a gentle, sweet ache as she wiped her face on her shoulder and picked up her chopsticks with a deep breath.

Shyte, Cadet Commander Too-Military-For-A-Name had some kinda heart or something.

And he'd heard from Njande lately. *Weakness is strength*—she'd recognize Njande's voice anywhere, in anyone's mouth, and even though she didn't know what the paradox meant, the voice she loved soothed her drained mind like someone had poured cool mint balm into all of the crevasses of her cortex. Whatever it meant, it was good having another Contaminated person here with her.

She took the phrase to heart; she whispered it during her bench press when her grip on the metal bar threatened to slip, let it occupy her mind when she was gnashing her teeth under electric shock because she wasn't a parrot, dammit, and dreamt it during the drug-induced hallucinations that reminded her just how fragile reality really was. She didn't want reality to break.

But was that what it needed?

Lem shook off the thought. A drop of sweat hit the grate under her as she pushed off the ground into a handstand push-up and purple chrome knives flew past her to hit the wall. If she swayed, she got stabbed. Just another day in forever. She didn't know the time, the day, the month, or whether or not she was dreaming.

But it now seemed like her feverish ache had value—that somehow Njande was about to use the essence of her weakness as the fuel for power.

The grays wouldn't see it coming.

CHAPTER TWENTY

Cinta

THE SISTER HE CARED FOR HAD A SCENT LIKE SWEET LEATHER, clean metal, and fermenting berries.

Her human family had laughed upon hearing such comparisons, but the nose rarely lied as the eye did—at least, so went the old Biouk saying. After spending enough time with humans and their weak nostrils, Cinta doubted the proverb applied to all species.

It applied now, for Cinta stood trembling on the planet Revelon just inside a tunnel in the sharp ivory mountainside with his sister's scent calling him at last. A guard outside one of the smaller Growen camps had somehow known the training center's location here on Revelon; a civilian freighter let Cinta buy a ride for five peacock-guinea-pig pelts. Asking questions had paid well.

Cinta's nostrils flared, black wet nose twitching with the signals of the foul lair above him. He glanced over his haunches at the cave's opening; a cool breeze moaned against the passageway with a musical hum, warning ... nature and her piney fragrances, the rush of the nearby stream, the gentle whiff of healthy bacteria breaking down the underbrush in the distance, all called him back.

But the tendril of his sister's smell guided him like a beckoning hand further into the darkness under the mountain.

Faith, he must have faith. How perfect was the shape of this tunnel for his small form, far too small for any human, Wonderfrog, or Bichank land-walrus! How perfect the guidance of his Njandejara.

The sharp whining acidity of cleaning fluids and the complex gagging richness of engine oils met his nose now. His muzzle wrinkled. Moist stone *squicked* under the touch of his leathery paws—disgusted, Cinta moved quickly, and lifted each step gingerly, dreading the next. Suffocating, suffocating, suffocating, buried under the alien mountain far from the treetops and the jungle sky, suffocating, dying …

No, certainly the tree-dwelling Biouks had some underground ancestors, Cinta told himself, and certainly to a child of Njandejara no terrain, no part of the universe, could truly call itself alien? *I can love any place, any person.*

But the oiled darkness, devoid of light, almost of oxygen, continued to tighten around Cinta's body.

And what if he should become *stuck*?

The horrible thought—Cinta recoiled a few steps, to where stone no longer touched his shoulders. The hoarse whine of his nostrils seemed loud, close, with no echo and no space for sound. His throat tightened. No light or space!

Slow down, slow breaths—Njandejara had given him this passageway. The Being did not believe in dead ends.

More steps forward, squishing through each smaller and smaller cranny. Tighter the mountain squeezed, now compressing his ribs. Rock wall scraped the ears tucked tightly against his head.

His heart pattered, buzzed like a dragonfly. Breathe, *deeeep* breath like he'd taught—

Not with the walls wrapping his body like a wrestler's embrace. When he took a deep breath, his chest pressed against the crushing rock. He could not expand his lungs. Shallow breaths only.

He could not breathe!

Cinta squirmed and began to flail. His shoulders caught—he could not go backwards! His hips caught forwards? He could not—!

I can do all things through Njandejara! He squealed and kicked forward, and bumped into a wall. A dead end! Gasping, he patted his paws all across the wall, ordering himself not to claw, not to claw the stone, to calm down!

Empty space to the left. The wall turned left. A turn, not a dead end. He scrambled through it, now able to run again, and took a deep breath as light appeared at the end of the channel.

A grate—an exhaust grate, perhaps, or perhaps the air vent into an access tunnel. Coolness washed over Cinta, and his fur rippled in a wave to lay flat against his relaxing muscles. His normal breathing returned.

Oh thank heaven.

Horrifying, that experience, but *forgetting what is behind and pressing on to what is ahead* ... he quoted more messages to himself from his Njandejara, and drew his laser knife to loosen the edges of the metal grate. Like butter the metal gave, and soon he'd left the tunnel behind. Thank heaven, thank heaven, he would not have to return through that horrible passageway.

This dark hallway, still floored in rough stone, seemed to turn in a large circle around an enormous, seemingly bottomless central gymnasium, visible through small viewing portholes every few meters. Cinta looked around, ears erect for the slightest sound, and then dashed to the nearest porthole.

At long last he saw his sister.

BEREENS

After enough indeterminable time in the training center I hit that point where you're so tired you're not tired anymore, and you relax, and the endorphins come out, and you're one with your body. My first trainer back on Alpino, a winged Draconian with violet scales, always called that his "second flame."

But my volcano-dwelling teacher left my mind as quickly as he'd slipped into it—I was busy. Flipping over the abyss in the now-familiar gym, spinning through rings of fire, landing on a shining, oiled platform with my arms spread as I slid towards the edge— Diebol across from me with his fists raised.

His finger never left the trigger that controlled the gym's wild fluctuations.

Sparring Diebol was always my favorite part of the … day, or week, or whatever, and I was getting better. He kept calling for his Bichanks earlier and earlier, and today I saw him stumble. Step by step I was catching up to him.

I'd earned this closeness. I was friendly, cordial, *obedient*, to a fault. When he wanted me to say something, I said it. Every obstacle course he threw my way I took with a smile. He sparred me because I'd almost built *trust*—because he wanted to see what was really inside me, and you know where a man stands when you're staring him in the face as he strikes at you. His eyes tell you whether he wants you dead or not.

My eyes said *it's all just a game, right*? I hoped. Now I had him on the ground, under me. I could see the pen in his jacket pocket. His transmitter; my phone call home. I raised my left fist to punch him, a wide, dramatic, aggressive arc—

And with his eye on that left hook I slipped my right hand towards his jacket as if to grab him by the collar and *slipped* his imaging pen out into my sleeve.

My everything tensed in triumph. It would've been a dead give-away had he not blocked my punch and decked me in the gut at the same time. An em-push hurled me across the platform, away from him, and I tumbled into a roll and stood up, trying to relax my shoulders and keep a straight face because *ha! I have his pen*! Now I just needed a moment alone to make the call!

He didn't see me struggling to control my breathing because he was staring over at the platform near the door where a Wonderfrog was licking his lips and raising two webbed fingers. Diebol nodded.

"I'll be back in a bit," he said. "Meanwhile, here's your sparring partner." He waved his hand and pressed the trigger on the little black control stick in his hand. With a flash of smoke Lem appeared on the neighboring platform, looking around in confusion. "Match goes until someone taps out. Winner gets to eat today."

With that, his side of the platform detached to carry him over to the glass doors. Lem leapt over to me.

"How does just one button do all those different things?" I wondered.

"Bet it's placebo effect," she said. "Stupid button doesn't do anything, it's all choreographed. Like dumping me through the ceiling in a cloud of smoke. Oh," she twirled over behind me and tapped me on the shoulder with a smile. "I tap out, I lose. Your turn to eat today, Abejundo."

I grinned at the new name guess, but I needed to tell her about the pen—and if the match ended now I might not see her alone for a while. "No, I actually want to spar."

"Oh, do you? A'ight." She dropped to the floor to slide-kick my knees out from under me.

I jumped over her attack—wow, chipper today, was she?

Lem slid back up to her feet and lashed her open palm at my chest. I blocked; she grabbed my wrist, twisted my elbow behind my back—hm, this was actually really bad form, if she wanted to hold me she should really tighten her—wait, she was tickling my palm with her fingertips?

No, she was tapping out Frelsi tactile code!

My meds aren't working today, she said.

I whirled to face her with a wink. Nice. I got it. She kept her hand on my wrist; I stepped to the side to pull that arm up around her into a choke-hold. She ducked out before I stabilized it.

"They're probably alternating your drug doses with a placebo," I said aloud, striking open-handed towards her mid-section. "So your brain doesn't get so used to the meds they don't work anymore."

"Drug holiday," she nodded, blocking. Yeah, she'd heard Dr. Pattie talk plenty of times. I snatched her wrist and tucked her arm under mine into a lock.

I have his pen, I tapped into her imprisoned palm.

Her eyes lit up. She gripped my hand as I released her arm. *I'll make for the door and distract 'em*, she replied. We both knew our recipe for success by now. Her in the spotlight, myself in the shadows, her bold defiance and my quiet strategy …

We were supposed to drop our hands, then. But we didn't. We hung there in stasis, fingers intermingled, mine wider, calloused, hers longer, kind of leathery, both our palms laced with scars and speckled with sweat, neither very nice hands—but hers was the first non-violent touch I'd felt in weeks, maybe months. A buddy's pat on the back, my dad tousling my hair, all those kinds of meaningless things that mean so much might never happen again. This was it. I was going to send this message, and then we were going to die.

"My name's Jei," I said.

She smiled.

"Pleased to meet you, Jei Bereens."

And she let go.

CINTA

Through the viewing port Cinta saw his little-big Jaika whirling with a blond human, their fight like a dance. The boy twirled her into him, arm around her throat; she ducked out like a flighted bird, her wrist in his as he feigned a strike with his eyes locked in hers. She seemed to blow away his open hand, her block like the wave of a decorative fan as her boots marked time. The boy seemed familiar, like this, not just from the missing person report but—like the magical child, years ago, spinning in the woods before the saber-toothed cat, leading Jaika away …

Hmf. Likely a coincidence. Cinta knew himself to be over-poetic —Lem often teased him for this. He shook himself to think. Weapons? Guns protruded through the walls into the training room at even intervals. Here, by his porthole, was one. Each porthole had one.

Escape routes?

The glass door at the far side seemed guarded.

Perhaps down?

Oh goodness, down.

Cinta blinked in confusion. A huge gymnasium with a floorless mountain abyss, built by the Growen? No, too impractical—*found* by them, their center built over it for convenience and mythos. Staring into the depths Cinta could sense the mystical, almost spiritual something that perhaps the architect had felt when he selected this place. Holes and falls and cliffs, with floating platforms everchanging ...

Had Lem noticed this room was identical to her mother's secret garden?

Lem did not give Cinta any more time to think. Suddenly she swan-dove into the air and began to leap like a mountain goat from platform to platform towards the glass doors. *No, Jaika, no! Not the glass doors*—she should try to head down! Rebirth came from descent.

The gun-posts sputtered into action; panel after panel popped open in the room to fire at the rogue trainee. Cinta yanked back the slide on this one closest to him, switched its load from rubber bullets to shock rounds, and jerked it out of its mount. He would improve her chances.

Trotting in the dim light, Cinta's paws made no sound. He found his neighboring gunner, a Wonderfrog who cackled every time his shots made contact, and softly put him to sleep.

No need for murder, see?

Surprise and silence served him well. Next gunner, to sleep, and the next—and around in this spiraling hallway he ran, placing gentle shock bolts to the nape of each neck. Soon only one gun remained firing on his sister.

Hope! Deep calls to deep ... A prayer to the Dei of my life ...

BEREENS

I swallowed as Lem dashed towards escape. A sanitized Wonderfrog voice blared through the loudspeaker. "Stop. Stop and drop to the floor on your stomach with your hands behind your head!" He sounded faux-human, but even now he couldn't help the repetition. "Stop and drop!"

I "obeyed," slipping Diebol's pen out of my sleeve onto the platform under my face as I put my hands behind my head. The rubber training bullets came out in full-force. Lem plowed through them. I lifted the holo-pen with my mouth and started scribbling the "to:" address on the platform in front of me. A platform ahead of Lem burst into flames—they'd gone beyond warning now! She pounced on its edge faster than fire and bounced for the next one. I had the first sentence written out now. For some reason the guns stopped firing. She was colliding with the Bichank guards at the door. I was trying to figure out how to press the send button on the side of the pen without taking my hands off my head. Come on, almost there, dammit—

She screamed.

CINTA

No more monsters shot at his sister now, and looking through the viewport into the enormous training room it seemed only two guards would meet her at the glass door. Good! Good, very good. Cinta trusted his hunting skills. One more Bichank crouched by the last viewport, just ahead of him, and soon this one would sleep, too.

Odd. *This* one breathed through its mouth, loudly, and heavily, like something wet with pneumonia … the scent reminded Cinta of the illness on the rec center roof …

Cinta's fur stood on end.

This Bichank had no ears.

Burnt red-black scars marked where the large hearing discs once stood. The mutilation stole Cinta's breath—this poor enslaved creature! Acid rose in Cinta's throat as he steeled himself.

He took another step forward, tightening his grip on the sleep-pistol. Hurry now! Tap, tap, tap … the Bichank's fingerpads ticked against the barrel of his weapon with the regularity of a clock. In his other palm he twirled an electric razor.

Cinta's belly churned, his insides screamed at him to run away—

Why? His logical mind asked in response. This Bichank would be the easiest to stop, for he could not hear!

"Weakness is strength, isn't it?" the Bichank laughed.

Wha—

Cinta jumped back too late. The huge land-walrus pounced, Cinta's weapon bounced somewhere on the floor, a giant paw crushed his neck, and terror of terrors the huge face before him had stitches instead of eyes, and a stubbed wound oozed at the end of the Bichank's muzzle instead of a nose! How did—how—

"I can do all things through him who strengthens me—isn't that how it goes, little Biouk?" Okl chuckled, a deep, raw, *pleasured* chuckle as giant leathery hands roamed over Cinta's belly. *Don't touch me, let me go!* The whirring electric razor threw the little Biouk into a full kicking and shrieking panic. His ears flattened against his scalp to get away from the throaty hot whisper against his muzzle:

"Looks like Njandejara brought me a present."

JEI

Lem screamed.

I should've ignored it, I shouldn't have jolted, dropped the pen, but shyte I hadn't heard a scream like that since my mom died! Full, high, throaty, a cry ringing rich with horror, the kind of roar that takes your whole body, stiff, primal, haunting, and I cursed in a panic and tried to start the message over again, but Diebol was suddenly beside me, over me—I nudged the pen back into my sleeve as he crouched. My heart pounded against the platform. He didn't see that, right?

No, because he was too busy gloating. He punched my shoulder and pointed toward the door like we were beer-buddies enjoying a show.

There by the glass door, flanked by twelve Stygges, on the end of a metal chain, shaven and small, lagged a Biouk.

Oh no.

"Cinta!" Lem cried. The hope, the fire, the ever-present promise that *someone was coming* drained from her face as if the scream sucked out her soul. Ashen cheeks almost gray, eyes almost inhuman in terror—she leapt towards them—

The Stygges drew their maces. She skidded to a stop on the edge of her platform. One of the Stygges pointed behind her, towards Diebol and me, and she whirled, hands outspread to catch her balance, palms up as if in supplication. "Don't," she gasped. "Please —tell me what you want."

Tell me what you want?

Just like that, he'd tamed her.

I dropped my head to the platform. Dammit. I clenched my teeth. Dammit! I'd thought it was impossible. Here I'd almost become infected with her brutal hope, too.

No, I was right, and she was wrong, and I suddenly hated her, Njande, and myself for making it so. I'd wanted to believe in last minute rescues. I wanted to believe in her.

Instead I closed my eyes and didn't see her defeat.

BRICANDOR

The Master sat cross-legged in the center room of his ship. Candles flickered around him ... he reached out with his soul, and stilled their flickering to a straight, perfect burn.

He could feel the assassins around the galaxy with each flame.

On Alpino, several distant relatives of the Bereens family met their electromagnetic end impaled on the spears of the tentacled wonder.

On Forge, several key generals suspected of em-pushing found themselves pushed into a fiery crevasse, their flesh melted from their skulls.

Down the list he continued, weaving each death into the tapestry of monopoly; then, only then, his soul moved on to sense the Awakeners positioned around the Galaxy, Awakeners ripening abilities in those he controlled. Soon he would own the only electromagnetics in the universe, just in time for the invasion of Fort Jehu.

And of course, most delicious of all, on Luna-Guetala, the Ebon Shadow had killed three military officers before taking the little girl who would soon satisfy the hunger of the Flickerform.

"Send my public statement of condolence to the last six families," he murmured to the computerized console hanging around his neck. "The one describing our dedication to honor, and to the treaties ..." The one that subtly raised the question: if people in Undecided territories were killing the Frelsi, didn't that mean even the Undecided wanted the Frelsi gone?

Speak it, and it will come to being.

An irritating itch on his left buttock reminded him of young Diebol's foolish project, and with a grumpy sigh, the peaceful master rose.

CHAPTER TWENTY-ONE

Jei

I TRUDGED INTO THE ELECTRIC "THERAPY" ROOM WITH MY HEART heavier than I'd expected. I kicked one of my Wonderfrog escorts in the shin just because. I bumped the other against the wall with my shoulder, and didn't answer when the blitzers yelled at me. No comeback, no technique, no reason, no rhyme. I was just pissed off.

Diebol waited for me in a simple wooden chair, knees square, his hands folded, his head bowed. Utter peace radiated from his face as the guards seated me across from him.

"You don't need to be tied down today, do you?" he asked softly.

I didn't answer. His assumption—like beating Lem trumped me, like she was the last stick on the board and it was still a game, like what she did had any influence on what I did—it burned my stomach. My tongue became dry acid.

But I held it in and took my seat. I'd pretend. I'd bide my time. Until I destroyed him.

They left us alone.

"So let's talk about today," he said.

"I'd rather not."

He chuckled and sighed. "Alright. What do you want to talk about?"

I almost laughed out loud. This arrogance. Bloodseas, this arrogance! He'd asked an open question, but he'd already silenced any real speech. And he had the nerve to pretend he did it for my good. "Anything you want," he said. "It's been a rough day for you, so let's take it easy this session. You've earned it, friend."

"Friend" did it.

I em-pushed off the wall behind me, throwing myself against him, my fingers twisting in violent grip under his rough collar. His chair toppled as we crashed over it. Blood pounded in my temples; my vision tunneled. He em-pushed back, trying to get distance, get away from me—I em-pushed harder, crushing against him, slamming his back against the metal wall again with a dull'd ringing thud. He reached for his mace—I flicked my wrist—the mace flew away to lodge in the wall. I couldn't use it—it burned anyone without his DNA—but I could keep him from it—

The point of a flayer pistol jammed against my solar plexus, below my ribs, and knocked the wind out of me. Diebol's eyes met mine, cold. I winced. I let him go.

"It's a pity," he said, prodding me back to my seat. "You were pretending so well." He lowered his voice to a whisper: "May I have my pen back, now?"

Shyte.

I handed it over and sat down. What was I doing? I wasn't thinking. Green, color green. Damn, what was I even fighting for now? Freedom no longer seemed like a real thing, or at least not an achievable thing, and who cared whether or not I spoke to something I couldn't see? I didn't. But the fort, the Luna-Guetala fort, they were going to kill those people. I could fight for that. We were alone. I could take his flayer. I em-pulled—

He smirked and maintained his grip. "I will shoot you," he said. "Curing you is important, but I won't give my life for it."

I stopped pulling; his face softened.

"Listen," he said. "I know you're confused and upset. I imagine it's scary to see someone break like that, and I understand that. But it's necessary. Benzaran merely realized that Njande's only using you. It's not *about* you. Once he's collected enough portals for his invasion—it doesn't matter *who*—you're out, and once you see that, once reality opens up before you and you break your chains, you break a little, too. That new birth is painful. But it is worth it."

"It sounds perfect," I muttered. "I get it. But it's almost impossible to 'free your mind' when you've seen—look, Njandejara, he's elsewhere now, in his own dimension, saving that world, but when he visits, he brings …"

"Miracles, sweetness, good feelings, a presence you've never known anywhere else that enhances the joys of reality and masks your existence's brokenness—I know." He leaned in closer to me. "It's all drugs, Jei. I can do the same for you with pills, at lesser cost. Is that what you really want? I'm not saying that's wrong. Whatever it is you truly want, in your heart of hearts, we need to uncover that so we can use it as your pathway to freedom."

"You're looking for my price, in other words," I muttered.

"Would you like to help me find it?"

I opened my mouth …

Pounding on the polymerwall. Diebol ignored it.

It continued. He rose with a grimace and tapped the panel on the wall that released the DNA lock.

Two blitzers tumbled through the wall. "Captain, pardon the interruption, but the Commander has returned—"

Diebol raised his flayer pistol.

"—And his reading of Benzaran came out positive!"

All the blood surged to my head.

She *still* wasn't cured? Wait, what did that even mean? Was this a hopeful thing? Was this hope?

DIEBOL

Diebol pistol-whipped the messenger across the side of the helmet.

"Do you think he needed to know that?!" he roared, pointing at

Jei as he loomed over the stumbling blitzer. So close! He'd been so close to getting a real response! "Do you really not see what I'm trying to do here?"

The second blitzer tried to step between Diebol and his fallen comrade. "I'm sorry sir, it's just we need to warn you *he* just arrived—"

He was interrupted by a form pushing through the polymerwall to enter the room. "My goodness, Captain Diebol. Your idea of reform does seem to generate a number of HR complaints."

Shyte! Diebol holstered his flayer and folded his hands behind his back. Shoulders square. Feet planted exactly shoulder-width apart—a centimeter off-stance reflected a lack of dedication and deserved punishment. Which he didn't. He stared straight ahead as the wall congealed back into place and Counselor Bricandor stepped in, silver cape fluttering and blue eyes burning.

You're early! I have another week! What are you doing here?! Diebol held his tongue, but he couldn't help his mind. *You can't kill them yet! I need more time!*

Bricandor sighed; that gentle smirk said he'd heard Diebol's thoughts. As he stepped over the fallen blitzer without a glance, like he was passing a dirty puddle, his pointed nod towards Jei told Diebol the worst before he spoke.

"This one has five more days. The other one dies today."

Diebol wasn't attached. He wasn't breaking from his training. He was just trying to save the world. He knew what could happen if he said it, but he had to try—he had to say it!

"No," he pleaded.

Bricandor's grizzled eyebrows raised. His hand slid to the mace around his waist, rustling his cape as he peered into Diebol's face, so close his breath warmed Diebol's cheeks.

Diebol stared straight ahead. No blinking. He wanted to cringe. Disobedience used to end with him bleeding on the floor. Didn't he just say he *wouldn't* risk his life for this?

"Explain yourself," said Bricandor.

Oh thank goodness. No bleeding on the floor just yet. "I will," he said. "One demonstration, and you'll see what I've been working on. Give me an hour."

"I've given a number of hours. I will have your explanation now."

"As you wish." Oh, this was hopeless. Diebol's peace disappeared under a dead stillness, but he didn't flinch. He'd dug his grave, and he'd lie in it. He waved several Stygges into the room to take Jei away, and with a deep breath and a set jaw he switched chairs and called for Lem.

LEM

Lem sat in the electric therapy room alone. Same old wooden chair for her. Same marble throne for him. Same place she always defied them.

Some defiance. Her face burned, and she squeezed her eyes shut to hide from her reflection. *"Please, tell me what you want!"* Some rebel she was.

Shyte, though, who cared? It was Cinta. She'd never have heard Njande without Cinta. Cinta's sense of smell found her as a baby when her parents hid her in a log before their first Growen capture; Cinta's leathery paws held her hands when she took her first steps; Cinta's bravery returned her to her human family after they escaped the Growen. And it wasn't just that he was *everything*. It was that he was the *one thing* they couldn't reach. Everything else in her life they could destroy, but he was hidden in the jungle, protected by his pacifism.

He was the only constant she'd known she'd never lose.

"Njandejara, you can't have him," she hissed. "He's mine."

"Well *that's* a striking statement."

Lem whipped her head around to face the polymerwall. Diebol leaned beside it, hands in his pockets, grinning. He was a good actor, but something forced and strained tickled around the corner of his mouth, and his forearms flexed taut.

"What're *you* stressing about?" Lem spat.

"You're not the only one making difficult decisions right now," he grimaced. "But what you said—I like the way you've framed it. In your mind, it's not just a choice between your interdimensional or your Biouk. You see Njandejara *taking away* your friend."

"That—it's complicated," she muttered. "We made a deal with him."

"Oh?" Diebol smiled, a real smile now, and turned his chair around to sit on it backwards, legs apart and forearms leaning on the chair's back. "A post-mortem deal, correct?"

Lem's eyes narrowed. How did he—

"It's the same deal he makes with everyone, Benzaran, don't act so surprised."

"You never brought it up before."

"It's not worth bringing up. He's not going to keep it. You're not turning into gods and goddesses—if anything he holds your powers *back*—and when you die, it's not going to be an ascension into his dimension. There's no gate between our worlds."

"He's making one."

"Oh, I'm well aware. But that's for his descent, not your ascent. It's never been about you. It's always been about him."

Lem's jaw tightened. The heat from her face trickled down through her muscles. Damn, didn't she just *ache* to smash in his arrogant—

"Why does that make you so angry? No one's that afraid of something they really believe isn't true. And—" He smirked. "Doesn't rage burn out your connections to him?"

"How the hell do you know all this?!"

"No reason," Diebol smiled. He glanced away and ran his finger along a crease in his leather vest. "You know, I don't really want your Biouk here. I have to torture him if he stays, for you, but he's only here because he followed you—what a faithful friend, right?" He raised his eyes to meet hers. "Tell you what. You defeat Jei at this afternoon's training game—without saying a word to him—and your Biouk goes free."

"What the hell's in that for you?" Lem cried.

"A good story. I enjoy tales of enduring friendship." Diebol rose to his feet. "I would hate to see yours end with the heroine climbing over the corpses of everyone she loves for an ideology."

And Diebol left the room.

CHAPTER TWENTY-TWO

Jei

Emerald and azure lights flickered on the floor, highlighting and shadowing my reflection on the plexiglass spread 360 around me as I stepped into the arena. An enormous lit grid spread ahead of me under my feet, a giant, updated, much more beautiful version of the tiny game-board Diebol and I had carved into the floor of our cage. In the cage, on our crude carved grid, we used twigs to mark "territory," capturing each other's grid spaces by placing a perimeter around them to score points; here, if I pressed a button on the sleek black console beside me, a shining green stripe on the blue floor would mark my placement. I could even use the touchscreen on the console to rotate my digital "twig," to build the triangles and diamonds that won additional turns. The entire room delighted me; in that glowing, colorful moment I almost forgot I hated him, and looked up almost to smile at his ridiculous nostalgia.

But he was seated on the other side of the curved window to my right, his elbows on his knees and chin on folded hands, watching me like a man praying for his life. He sat in the shadows of Bricandor's silver robe.

We were both prisoners, still.

I shook off the stupid thought with a healthy mental picture of stabbing them both in the face. Commotion, a cry—the polymerwall at the other end of the arena bulged and popped. Lem stumbled through, cursing at whoever had shoved her; I tossed an electromagnetic wave her way to help her catch her balance.

Her eyes lit up when she saw me. She stepped forward—

"Benzaran, stay on your side of the field," Diebol snapped.

Bitterness melted across her face. Lem made as if to dash herself through the plexiglass at him—

"Lem, stop, it's electrically sealed," I called.

She glared at me like I'd built the thing, but she let Diebol explain the rules. She seemed calm? She didn't mock every other thing he said, didn't say anything at all—maybe that was good? I couldn't see her expressions with the blue grid-light casting odd shadows across her face …

No—she was grinding her jaw.

Bloodseas, I really needed to talk to her. Fortunately it looked like I might get my chance: this was the same game Diebol and I played, definitely something you can chat over. At the very least I'd grab her hand after the game and code a quick status check into her palm.

After the game. But what would happen after the game? This was *the* game, the one thing Diebol decided to show Bricandor to prove he could cure us. So if he failed, Lem would die when we made the last move. Kill her now, and me next week, he'd said. So—so we needed to look curable before the game ended.

What did that even *mean* though? Was Diebol trying to fool Bricandor's reading somehow? Or were we actually in danger of losing Njandejara? Should we act—

Lem whacked the podium beside her. A square tile six feet in front of me lit up with a diagonal blue line through it. First move, done. No time for a game plan.

"Wow, someone's in a hurry," I laughed uneasily.

Lem crossed her arms.

Well okay then. My lower chest constricted; I tried to chalk it up to paranoia, to the fact that I'd spent too many hours in a mind-melding horror house. Nothing was going to go horribly, horribly wrong right now. Not for anyone but Diebol.

Except that if Diebol failed, Lem died. Our fates were intrinsically linked.

How did that work? What happened if Lem flipped, anyway? The strategy part of my brain didn't care if she, personally, talked to Njande or not, but it did care about Bricandor owning a Stygge *nuke* like Lem if she switched sides.

I rubbed my hand across the back of my neck, still sizing up the board. I didn't know what I wanted from this game. I could see Diebol watching me, waiting to play his trump, that despised face grinning like he did every time he dropped that stupid twig on my side of the board, right under my nose, only to somehow turn the dumbest move in the galaxy into a win. This was one of those stupid moves: *this* game to convince Bricandor? What? It'd never work. But of course my confidence scared me. Diebol only ever beat me when I was two moves from the win. Was that what this was? Was I winning, and therefore losing?

Maybe it wasn't Lem I should worry about. I hadn't heard from Njande since that *weakness is strength* quip, and while I didn't need him swinging in for the rescue or anything, it bothered me he hadn't checked in since then. Maybe my medications were silencing our connection? But that didn't make sense: I knew actual psych patients who could still talk to him, drugs or not. Maybe he'd dropped me in disgust after I talked about tormenting Diebol?

If *that* was the case, Njande sucked. What was Diebol's kill-count, something like three hundred on his own, more if you gave him credit for the blitzers under his command? Diebol deserved everything I wished upon him. If Njande didn't hate him, he—

A spark shot across the arena. Pain jolted up my shoulder. "What the bloodseas—?" I gripped my arm with a cry and a scowl.

Lem fumed in the shadows behind the playing board, shoulders square, hunched, almost menacing in the shade as her hand stretched into the blue light towards me. She'd—she'd shot me with her fingers?

Diebol leaned over to pull a microphone toward himself. "I agree with her. There's a time limit on moves. Five minutes per turn or that turret"—He pointed into the corner of the room, behind Lem. —"shoots you in the kneecap. Or she electrocutes you, I suppose."

My mind reeled. I tapped my podium quickly to drop a random diagonal green line on some square somewhere. She could do that? How much energy did it take to fling a charge that far? Was she okay?

No time to think. She'd made her next move already. Another blue diagonal line mirroring her original one. "Look, lady, it's in your best interest to think for at least four minutes," I snapped. "Are you okay over there?"

She ignored me. She was talking to herself about the board, leaning back on her hip with one hand over her mouth as she gestured to different spots, trying to work out a strategy. Bloodseas, she wanted to win, and win fast.

But I didn't have a plan yet! I didn't know what would happen when the game ended, or how to stay alive, or what we were even playing against here. I was playing blind. I needed more time.

I needed to keep her from winning.

LEM

Cinta, Cinta, Cinta …

Lem breathed hard, struggling to pin her mind to the board. She wasn't going to panic, or burst into tears, or fly into a rage and blind herself. No, she was going to win and Diebol would set Cinta free. Breathe. *Breathe.*

She pressed the palms of her fists against closed eyelids, walking in a circle around the podium. *Stop talking to yourself about breathing and just think!*

The goal was to rope off territory on the board, or capture the other person's glowing lines by surrounding them with a complete shape. Patterns had additional meaning. If she made a complete diamond it gave her another turn she could either use now or save for later; if she made a Z-shape she could move one of her already-placed lines.

"I can make a diamond right there, this turn," she muttered. "And I'll take that second turn now, and branch towards the upper right-hand corner ..."

Man, this kind of stuff always made her feel so dumb. She excelled at her academics, but the kinds of concrete thinking she used for that—memorization, association, creativity—didn't do shyte here. This was pure strategy, distilled logic, as undiluted as the engine fuel Cinta's father drank.

Okay, chill. So strategy's not my thing, I still got a shot! First time for everything ...

Shyte, he'd taken his move, and she'd spent way too much time trying to psych herself up. Did "possible-ness" even matter? She still had to play whether or not she had a shot. Maybe back on the freighter, when Jei kept harping at her to accept the possibility of defeat, he'd meant something like that—that sometimes you gotta fight whether you're gonna make it or not, just because of what's on the line.

But the prospect of not winning—

Not gonna happen. Not even thinking about it. I'm taking the top right-hand corner.

She built herself a decent stronghold over the next few turns, focusing on using diamonds to make extra moves right away 'til she'd fenced off almost twelve squares. Jei zig-zagged around her area—*dude, get your own territory, no way you're gonna break through this wall*—and didn't use any extra turns. He watched the game board with his palms pressed together, fingertip touching his lips. *Maybe I'll win pretty quick?*

But then he blew over his fingers in a sigh of relief and tapped his podium. One green diagonal streak in the tip of the corner, deep within her territory—

And all her lines disappeared. He'd captured them all in a bigger shape. Score was suddenly something like thirty to nothing. Lem gasped. Wait, how? That wasn't right. She cried out—

Diebol rose to his feet, eyes fixed on her.

Dammit. No talking. She gripped her podium, staring at her mini-board in horror, shoulders slumped and knuckles ashen. She slammed the replay.

Yeah, it was real. She hadn't seen his pattern before, but she saw it now: he'd roped her off, hemmed her in, and then with that last placement captured the whole swath, no liberties. Clearly Jei had played this before.

Diebol's gaze burned Lem's face. She ground her jaw and didn't look at him. She wasn't about to let him psych her out.

She had to tell Jei to let her win. There was more than one way to communicate—maybe she could draw letters on the board.

Deep breath. Lem clutched one hand over her chin nervously as she tapped her podium again. His move, whatever. She ignored it and tapped her next move, a diagonal line right in line with her first line. His move again—now hers—now she'd almost finished the first letter: "I win, they free Cinta …"

"Benzaran," Diebol sighed through the mic. "Remember our deal."

Seriously? Lem growled in frustration, slamming her hand down on the podium.

Now she was three more moves behind for nothing. "Njande, where the hell are you?" she hissed through her teeth. "This is getting a little last minute even for me."

Did he reply? She couldn't hear him. Didn't feel anything. That freaked her out, especially with Jei's next move, another capture. Her skin prickled. Her face chilled. Her chest rose and fell too fast, hyperventilating—

She was panicking. She didn't want to panic. She wanted to calm the hell down.

Board, think about the board. This can't be impossible. Focus, dammit!

Lem cursed as Jei fenced off the board's lower-left-hand corner, winning at least twelve more points. Shyte, this idiot, couldn't he tell there was something up and she needed to win? Cheating. She had to cheat. Was there a way to do that? *Dammit Jei!*

Well, she was allowed to electrocute him, apparently.

JEI

A spark shot through the ground, across the board, zapping through the hole in my boot; pain seized up my leg.

"What the hell, Benzaran?" I yelled, gripping my shin as I jumped back from the podium. "Calm the bloodseas down, I have three more minutes!"

She snarled and stomped her foot again. Another arc of electricity—I leapt this time, and it streamed past me into the wall, diffusing through the floor. She threw up a magnetic field; a wall of polarity repulsed me away from my podium.

"Okay, cut it out," I snapped, raising my left hand to divert her force, splitting her energy into two streams rushing past me as I called our captors. "Is she allowed to do this?"

Diebol shrugged. The corner of his mouth twitched like he wanted to laugh. "Better hurry up," he said. "Just one minute left."

Man, what the bloodseas did he have up his sleeve? Confusion gave way to suspicion as Lem continued to physically interfere with my moves while Diebol's fingertips crept higher up his chin, over his lips, barely masking a growing grin. *"Remember our deal,"* he'd said. What deal?

Bloodseas, had she turned?

I messed up my next seven turns or so, distracted by her bullying. Maybe—was that okay? I didn't want either of us to win too quickly—?

But Diebol's eyes sparkled as Lem's score rose, as if her victory meant his victory. I couldn't have that—couldn't let him win. *Deal, what deal?* My eyes narrowed into his as I dodged another blast from Lem, my nerves calming, the board seared into my mind's sharpening focus. I didn't even need to look as I placed another diagonal to confirm another capture. Diebol's eyebrows rose; that confirmed it. Beating him meant beating her.

Lem's cry of frustration drew my gaze back across the board.

"What's wrong with you?" I shouted across to her. "What's the deal?"

Her eyes met mine. Was—was she about to cry? She said nothing: she stood empty-handed, lips parted, palms open in supplication like with Diebol in the gym.

Begging me to—what? And why?

"Lem, what is the *deal*?"

She wouldn't answer. Not then, not later. Every time it was my turn she freaked out. Was I too slow? *But woman, they're going to kill you when the game ends!*

"Hey, talk to me!" I yelled.

She shook her head with a growl and turned back to her podium.

LEM

Lem's stomach folded in over itself, still, and dead, and her breath tasted almost metal as the despair approached. This was it. Two more lines and he captured her last stronghold on the left side of the board, probably in the whole game. Lem paused before placing her pin.

Shyte. He was a move ahead of her, and he still had all those extra turns he'd saved up from earlier in the game. There was no way she was going to win this area.

There had to be a …

No. No there wasn't. Even straight up frying him out of the game hadn't worked.

Lem's chest constricted, and for a moment she grew dizzy. Dammit. She'd lost. Njande had let her lose.

"What the hell," she croaked. "Maybe he is far away."

And then, at the worst moment possible, she saw him.

He stood in the shadows behind the board, a marbled blend of light and shadow with biped form, gazing over Jei's shoulder. Jei didn't seem to notice him, but Lem saw Njande point at the podium and whisper something in Jei's ear; Jei slid his finger across the podium, nodding, chewing his lip as if he'd just decided his next move.

What. The. Hell.

Charge splashed from Lem's enraged body; the wave hurled her across the board, smashing towards Njande's flickering form with a wordless roar.

She slammed into Jei instead. They tumbled across the floor as he cried out—

"Benzaran!" In her peripherals she saw Diebol leap to his feet— Bricandor held up his hand to stop Diebol. Well screw him! She was licensed to cheat, but who gave a lizard's tail about licenses. Lem untangled herself from Jei, jumped for his podium, and made his move for him in some stupid corner of the board. She slid her finger again, to make another move, use up his stored advantages—

"What the bloodseas—" Jei's palms gripped her shoulders to *shove* her away from his podium. Oh, so he was pissed now? Did it feel unfair, maybe, that they let her get away with everything? She laughed. Screw him, too, he was torturing Cinta.

Lem kicked Jei in the knee and elbowed him off her. He dodged the knee-kick, side-stepped the elbow, and pushed her from his podium with an electromagnetic surge. She met the floor butt first.

"What's this deal he's talking about?" Jei hissed, eyes narrowed, his glance flickering from Lem to Diebol. Lem shook her head, reaching for his hand to stop him—

But he made his move.

One more and she'd lose. She body-slammed him from the podium, desperately whacking the touch-screen interface—tap, tap, tap—using up all his movement, buying herself a chance. Jei elbowed her; she shocked him. It seemed so easy now that she didn't hold back, didn't care about seizures. Bloodseas, she'd welcome a seizure, a coma, anything that took her out of this moment. Charge tickled naturally through her fingertips to crackle through the air ...

Jei snatched her wrist. She fired up for another shock—

Jei yanked Lem against him, holding her hand up in the air, diverting her shot into the ceiling. His fingertip brushed her wrist.

Tap.

She kicked him in the shin. He growled and kicked her back. She stepped out of the way.

What is he doing to you, he tapped into her palm.

She froze. Could she reply? She slid her fingertips down across his palm—

Bricandor whispered something to Diebol.

"Back on your side of the board, Benzaran," Diebol said. "No more cheating."

She tapped before she started to step away. *Ci—*

"Now!" Diebol roared. A wall of force threw Lem backwards as Diebol thrust both hands forward. Lem tumbled and slid across the playing field, skidding to a stop with a thud against her podium. No. No no no no! Her back stung; she had to force herself to breathe through her winded chest in heaving gasps that quickly devolved into sobs.

"Jei, this is your last move," Diebol said.

Jei panted over his podium, sweaty hair sticking to his forehead as he stared in utter bewilderment across the field at Lem, his gaze suffering with hers. "It's just a stupid game," he mouthed.

But he didn't mean it, and Lem knew that. He had to say what it should have been. To protest the universe that pitted them against each other. He didn't know what to do with her incomplete message, with Diebol, or with her wild terror, and he didn't want to end the game like this, or even at all. Bloodseas, that was why he'd saved up all those moves instead of using them. She could've lost a long time ago if he wanted.

How pitiful.

A tragic laugh bubbled within Lem's chest, spurting out past the hot tears clinging to her cheeks as she shook her head.

They lost track of time.

The crack of firepower. Lem jolted through blurry vision as Jei cried in pain and fell to a kneel, gripping his shot knee. The poly-merwalls bulged with giant reaching forms, then popped like splattered alien eggs to deliver thirteen Stygges into the room. Lem heard only vaguely as Diebol declared the game over. She felt only vaguely as her fists pummeled the hairy chest of the Bichank nearest her, as her electric shock singed the cold hand of the human pinning her down, as a long scream, a stream of all the words she'd held in, all the things she hated in the world, echoed through the room in syntactic chaos.

"I hate you, Njande!" Lem screamed. "I hate you!"

CHAPTER TWENTY-THREE

Ebon Shadow

DARKNESS ENGULFED HIS MIND, SWALLOWING EVERYONE WHOLE. People ran through smoldering streets screaming, trying to bat the shade away from their heads. Shrieks faded into whimpers; resistance faded into obedience. Marching, silent creatures morphed through gurgles and the scent of sulfur into one agglutinated whole, a monstrous beast with glorious colors and terrifying fangs, radiating power down its spiked back ...

It turned and looked at him.

He ran, firing off all the torpedoes his jetpack could carry, but It beckoned, promising in some unknown tongue that he *belonged*.

And then, at the end of all things, it died, and its body melted into the earth, and the earth into the stars, and the stars into each other until everything became one, a vast, cold whole, and in the silence rang only the distant scream of a man left alone.

Carl Hampt jerked awake, sweating beneath his armor. He ripped off his helmet, gulped in recycled air, and reached for his utility belt, hands shaking. He steadied his fingertips and popped open a canister of white pills.

It was over. He wasn't asleep anymore. He was seated in his black leather chair, with his thirty-five-million-drachma compuwall spread above and around him, 180 safe degrees in every direction, humming with reassuring engine stats and a long, clean view of space. Not the uniform space of his nightmare: messy space, with stars scattered in clusters and clumps and dirty ice hurtling past his starship at twenty-five kilometers per second. The numbers comforted him.

He'd never had nightmares, or even dreams that he remembered, before this mission. His computer's psychological analysis recommended a cocktail of sleeping pills and a full conversation with a doctor. The latter he didn't have time for, but the former wasn't working.

"Computer, repeat psych eval."

"Certainly. Please replace helmet."

He slid the black mask over his head. Cool protrusions extended through the top of it into his scalp. A new graph appeared on the compuwall beside his prisoner's health stats. Both graphs read "human"; both showed skyrocketing stress levels.

It was illogical to deny it: the dreams began when he acquired the girl. It had nothing to do with K'arl's death—Carl knew, objectively now, that pulling the trigger on his twin at point-blank felt no different from ejecting him into space, drowning him, or burying him under an avalanche. Hopefully the chatty pest would *stay* dead this time: Carl was starting to run out of ways to come back from the dead himself. Armor-upgrades didn't come cheap.

Neither did psychiatrists. The computer beeped. "Unresolved guilt" was a possibility.

Guilt? Carl almost had to look up the definition of the word. He knew what people said about him, but he was objectively reasonable. He'd given the family a chance to buy the girl back. It was too bad they couldn't afford her: despite all the rumors of weapons' manufacturers funding the Frelsi, a little bank-scouring showed the Growen out-funded them ten to one.

Perhaps he felt guilty for putting the Growen on hold for a few days while he looked for a higher bidder. That was a matter of principle, though. Only the true Ebon Shadow dared go behind *Bricandor*'s back, so Carl had to or his brother won: it was quintessential to the identity. Anyway, anyone who *knew* the old man knew he was an ass. If you didn't, your opinion depended on the planet you lived on and the media you trusted, but among those who listened on the inside Jared Diebol was definitely the favorite for Growen Commander. Bricandor was a politician, not a general —why Diebol didn't just shoot him already, Carl could only guess.

Come to think of it, the decrepit dictator was probably exposing him to mind-altering chemicals right now. Every time Carl stepped within three feet of little Juju Benzaran his hair raised on end. That wasn't normal. His equipment didn't pick up any standard biological agents, but he didn't know what to look for—his computer didn't have a category for "chemicals that echo the scream at the end of your nightmares."

Best confront the old man. Carl tapped the ceiling and dragged a contact profile down the window in front of him, right next to the view into space. He checked his anti-tracking software, double-checked transmission security …

"Ebon Shadow, it is good to finally hear from you," creaked the gentle voice when Bricandor answered. "I assume this means you've decided your pay is fair?"

Carl scowled. How the old man knew he'd been running around on him, Carl didn't know. He didn't like not knowing.

"We decided that by contract," Carl said.

"I thought so, too. When can I expect your arrival?"

"Seven-day, 2100."

"Next week? My, you're slow."

"Space is big," Carl shrugged. "Is the child a bio-weapon?"

"No, why?"

Carl didn't say.

"Does she seem gifted?" the Counselor asked. "Can she read your mind?"

"I don't believe in mind-readers."

"Well that's certainly foolish. What's happening with her, then?"

Bricandor's curiosity confirmed it. The old man wasn't telling him something—but Carl didn't plan on sharing his newfound mental instability with a client. "Why do you want her?"

"Why do we ever want children? For what she can grow, Shadow."

Pretty proverb. Carl didn't appreciate it. He didn't know what to say, though, without sounding like a child whimpering to Mommy about bad nighty-nights.

Bricandor interrupted his pause. "I know I requested the initial delay to confound my son's side project, but this is becoming just a bit ridiculous. The faster you bring her in, the faster you'll be safe," he said. "There are beings at work here that want you ... Carl."

Carl! He jerked upright. No one knew his name. He'd once married a woman without telling her. What else did the Stygge know? Did he know about K'arl?

But Carl's voice didn't betray his shock. He doubled down. "I'll see you seven-day, 2100."

And he hung up.

Carl ripped the helmet off his head again and mashed both hands through his matted hair. He was sweating. This was ridiculous. He needed to take control of this situation, and if he couldn't get answers from his client or his gear, he'd have to go to the quarry. Maybe the kid knew something.

Carl swiveled in his chair and crossed the gleaming black cockpit floor to push through the polymerwall into the hallway. His reflection repeated on each polished dark wall, echoing his stealth armor into infinity as he stalked to the spot that opened into the hold. As he pushed through the polymerwall, he *expected* to stand atop a cage-link metal staircase, looking down into a huge open area stocked with crates and cages.

What actually happened was that as soon as the polymerwall released him Carl found himself hurtling through the air towards a sucking gash in his ship's side. His rocket-boots kicked in to stabilize him; his sealed armor linked him to his oxygen tank as his pressurizer kept him from snap-freezing. He drew double pistols.

A female Bont lizard in ratty civilian-grade space-gear was

dragging Carl's prey out the hole, whispering things he couldn't hear to the little girl. A quick glance through the gash showed Carl the now-dissolving grey goop outside: a makeshift polymerwall connected Carl's ship to a Leech vessel that'd somehow latched onto his *Huntress* without triggering her alarm. It'd bought the intruder enough time to open a hole *and* get the girl into a spacesuit before the goop fell off.

Seeing all this took nanoseconds. Carl was still spinning upside-down when he fired on the lizard. A one-use energy shield flashed blue on her uniform, absorbing the shock and fading; the lizard kept going, firing behind herself at Carl as she backed into her ship.

Carl's armor took two hits without any damage. He dashed across the hold and whizzed through the gap after the lizard. He slid into the lizard's parasitic Leech ship just as its roof closed.

Carl landed on his feet as gravity turned on. He almost couldn't do anything *but* land on his feet: the tiny decontamination room had barely enough space for him and the lizard to stand chest to chest. At this proximity if he shot her the flayer bolt would pierce through her body into the child smushed against the wall behind her. He drew his jagged hunting knife.

"This is the worst birthday ever," cried the little girl, her voice muffled by her helmet.

"I've had worse," said the lizard. With a flick of her glow-whip she knocked Carl's knife to the ground, killing one of the flash-shields on his forearm—not bad, but in three spins of his wrist he'd disabled her.

He drew his crescent blade. Gripped it in the middle between the two sharp curves. Tangled her whip around it. Yanked upward, pulling her arm away from her body. It was all mathematical.

She tried to knee him between the legs; he let his armor take it and punched her in the gut full-force.

It was like smashing a baby with a club; the armor-less lizard doubled over. Carl reached past her, yanked the little girl over her body, and fired the grappling hook from his blade's handle back up through the ceiling, through space, through the hole in his ship into an open holding cage.

Air hissed out into space when the ceiling broke; the little girl's scream faded like someone was twisting reality's volume dial. Carl sliced a bigger hole in the roof. Kicked the lizard again as she tried to rise. Wound the grappling line around the girl, two quick twists. Released the crescent blade.

The line tightened, dragging the girl back into Carl's cargo bay where she belonged as the lizard wheezed, struggling to rise to her knees. Her forehead met the barrel of Carl's cocked pistol. "She's just a kid, Shadow, let her go," the lizard coughed. "This isn't about the bloody job anymore, mate, she's a baby. Letting her go won't make you less of a legend."

Carl didn't bother taking the time to mock her. Of course she was lying—of course it was about the job, no one went up against him for anything less than money or fame—but it wasn't his business to point out other people's delusions.

"Fear is a good preservative," he said. "You should have been afraid."

He shifted the gun to aim, and left her with two holes in the brain.

CHAPTER TWENTY-FOUR

Diebol

HEAVY BREATH MISTED IN FRONT OF DIEBOL'S FACE AS HE LEANED his head against the hallway wall, waiting for Bricandor to exit the arena with his prognosis. *Did it work? Did it?* Diebol's stomach churned in rhythm with his tumbling thoughts. His shoulders trembled. *Pathetic.* He tightened his stance and clenched his fists.

We all die; like she said, today's as good as any day. Let go! Release the attachment!

Curse this wait.

Bricandor slipped through the polymerwall at last. Diebol snapped to attention as the great lord swished past him like a ghost, head down, hands folded behind his back. The cloak moved several steps beyond the young leader; Diebol stared straight ahead. *Hold the stance.*

Don't kill them yet!

Hold. The. Stance.

Bricandor glanced back over his shoulder. "Walk with me," he said. He didn't smile or frown—just said. Diebol searched the crow's feet at the corners of Bricandor's eyes as he fell in beside the old man, and saw no answer there, but somehow the ancient blues still calmed him. He let it go. He breathed.

"You've made better progress with Bereens than Benzaran," Bricandor said.

Life! Diebol's shoulders relaxed and everything in him lifted. He had the galaxy before him—

Caaalm down.

But he was happy.

"Benzaran attacked the interdimensional only in the heat of the moment. You'll have to carry that momentum forward quickly if you want to convince her she really feels that way. But Bereens—" Bricandor grinned. "You couldn't see it, of course, but Bereens had the creature by his ear the whole time and ignored him completely. He's an upright man who always places the mission first, so if you can give him a choice between the Contagion and his mission, you make it easy. His head will clear, and then we'll pounce."

"*Then* we'll pounce? Teacher, once he's chosen we've won."

"An empty room can always receive an occupant; nature abhors a vacuum. You exorcise one monster, without replacing it with something, and seven take its place; eliminate all the microorganisms in your intestines, and you will die of a super-antigen."

Diebol stiffened. "Are you—implying there's another interdimensional poised to befriend Jei?"

"Not befriend so much as possess," Bricandor chuckled.

"How do we prevent that?"

Bricandor smirked, his gaze unwavering straight ahead. "There's still a great deal you aren't ready for, I suppose."

They continued down the hallway in silence. Diebol scowled inwardly, grinding his teeth into his tongue to silence the protests that welled within him about "readiness": his kill count, the entire armadas under his command, the planets he'd conquered—!

Diebol swallowed his pride for the task at hand.

"Teacher, so then what should I do about Jei?"

Bricandor whirled. A morphed, otherworldly grimace wore his normally mild face as the Teacher disappeared under the Dictator. Claws gripped Diebol's jacket collar, chafing his neck. Bricandor's teeth flashed. His soft voice wheezed in a throaty shriek. "Do not change the subject! What I had to tell you about your readiness far out-values your miserable pet, you bleeding-heart housewife—now cease pestering me with your doomed experiment!" Spittle splashed between his teeth; a rancid breath like dragon smoke oozed from his lips.

Diebol breathed slowly, hands in the air, palms up. This was the second time today someone had snapped and thrown his back against the wall. Somehow that was amusing.

"Yes, Commander," he murmured. "I will not fail you."

The crazed glitter flickered out of Bricandor's eyes and his snarl relaxed. The intelligent spark returned as his shoulders drooped. A soft, begging pain lined the small face. "You will not fail me?" he whispered. "Oh my child, we both know you hate me. And one day your hate shall act. The alpha wolf only finds his place by murdering his father."

"That—thought has not occurred to me before," Diebol said slowly.

A gentle smile rose from the old man's face like dawn over the tangled crags of a burnt forest, and Bricandor sighed, patted Diebol on the shoulder, and walked off.

It was strange, sometimes, working for a psychopath. A good psychopath, with an uncanny brilliance that bespoke his wisdom even more than to his ability to tell the future and read minds—but a psychopath nonetheless.

I assume that assessment does not offend you, Teacher, Diebol added in his head, knowing the old man could be listening.

The silver figure paused at the end of the hallway. Diebol stiffened into ready stance, both hands folded behind his back. The old man did not turn around.

"You need to put Benzaran in room 256 immediately, with the furry. Administer the same treatment to both."

Acid rolled up Diebol's throat. He swallowed it. "I'll send one of my best right away."

"No. You go."

No! He almost stepped forward, almost cried out, almost—

almost what? He'd told her he'd torture the furry if she lost, and he was going to do it. He just hadn't planned on touching *her*, himself —but it was only a bit worse than what he'd already done to her. It was for her good. It was—

Diebol swallowed his thoughts. "Forgive my hesitation, Commander. I will proceed."

"And Diebol?"

"Yes, Teacher?"

"Don't bother me with Jei again."

He rounded the corner and disappeared.

Diebol stuffed his hands in his pockets and walked in the opposite direction, his head lowered. Jei was *at least* as likely to end Bricandor's life as Diebol was. The old man would do well to remember that.

"For the last time, you do not *need* the soldier's brain. I'll be giving you a better one."

What? Diebol stiffened, and turned in the direction his teacher had gone. Yes, that was Bricandor's voice. Who was he ... who was he talking to?

Diebol didn't dare follow without the Teacher's knowledge. That was disrespectful. But he was angry, and—just a step or two wasn't disrespect, it was accidental. He could pass this way anyway to reach Room 256. Right.

"I must ask you to stop digging your claws into my spine, Child."

Digging into his spine? What? Teacher, was his teacher alright? Diebol darted silently around the corner, but when he looked Bricandor was walking, head down ... alone.

"Or I shall consume you," the old man said. "Who consumes who is moot—it is really one and the same, either way. Distinctions do not become us. Go, bother Diebol if you want Jei Bereens's brain, but as I said I will give you one better. The child will be here soon."

Diebol sucked in his breath. This was a rather world-shattering image. He pulled back and walked the other way. He couldn't see this. It would destroy everything he knew to see this, everything he was brought up to believe. It *seemed* like a man talking to an interdimensional. It *seemed* like his Teacher betraying them all.

"What do you mean, they can hear *you*?" Bricandor laughed. "Who else in the building can hear *you*? Only I can hear you! You are in my mind only. My Brain-Child, my Muse, my insanity."

Or—or, his Teacher was, as he'd already established, a psychopath, and perhaps suffering actual psychosis because of his stress. Strange things happened to the minds of aged men. Besides, Bricandor would have no reason to train Diebol to rid the universe of interdimensionals if he, himself, entertained them. Diebol would send Cindy to evaluate the old man's health.

And of course, there was always the possibility that Bricandor was testing his faith. First he asked Diebol to kill him, then sent him to do a task beneath him, then walked away talking to himself—it bore every mark of a test.

A test Diebol would not fail. He clenched his fists, obeyed his Teacher, and left to keep a promise to a girl.

CINTA

Exposed, strange flesh, with goosebumps that raised no hair—Cinta ran his paws over his shoulders, huddling against the metal corner in naked humiliation and terror. *How did he know?* How did the blind Bichank *know*?

Cinta heard a voice in the darkness and could not judge its distance.

The cage was too small for the voice. Cinta could not even lay down or stand up in this cage. The voice could not be *here*, for it sounded outdoors and open, and this room was metal and dank and closed. He could smell no body, only spilt blood, rust, and the sharp nasal whine of an open medicine cabinet or chemical vat. They did not bode well, these scents; somewhere something dripped, and a chain swung.

The voice sounded like Njande, but smaller, eerie, and cold. Much further away, speaking to someone else, yet with that same quality as if it lived in your ears. *Could it be a … ?*

It wanted to eat the brain of a Jei Bereens.

Oh yes, it was! Cinta's ears popped up like soldiers at attention —he tried to pull them down over his face, but he could hear all the same. He didn't want to hear! He wanted no part of this in his head! No wonder the Bichank knew!

The voice taunted in a sing-song like a playground bully. "You know you're not the only one who can hear me, right?" it said.

Oh no oh no oh no … it was talking to someone else, but basically winking to Cinta! It knew he could hear! He squealed and drew his claws, his heart thumping against his sternum like a man trying to escape a burning hut—because yes, yes it was true, there was a *ba-eater* nearby! He'd heard one before, hovering over one of the doctors in a town leagues away from his, and he'd heard tales of the sapients, religions, civilizations they haunted—these were the soul-eating monsters the Stygges claimed Njande was. He did not want to hear this! He closed his eyes and breathed faster—

And soon he could not hear. In the silence the terror died down, leaving only the names he'd overheard. Bricandor. Bereens.

Cinta was left in the darkness only to feel numb.

Numb? He bared his fangs, frustrated with the unnatural calm now inside him. Look at him, fearing only for himself, while somewhere in the building a ba-eater hunted a man's mind, and Cinta's very presence brought his sister screams! Cinta deserved to feel the cold, the nakedness, for shaming them both.

But—but he had expected none of this. He was not so important that Commander Diebol should know of him and intercept him. He was to hear rumors of rumors and follow them to a doorway he could shadow-stalk through! He was to fulfill Njande's rescue mission!

Was he not?

Cinta's ears sagged down the side of his face, cold and leathery against his muzzle in their bareness.

"I don't understand," Cinta muttered.

A conflagration of dark and light shimmered in the opposite corner of the cage like fading smoke. Cinta snatched at it— "Njande?"

It disappeared, leaving Cinta only with a floating thought. *I sent you to deliver a missive. That is your mission. Everything else is side-story.*

And no more.

"Wait! Njande!"

No one answered.

Cinta ducked his nose down into his knees, blinking hard and breathing fast. The mystery in the darkness, the ba-eater, mind-reading, the message … this was too big for him. He did not want this. He wanted his small-town safety, his bed, and a bowl of lechichi covered in warm jaguar milk. Did this captivity even matter to Njande? Did it happen on purpose?

"Njande," Cinta muttered. "Why am I here?"

The feeling of butterfly wings floated by his muzzle.

CHAPTER TWENTY-FIVE

Jei

I CLUTCHED MY FRACTURED KNEECAP, CURLED ON THE FLOOR OF THE game room as the giant board went dark in a cascade of dying green, and they dragged Lem away kicking and screaming.

That meant we'd done the right thing, right? She was a few synapses short from breaking with Njande completely, so they wouldn't kill her?

Bloodseas, was that what I wanted? If I'd asked her, she would've told me she'd rather die. But I didn't want her to die!

Shyte, that didn't sound well-trained or professional. That sounded like an emotional *idiot* who wanted to create a new Stygge enemy for himself because he couldn't handle a little loss. What was my mission, again?

Warn Fort Jehu. That. I was losing sight of it in all Diebol's mind-games. Maybe killing him should be my mission. I was fully aware my racing thoughts came more from the pain in my leg than from logic or training, but I couldn't find the color green and couldn't recover from the flip-flopping uncertain reality Diebol and Lem had created for me. *Escape.*

Four female human Stygges melded through the polymerwall, two prancing like beauty queens and two marching, straight-faced and short-haired, soldiers with a grudge. I sat up and gripped my podium to stand on my good leg. The Stygges didn't say anything, but one of them, a tan princess with dark, curly hair floating down her back, wrapped her arm around my waist to help me walk, and together the four escorted me across the hallway.

I didn't talk to them. I pretended to focus on limping. The contrast between my escorts and Lem's heated my face. Bloodseas, Diebol was letting me know he appreciated my help.

They left me in an open, empty courtyard, tiled in blue and white arabesque designs mimicking the sky that shone through the metal prison grates overhead. Five-fingered jade leaves the size of my torso sprouted from potted plants lining the yard, and in the middle a table showcased six platters bursting with delicacies: smungworms from Floran baked with apple and onion until they became savory and tender; orchid blossoms from Burburan hot-houses, crisp and colorful alongside chips made of fish and algae; roasted parrot seasoned with cocoa, cumin, and ginger, from Luna-Guetala, with a side of lechichi; baked sauer-roots from Alpino, my home-world, starchy and rich in a thick mustard sauce laced with sausage; and a number of other things.

My stomach gurgled as they sat me down, and that normal biological reflex disgusted me. This whole victory celebration—I wanted no part of it, but then again I did want a part, a big, juicy part, and that pissed me off. As soon as they left I got up to pace, dragging my bleeding leg, punishing myself for my hunger. It was destructive. I justified it with something like honor.

What would happen to Lem if she lost Njande? He was her everything. Bloodseas, they'd taken her everything, and now made me a part of it. I just wanted to slow down the game to keep her alive, and then she'd freaked out, and I'd freaked back, and I'd misunderstood, and I thought she and Diebol—dammit, I didn't get it in the heat of the moment, but I sure as hell got it now. Whatever deal she'd made with Diebol, her screaming fit and this feast made it painfully obvious the agreement hinged on her winning without my help. But there was no way she could ever beat me at a game I'd helped invent.

"That was unfair," I muttered.

"I did what I had to," said Diebol's voice behind me.

I whirled; I hadn't heard him come through the polymerwall. A cool breeze evaporated the sweat on my neck and face, sending chills across me, and suddenly I was afraid to hear what he had to say. *Don't tell me she's dead. Don't tell me she's a Stygge. Don't tell me anything, anything at all.*

He didn't speak for a bit. He sat down, ripped a leg off the parrot with a tendinous cracking sound, and began to eat.

Dammit, tell me what happened to her!

I sat down. I couldn't pace anymore; I gripped my knee and struggled not to grimace, clenching my jaw shut.

"I've got somewhere to be in ten," Diebol said. "So I'm not going to bother playing with you. I want you to get rid of Njande-jara, and I want that more than I want Bricandor's attack on Luna-Guetala to succeed. That's just more killing—you're the dawn of a new era. So if you'll convince the interdimensional to leave you, I will let you go and try to warn your fort. We'll just set you free in the wilds of Revelon." He waved his hand dismissively, then paused to wipe his fingers on a white napkin embroidered with blue florals. "Two conditions, of course: if we let you go, we won't fix your knee, and won't feed you after this meal. So … eat."

I lowered my head onto my fist, dizzy. I almost couldn't pay attention to his words with my knee screaming at me. "There's gotta be another catch," I mumbled. "You *do* care about that attack—you're not stupid. And if we are really on Revelon, this whole operation's illegally based on an independent planet. You'd never take the risk that I'll run into some civilian on my way and rat you out. You think I'll be back. You don't think I'll make it there without Njande."

"You're absolutely right," he said. "But you have plenty of friends in your Frelsi who don't talk to interdimensionals. So losing Njandejara doesn't guarantee you'll fail your mission. And I have other mechanisms in place to protect my center from rogue accusations from escaped convicts." He leaned back and crossed his arms. "At any rate this is the only way I'll let you try right now. Consider it a … loosening of the leash. But I do have another move." He glanced at his wristband. "This schedule is ridiculous. I hate the Teacher today. You know he told me to kill him?" He glanced up at me, like he wanted advice on that.

"You should," I said.

"Well. I'll be back in forty minutes. Eat up—after I'm back you won't want to." He rose and glanced over the table at my knee. "I'll send someone to keep that from bleeding, but that's it. No exo-support on it or anything."

I nodded, licking my lips with a drying tongue. "Wouldn't expect otherwise."

"Ay-ay." He flicked me a cheery salute, spinning and walking backwards through the polymerwall.

Yeah, I'd messed up. My head sank into the crook of my elbow. I just listened to the wind; just felt the pangs shoot up and down my leg. I always waited until the very, very last minute to ask for Njande's help—if you want something done, you do it yourself—but I liked having the option, the extra possibility of a save in case he happened to be in the neighborhood. The idea of losing that and heading across the wastelands of this unfamiliar planet alone with a banged-up knee in search of someone with a phone to call home—that didn't excite me, but I could do it. Would Njande … understand? Could I cut off our connection just long enough for Bricandor to read me? Did it work that way? I wouldn't end up like Lem if I lost him, right? He wasn't that ingrained in my life. I wasn't an addict.

Fingers trailed along my calf. I jolted and opened my eyes—in my painful stupor again I hadn't heard anyone enter—and almost kicked the girl in the face. She scowled at me, electric blue eyes brimming with fury as she jerked wrapping tape tight around my knee. Agony surged—I clenched my teeth—

After the initial shock I sat still while she stopped the bleeding in my leg. I wondered where Diebol got so many pretty girls in tight leather to follow me around and remind me I'd beaten a beginner at a board game.

"You got the job no one wanted, huh," I said.

"You're scum," she spat. "I'm not fond of playing eye candy to scum. No hard feelings—" She snapped the knot tight, sending another pang up my leg. "But I hope you die."

With that, and a glittering toothy smile, she rose and stalked back to the polymerwall to leave, dangling her fingertips like she'd touched a rotten carcass. I didn't blame her for being pissed. No one liked this center, not even Diebol. Here, hunting the next step, the mission, the plan, required completely offending who we thought we were.

And my plan required survival. So with a knot in my stomach I put aside my repugnance at the lavish fake victory and began to eat. I tried a bit of everything, and for the first time since my capture I felt full.

LEM

Lem tripped as the Stygge trainees dragged her down the hall. She tripped, maybe, because she didn't really wanna get where they were going. Or because she tried to trip one of them? She didn't know. Didn't matter. Cinta was gonna get hurt. She'd failed.

She fell—stupid human kicked her sharp in the shoulder. A tree-trunk-sized paw thudded into her hip. An insectoid joined in—soon everyone was kicking her, yelling at her to get up, and Lem was trying to wrap her shackles around something, trip someone, but in the time it took her to move three centimeters she took four more hits to the side …

Why is everything so slow?

Her head. Headache throbbed. *Gah.* She curled in on herself, clutching her temples and choking on grief, and just took the pounding like a cold, dead nail.

Everything stopped.

The Stygge trainees snapped to attention, leaving Lem lying on the floor. An opening for escape? Lem commando-crawled forward—

No, she didn't. Even now they held her frozen in an electromagnetic field. She pushed for a second—her headache flared like firecrackers in her temples. She groaned and dropped her head to the floor. The cool bronze soothed her heated face, and she took comfort only in that, in that one thing, because everything else sucked.

She couldn't believe she'd seen Njande helping Jei win. She actually couldn't. But if she was just seeing things, maybe she'd been crazy in the first place. Maybe she'd never seen Njandejara at all. Maybe she *was* climbing over her friend's dead body to love or hate something that didn't exist—like slamming into Jei to attack a hallucination.

Maybe she did need a cure.

A shadow embraced her. She glanced up.

Oh, that was why they'd snapped to attention. He'd come to her rescue. Like with that blitzer in the conference room. Emerald eyes shone from under the shade of a dark hood, and a tired, dark face drew near Lem's as Diebol knelt.

"Hey," he murmured.

"Hey ass-face," she grumbled back.

"I'm so sorry," he said.

"No you're not."

But his quiet tenor rasp wore away her tired resistance, and when he touched her face she didn't move. "I have to put you through one more room," he said. "You'll hate me more when you're done, if that's possible, and I deserve that. But just stay alive for this. Preserve yourself, please. You're so close."

Lem chuckled in desperation. "Damn your friendliness. You're about to put me through some kinda torture and here I'm thinking you're my coach giving me a pep talk."

"This is a strange thing to laugh about. You're laughing."

"If I don't laugh, I'll cry." Lem buried her forehead in the floor again. "Let's get this over with."

The Stygges led Lem to a door with a red smear below the handle. Cold air filtered through the cracks as one of the humans turned the door-handle; Lem had just a moment to notice a long burn mark on the human's wrist, and darkness blacker than the back of her eyelids peering at her from inside the room—

They whirled her around and wrapped an aluminum cloth around her eyes. She sucked in a deep sudden breath at the blindness, stumbling as they pulled her backwards. She slipped on her heels—she cried out trying to catch her balance—but she fell, or they dragged her down and her feet didn't touch the ground again, and either way her back thwacked against icy metal, and she bit her lip to hold back the weaselly cry that almost escaped.

In seconds the chill erupted through the back of her jumpsuit, pinpricking into her back, thighs, rear, shoulders. She wanted to yell, ask questions, do something as hands, paws, claws stretched out her limbs, spreading her like a spiderweb as far as she could go, everything open and vulnerable, but she held her tongue because here and now she began to think about that noble death Jei'd mentioned. This was going to happen whether she liked it or not, so she could embrace the suck or—

No, I can do something about this!

Clamps snapped shut around her wrists and ankles. She pulled against them—and felt only the strain of her muscles stretched too far, and a pounding warning from her aching temples. She relaxed, but could not relax; she was held taut, and now as the door creaked shut, she was alone.

Was she? Dammit, she hadn't counted footsteps. What the bloodseas was about to happen? Diebol made it sound pretty bad. Red on the door-handle—blood? So then they'd break her skin at least. Or these wires she felt through this aluminum blindfold? For electrocution, blinding, or maybe something to trigger her powers? *Shyte no, this headache sucks already. I think then I'll straight up die.* Or spread-eagled like this, everything about her open to —everything.

So ... rape. Rape was a pretty standard torture procedure for the Growen under Bricandor, because it worked, and it didn't sound like Diebol was planning on protecting her anymore. Lem cringed, and her abs clenched, and she tried to make herself breathe and relax, but scenarios coursed through her mind, playing over her body, and she wondered—should she hope for a human or not? A human would hurt a lot less, without jabbing bits and things that didn't fit. She forced herself not to shudder. But shyte, she wasn't ready to be a mom! Less ready to be a mom with her baby ripped outta her for torture's sake, or a mom who years from now got home to her kid's burnt corpse because mom talked to invisibles ...

Njande, why do you cost so much?

As if in answer: "Jaika, are you alive?"

The soft growl, in Biouk, threw Lem into uncontrollable shakes. She whimpered, and all memory of bravery and standard torture procedures and resilience training fluttered off into the darkness like moths dispersed by bug spray. She cried out in the moon dialect they'd learned as a code: "Cinta, is that you?"

"It is."

"How do I know?"

"Because you are the white bird, and I am the cocoa plant where it lives."

A hot breath erupted from her lips, carrying with it something like a cry, a gasp, or a yes. "Are you okay? Where are you? Can you move?"

"We do not have time for me, Jaika. I have a message for you from Nja—"

The door's slam cut him short.

CHAPTER TWENTY-SIX

Lem

THE DOOR SLAM WOULD'VE MADE LEM JUMP, IF SHE COULD MOVE. Her limbs continued to strain unintentionally against the chains that had her splayed out to the limit of her length; the icy floor against her back made her muscles twitch and shudder, and each tiny twitch sent pangs of discomfort shooting through her stretched joints.

She heard Diebol's voice somewhere to her left. "And that's the end of that waste of time," he sneered. "You can thank my insane commander for the fact that you have me and not the Bichank I'd assigned."

"What, you didn't want to hang out with me?" Lem murmured. *Think. Think of a way out.* She squeezed her eyes shut to keep them from straining in the pitch blackness of the room and the blindfold, and opened her mouth a little to loosen the muscles around her ear canals: she needed to *hear* the room.

"This is below me," Diebol snapped in answer to her weak sass. "And since I plan to be working with you in the future, I don't very much enjoy the prospect of—doing things to you." He ended in a growl. "Enough talk." His boots snapped through the room past her, and Lem heard metal clinking.

"But talking is the best torture ..." Lem trailed off. Her heart wasn't in it. She was trying to listen to Diebol's preparations. She heard him drag something heavy, something with mechanical whirring parts, over to the area where Cinta's voice had come from. Fur rustled—

"What's he doing to you?" Lem snapped.

"Nothing," Cinta said. It was a lie. In the crisp silence, she thought she heard his claws extend. Something was being strapped to him. Some kind of robot or something? Based on all the whirring sounds, and now the button beeping—like Diebol was selecting settings?

Diebol's bootsteps returned to her now. Her heart sped up as his every step slowed. *Just get it over with!* The anticipation was terror; she heard buttons snapping, like he was taking off his jacket. Or maybe something else … Her breath came faster. Dammit, he'd hear her panicking. She slowed it down. She tried to pull against the shackles, slow and even, a nice long magnetic force, none of this crazy spark stuff—

But the charge trickled down her wrists and escaped into the metal.

Oh no, Cinta, what was he gonna do to Cinta?

A hand rested on Lem's stomach, soft and heavy. She wilted away from it, grimacing in cold rage. She hated this feeling, this hard, bitter resentment without fire and action and screams, this shivering that looked like trembling, so angry and frail and tamed and so utterly take-able.

She could do nothing. She wanted to explode into angry tears.

To her credit, she did not. The hand withdrew. The absence left Lem's belly colder than before, and she hung for just an instant in tentative terrified relief before—

A blow echoed the touch, a fist in her gut, like splitting her in half. A Biouk's whelp smothered her yell. She choked on her own voice.

"What'd you just—!" Cough, wheeze, bloodseas punch that hurt. "Holy shyte, what'd you do to him?"

"I'll let you guess."

Lem shouted something obscene, but he ignored her. He faded into darkness. Lem listened for his breathing, for Cinta, and heard neither of them. "Cinta, what happened?"

"Nothing, I—"

"Don't you dare lie to me!" she roared. "What the bloodseas just happened?"

A grip laced with callouses wrapped around her ring finger. Lem dug her thumbnail into Diebol's hand; he ignored her, his breath even, and did not let go.

"Cinta, answer me right now!" Lem snapped.

"Please, focus on Njande; I am not here to—"

Diebol let go of her hand. Again came the rush of cold, the instant of apprehension, and then—

Crushing agony in her finger as he snapped it.

This time Lem screamed as loud as Cinta did; red flashed before her eyes, and she groaned and panted to recover, trying to sort out the throbbing, the stabbing, the confused jumble of sensations in her hand. *Assess. Assess! Something broken? Probably. What's wrong with Cinta? Is it his paw, then? Are we feeling the same?*

Forget assessing! "Cinta!" Lem cried, yanking against the cuffs, only straining her joints. The muscle pain distracted from the jagged shrieking grief in her fingers. She tried to focus on that—her ragged breathing wouldn't let her—was this how Cinta felt? No, not for her—!

Diebol closed his hand around her forefinger and middle finger.

"Okay, I get it," Lem gasped. "Whatever happens to me happens to him. You've got some kind of robot or something, copying on him what you're doing to me. You know that's stupid shyte, right? Please stop! I'll give you—" Damn, she was beyond rage into bargaining now? What would she even offer him to make him stop?

"Please, I'll let you—"

No, she couldn't do *that*.

"You can have—"

She ended in a cry of frustration.

"There are two people here who can make me stop. You, and your interdimensional. But you know *he's* not going to." Diebol's voice was more bitter than mocking. "Something about autonomy and noninterference, blablabla, I'm sure you're tired of it." She felt his breath against her ear. "It must *piss you off.*"

She wanted to bite him, but bloodseas he was right! She was pissed! And maybe she did need to be cured! But it didn't matter what she thought she needed, because this was happening whether she wanted it or not, and she had no power over her feelings about it, no power over her pain, no power over what happened to Cinta or herself or anyone, no power over whether or not she spoke to Njande because the choice was made by whoever could trigger her anger, and she could do nothing and in all that nothing Njande was supposed to rescue her but he wasn't here and she could hear Cinta whimpering from somewhere to her left and she smelled blood and now Diebol was touching the fingers on her other hand and she imagined Cinta's paws crushed and then it was already happening, already over, she was already screaming and now both hands screamed with her, and her head swam and tears stuck to her sweaty cheeks and she didn't know anything except yes, she was pissed, and Cinta cried out, and Diebol touched her cheek, and Cinta's muzzle flashed before her eyes—

"Wait, I can do what you want," Lem blurted.

"Jaika! Jaika no, hold your connection to Njande! It is to save the universe!"

What?

"Shut up!" Diebol hissed. A crunch, a cry—

No, no! "Leave him alone!" Lem shouted.

"From heat death, Jaika!" A garbled cough—? "Njande told me!"

"Silence!" Another thud—and there was silence for a moment. Diebol inhaled to speak, then—

A moan, like the low nasal whine of a dying moon-wolf. "There is a ba-eater, Lem, trying to consume your friend Bereens! The Commander Bricandor, he has a ba-eater!"

What? At *that* Diebol growled—Lem felt his heat leave her side, heard his footsteps rushing the cage—

"No, stop!" Lem shouted. "Please no!"

"Jaika, the universe, the whole universe—"

"Silence!" Diebol roared now. Crunch. Scream. The Biouk was screaming now.

"Needs you to hold to Njande!" He shrieked.

"Shut up, Cinta, please shut up!" Lem screamed back. "Diebol please, I'm not listening to him, what do I have to do with the universe? Muzzle him if you want, please stop hurting him!"

The heat returned to her side. Cinta's whimpers died into the background. The whole world boiled down to Lem and Diebol. Lem hated it. But the scent of blood, of Biouk blood—"Please," she said.

"He's muzzled." Diebol's voice was gentle, so gentle Lem felt herself starting to cry. "I need to leave you for ten minutes, in silence, to make sure I have your will involved here, not just your emotions. Then, when I come back, you'll repeat after me, and we'll start your freedom."

"Okay. Yes. We will. Please—please just don't hurt him anymore."

JEI

This time I noticed when Diebol re-entered my extravagant, tiled victory room. My gut twisted as he approached—he hid it well, but something was off. His fingers curled and uncurled; he sat down at the table across from me, stretched his neck, then *slid* both hands forward like a jungle explorer parting branches to clear a space on the table between the parrot and the orchids.

He flipped out his holo-pen and drew a square.

I choked on the sauer-root in my mouth and spat it out.

Lem lay splayed out and blindfolded on a frosted silver floor, blood caking her fingertips, puddling in her palms, and streaking down her forearm. It was a video: I could see her shivering, gritting her teeth, hear her pleading something I couldn't catch. A fist flashed across the screen and slammed her stomach.

Diebol cut off the video.

"*Shyte* I messed up," I breathed. "Holy—*bloodseas*, what the hell are you doing to her?!" My voice rose; I found myself rising in my seat.

"You might better ask why her beloved interdimensional doesn't stop it," Diebol said.

"It's not Njande doing that to her, it's *you!*"

"Isn't standing by passively the same as actively participating?"

"What?" I screamed, whacking the table with one hand. "No! No, we are not having this conversation! *You* stop pushing responsibility on someone you can't even see! If you want it to stop, *you* stop it! Maybe—" I paused, panting, trying to push aside my hatred for him just for a moment to grasp at whatever strand of reasonableness I could find in his skull. The little boy in the cage who'd grabbed hands with me after being beaten, that boy, I was reaching out to *him*, not this monster, I—"Look, Jared, maybe *you're* Njande's answer to suffering. He's not a demon—he works through wind and circumstance, and maybe in that wind and circumstance it's been arranged so *you*, someone who actually wants to end this shyte, would end up in charge of the Growen. Maybe it's your moment to stop this, turn this ship around and save us all."

Diebol stiffened like I'd stabbed him in the face. Really? There was something there? I opened my mouth again, begging for words to come before his training took over to kill the thought.

"You can save her, Jared," I went on, pulling myself forward along the table toward him. "Come on, I know you like her. What's not to like? She's smart, even *wise* sometimes, and thoughtful and persistent, and she's got one hell of a punch. You've never met anyone who thinks like her. You want her."

I was making shyte up at this point, but if it worked—if it could work—

"How do you know I *want* her?" He lowered his eyebrows.

Too far? Bloodseas, I didn't want to get her in more trouble. "Her soul. You don't want her to suffer."

"I don't want her to live in slavery, either," he said.

I choked and grabbed at the one piece of crap I had left. "I know you think you're born to set us all free. Think, just for a moment, about the possibility that maybe you were born to do that by taking these debates out of the battlefield and out of the torture room. You could just decide, right here, right now, *not* to do this to her." *Revolutionary, I know*, my inner sarcasm growled, almost throwing me into a fit. My arm shook as I gripped the table, and my chest heaved with the effort it took to rein in my frustrated panic and just let my mouth run. "Come on," I was begging now. "You don't want to do this. You're better than this." *No, you're not. Dammit, you're not. Please just shoot me now.*

I searched his face; he searched mine, his eyes sliding back and forth as if trying to figure out how much cow-shyte I'd eaten—as if wondering if this was for real. I wondered myself. What was I even doing? This wasn't me, this was a Lem move. A desperate Lem-move that saw openings that weren't there. There was nothing here. This guy was a cold-hearted killer. He wasn't going to budge.

Maybe if I'd given him just a second more. Maybe if I'd really believed in his change or something, I would've calmed down and done it right. But I couldn't convince him to believe something I didn't believe myself. Njandejara, setting Diebol up to be a hero? I didn't even want that. I wanted this guy dead. If he turned his back, I'd throw the butter knife that lay six centimeters from my hand. I'd dig out his spine.

I dropped my gaze with a curse. *Forget it.*

It wasn't until I heard his voice that I realized how close I'd come. His first word started with a tremor.

"She—"

And then he swallowed it, in silence, shaking his head and

leaning a fist against the table. "You," he croaked, shaking his fore-finger at me. "You would be so dangerous if you actually believed in something."

He rose and straightened his jacket with a nervous laugh, stepping back from me. "We're deploying in two weeks. You have 'til then to get rid of Njande and save your people. Oh, and—" He smirked as he backed into the polymerwall, fully recovered. "Teacher says he saw Njandejara beside you throughout the whole game. Odd how ineffective he was, isn't it?"

Sploosh through the polymerwall, and he was gone.

My jaw dropped.

"Bloodseas, Njande, is that true? Were you really here the whole time?"

Yes.

"Why didn't you *do* anything?"

I did.

"Bloodseas." I put my head in my hands. "You've really screwed us up."

You need to trust me. You can't see everything I can see.

"Well, you could show me!"

Show you everything? Your head would literally explode.

"You could have given me what I can handle, then!"

I did, but you didn't take it. You never asked me, and you've closed off a lot of the parts of your mind that connect to me.

"Well, open them up, then!"

Are you actually asking me to do that?

I growled. "No, actually, not now, no. Thirty minutes ago would have been *ideal*. Right now I need you to leave." I ran my fingers through my hair. "Bloodseas, I can't *believe* you've been here the entire time. So Lem was right?"

Yes and no.

"Okay, you know what, forget that poetic crap. Get the hell out of here."

No.

"What do you mean, 'no'?!"

You'll lose your mind if I go. There's someone out to get you, and I'm trying to protect you. You literally mean the universe to me.

I threw my hands in the air. "I can't debate theoretical philosophy right now. I need you to get out of here! What happened to noninterference?"

I never *promised noninterference. I said rain falls on both the evil and the good, and that I withhold my hand sometimes, and that you could choose to reject my friendship when we first met, but nothing beyond that.*

"*Can* I get rid of you now? You said before—!"

If, in your heart of hearts, you want nothing to do with me, then I was never with you in the first place. No one who's tasted air can live without it; if this is how you feel, then you were never alive to me, you never breathed and I was never tied to you, and you were only communicating to me on the outside like your radio signal to Diebol.

"Not that it matters, but I remember it differently," I muttered. "My choice *now* doesn't change our past."

Time does not pass me. It is relative. It is a place I live outside of and step into only if I want. I am, right now, in both your past and your future, and I can say this moment, right now, and this decision, is infinite.

"But my decision doesn't matter to you, apparently."

It absolutely does. I see a different person in you, right now in your future, because of the decision you make now.

My eye glittered. "So you see us alive in that future, then?"

I did not say that.

"Holy—" Enough! My lower jaw froze and I threw the nearest plate. It was plastic apparently—it bounced as dead parrot flesh stained the white tiles. "Go away!"

No.

"I have to warn the fort! Go away!"

He said nothing this time, but now I could sense him nearby, the way you feel mist rising from a waterfall, or sense someone sitting next to you even if you're blindfolded and wearing earplugs. I couldn't believe I hadn't noticed him before.

But if I hadn't noticed him before, I could ignore him now. He said I'd already turned off a lot of our connections that way. Maybe I couldn't burn the connection out with rage like Lem did, but the axons of many nerve cells worked like muscle fibers: if you don't use them, you lose them.

I closed my eyes and focused on the color green.

CHAPTER TWENTY-SEVEN

Lark

For the first time in her life Lark Scrita was truly happy to be human.

That wasn't her first thought. There, lying in a pool of her own blood as it iced over, squinting at the stars through her broken roof and blurred vision, *three lives on my hands*, was her first thought, once the agony searing her thighs cleared a space in her mind for it. Her parents, and the little girl.

She rolled over, stretching for the door into the cockpit. Her helmet clinked against the floor. Her breath misted her visor. She hacked to breathe past the pain.

Not four. It wouldn't be four. Lark had to survive this. She had to survive this because she'd fooled the Ebon Shadow, and by gum she *would* live to say that to someone.

"I fooled him," she grunted aloud. He shot her in the thighs, believing she was a Bont lizard; but as a human, her brain was in her skull, and her disguise projector was off center enough that he'd missed her femurs. "I fooled him." Her breath stuck in her throat— most of the oxygen had drained out of her ship. She turned down the oxygen flow in her mask. *Make it last longer.* She needed more than the hour it held.

"I fooled you, you gormless piddle-twit, I fooled you," she muttered as she yanked the heating pad off the wall and dragged it with her through the tiny porthole into the cockpit. Her belly slipped in the ice on the floor—blast, if *that* blood was freezing, it wouldn't be long 'til her limbs froze, too—and then scraped along the edge of the porthole. She fell into the pilot's seat with a gulp of jarring pain and closed the opening above her. One thing at a time. Not enough air to think about more than that, eh?

Lark leaned back against the plastic seat with a burdened breath. Three lives, blast it all, what had she done? She might not even have a chance with the electromagnetics now—would their deaths be her fault, too? Five?

One thing at a time, or she would die. If she died, she couldn't lord it over the Shadow. It was a shallow, selfish thought, but Lark knew better than to fight it. A lass had to have *some* reason to live.

One thing at a time. She arranged the heating blanket over her legs. Her legs, where the main brain centers of a Bont lizard were supposed to be. Ha. Very savvy of the Ebon Shadow, not to shoot her in the head—that would've thrown a Bont lizard into a wild power-rage, with no higher thought, no pain to hold it back. But she wasn't a Bont lizard, was she?

Inspect bloody burns. Reach under seat. Adrenaline shot. Morphine shot. Probably bad idea to use both at once.

Lark used both at once. Jammed them into her thighs. Shook her head like she could shake the grogginess right out. Beans, she needed more air. Looked like if she sealed the porthole to the other room the cockpit still gave a decent air supply, and she could crank up the heat as much as she wanted.

Next. Nearest planet. *Forge.* She was still on track, then. As she'd predicted, the Biouk chasing her electromagnetics had disappeared, and Lark heard he'd ended up on a Growen transport bound for Revelon, Forge's neighbor. She could refuel on Forge, then jump ship for Revelon. *Let's go.* Lark lifted her finger towards the compuwall to steer—and dropped her hand.

Damn. She was knackered. That fight had drained her, wrung her out like a barmaid's grey towel. She wanted to sleep.

That'd be the morphine, the cold, and the lack of oxygen, mate. And the adrenaline? The super-human strength or focus or what have you? When did *that* kick in?

Perhaps her heart pounding at two hundred knots a minute, perhaps that was the adrenaline. She wished she cared. She didn't. She'd mucked everything up. She wanted to sleep. Damn the adrenaline and her heart-rate, why shouldn't she sleep? This was a bad day. This was the kind of day you wanted to sleep and forget.

Aw, come off the whinging, you're Lark Scrita! She took a business card out of her belt. Glossy. Embossed. She'd kidnapped a lass for it. Classy!

It wasn't doing anything for her. She couldn't make herself move. The little girl's fading scream weighed on her chest. The grey ghost hung around her like a straitjacket. She hated it. She hated herself and she hated it.

"Quit watching me," she muttered. "I fooled the Ebon Shadow, I'll fool you, too."

She didn't quite know what she meant by it. But that thought got her going. Her fingers slipped across the compuwall, and with a slow push she started the ship towards planet Forge.

Lark unbuckled her seatbelt with one hand, eyeing the dead parking lot ahead of her as she eased the broken Leech to a halt.

She collapsed against the back of her seat with a sigh. It was alright now, it was.

Forge, Revelon's Growen-owned dust-dump of a neighbor, was a planet coated in colorful sands with oodles of metallurgic and biological properties. A pretty pound of radioactivity in those sands —a place you packed your breathing mask. Most people visited for the art displays or wildlife. No one wanted to live here.

Except Growen outpost sentry Jake Veradan. The gangly weather-skinned human wanted to scurry into a cave somewhere and study dirt, and Lark could tell as soon as she landed the Leech at his empty Growen checkpoint to buy medical help and a re-fuel. *As unmilitary as they come* ... he dangled his helmet in one hand as he waved Lark to step out of her ruined Leech. He also kept leaning on the equipment of the fuel tower next to his tiny sentry box, like he couldn't remember to stand up straight, and he was anything but snappy, taking his bloody sweet time to hand her the fist-sized med-bot-ball she needed to re-graft and stitch her thighs. She had to fight herself not to snatch it out of his peeling hot gloves. Finally he got to inspecting her ship—and she started him off talking.

Lark liked small talk. Traveling and meeting different kinds of people made this job sexy. But this small talk, in particular, Lark could have reported on her taxes, if she'd paid them. This talk was money.

Veradan had a nervous habit of running his fingers over the edge of his uniform and shuffling his feet, stirring up pink dust as he waved his chem-sensor-wand around the Leech's cockpit. While he rambled Lark sat on a crate behind him, estimating just how much the blitzer hated baking in his tiny sentry box in the empty parking lot while the colorful shops and tourist tents three kilometers down the road taunted him under wavy heat lines.

"I joined for cultural unification," Veradan rambled. "But what do I get? Psh, the jack-heads up top couldn't see culture if it was pissing in their mouths."

"You're not alone," Lark interrupted for the first time. She slowed her gravelly grunt as the robot-ball on her leg finished its stitch-work. "A lot of people have worker drone lives they hate. A lot of people want an *out*. Sometimes ... I give them that out."

She knew it sounded bloody sinister. The sentry dropped his hand to his gun, but he didn't say anything. He waited. *Good sign.* Lark unclipped a thin rectangular film from a box in her utility belt. "If you were a different species, what species would you be, mate?"

He answered right away. "A Trojan sand-crawler."

"You want to be an underground ten-legged parasite?" Lark scowled. "No sir, must be sentient."

"They have feelings! All creatures have—"

"Fine, sapient, then. Hurry before another ship lands."

"Eh, we only get one or two a day at this lot. And—" He paused. "I suppose I like being human."

Lark rolled her eyes. "Let me phrase this question differently," she said, sliding the pad of her claw across the slip of film in her hand. "Time to wake up, sheep."

And she slapped the film across his cheek with a resounding *thwack!*

Veradan fumbled with his flayer, stammering in shock. No one slapped a man with a gun! Lark grabbed his reflective helmet from where he'd dropped it: "Check your reflection now, mate," she said. "Preferably before you shoot yourself in the foot. Ought to keep your helmet on in this atmosphere, anyway."

The colorful insectoid jumped back from the mirror, stumbling against the metal shack behind him. Lark didn't blame him: the illusion was fantastic. Former human Jake Veradan now had six legs. Two of them shriveled against his belly, lame, jutting uncomfortably out of his humanoid blitzer armor. His jaws shone black like an ant's, and his body would show bright pink and forest green striped over ebony once he washed off all that desert dust. His long scorpion-like abdomen curled over the back of his armor, tucked weakly over his shoulder. All in all he was an ugly, wrinkled, injured specimen.

"You'll look a mite better when you get out of that stupid uniform into something the hologram can work with. It's difficult to warp your insectoid body to humanoid clothing, especially with something that bloody form-fitting. For now, however, welcome to your new face! And your new culture, new handicaps, etcetera. Practice with it—see, if I touch you here—" She poked his hard jaw. "It feels to me as if you've got an exoskeleton. It's not just a sight illusion, but sound, pheromones, and touch, too. What'd I just poke, your nose?"

"Y-yes?"

"Ought to get used to thinking of your nose as your jaw, then. You'll have to get in the mirror, and poke yourself 'til you know what's what. Oh, and learn Scorpish, of course, or come up with a heart-breaking refugee story for why you only speak Grenblenian and why you've got two lame legs clinging around your midriff like that. If you want to stop the illusion just peel the chem-filter off your cheek. Bully, it'll hurt like hell, but you—"

"Excuse me. Just stop for a moment. This is just all too fast." The blitzer clicked his jaws as he staggered back and forth, staring at his claws. "How—how does this work?!"

"Magician never tells her tricks," Lark said. Mostly because she didn't know. Something about DNA collection, chemical warfare, and parietal lobe triggers, blabby-bla unknown science words. Who bloody cared. "Now you better get out of here and start living your new life, mate!"

"But—but—"

"Because if you don't, you'll be court-martialed."

"Wait, why?"

"Because you, Private Jake Veradan, just deserted your post and stole your Growen-issued spaceship."

"I—I did?"

Lark smiled. She tapped the side of her mask to access the pictures she'd taken of him as he talked, and reached inside her leather jacket to stroke one of the strips of film she wore on her own collarbone. Then she took off her helmet. "Yes, you did."

The blitzer stammered as he stared into his own face, on Lark's body. Lark bet she wore Jake Veradan with a much more cocky and battle-sure smile than he ever did. "I'll need your ship codes, your armor, and your helmet," she said. "You'll get out of here fast as you can, and I'll assume your hated post."

"Are—are you *Frelsi*?"

"Why does everyone always assume that? Shyte, hell, beans, blast it all—shoot me in the face first," she spat. "No!" She gathered herself. "I'm merely someone who, like you, wants a better life. Here's my card." She flipped a business card from her sleeve and held it out to him.

The blitzer didn't take the card. He glanced around the empty lot, the empty street, the empty life he hated, with no family, no friends, no reason to stay but a signature on a dotted line ... *Wait for it in three, two, one ...*

Veradan stripped down to his jumpsuit, right there and then, and shoved Lark aside to scramble into her Leech.

"Uh, hold up there, bug-boy, that's still not space-ready!" Lark started to say—

No, no holding up bug-boy. He fired up the Leech and took off across the desert, leaving Lark covered in pink dust.

The wind of his exit died down. The sun beamed. The medical robot beeped.

Blast it, no one ever wanted a business card.

On the bright side, that worked in record time. Normally it took them at least two hours to buy Lark's spiel. This was Lark's *modus operandi*. She'd borrowed the Leech from a tired gas station attendant who wanted to join the rodeo; hitched a ride to her last mission on the barge of a wealthy Vibrant prostitute who longed to study engineering; found Zhirskahm Frland by selling a cat identity to a deformed Scorpish beggar. Lark was a no one so she could be everyone, the liar who bought people their new selves.

And now she had another self to play with. Jake Veradan. Lark glanced across the parking lot at the gray Maggot that belonged to him. She'd seen Growen Maggots in space, writhing their flexible ring-plated bodies and spewing firepower everywhere like baby worms vomiting hot sauce. They didn't fly easy, but at rest in their egg-like-shape they looked like the Leech. Perhaps the engine systems were similar. She imagined she could do this if she kept the ship compacted, and avoided that whole undulating-worm nonsense.

"Incoming ship," beeped the metal sentry post.

"Aah!" Lark yelled and scrambled into the abandoned uniform, tripping over the big boots into the steaming metal hut. "Computer, run standard protocol!"

"Affirmative. Incoming pilot identified: Civilian. Mercenary. Commander-level pass for parking. Call sign—"

The next words sent cold sweat down Lark's back.

"—Ebon Shadow."

CHAPTER TWENTY-EIGHT

Cinta

In the darkness of the torture room Cinta spread his paws as far from his body as possible, hissing through his fangs to keep from whimpering. Breathe. Breathe. Only keep her from knowing ...

It took him a while to realize that the robotic hand had released his fore-ankles and paws; the agony relaxed into a pulsing sting so he could think again. *Ratschica—*

No. He would not *be violence*, not even in his head. Cursing was unacceptable.

But they had declawed him, removed his transportation through his homeland forests, his connection to the tree bark; they had maimed him so he could not protect a mate or young, and the horror —*no claws, no claws, no claws*—the horror amplified the pain as if they had castrated him. *Njande! Claws, no claws!*

Jaika cried nearby.

Crying. No, not that. When humans did that it terrified him, and more when *she* did it: not many other species ooze liquids from their eyes without deep physical trauma. *She is not dying. It is a human thing. It is just a human thing. She is crying, not dying.*

But—but crying only happened when something went horribly wrong, sometimes right before a human died, and the sound reeked of choking, drowning—who knew whether falling tears were the leaking blood of a human's soul?

No, stop, I am a scientist, I know it is not so. I must help her!

Help her? He could say, do, nothing! *Njande, you promised to step in when I came to my end! I am at my end! I cannot help her! Please, answer her! She is calling for your voice! Will you do nothing?*

"Do you believe I will do nothing?" The words seemed so loud, Cinta thought for a moment Jaika must hear them—but it was clear she did not.

Speak louder! I am silent, with this leather on my snout, you must speak now, you!

"You're not at the end, not yet. May I use your will for a moment?"

If that will help her, absolutely! Please, she is leaking!

"Have peace, then. Rest."

Rest? He did not want to rest! He wanted to—something! Perhaps unite his will with Njande's and suddenly burst through the cage a new Biouk—

Ach, he was delirious. The pain swelled through the pads of his paws, up his forearms, as if his missing claws sought vengeance, scraping through his bloodstream to his heart. She mumbled something he could not hear, a groan. Stiffness overcame him …

Her voice. "A ba-eater, you said. Is that—mebbe that's why Njande spent the whole game huddled around Jei? He shielding him? I didn't see a ba-eater …"

Ah—perhaps that was why Njande had told him to rest. Perhaps she would work this out herself? She used to do that, walking through the tree-tops, talking out her problems. Perhaps she did not need him. Perhaps he should … sleep … disappear into …

"Heat death," now she scoffed bitterly. "You were ranting about the apocalypse. *Ratschica*, Cinta, how d'you expect me to believe that?" The violent word, *ratschica*, broke Cinta's heart. "Even if I believed in heat death, how'm I s'posed to believe my connection with Njande's gonna stop it?" She was so unhappy, so angry. *Njande.*

The black and white coalesced to a form like a Biouk in the shadows. Not quite solid. Not quite real? "I'm almost there, little one," Njande said. "Just one question. If this is to work, I need this one question."

Yes?

"Do you believe I will help?"

Cinta didn't blink. *Of course you will. You love her.*

"That's all I need. Thank you, dear one."

That was all? Didn't he need his will or something? Some effort? Wasn't he about to possess him or something? Was that not how this creature did things?

Nothing happened. Jaika was not crying now. "Talking crazy like we're pawns in a duel between spirits," she spat. "Gah, I gotta get to Jei. He'd tell me you're full of it, of course. But man—if you're telling anything like the truth, I really don't know what to do!"

Silence fell again. Cinta wanted to argue, but his eyelids drooped, his muscles ached, his paws, his paws …

In his delirium he heard his mother singing.

NJANDEJARA

Cinta is not his real name. I know his real name. I have it written on a smooth, white stone, stored away in a pearl temple guarded by winged artillery, and one day, when he is strong enough to bear its weight, I will give it to him. Then he will know himself.

He will know that he can read her thoughts, and mine, and that in this moment, his electric mind is the connection, the wire, between the power source in my dimension, and her. And when I finish this circuit, plug in this lamp—there will be sparks, and shad-

ows, and it will be ugly, but I make no apologies, not to you, not to him, not to her. There will be light.

LEM

It wasn't Cinta's mom singing.

Gotta stay awake. Couldn't let the chill coax her to sleep—she needed every neuron sparking to get them out of this, and with the pain and Cinta's slow breathing and the tugging in the pit of her stomach begging her to just flop back and give up and sleep and die —her voice kept her on. It rumbled over dry lips, dragged her spirit forward these last few steps until Diebol returned to set them free.

It was a silly little ditty—shyte, it was pathetic, about seeds in warm soil and sunshine, seed husks dying to birth new plants, and sunshine, sunshine, filtered through the atmosphere, deadly fusion sunshine, filtered to gentled fingers that coax flowers to grow, the atmosphere won't let the flowers get more than they can handle … Something something something stupid. Sentient clouds and shyte like that.

But the song distracted her. It brought her back to days spent lounging in the moss, dancing with Njande in filtered sunlight under the banyan tree's thirteen sprawling trunks. Even after she found the Frelsi, Njande had wrapped himself around her to bring happy pranks and whispers of relief into unending weeks of combat drills and classes. She couldn't imagine going back to that shyte without him. She didn't want to stay here under Diebol's thumb to fight her friends. But she couldn't kill Cinta.

But—but she didn't really believe Cinta was crazy, or lying about Njande, not now! Maybe *she* was delirious. Maybe her connection with Njande did matter for something? But did she even want him anymore? Did it matter what she wanted?

She couldn't even be angry anymore. She was so tired, and dizzy, and strangely alone in this big dark pain-room, and …

It was so nothing. She was suddenly so empty. She'd lost all her fight.

And suddenly, that was completely okay.

Because now, with herself out of the way, she could see Njande.

Clarity dawned on her like spring showers over a tilled field as his hand—or claw, or paw, or branch, or the best of all those things put together—drew a line across the darkness. She found herself standing in his shadow in a field of stars with the ache a memory at her back and this brilliant star-thing-person flashing before her, and she didn't know what had happened, and she ran forward and wrapped her arms around him and buried her tears in his warm heartbeat even as she whacked his chest with her fists.

"Why didn't you help us? Why didn't you help me *win*?" she wept.

"Do you know what would have happened if you'd won?"

"Cinta would be fine now!"

"No. You would both be dead." He gripped her shoulders and pushed her at arm's length so he could look into her face. "Bricandor's grown weary of the whole affair, and he planned to shoot you right there if he didn't see real change in you."

She stepped back for a second, staring into the grass beneath her bare feet. Okay. Yeah, she couldn't have faked that. "But what about everything *else*? Where have *you* been? You're supposed to get us out of here!"

"I have been fighting in my own dimension. *You* are supposed to get you out. You are the protagonist."

"Bloodseas, that sucks!" she spat. "So—Jei was right? You're not with me, and I'm stuck on my own to deal with truck-tons of impossible shyte?"

"No. I'm here with your things. And I'm off doing bigger things. Both are true. I'm quantum."

"So you're two sides of the same coin, then," she hissed. "You're flippant, two-faced, and unfair." She was in pain again, bound down on the icy floor, and furious.

He waved his hand across the ceiling, and it opened into stars.

He plucked a sun and pulled it down for her in all its fiery majesty, and pulled it into pieces, smaller and smaller, until he reached a tiny blotch, a blur, an atom. He held it before her and asked, "Where is the electron?"

She pointed, and the electron looked for a moment like a dot, a perfect round orb.

"Now can you tell me how fast it's going?"

"I don't have anything to measure that with."

"Hold out your hand and think with me." He gripped her palm and placed a glowing beam in it. "Find its speed." The beam lit up with numbers when she pointed it at the grass beneath her feet, or at her own hand, and when at last she thought she had the hang of it she pointed it at the electron. But when she got its speed it became a wave, slipping around her, dancing—and she found that if she knew where it was, she couldn't find its speed, and if she charted its speed, she couldn't tell where it was.

"What is it? Is the electron a wave, or a particle?" Njande asked.

"It's ... both."

"So am I. Because of who I am—because I am Spirit, a wave, and I can flow through you, and because I am Person, a particle, and I am autonomous and me and separate from you—because of that we live in Paradox. So I will always guide you. I will be the wave that moves your ship, and you cannot get to your destination without me. But as much as I love that oneness, and being with you and protecting you, I love your identity, your separateness as a particle, because I love my own separateness. You must be separate as I am separate. I cannot deny the goddess in you because I cannot deny myself, and so I must let her grow and fight and become something greater. The suffering is only extreme because you are extreme. The greater the glory, the greater the price; the greater the heroine, the greater trial she overcomes. Not just endures—overcomes. You were meant to triumph."

"A goddess? What are you talking about?"

"I will make a goddess out of you. A true goddess, not a supreme being to be worshiped. I will always be Ultimate, and I will always be above you." Lem marveled: If anyone else said that they spoke arrogance, but when he said it, it was a simple admission of fact. One plus one equals two, confidently. The bird doesn't think less of the fish for being bad at flying: nature is nature, and it needs no false morality or fake modesty. "I must be true to Who I Am, or everything falls apart. And you must be true to yourself, which is a different kind of being entirely.

"For there is a reflection, a spark like me in you," he smiled. "And I long to see that reach full glory. So you must stand on your own two feet, and yet you must never stand without me. You can handle this alone, strong; and yet you cannot, and you are weak. *Weakness is strength.* It's a Paradox."

"This is so hard to understand."

"If you understand only one thing, my love, understand this: I know the plans I have for you, and they are plans for your good, not for evil, to give you a future and a hope. And in the end, I will be found by you."

I will be found by you. He used the passive voice there. Another Paradox? He the passive, and she active—*you will seek.* And yet he was active, for he was planning, he was drawing, he was Master, and she would be planned, drawn, and mastered. And in that Paradox of active and passive, of agency and surrender, Jerusha-Lem and Njandejara were a harmony separate and strange from everything around them. Diverse and different. There was nothing in the universe quite like him and her.

And that differentness was the evil Diebol feared.

Weakness is strength.

"Cinta, I'm going to try something."

CHAPTER TWENTY-NINE

Diebol

DIEBOL PAUSED OUTSIDE ROOM 256, HIS HAND HOVERING ABOVE the doorknob as his heart raced. So close to the cure.

What was she saying in there? Was she trying to comfort the delirious Biouk? *Oh, Lem, I'm so sorry.* It would be over soon. He slipped inside and crept over to crouch beside her.

"Hey," he said.

"Did you know Bricandor talks to a ba-eater?" she asked.

Diebol groaned. No. No, she wasn't cured, and she wasn't discouraged. She was stalling. "Really, you're going to give me more trouble now?" he asked.

"I'm serious."

He laid his left hand on her belly with a heavy sigh, and with his right threw an em-push to re-activate the robot by the Biouk's cage. "You know what comes next."

But she didn't cringe. She breathed, softly, and Diebol did nothing for a moment. "Are we continuing or not, Lem?"

"Can I ask you something first?" she asked.

"No, you answer me first. Do I have to keep going with this shyte?"

She sighed. "I think all that's *left* in me is Njande. So now if I lose him, I lose everything. Maybe Cinta, too. Maybe literally. I don't know. The universe is somehow tied up in this, apparently."

He withdrew his hand. He lifted it to strike, every modicum of his being weary. No! He didn't want this anymore!

"Just hold on and let me finish," she whispered. "Then you can keep going. Put your hand back so I know you're not gonna hit me yet."

Yes. *Then you can keep going.* Her request for respite gave him a way out, just for a moment; for a moment, he could hide from the torture. *Thank you, thank you, thank you ...* He laid his hand back on her stomach, listening to her words and her warmth and her slow rise and fall ...

"I hate Everyday Life, you know," she said. "And I don't know how to explain this to you," she breathed, wincing. "But he's my solution against Everyday. So war and work and drills can't touch me inside; so even if my whole world falls, I got no attachments to any of it, and I can let it all go. I'm not quite there yet, but I will be, and when I am resting in him it's pretty much the best. It's a —*Paradox*, I guess: I'm completely unattached, so nothing can faze me, but I can love and enjoy everything, so I'm totally attached. Point is, he's what makes this stupid life work.

"So—so I've been so scared that you can take him from me, and own me, and it's—" She choked, and breathed again. "Man, it pisses me off. I can't do anything about this. You could take him away, maybe, with some kind of brain surgery or something, or burn out all my synapses, and that's terrifying. But—but if there's nothing I can do about it, no way to hold on to him, I guess it's up to him to hold on to me. So—I guess everything's gonna be okay?"

She was delirious, speaking contradictions, and Diebol heard her breath speed up as the air brimmed with her panicked bravery, her terror at her own words, at everything she might lose now ... he found himself frozen in the face of her calm wildness. What could he even do? She was invincible. They were wearing him down, she and Jei, and bloodseas, he didn't want this anymore. He *could* choose to end this.

No. No he could not. He had to save them.

"Diebol?" The smallness of her voice was overpowering, spine-tingling, gut-wrenching. "You'll have to do your job now, I guess."

No, no, he didn't want to do this! It was impossible, wading against a tsunami—but they'd come so close! *Steel yourself, man.*

He removed his hand. She stiffened in the cold. His stomach pitted.

"I don't understand," he breathed. "What happened in the ten minutes I left?"

"Njande showed up. I'm—sorry I'm not sorry, I guess. You gonna get in trouble?"

He buried his face in his hands. Yes. Yes he was going to get in trouble. One visit from the interdimensional, one flash of nauseous delirium, and everything undid itself, leaving him another mountain of brutality to scale as Sisyphus rolled his stone over crunching bones. What could he do now? Flay the Biouk, break the girl's arms —how far would this go? "There must be another way," he groaned. "This is only more of the same refuse I'm trying to reform. I just— just don't have *time* to develop this properly!"

"Why, because of Bricandor? Who put you under him, anyway? He's kind of a freak."

Bam—her stomach curled under his knife-hand blow. It was instinct. "Have respect," Diebol snarled. "My Teacher's wisdom—"

"You have Stockholm Syndrome," she coughed. "If he's so wise, he'll understand that torturing my friend ain't doing it for me."

"The advice he gave me was sound." Diebol clenched his teeth and mustered his faith. *I shouldn't talk to her. I should keep going.* "I should continue with his recommendations."

"Then what's holding you back?"

His hands trembled. "What would goad you to ask something like that? Do you *enjoy* pain?"

"No. I really wanna know what you're thinking. Are you smarter than this? Do you really have a better plan? Or do you maybe just feel bad for us, and—" She paused, gasping for panicked breath. "I mean, shyte, we're having a real-life conversation here, with like, rapport. Why? Are we some kind of twisted—something, like a something that—doesn't—hate each other?"

Her voice ended in an uncertain whimper; her shoulders shuddered against the icy floor—bloodseas, Diebol realized, she meant every word.

His voice grew hoarse. "I never hated you," he murmured.

"If you don't hate me," she whispered. "Act on it."

If you don't hate me, act on it.

No!

With a strained cry he grabbed her wrist, his palm sticking in blood and sweat as he unclasped one manacle, snatched at the other, and slid his arm under her shoulder-blades to pin her against himself as she fell free. She cried out and cringed away, wrapping her arms around herself to shield her hands and belly.

"I'm not going to hurt you," Diebol growled, yanking her closer, heaving her to sitting so he could reach her ankles without letting her go. She protested, she cried something; he snapped open her bonds with a snarl. "Lights, on!"

Sensors recognized his voice; he snatched the blindfold off her and pointed to the Biouk shivering in the iron cage, blood spattered across his naked skin and the multi-armed robot beside it.

"What you said goes for you, too, beautiful hypocrite," Diebol hissed in her ear. "If you don't hate him, act on it!"

He drew his flayer, still holding her tight as he rose from his crouch. He yanked her drooping form to her feet, his forearm across her throat, her shoulder-blade pressed against his chest. "Maybe the connection isn't direct enough for you," he snapped. "Maybe you think by passively lying here taking blows you aren't participating. Well here!" The inspired rage pounded in his temples like a headache as he gripped her wrist and shoved the flayer into her hands, pinning her broken finger over the trigger. "You will either shoot him, or you *will* order the Contagion to leave! No more games: the choice happens now!"

LEM

Lem froze. Diebol's chest rose and fell against her back like burning bellows, scalding after the room's chill. The temperature change threw her into shivers. She didn't struggle. Didn't risk a misfire from her suddenly impulsive jailor. Cinta's life was no game.

There was no emotion. No panic. Everything was light.

The room was silver and mirrored.

Six surfaces splattered with blood.

A self-cleaning mind-game cell, like the others, but with buttons.

A panel above Cinta's cage bore a label: lights and refuse removal.

… Just like the mind-cells with the moving floors that opened to clean …!

Diebol counted down in her ear.

DIEBOL

"Three," he said, tightening his shoulders and forearms around hers.

"Two," he said, tensing for any escape as she shivered.

"One," he said.

He forced her to pull the trigger on her friend.

The gun jerked upward; the shot hit the panel on the wall! The lights blew out. The walls hummed with a soft mechanical whir. Lem's boot scraped Diebol's shin. His whole world tilted to the right; he stumbled, firing again, crushing her injured fingers in his grip. She cried out in pain; the shot clanged on metal. The floor, the tilting floor, preparing the room for cleaning—! Diebol and Lem fell together, tumbling to the right as *screeeeech*—

The cage slid by them. Lem thrashed—but she wasn't trying to get away? Diebol didn't know what to counter, he didn't know what she was—she wrapped her legs around his stomach—*wait, what?* —and threw herself backwards, dragging him across the floor, knocking them both against the cage—

Oh, shyte!

Lem slammed Diebol's hand against the cage door, screaming throaty growls and bird-noises to the Biouk. Diebol heard the lock open as it recognized his DNA—

Oh no! He fired. He fired again. He let go of the flayer with one hand to tap his belt, turn on his transmitter, and roar for backup. He threw her away from him with an electromagnetic shove, tearing the flayer out of her hands, and whirled in the direction he'd thrown her. He needed distance. He could sense her. He fired.

The shot hissed through flesh. She groaned. The Biouk cried something—more bird noises, Lem replied. Diebol interrupted with another shot, same spot.

That one hit metal. She'd moved. He ran for the door sneering. So predictable, her damn escape obsession—this girl would *never learn!*

He reached the door. She wasn't there.

Something heavy slammed the back of his head.

She'd learned.

CHAPTER THIRTY

Lark

THE HEAT WAVES OVER FORGE'S COLORFUL SANDS SEEMED TO PART as a shimmering bullet-shaped hunter ship plunged through the atmosphere towards the area's Growen fuel station—where Lark Scrita had just assumed the role of the blitzer sentry.

Lark choked and got her finger jammed in the pants-joint of the armor. She cursed, hopping on one leg half-dressed as the computer kept talking.

"Grant permission to land?" it asked. "Verbal confirmation desired?"

"No! No verbal nada, I don't want to talk to him! Yes, land-land-permission!" *Get it together, piddle-twit, you're a blitzer now! Lie!* "Permission to land granted!"

Lark dragged her glove on with her teeth while she checked the charge in Veradan's flayer gun. Come off it now, mercenaries stopped on Forge all the time to refuel. The Shadow wasn't here to finish her. Right. Right?

Fool him once, shame on me, fool him twice—and—and he knows where to shoot next time? Ick, no good. Lark couldn't think of anything snappy. Had anyone *ever* fooled him twice? Beans, if he didn't kill her, the performance anxiety would!

The *Huntress* landed outside. It gleamed like the carapace of a giant, legless black beetle. The broken hole in the side glared at Lark, accusing her.

Yup, no, I'm out. Lark was diving to hide in the porta-potty— when she caught a glimpse of her reflection in the metal wall.

Young, handsome ... bored.

Bored. The lie took over. Lark slipped the helmet on and didn't think. Didn't fear. She distanced herself, strapped the blitzer to herself like a puppet, and the routine checkpoint passed like a dream as Lark watched from the outside and the blitzer worked.

Jake Veradan did this every day, and he was tired of it. Wave in half-hearted disinterest. Verify the visitor's pass; waive the usage fee. Start the fuel pumps. Wonder if he could get off work early. Sigh with job dissatisfaction.

Lark snapped back into her own mind when she saw the little girl.

"Gotta take her out for sunlight," the Shadow muttered. "She asked for sunlight."

Sunlight? What does he bloody care if she gets sunlight?

The Ebon Shadow hooked the little girl on a chain and two stasis fields to the ladder underneath the *Huntress* and walked a few paces away, clenching and unclenching his fists, leaving Lark tending the fuel hose while two thin, multi-armed glue-bots repaired the hull damage, extruding reinforced polymerwall through their hoses.

Lark's heart leapt and fell and leapt again in a frantic ballet. The girl was *right there!* Lark was stepping around her bound legs to manage the fuel hose. She could—she could—

She could do nothing about that stasis field without a key.

"Hey," Lark whispered. The girl ignored her, staring with pursed lips and wet, hollow eyes at the pink sand. Blast that stare, Lark saw it too often on slaves; it wrenched her chest.

Lark stepped over the girl and stood with her back to the Ebon Shadow, keeping her arms up against the bottom of the ship as if inspecting the glue-bots' work on the hull. "Hey!" she repeated.

Lark lifted her helmet for a moment and rubbed the film on her shoulder to flash her lizard-face. "Remember me?"

"… No?" The girl whispered back. *Not without the Bont helmet I wore during the rescue, I guess.* The child's lacquer nose wrinkled as a stray blonde hair tickled it.

"I know your—er, family," Lark said.

"You do? Do you know where Lem is?"

Beans, did she mean … "Lem Benzaran?"

"Yeah, my sister! Did she send you?"

Beans, those big, bright eyes just glowed in the child's pretty face. The inevitable fairytale leapt to Lark's lips—she couldn't *not* lie.

"Quiet. Yup, Lem sent me." Lark reached into her pocket for a white plastic wrapper, glancing over her shoulder at the Shadow still pacing in the distance. He wasn't paying attention … busy plotting some get-rich-quick blood scheme, no doubt. Lark unwrapped the candy and held it up.

The amber honey-drop glowed between her fingertips as the evening light flickered through it, illuminating the silhouette of a safe little tracking device. Lark couldn't free the girl now, not with the Shadow here. But if she knew where to find them, she could bide her time. Catch the Shadow with his britches down. "Swallow this candy whole," Lark said. "Don't chew it."

The little girl obeyed. Lark smiled.

A hard glove gripped Lark's wrist.

"What did you just feed her?" the Ebon Shadow asked. Asked. Not snapped. Not snarled. If he caught Lark feeding tracking devices to his prey he'd shoot her. No hard feelings. Just business. His black mask stared eyeless, just the empty outline of a human face peering into the helmet of the terrified—

Of the terrified *blitzer.* "C-candy. What, do you want a lil bon-bon, too?" The blitzer reached to draw a candy from his belt—

The Shadow snatched Lark's wrist to keep her from pulling a gun. Lark shuddered. Two hundred pounds of killer, right here, holding her hands, almost chest to chest, breathing her helmet exhaust, pinning down her pulse—

The blitzer burst through her lips. "You have five seconds to drop your hands, civilian!" Veradan/Lark yelled. "Or forfeit your person to *Growen Justice*!"

The Shadow stood fast. The blitzer leaned closer. "Drop. Your. Hands!"

A pause. They breathed.

The Shadow dropped his hands to the flayers on his belt.

Lark wanted a moment to breathe, but the blitzer was offended now. Pseudo-Veradan waved another candy in the air to show the uptight civilian mercenary a thing or two. "Look, you paranoid freak, it's a freaking candy. A candy! You think I'm trying to mess with your clients? You think I joined the Growen to get stupid and killed?"

"Yes," said the Shadow.

Lark resisted the urge to giggle nervously. "Get out," the blitzer fumed. "Your repairs are done." He turned his back in disgust. He marched towards his sentry-box, throwing his hands in the air. One step, two steps, three steps—turn, toss the comment over his shoulder: "Stygge Bricandor doesn't like to wait, civilian," he hissed.

And he shut the door.

Ho-ly blasted bloodseas.

Lark fell against the wall, sweat bursting over her as the tension broke. Bricandor doesn't like to wait? Where the bloodseas did *that* come from? *Brilliant!* The Shadow respected no one, not even the Growen. Everyone knew that. But he didn't shoot his clients. *And that's why he didn't shoot me.*

Beans, what a discovery, then! If Shadow's client was Growen, and the girl was Lem Benzaran's *sister*—aces against twos Lark bet Bricandor either wanted to manipulate Benzaran with her, or the girl had electromagnetic abilities for that Stygge army. So aces against twos, if Lark followed the Shadow she'd find Benzaran with Bricandor. No wonder the Shadow chose to refuel on Forge, so close to Revelon.

Magical.

Breathe. Wait. Breathe. Lark glanced out the window as the Shadow lifted the girl back into the beetle's underbelly. The girl gazed over her shoulder toward the sentrybox, waiting, expectant, hopeful as the polymerwall absorbed her ...

Lark looked away and held her ground. *No heroic rescues today, sweetie.* She heard the girl burst into tears. She heard the *sploosh* as the polymerwall sealed. She heard the engines roar—she poked her head outside as the ship flung itself over the horizon.

No heroic rescues ... yet, Lark revised as she dashed towards Veradan's Maggot-ship to trail the mercenary. Her heart ached for the girl who'd expected more than a candy, but a solidness, an anchor deep in Lark's stomach, held her on track. This solidness told her what card to play the night a drug lord gambled against her target's life; it'd made her duck the axe swing from behind the day she lost herself in Guetala's jungles; and it hid her under the roof after the Growen killed her family. *This* plan was solid.

Lark's boots clonked in the pink sand, a muffled snare drum against the flute of the desert wind. The sky was clear. The distance was safe. A glance at Lark's wristband tracked the little girl's blip breaking into space and heading towards Revelon.

Where the little Biouk had disappeared.

Yes, yes, yes. Benzaran's gotta be there.

The gray Maggot-ship glowed as the blitzer's uniform neared. ID codes embedded in the helmet told one of the ringlets to slide back. A panel popped out; Lark glanced at the cuff of the over-sized glove where lazy Veradan had scribbled his second ID instead of memorizing it, and Lark punched that into the panel.

She slid into the plastic army-green chair, wrinkled her nose at the mildewed air, flexed her fingers at the wall of buttons before her, and let the engines whine. The ship shuddered, creaking, and soon the pinks and greens and blues of Forge disappeared as Lark dipped into the black-and-white silent film of space.

CARL

The Ebon Shadow had a stomachache.

This never happened. Carl never felt sick, or guilty, or the need to give his targets "fresh air" or "sunlight" or whatever stupidity he'd muttered to that blitzer. Now, what with the probable damage to his professional reputation, he regretted his lapse.

Every ten to ten-point-five minutes Carl's rear radar detected the Growen Maggot trailing him. It stayed at a distance, clearly trying to remain invisible. Perhaps the driver had some trepidation about following the most feared mercenary in the universe. He should: one of Carl's rear gun turrets packed enough firepower to take out the Maggot in one shot, shields down. Shields up, it might take two shots.

The risk of destroying a client's scout outweighed the insult of getting tailed, though. Sometimes thieves disguised themselves as Growen for legitimacy, but it was best to call Bricandor to check the ship. Make him call it off.

"Silver Knight Six, this is Ebon Shadow, I need a direct line, over."

No response. "Silver Knight Six, this is Ebon Shadow on freq 4550. Please confirm frequency security, over."

"Ebon Shadow, this is Silver Knight Tree Two, Captain of Stygge Bricandor's security team. We're currently dealing with a security breach here, so the Commander cannot take your call personally. I can pass along your request. Over."

Carl grimaced. "Silver Knight Tree Two, I only deal with clients directly."

The voice on the radio grew testy. "I am authorized to take the Commander's calls, civilian." They overused civilian like a dirty word. Some psychological insecurity that came with wearing a second-rate uniform with no individuality.

"Silver Knight Tree Two, I have a Growen Maggot trailing my craft. That is unacceptable. Get Bricandor on the radio or cut off."

"I'm sure if Bricandor has a tail on you it's for a reason," the peon spat. "But for right now, we have an emergency situation with some escapees, and I am authorized to—"

"Over and out." Carl cut the call. He'd seen enough bait and switch to learn to avoid people who tried to talk for their bosses. He planned on getting paid for this job, not dropping his cargo off with an underling who'd turn and sell to the highest bidder without delivering to his boss. *Get things done yourself. Get them done at the source.* Dealing with "chain of command" only wasted resources, fostered corruption, and started a ridiculous game of radio-tag Carl didn't have time for.

Carl wanted to lose this Maggot, though, whether or not it belonged to Bricandor. He tapped the upper left-hand corner of his window and dragged a map and schedule to center-screen. Perfect. Local meteor showers. A speed more than twelve thousand knots through any field more dense than one body per square meter would tear the tiny Maggot apart, and at a speed slower than that the Maggot would fall behind. Carl liked those numbers.

He liked the numbers a lot. It didn't take him long to escape. He almost stayed in the meteor shower longer than necessary: it comforted him to weave back and forth with his consciousness engulfed only in the *Huntress* and the stones. Navigation. Shield management. Rocks. These were things he knew. Things without ephemeral whispers and cow-shyte. Things he missed when he broke out of the chaos into the stillness of open space where glittering galaxies reminded him of the presence driving him insane.

At least he'd lost one stalker …

CHAPTER THIRTY-ONE

Lem

LEM DROPPED THE BLUDGEON-LICIOUS METAL ROBOT NEXT TO Diebol's unconscious body, panting as she staggered for the door. She winced on her shot leg—but forget the burnt quad, she'd done it! She'd gotten Cinta out: dumped him into the refuse trough under the room, because he was small enough to fit between the wall and the floor when it tilted open, and maybe now if she went the opposite direction they'd ignore him and he'd escape out that pipe she saw on her first day. Thank Njande for that moment in the light.

Thank Njande, huh? That was something Cinta said often.

Lem found the door. She gripped the handle with her palms and wrists—shyte, that was gross. Her blood was sticking to it. It turned no problem. Now to find Jei.

JEI

I guess you never notice some things until they're in your way.

I paced for the greater part of an hour, intentionally putting weight on my injured knee now and then so the pain would take my mind off Njandejara. Sweat laced my back and chest, and I began to get dizzy. I found my mind fighting a force as much greater than myself as a tsunami towering over a rowboat.

Why wouldn't he *leave*? I didn't like considering that Diebol knew his stuff, but maybe all along I'd needed a cure because Njande fed off my brain. How would I know?

I did know it was all friendship and promises until we needed help.

But actually that accusation was only a veneer on the true reason I didn't want to imagine Njande that close. What really, really bothered me about this new proximity had nothing to do with morality and everything to do with the *invasion* of privacy his ephemeral presence constituted, with the voyeuristic paint my mind drew on the whole situation—and with the *alienness* of such a being. He was that close, all along? A core xenophobia cried *no* within me: he could have his space, his country, but once he crossed the border into mine I needed him deported.

On some barely conscious level my thoughts struck me as ignorant: by his very nature he could no more avoid knowing my thoughts when he stood near me than a magnet can avoid drawing iron to it. But that made him worse! Dangerous, too intimate. Creepy. I wanted him away. I needed him away. I'd had enough! And I didn't need to defend that—it was my mind, and I was within my rights to exile whoever I wanted!

So then shut up! Shut up and meditate him away!

But the more I tried to shut up the more I found the floodgates opening. I hadn't even noticed that over the years I'd built walls around my communication with Njande, walls like the ones blocking Diebol's radio out of my inner mind. Now, when I needed those walls, I found them shuddering, thin ... as if I'd locked a Crajk-beast in my closet, and he'd shaken his mane, flexed his lizard claws, and slammed his entire chimeric form at the tent fabric I'd used to cover myself.

A Crajk-beast from the wastelands of Alpino. I could envision that, meditate on the image. Scales all over thick as woven metal. Tail like an apatosaurus. Legs like a man in a permanent pushup. A wide face, like a Komodo dragon, but then a hairy lion's mane, and webbed feet.

A Crajk-beast I'd locked out of his territory.

"What the hell kind of thought is that?" I cried, gripping my hair with both hands. I knew nothing! I'd claimed this dimension-traveler as "friend" for six years, but we talked what, once or twice a month? I didn't know what he liked. I didn't know what he wanted. I knew what he could give me, and I knew I didn't like some Growen overlord telling me who I could or could not talk to; I knew my rebellion against them, and Njande's kindness towards me, but now I found myself facing something solid and warlike and *different* … I needed Diebol's help. Maybe the drugs or the EZT therapy would work now that I wanted them to. Maybe—

And then the polymerwall bulged, and I was strangely unsurprised to see Lem burst through it.

Red crusts streaked down her forearm. A star-shaped burn marked her quad, speckled with colorful flayer-shot oxidizing gel. Long lines of pain crossed her smooth face.

But her cheeks glowed, and her eyes glistened.

"Holy shyte, am I happy to see you," she breathed.

I could say nothing. My mind suddenly came up blank, as if I'd broken my word-bank slamming it up against that rock in my head, and I couldn't tell her how happy I was to see her. A jumble of shocked questions bumbled through me. How …?

She wrapped her arms around my neck for a hug, and ran out the polymerwall.

I plunged after her, trying to figure out how she'd bypassed the wall's DNA check—I almost tripped over Diebol's leg.

"What the—"

He lay in the hallway with a smear of blood on the back of his head. His hand draped up the wall toward the panel that disabled selective DNA control. Lem had used his body as an override key to disable all the building's polymerwall locks. He was breathing. A hostage.

I wanted to ask how she'd gotten him here with those mangled hands, and how she'd knocked him out, but *you know what? Forget it. Just adapt to what she does and channel it into what works.* No more wasted time trying to control lightning.

I knelt to snatch Diebol's knife, mace, and extra flayer, and I slid up beside her. Even if I couldn't touch his mace because of the DNA-lock on it, I could at least em-push it into the other room to keep him from using it. I fired his flayer and blew out the security camera ahead of us in the hallway.

"Where to?" I asked.

"I was hoping you could tell me." She squeezed Diebol's wrist between her palms, trying to mash his hand against the wall to show me the map. I took his wrist from her—she grimaced, but I got the map to load.

"Where's the transmission tower?" she asked.

I scanned the symbols—nothing but training rooms and medical cells.

"Either it's hidden somehow from Diebol, or there isn't one," I said. "I have trouble believing the first option, so—I guess communication only leaves here through Diebol's holo-pen?" I pawed through his vest.

"Yeah, I couldn't find that," Lem said.

"Let's check his living quarters." I pointed on the map to the right along the hallway.

"Nah, that's the way I came from, dude, and he definitely called for help, so if I missed the blitzers by leaving left they were coming from the right."

"Alright, we'll bypass them, then. Detour through the mess hall and the gym."

I heaved Diebol over my shoulder with an em-lift, concentrating physical pressure off my body by magnetizing the metal around us to repulse him into the air. Lem leaned against the wall as she hobbled beside me.

"Wish I could lift like that," she panted. "You're a much better magnet than I am. I'm all shoving him with my elbows and kicking him and shyte to get him here, and then you just lift him like a doll."

"Just takes concentration," I grunted, sliding forward. We neared a corner. "I take left, you've got right."

"A'ight."

I hit the left wall; she hit the right. I aimed and fired around my corner to take out three unsuspecting Stygge trainees while she sent electric arcs racing the other way at two blitzers, paralyzing them momentarily. We raced past the blitzers, and I strapped their rifles over my back.

"See, I wish I could do *that*," I said, nodding towards the sparks still popping over her fingers.

Lem was too busy breathing to answer as we veered right, ducking into the little mess-room. The door slammed behind us. She stumbled to our table. Red mist smudged the white speckled plastic under her palms. I dumped Diebol beside her and grabbed the intercom in the corner.

Lem stared at me, eyes narrowed. "Hey, you okay?" she asked.

Was *I* okay? She wasn't breathing like that because she was tired—she was huffing and wheezing because everything hurt, and I knew that. She wanted to know if *I* was okay?

"You're crazy," I said.

"Please don't say that. I hate that."

"Roger." I flicked the intercom on to threaten the Stygges with the death of their leader, reciting some formula I'd learned from a guerrilla tactics class as a thirteen-year-old. I'd memorized it; I didn't even think as my mouth rumbled. Except—"Next Growen face I see, I shoot Diebol," I ended. I meant it.

I clicked the red switch back off and stumbled to Lem's side. Damn my knee.

"You didn't answer my question," she wheezed, eyes shut.

"Well, you've taken more heat than I have. Which is becoming the norm, I guess."

"That's not what I'm asking," she said.

I smirked. "Hey, you need a hand to keep moving? We've still got the training room between us and Diebol's room."

"Jei!" Her eyes flashed and her teeth bared as her head snapped around to face me. "You avoiding the question puts us in danger. There's a ba-eater in this building that wants you. You, specifically. I need to know you're okay!"

Yeah, and that ba-eater was Njande. I glanced at the door behind us. "We gotta keep moving. They can already see us by camera, and they're only being careful because we've got Diebol. If the blitzers catch up to us they'll gas us out and we'll fail."

"'Kay." She wrapped her arm around my shoulder, allowing us both to lean weight off our injured legs as I lifted Diebol again. He felt lighter now—

"Lem, quit helping me. Save your firepower for offense."

She released him, and we passed into the gym. It was quiet, empty except for the floating platforms hanging in its multi-story abyss.

"Jei. Ba-eater. In this building. Listen to me."

"It can't be 'in this building.' They can't enter our dimension like that." I focused on my footsteps, on the corners, on the shadows.

"Jei! I really need to know! Are you cool with Njande?"

"We need to keep moving or it won't matter."

"Dammit, Jei," Lem groaned.

We hobbled across the first platform in the room, the T that jutted from the glass doors over the abyss. My face felt dry and pasty, like the salt in my sweat had sucked the life out of it, and my tongue thickened … shyte, I couldn't answer her. Of course I wasn't cool with Njande, and I didn't want to be, but she'd suffered so much for him. At what point would I burst that bubble of hope to tell her he'd jeopardized our mission? Not now. Not fifteen minutes before her likely death. Let her die brave and happy, without her world shattered, and if we survived, I'd tell her. I'd tell her he'd betrayed us.

We reached the end of the T. The abyss yawned below us; a meter or two from us floated another platform. We backed up to start our em-leap towards it—

I suddenly saw, in my mind, a crack. A shadowy arm twice as

big as my waist pushed on the other side of my thoughts, bulging with untapped, sinister power.

I tried to shut off the image, and in my panic I shut off my electromagnetic hold.

I dropped Diebol off the platform.

"Bloodseas, no!" Lem cried, reaching after him. But she fired a spark, not a pull, and he plummeted into the shadows.

The room roared to life. Knife-panels opened in the walls; gun turrets lowered from the ceiling; twirling sunflower blades rose towards us from the depths; blitzers poured into the mess-hall behind us; jet-streams opened below us and the room began to fill with dark liquid too blue to be water. I'd killed Diebol, I'd lost our hostage, and they knew it. And now they were going to kill us.

CHAPTER THIRTY-TWO

Cinta

CINTA TUMBLED THROUGH A DARK, RANK-SMELLING CHUTE, THE stubble of his fur slick with acrid slime. His joints jolted against every corner; nausea stroked his forehead and stomach in waves, and he vomited all over himself as he fell.

I am going to die in this hole, I am going to die—

A hint of fresh air penetrated the musk. Cinta's nostrils perked open; his body leaned forward without his will, hunting that air—

He tumbled into cool liquid before he could catch his breath. His paws stung and his eyes burned in the blur and his nostrils soaked in choking fire as his heart flip-flopped against his chest like a drying fish—he could not swim!

His hind paws found a slippery rock. He pushed off it towards the surface. His muzzle broke into brilliant light. A shore came up on him fast. The sewage carried him forward, splashing him against a sandy, dirty bank littered with sharp pebbles, and he scrambled out of the water hacking and coughing.

He was out. The nightmare was over.

Cinta breathed, cold and strangely *alive*, on a bed of pine needles and sharp rocks beside a stream guarded on the left by a towering cliff face. A white, many-spired twisted building crowned the cliff, and a chute jutted out of the rock just above the stream, vomiting silt and waste—and apparently also escaped prisoners—into the water.

Cinta dragged himself towards the spindly roots nearby to hide, partly just out of tree-dweller instinct. Downstream from him, the stream banks on both sides tightened and deepened until the rapids danced through a gorge, sucking into a water-treatment turbine at the canyon's narrowest part. Besides the turbine, guarding it, stood four blitzers in shining, reflective silver.

"Just a little longer until the offensive," one commented, taking off his helmet to spit into the river.

"Should be easy. Heard they've got a Stygge awakener on the inside over there."

An awakener? Cinta's near delirium couldn't take more secret information now. He forced himself to file the fact away, and blinked.

Emergency transmitters hung on their belts.

Local SOS. Anyone could hear a local SOS distress call. Even the Frelsi.

They had not seen him yet, those humans. He slipped into the shadows of the gangly trees, his body hugging the bark and earth as he faded almost into invisibility.

One last action before he died. Then, he told the pain, Njande would take over.

LARK

Lark was making good time behind the Ebon Shadow. The moldy-smelling Growen Maggot-ship was no Leech racer, but it cut through space just fine. Beans, this creep was leading her straight to Revelon, just like the Biouk—but better than the Biouk, the Shadow had an invite from Bricandor. Soon she'd rescue the little girl *and* bag the Frelsi electromagnetics. Lark felt so good she almost started to whistle.

Suddenly a high-pitched beep whined in her helmet.

"Eeep!" Lark yelled and ripped the helmet off—the sound faded, but a red light blinked in the upper left-hand corner of her dashboard.

"Hey, Eardrum-Impaler, what do you want?" Lark snapped. "Beans, what does the blasted light mean?"

She ducked under the dashboard, checking for engine hatches to worry about, anything smoking … ? No. As she sat back up—

Meteor to the face!

Lark mashed the buttons on the dashboard's left, swerving the ship left. The cockpit rattled as the meteor scraped the ship's right side. The Maggot hurtled head-on towards another ragged iron boulder. "Shields, blasted shields, where are you?"

Lark tapped the button panel, tapped the lights, tapped the unlabeled things—a drawer popped open and dehydrated food poured out over her. "No, no! Shields!"

She snatched the helmet. "Voice command?" she asked it.

"Not available for this model," flashed a message in its inside screen.

Too many blasted buttons! Lark whacked the unmarked sector below her steering area, trying to find those shields, or weapons system, or—

Piddle-tarts! The ship flew out of control. The rings separated and the back whipped around, missing another meteor by a hair's width as the Maggot hatched from easy-to-drive little egg into wild, hot-sauce vomiting worm. "No, wait, undo that!" Lark whacked that lower panel again with her left hand. The tail swerved left. "Beans, two separate sets of controls for the front and back? *Why?*" The tail dangled through the meteor field, wobbling her off course, taking pings from small debris. Fist-sized lumps vibrated soundlessly against the hull, throwing Lark every which way, and *blast it all*—

Two more meteors dove straight at the blinking windshield.

Instinct replaced intellect. In panic Lark slid her hands along the buttons from outside to in, like a clap, like she'd do with compuwall controls.

The ship straightened; the rings grew taught; the Maggot squeezed between the two meteors, as compact as an egg.

Beans, that was close. Well, perhaps the answer wasn't in using different buttons. Perhaps she needed to hit the same buttons in a different pattern. She tapped faster on her left and right panels instead of pushing against them.

Two torpedoes rocketed out in front of her. One shot out into nowhere; the other collided with a meteor. The close explosion threw the ship backwards. Lark whiplashed forwards—her wristband cracked against the wall—she glanced out the back window where an infinite spiked stone surface careened towards her—

Death stared her in the face. That solidness gripped her gut. She floated mid-momentum as the grey ghost—

Grey-green button top-left!

Lark whacked it. "Shields engaged," flashed the words on her helmet screen. She braced herself—and the newly magnetized ship bounced off without touching the meteor. The high-pitched alarm did not stop screaming, but Lark was alive.

"Blasted Shadow," she growled at the broken monitor on her wrist. No more tracking device. Now she'd lost him. She veered around the next few meteors as best she could, taking blows here and there as the magnetic repulsor shield pushed the iron rocks away—but when the Maggot shot back out into open space, Lark saw no *Huntress*.

She was lost.

CINTA

Cinta's headache ceased pounding. His legs drew him through the trees without his command. The blitzers paced almost in place, small footsteps marking circles as they watched their area by the stream, heads swiveling in all directions. One of them leaned back against the pine tree nearest Cinta.

Cinta's paws stretched for the blitzer's belt. He wound around the tree like a snake, back claws clinging to the bark as his de-clawed forepaws flexed. They screamed, his forepaws, but he bent them forward regardless, accepting the agony, wrapping bloodied paws around the transmitter and unclipping it from the belt—

"Hey!" The blitzer's hand flashed to his belt. Cinta scuttled away—but the hand caught his back leg. Cinta swung off balance, hanging in the air upside-down, trying to get his paws around the lock on the SOS button—he vaguely knew the blitzer had his leg in one hand, but *come now, button, open!* A human whined; fingers in gloves, the blitzer's other hand, snatched at the emergency stick. "Gimme that!"

Cinta bit down on the glove.

The blitzer cursed; Cinta flew, hurled through the air. Cat-like instincts kicked in. *Land on my paws—*

No, too late. Cinta curled against the ground on his back. It stung, slapped. Dust dug under the stubble of his shaved fur, scratching exposed skin.

The sides of Cinta's vision lit up with alarms. Alarms he ignored. *Move, button, move!* He knew the blitzer was drawing his weapon. He knew the blitzer had no reason not to shoot him. And he knew he did not have time, in this split second, to hide anywhere.

I won't give you more than you can handle. Something like that, Njande had said. So he could handle this. This button built for unin-jured human phalanges—he could wrap his damaged paws around it.

No. No, he could not.

A flayer shot plunged into his shoulder. He yelped, scraping the button with a whine. The blitzers mocked their comrade: "Come on, you can't kill the thing at this range?"

"Hey, I got it clean through his shoulder! It's target-practice, like our deployment on Luna-Guetala, remember? Watch, you call a target, I'll hit it."

"I'll do you one better. Watch me—rear left paw." Another flayer drew somewhere.

Ratschica, this cursed switch! As the next shot fired up, Cinta's life did not flash before his eyes. What could have happened flashed there instead, plaguing his pre-death hormone-freeze with the hundreds of ways he could have done this better. The right training, the right resources, some way to defend Lem, some way to fight off Diebol—anything could have changed this moment. *I can still do that. I can still get Lem free.* Press this worthless button, that was all he had to do, and he could not.

Something hit his rear left paw; agony flashed up his left side, blinding him for a moment as someone laughed. Laughing, with the fate of the universe at stake? Justice screeched in his fingertips. This was not fair!

Then he understood: *this wasn't just happening to him.* Somewhere else, these monsters were taking whatever they wanted, playing games with people who couldn't fight back. This wasn't warfare: this was oppression. Suddenly the past colored a different shade, and Njande himself sounded warlike. *Save those led off to the slaughter* wasn't a metaphor. Maybe he could turn the other cheek for himself. But hiding in the jungle while children died and these fools *laughed*—was that turning the other cheek, or a blind eye?

Njande, give me one more chance to save her.

I did. Take it.

Cinta jammed the transmission stick into his mouth and bit down until it cracked.

Click—the SOS signal went off with a screech.

Crack—another flayer fired.

It was as if a river burst through Cinta's back, blasting away all his air, covering him in a current of fire. He could not hear himself scream. He could only see agonizing gray. Gray people, gray stones, and a gray maggot-shaped spaceship appearing in the distant sky like a star. Hot wind battered them all.

LARK

Open space didn't give a damn how much Lark raged or sighed. So she wheeled towards Revelon's surface without doing either; she let the deadness sit in her stomach like a bad dehydrated meal, and drove on in silence.

With that Shadow-lead lost, she'd never find the electromagnetics. "Oh, bloody good, they're on Revelon! Congratulations, you just have eight continents to scour now." Sod it all. Perhaps it was time to quit this job and start fresh with a new identity.

"SOS at D9257893, Revelon, Sector 12." Her helmet screen flashed.

Well. What else did she have to do right now? She brought the ship down, weaving it through the spires of Revelon's Alto Mountain Range. Lost hikers, perhaps. A chance to give out business cards. After all, she'd kidnapped a manager for those …

Oh beans, no, it was a Growen SOS. Those were blitzers, gathered around that turbine, at the foot of the cliff.

Mmm, no thank you. Not in this ship. Until she got paid again Lark drew the line at uniformed kid-killers *and* Frelsi extremists. She pulled the ship back up.

Eh, hold on—what was that they were gathered around?

Lark glanced out the window one more time.

A Biouk. It was a Biouk. What was a Biouk doing on Revelon surrounded by Growen blitzers oh goodness could it be could it be *could it be*—

Lark's fingers danced like a concert musician's across the weapons panel: the three surprised blitzers around the Biouk died in showers of colorful oxidizer torpedoes before Lark had the Growen Maggot straddling the creek. The Biouk looked dead, too. Was he dead? Lark tightened the valve on her mask and leapt out the door; the heavy boots felt light, light as sandals as she crunched on the rocks, sloshed through the stream, and clunk-trotted back into the Maggot bearing the furry. An aid-bot hung on the cockpit wall, ready to keep this heart going, ready to patch that punctured-lung—

"Get the Frelsi," he gasped. "My friend's trapped in there."

She'd found them. Oh goodness, she'd found them!

CHAPTER THIRTY-THREE

Jei

THE GUN TURRETS IN THE CAVERNOUS GYM WALLS SURE AS HELL weren't shooting rubber bullets now.

Neither were the blitzers in the doorway behind us. A storm of colorful flayer cartridges flashed through the bottomless training room, echoing and bouncing off its floating platforms. As the blitzers behind us charged, I leapt away to the platform with exercise weights on it and ducked behind the weight-rack. An em-push from my left hand diverted the blitzers' aim; Diebol's pistol, in my right, returned fire.

Lem dove for the platform behind me onto the running track. Her entire body lit up with an electric field. I doubted she was doing that on purpose—it probably meant she was going to overload and kill herself—but hey, it made the turrets' oxidized flayer cartridges swerve away from her at the last second.

Torrents of bright blue liquid rushed towards us from the abyss in the bottom of the room: if they couldn't shoot us, they'd drown us. We couldn't escape back the way we came—the blitzers covering that door multiplied every second—but there was a platform on the other side of the gym with a second, small stone doorway. We had to get there before the room filled up.

Walking was agony. *Shut up, knee.* I didn't need a knee. Who needed a knee? I had electromagnetic powers.

Oh. Keyword *had*. As I leapt to the track-platform after Lem, I found out, mid-air, that my abilities just up and quit on me.

"Shyte!" I wasn't going to make the jump—

Lucky for me, poisonous burning water caught me when I fell. Repeatedly. From platform to platform. And if I ever got tempted to just enjoy that little swim, ignore the tingling in my skin and let the "water" float me across the room, every time I splashed hordes of mechanized aqua-bots charged me from below, buzz-saw teeth whirring in their sharkish mouths. This one snapped at my heels—

Rifle to the teeth! I swung one of the blitzer weapons we'd confiscated in the hallway, splashing myself in the face with stinging liquid. The gun jammed in the bot's jaw. The metal ground, ground, ground, and the bot sank, taking the rifle with it, and yeah that whole jam-a-gun-in-its-mouth trick worked great with the other rifle, too, but the number of aqua-bots, unfortunately, was greater than two.

I dragged myself weaponless onto the next platform, clawing like a soggy cat at the metal. Dizzy. I couldn't find the color green. Couldn't center. Everything was blue, so damn blue, and the Crajk-beast pressed through the walls—blue light seared through the cracks—

I tumbled into the sharp-smelling water again. Another aqua-bot swayed at me from below. Silver longitudinal stripes glinted against its gray body; red light glowed in its eyes; bubbles turmoiled in its mouth. It would get me, consume me—*you are mine*, it whispered.

Whispered? It didn't whisper anything! I was hanging in the water staring like an idiot while a whirring machine charged me. I dashed to the right at the last second; the aqua-bot's left fin whacked my injured knee; I cried out. Water gurgled into my throat and burned.

The poison slowed my body right away. Diebol's pistol slipped from my hand and sunk into the depths ahead of me. I could just see above the water as I froze, see that we were halfway across the room. Halfway, the beast halfway into my mind as I sank …

The aqua-bot spun around to attack again.

Fingers curled around my wrist from above. I jerked back, startled—but Lem pulled back harder, yanking me out of the aqua-bot's path. She drew my hand to the rubber platform she was lying on: we dragged me up together, scraping the platform's edge across my chest.

I was up, I was safe, but she kept pulling me, yelling something —oh shyte, the aqua-bot! Its fins burst from its side to split into feet, fore-fins rolled into a cylinder to become a gun barrel—it clambered after me. *All* the bots rearranged their limbs like skeletons rising from the grave, morphing from aquatic beasts to humanoids, creeping towards us with poison dripping off their jaws. They had thirty guns, at least. We were surrounded. I raised my hands in surrender. This was execution time, and I couldn't control a single weapon.

Lem fired an arc of electricity into the water.

The room lit up like a thousand supernovas. Tangles of electricity leapt over every wet bot like a sea-monster's tendrils—each bot still had a limb in the water. They shuddered backwards like men shot in the spine. High-pitched radio feedback screamed through the room. The aqua-bots sank, shorted out.

I didn't get a second to appreciate Lem's rescue. The voice whispered again—*You are mine …* I jammed my palms over my ears. "No! No, I—"

Lem kicked my legs out from under me. A knife zipped over me as I fell.

"What are you doing?" she panted. Her eyes glowed red. I could see scales creeping across her face, the disease of the Crajk-beast—I scrambled to my knees away from her and dove towards the next platform. *Get away, get to the little stone door!*

Nothing, nothing in the room was green. I knew I wasn't thinking straight—I knew monster-Lem just saved my life twice, three times, maybe—but her *Contamination*, my mind, keep her away, keep it empty, keep it *mine*—

"Jei, what are you doing?!"

Why was I fighting him? I didn't know. Because it was mine. My emptiness—he couldn't have it. He didn't deserve it. He didn't save us. I decided. I decided he had to go.

I shook my head to focus—Lem was about three platforms behind me, about three-quarters across the room. I'd reached the platform nearest the small stone door now; I just needed to cross the mini-runway to the door, short out its lock, and escape.

Suddenly an icy claw ran up my spine, seizing the back of my neck and wrapping around my throat, spreading through my skin like cool oil. I gripped at the something, trying to tear it off—

"Jei, stop!" Lem screamed. "Holy sh—stop clawing at your throat! Stop that!"

The Crajk-beast did not get in. Something else did. A dark flood of gleaming oil rushed through the hallway of my mind, penetrating some back door I'd left open in my panic about Njande, pouring over the walls, seeping out into the cracks, running over me until I couldn't breathe. My spine wept; my fingers burned; suddenly I understood.

Nature abhors a vacuum.

LEM

"It's the ba-eater, holy shyte it's the ba-eater!" Lem was frantic. She'd fallen in the water. Twenty-five meters away Jei slammed himself against the exit platform with an unearthly cry. Flames engulfed the platform nearest Lem. She dove under it, eyes squeezed shut against the poison, trying to keep her body stream-lined underwater, to beeline *faster* towards Jei. The water heated above her, boiled under the platform—*dive down, further down*—but she needed to see, needed to breathe—*up, come up!*

The weapons' fire intensified, throwing up a wall of burning colors in her path. Lem was forced back under. *Throw off the turrets' aim—water diffracts light!*

Up for air. A cartridge bit her shoulder. Her arm, poison seeped into her arm … she was sinking …

She wasn't gonna make it. Jei was gonna kill himself. Everything was too fast and she was too slow.

"Njande, kill it!" she gasped. The goddess conversation flashed in her mind. "Or—or use me to do it!"

Open your eyes and see what I see! Njande cried back.

Lem was twelve meters from Jei.

She saw.

Njande broke through the colors, a form like a Crajk-beast pulsing around his limbs as he leapt at Jei. The wounded warrior fell; the Crajk-beast's scales glistened with black blood, blood that belonged to *that*, to a black hydromorph with sixteen spiked tentacles, the ba-eater tearing over Jei's face and spine.

The hydromorph's shimmering limbs strangled Jei; Jei clawed his own neck, drawing blood as his fingers faded through the tentacles like mist—Jei the mist, the beast the reality. Njande's teeth sank into the hydromorph's limbs, but the thing seeped and rolled around him like a swarm of bees. Jei kicked at them both, shoving a boot into his rescuer's stomach—and Njande took the blow, at once solid to Jei and solid to the hydromorph as the three of them folded through different phases of being like flickering lights in a fog.

"Jei, let Njande help you!" Lem panted, trying to scream over the thunder of the firing cartridges. Water licked her lips in an unwanted kiss. Her lungs inflamed with the scent; adrenaline hyped her muscles. Swim—gasp—swim—Jei struggled against Njande, one hand on his own throat through the tentacles and the other clutching the Crajk-beast's neck, choking his *friend*. But it wasn't his fault, he couldn't see! That thing, shyte, it could roll around both its attackers because it didn't *care* if they got hurt—Njande was playing gentle, like a surgeon, not tearing the spines out of Jei's neck, not ripping the creature to shreds through Jei's hands, and it was *so unfair*!

Fury bubbled within Lem, this time in a searing white heat that cleared her head, washed her neurons, highlighted every connection she'd ever formed with Njande—a fury as different from her former rage as a hero's sniper rifle differs from shot-gun spray in a crowd, and this new wrath opened her mouth and shone from her eyes and she cried out: *"Release him, Wurm, and return to your wretched home! He is not yours! He is ours!"*

The hydromorph shuddered backwards as Lem's words reverberated through Njande's body like searing light through a prism; Lem sputtered and renewed her strokes, devouring the last few meters between them.

The hydromorph tightened its hold. "Who are you?" It hissed. "How dare you challenge me?"

Njande reared his head and Lem cried out with him, their voices synced: "Insolent whelp, who are *you*? We are the Master of Paradox and his Warrior-Queen—what are *you*? A shadow, a slime —give me your name, slime!"

The hydromorph screeched in pain. Lem reached the platform— the platform still floated about an arm's length above the water's surface—and grabbed for Jei's wrist. She wanted to move his hand so Njande could get that tentacle off his neck—but cartridges pinged near her arm. She jolted back, hiding her body under the platform. Her shoulder-pain flared—she couldn't lift herself that far out of the water, onto that slick surface, not like this! *Just try!* She reached for Jei again …

"He doesn't want you meddling with his mind," the hydromorph hissed, raking its dry tongue over Jei's cheek. "And that makes him *mine*." He chuckled. "If it's not alive it's dead, right Njandejara?"

"I'll show you dead, freak," Lem said. But she couldn't reach Jei's wrist—she began to slip—a line of bullets threw water up by her face—

"Jei, please, let us help you," she gasped.

His fingers spasmed like claws.

JEI

I could choose. I had chosen.

But now, no I was being forced. *Why?* Why was it dark when light left? Why couldn't I have neither? *Mine, mine!* The oil in the hallways of my mind sloshed towards the ceiling, drowning out my identity; Njande's blue light began to die in the deluge.

Njande screamed to me from somewhere beyond the oil. *I own the cattle on a thousand hills. All that is mine is yours—you are heir with me in this promise! To him who overcomes I give the iron scepter, the new name: his own realm, his own identity. If you are mine and I am yours, then everything that is mine is yours. So make your mind mine so I can make it yours!*

That Paradox—that if I wanted to see I needed light, that if I wanted to breathe I needed air—that to be independent I had to depend on so many things—it was altogether natural but repulsive to the slime filling me and closing my airways. The ooze seemed to have been a part of me for all time. I shuddered; I heard myself shrieking back at Njande. *Mine, mine*, screams the child, clinging to a broken toy even as his father pries it from his fingers to repair it for him. *Mine, mine!*

Black drowned out the blue. I could not choose Njande even if I'd wanted.

"No, Jei! He's your friend! Let him help you!"

Green. Bloodseas, a flash of green. Where? Where was the green?

My eyes flickered back to the outside world, and I saw Lem's hand stretched towards mine. A strand of green light traced her wrist and wrapped around mine, binding us together.

Lem was green.

Lem was green!

I grabbed her hand.

CHAPTER THIRTY-FOUR

Lem

JEI'S FINGERS CLOSED AROUND LEM'S WRIST AS SHE SANK.

Yes! Lem climbed Jei's arm and struck towards the hydromorph with a snarl. Njande's scaled paw jammed down on Jei's forehead; Jei's airway opened and he gasped. Was it Njande's claws that ripped the spines from the boy's throat? Or was it that Jei's fingertips suddenly became solid? Jei's hands and Njande's claws blended across dimensions like pictures superimposed on each other; they loosed the hydromorph's grip.

Njande struck with his other paw juxtaposed in Lem's hand. Their conjoined light hurled the being into the shadow of the doorway. "Begone!"

The ba-eater faded into the darkness, its eyes glowing gray. "My name," it hissed as it dissolved, and Njande faded, and everything became one dimension again. "My name is Accuser. My slaves call me Flickerform, Brain-Child, and Muse. And you, Jerusha-Lem, will be hearing from me again soon."

Jei hacked, coughing; his hands wrapped around Lem's shoulders.

JEI

When I came to, gasping, still coughing from whatever had just happened to my throat, I saw Lem lying with her torso on the platform and her legs dangling into the water, one hand outstretched over me and one wrist in my grip. She looked uncomfortable, but neither of us moved. We'd made it to the platform across the room. We were less than a meter from the stone doorway. We'd made it alive.

The guns on the left wall swiveled towards Lem.

Twelve knives shot from the ceiling at us.

I threw an em-shove at the guns, swiveling them to destroy the mirroring guns on the right wall; I grabbed Lem's shoulders and yanked her out of the water, rolling her with me out of the path of the first eleven knives. I counted their thuds as they hit the platform behind us. Ten—eleven—in a moment I'd make it under the overhang of the doorway, where we'd be safe—

Not fast enough. One of us was about to be skewered.

I stopped mid-roll. I braced above her—a sharp sting shuddered into my right shoulder-blade just below the joint. Pain broke out along my upper back, but I stifled my groan with a grim smile, for Lem, below me, was safe.

She cried my name. For a moment a glow of heroism engulfed me—

"You crazy idiot!" She yelled, pushing me up and dragging me that last step into the shadow of the exit doorway, where nothing else could hit us. "You're our last shot at warning the base! Me, I can't freaking—fingers! Gah, why'd *you* get stabbed? Now what're we gonna do?"

This girl.

LEM

Lem didn't mean to scold. She wanted to cry out in thanks because *of course* she didn't want to die pinned to the platform like a wanted poster but the freakishness of the creatures she'd just seen and the warm glow that'd come back to Jei's pale face and the suddenness of his movement and the raging adrenaline in her body and the pain in her everything—

Holy shyte, he had a knife in his shoulder blade. Okay. Medics said you shouldn't take that out? Right.

"I'm sorry, I'm so sorry," she mumbled. Gah, she was cold. Jei leaned against the stone door, blood trickling down his back as he flicked his fingers across the glowing lock in its center. The diamond-shaped compuscreen offered him a space for a password.

"We just have to break this code," Jei said. "And we can escape through this door."

Control the bleeding, that's what they said, right? Lem snagged the nearest knife from the platform and ripped Jei's tunic to use as bandage.

"Whoa there, lady." A wry grin broke his pained grimace; his fingers kept dancing across the keypad, trying to get them through the door before the water rose again or the blitzers came back. "We're not *that* close yet, Lem, but I'm flattered—"

"You make one unprofessional comment and I will stab you," Lem grumbled. But there was a laugh under her grumble.

"I was only going to say, use your own shirt." He tapped something else into the door.

"Now I really should stab you."

"Someone beat you to it. Besides, I like my shirt."

"Uh-huh. My little sister has the same one." Lem kept bickering with him to keep the nausea at bay … her fingertips stiffened with the strange chill creeping over her. She wrapped the cloth through his underarm, up around the knife, and over his shoulder several times. What was under there? Lungs? He was breathing fine, so it hadn't hit a lung. So it'd stuck in his shoulder-blade, and he was gonna be okay?

"Lem, you're shot. Stop and do yourself. Lem? Hello?"

She couldn't really hear him. Her vision blurred. She wanted to pass out. She kept wrapping his injury, mechanically, biting her tongue as she leaned against the stupid door. Tongue was thick, stiff. Broken fingertips didn't hurt anymore. Her stomach did. Why couldn't she just faint? *Get me out of here.* All that effort, and they still had this door in the way. The high of the pure rage wore off, and she wasn't a Warrior-Queen goddess-thing anymore, just another tired teenager dying of two burnt cartridge wounds, dehydration, and a slow poison, leaning on a stupid door.

Nope, not leaning. Her support disappeared; Lem fell forward into the hallway. Oh, the door opened?

But Jei hadn't opened it. A silver robe fluttered around silver boots before her face.

"Kill me and let him go," she told the tiled floor. It was ridiculous. Bricandor would only kill them both. But Lem tried. "Please, he didn't want to leave, I had him hostage …"

"The password to the door," Bricandor said to Jei, "was Contagion."

JEI

Lem was being crazy again, but this time probably because of nausea. Sure, they'd pretty damn near killed her already, but I wasn't an idiot for keeping her alive. With her powers and that Njande-connection behind her I planned on literally betting my life she could make it across the hallway alive to warn the fort. I could see the open door to Diebol's chambers under Bricandor's arm.

I stepped between Bricandor and my training partner, slowly, waiting for him to strike me down, my eyes on his wrinkled smirk. Six Stygges flanked him on either side. I didn't ask myself if I could beat them—I never tried crazy things like that. I think around obstacles. And with my mind back I had a few fairly good thoughts.

"You were so close," Bricandor sighed as his Stygges raised the staff ends of their maces like javelins. They wouldn't try to shoot me, not now that I could manipulate standard weaponry again. They'd hurl their neodymium into me with their full electromagnetic power behind the thrusts. "So close."

"I'm still pretty close," I said. I knew my next move, my body knew it, but I kept it out of my head so Bricandor couldn't read it.

"No. You're pretty dead."

He flicked his fingers.

I channeled *everything* at Lem. Forget me, forget blocking the staffs; I em-pushed her along the floor, under their legs, across the hallway, into the other room.

I dropped to the ground. The first four maces whistled over my head. Then searing, crushing fire coursed through the back of my left thigh, right calf— two maces hit their mark. I cried out through clenched teeth, braced for the finishing blows—

There I am, Njande whispered in my agony.

What?

Whatever you do for my friends, you do for me. Here I Am.

Instinct took over. I lowered my head and waved my hand; the next two maces swerved to the side and slammed into the doorjamb. The Stygges swung—I thought nothing and dodged—and in that strange absolute calm my em-push threw them back. Maybe all Diebol's training worked. Maybe it worked *better* because they treated me like shyte. I'd learned, somehow, to channel pain into power.

But Bricandor put a stop to all that. He waved the Stygges away. "Enough of this. Go kill the girl."

"You against me, by yourself, old man? You're brave," I grinned, straining to sit up and lean against the wall as the trainees left. My smirk took more effort than I'd expected; my voice sounded so weak and breathy out loud.

Bricandor sneered back. Gray pinpricks marked the center of his blue eyes, and I saw a flicker of something familiar, something that shouldn't have been familiar, and the hair rose on the back of my neck as his shadow crept over me. A droplet of blood burst from the corner of his forehead, beading on his ashen skin. I sucked in my breath—

And it would not suck back out. I couldn't move. Not my lungs, not my chest, not my hands, nothing. My thoughts began to shut down as an emptiness spilled across my cerebral cortex down towards my deepest brain centers.

I ... think he just killed me with his mind.

LEM

Lem blinked, struggling to orient herself. Jei had thrown her across the hall, into this room, and with the single mirror, and the bathroom on the side, and, okay, some folded black clothes with too many pockets—it looked like Diebol's quarters from the map.

It was. There was a bed. Lem crawled for it. She could see Diebol's holo-pen lying at its foot, glowing over the blankets ... like it'd just been turned on.

She glanced around and saw no one. She reached for it.

"So that's it, then."

Lem started; the door flicked shut behind her.

Lem whirled on her knees. Diebol leaned back against the wall behind her, his left hand outstretched over the door he'd just closed, and his other hand resting behind his back. A grim coldness rested over his face, barren of smirks or levity or idealism. Just ashen pain. Lem paused, her hand hovering two centimeters above the pen.

She didn't ask how he'd survived. It made sense that the fall didn't kill him, somehow. He was Diebol. He planned for shyte. Maybe the abyss opened into a series of momentum tubes to catch him, with fans and shyte to slow him down, and then they resusci-

tated him from her blow or some other imaginary filking shyte—
who cared, though? Lem only wanted to know one thing.

"Is it a mind-game?" she asked. "When I grab the holo-pen, we
disappear or something?"

"No. I'm just going to kill you. After everything that's happened
—that's it." He drew a silver pistol—blitzer standard issue—from
behind his back. "That's it."

A shot rang out in the hallway.

JEI

There was no thought, only what I could observe. I was no barrier to
the outside world; its observations filled me, and I formed no
response, only open, only receiving.

A million other colors washed over the green in me, eliminating
that which made it green. This was homogeneity; this was death.

*"Life's not a video game: these levels aren't designed with a way
out."*

*"But that's when I make a way out. You know, bust a hole in the
wall."*

When they've stopped your heart you can't strategize to get it
going again. At that strange juncture between the vacuous science
of positive psychology, and the reality that sometimes you just die,
cleverness doesn't matter. Only fortitude wins the day. Only brute
force and will.

I pushed back on the wall with Lem's brute force.

Two more seconds. I lived two more seconds in my vegetative
state.

A blitzer came running down the hallway, screaming Bricandor's name. Bricandor's concentration broke enough for me to *feel*
myself suffocating. Bricandor hissed something at the blitzer—the
blitzer yelled back—Bricandor turned his head—

The blitzer shot him in the face.

Bricandor released me. Air rushed into my lungs and over-whelming pain crashed around my head and chest as my nervous system turned back on. *"Hey, I almost died!"* my pain sensors were screaming. *I know, I know, shut up.* I hacked and cried out, gripping my chest in agony. I squinted up at Bricandor—

He was still standing?

The flayer cartridge floated a millimeter from his eyes. The excruciating torment on his face out-paced mine as if I'd scraped my knee while he got flayed alive. Blood seeped from all the pores on his forehead.

The cartridge fell sizzling at his feet. Bricandor closed his eyes and his wrinkles relaxed as he fell backward. He hit the floor hard. But he hit the floor breathing.

He'd stopped the cartridge.

"Blast it all, the bloke can stop bullets," muttered the blitzer. "But he's out. Beans, he's out. Alright you, let's go."

Was the blitzer talking to me? He waved a hand at me like I *didn't* have two broken legs, like I was just lazy and needed to get the bloodseas up off my pansy ass, and then he yelled across the hallway into Diebol's room.

"Hallo in there, I'll execute the old timer here if you mates don't send Lem Benzaran out of that room alive. With all you freaks crowding the blasted door I can't see her, so I'll kindly ask you to step aside. You hear me?"

Diebol stepped out into the hallway with his hands raised and his face drained.

Wait, Diebol?

I clutched my palm over my temple, trying to calm the pulsing stab there as I leaned myself back up against the wall. Somehow I wasn't even surprised anymore.

CHAPTER THIRTY-FIVE

Diebol

WHEN THE GUNSHOT SOUNDED IN THE HALLWAY A PAINFUL DREAD dropped into Diebol's stomach, sinking through him like a weight into mud, for somehow he *knew*. His head snapped around to face the sound; he saw his teacher hit the floor. Revenge welled up in him—relief, a horrible, confused relief, smothered it before he could fire a vengeance shot. Bricandor lived! His teacher lived. Everything he'd told Diebol about death was true.

But even Bricandor could not stop another cartridge. Not unconscious. Not after the strain of life-bending.

Diebol stumbled out of the room in a fugue, a drunk man in a nightmare. The renegade blitzer was crouched with his back to Jei, weapon in the Stygge Father's mouth, finger taut on the trigger.

"Good. You're a smart lad, you are. Just in case the rest of you blokes aren't familiar with basic anatomy—" The renegade looked around. "You can't divert this gunfire to the side, with your bloody little magicks or what have you, because the gun is *in* his mouth. You try to swipe the gun to the side, well, you'll have to rip through his face."

Diebol's chest tightened. *No. No, clear your head. Let go of the attachment. Release the feeling. Only think!*

"No way out of this one, Mr. Powers. You try to swipe it backwards, swipe me backwards, you trip me, the gun goes off. See? Trigger's already pulled. It's a little trick, with revolver-type models. Cock the gun and pull the trigger at the same time, let the trigger go, hold back the hammer, see? I trip? I don't even have to pull the trigger. My finger falls off this little doo-hicky, lets go, well. He lets go, too."

Diebol's teeth clenched as his chest began to rise and fall in panic. He raised his fore and middle fingers, and flicked them forward twice. The Stygges obeyed, and carried Lem out into the hallway. She tossed the holo-pen to Jei.

And Diebol watched as his enemy scribbled his message on the wall and sealed his triumph with a sigh; and Diebol watched as some punk renegade dragged his father down the hall with a gun in his mouth; and Diebol opened the outside polymerwall so his Stygges could bear Lem, Warrior-Queen with her head held high, outside to her freedom …

No. He swallowed his panic with clenched teeth. Look, they couldn't bring Bricandor *with* them in their—they had a Maggot, apparently, sitting on the cliff in front of training center, a big worm-like blob ship blocking the view of the mountains beyond it.

Well. They wouldn't bring him with them, for when he awakened he would kill them all with his mind. So they'd have to kill the Teacher *now*. But they knew that if they did, they would die. So they had to put him down, here. Unless they were out for a Lem-like suicide mission to assassinate Bricandor. But Lem wasn't holding the gun. She was struggling not to faint as poison seeped through her veins.

It's just the game again. Just like every other time he'd beaten Jei on the board. They had Diebol's pieces surrounded, but Diebol had a move, right in the middle of them all, out of all the options available—one move to win.

The wind rustled Diebol's light leather vest. Diebol reached behind his back, into his belt for another gun as his Stygges loaded Lem and Jei into the Maggot. Three quick shots would take them all out the instant they released Bricandor. He had that kind of accuracy. This wasn't a problem. He whistled—his Stygges raised their maces, free hands up and open like scorpions' tails.

The renegade blitzer was last into the ship. The Maggot's side gaped wide open, rings drawn back. The blitzer still had his gun in Bricandor's mouth; Bricandor's body trailed on the ground. Diebol stepped forward. He could see, inside, as Lem crawled to the pilot's seat and started the ship. He still had a clear shot. He walked as the Maggot lifted inches off the ground. Diebol smiled. The blitzer had realized it by now: he was trapped.

The ship hovered at the cliff's edge; Diebol could *feel* the prickling in the air as his Stygges prepped their em-pull to bring the ship down the moment the rogue released Bricandor.

"Send them inside," said the blitzer.

"Why?" Diebol smiled.

"Because apparently you care about Mr. Senility here," the blitzer said.

"If I send them inside, you have no reason not to shoot him."

"I have one. I know you're holding a gun behind your back. I know how long it takes for this stupid door to close. I know you've got aim, everyone's heard about the Beryllian mines. I'm not daft, mate."

"I have no reason to send them inside. You won't shoot him with them out here."

"I won't give him back, either. We planning on spending all day here, then? Because my finger's rather small in this damn glove, and it's going to slip eventually, mate. Perhaps then you kill us all, I don't know, but I haven't got a choice now, do I? So he dies, we all die, no one's happy." The wind picked up, distorting the blitzer's metallic voice. "Or you could send your boys inside, I put old Fartsy down, and we part friendly-like. You can take your chances, or you can make his death certain. Your choice."

Dammit, Diebol didn't know this player. He assumed the rogue blitzer would put his own life above the win—that he wouldn't play a "we all die" move. But some of the younger Frelsi cadets, the idealistic rage-filled boys just itching to get their names etched on some mythical wall of dead heroes, they might …

"Who are you?" Diebol growled.

"Look, imbecile, quit stalling. I don't know if you noticed, but I'm wearing armor. That pistol you've got there? No armor-piercing rounds. That means if I shoot Mr. Eye-bags here, you kill the two Frelsi nutters, not me. I can afford those losses. It's just cash for me. I'm gambling low stakes here."

A mercenary? "You're a fool, then," Diebol said. "If he dies my Stygges can rip you limb from limb, even at this distance."

"You can say that, but since I've never seen a Stygge do that, I'm not inclined to believe you. Don't these metal rims on this here ship divert your electrics or some such? You can't reach inside it for me, now can you, mate?" The blitzer's head tilted to the side, cocky now. "We both know you want these two, not me. This little deal goes south, I've got plenty of time to cut out while you kill them."

Lem mumbled something angry Diebol couldn't catch.

The blitzer's arrogance disappeared. "Shyte," he snapped. "Shyte! Alright, look piddle-twit, I'm losing the boy in here, and if he dies that's a pay-cut for me, you savvy? I don't have time for your ninny-pinching! You make me lose this bounty, I take it out of Mr. Saggy's hide. I know a Wonderfrog who pays handsomely for Dictator corpses. You've got Ten! Nine! Eight—"

He was jumpy. The blitzer was shaking, nervous, each word shuddered through clenched teeth. If his finger slipped—shyte, reason didn't work on unstable gunmen! Diebol's heart-beat rose again, insistent, begging in repeated rhythm: *He's going to die! He's going to die!* "Okay, calm down now, calm down. Let's work this out—"

"Six! Five!" The blitzer was screaming the words. Shyte! No panic, calm down! "Four! Three!"

Ah! "Okay, okay!" Diebol held up his fist, trotting backwards to unlock the polymerwall as the Stygges took the hint to stand down. "Look, I'm sending them inside. Calm down!"

The Stygges retreated into the tower. It slurped shut behind them.

The countdown stopped. Diebol raised his pistol. Shyte, thank goodness. This ended now. They could disarm his Stygges, but they still had to contend with him. *Put him down so I can shoot you now.*

The blitzer laughed. *What?*

And the blitzer threw Bricandor off the cliff.

The blitzer's released gunshot slammed into Diebol's arm at the same time, terrible aim, but Diebol didn't care, he didn't give a shyte, because in this eternal moment he could either spend Bricandor's last breaths killing his enemies or he could channel every electron in his being to rescue his leader, his guide-star, and dammit he chose, he dove to the cliff's edge as the Maggot took off, he reached down towards the falling father and begged Jei and Lem to just die of their poisoned wounds on their own because here, now, this one person was worth the whole universe to him—

And he would not let him go.

CHAPTER THIRTY-SIX

Lark

LARK WAS ALONE.

Lark was alone, because as soon as she leapt into the pilot's seat, shoved Benzaran to the side, threw her weight forward against the panel of green buttons, and slammed back into the moldy chair as the force of the Maggot's take-off plastered her there—everyone else passed out. She ripped the blitzer helmet off her head with one hand—bloody hard to see in that big thing—and whooped, laughing at her success as she glanced back at the two lads behind her seat.

The Biouk, Lark had strapped in to the med-pod. The pod's tentacles glowed in his mouth and wrapped around his chest, artificially forcing his heart to beat, breathing him like an iron lung. She had no idea if his brain had died or not.

The human, Cadet Commander Bereens, had strapped himself to the floor before passing out. He looked like Death at a wedding. His face was turning blue, but not like the purplish pale people turn when you choke them: a deep navy grew like vines up his neck, bulging under his skin.

Lark reached over with one hand to fasten Benzaran's seatbelt. The girl's head lolled back against the seat; her lips fluttered, she murmured something. Her skin was blue-ing, too.

Er, yes, so this was not the best possible outcome. But! So far none of the Maggots parked at the foot of the cliff had risen to give chase. Lark was getting good distance between her bluebirds and their cage. And damn, she'd out-foxed a Growen Admiral today! With a shaky gun-man routine! Time to update those business-cards, perhaps?

"Just stay alive 'til we get to the hospital, mates," Lark grinned. "See? City's right there on the map, just outside the park. Did you know you were hidden in Revelon's tenth world wonder? Any moment now, we'll come up to a sign, 'Thank you for visiting Drachmore State Park, Come Again Soon.' Though I won't bet on you coming back now, eh?"

The engines grunted with dull disinterest; the passengers' breathing slowed and thickened like the air, viscous with disapproval—the Grey Ghost had tripled, somehow, solidified, with the arrival of the bluebirds. Lark slumped her shoulders.

"Hmph," she huffed. "You lot are no fun."

Come now, you'd think *Emergency Room* would mean everyone here had *emergencies*. What was that, a Bont lizard who'd stubbed his claw? Oh, he was "bleeding profusely"? Hemophilia? That couldn't possibly be a real medical condition. *Suck it up and wait your turn, piddle-twit.*

Thank goodness the Revelonians got it, sort of. Four nurses had already started assessing Lark's cargo away on little floating beds while Lark hopped impatiently from one foot to the other by the Emergency Room door. Damn, the Revelonians were tall. Twice Lark's height and half her girth, jagged cheeks and skin shaved of straw-like fur to expose the crusted surface beneath. They looked like tan rock-people—instead of keratin their skin excreted a strange hard mineral layer, tougher than scales, and with their gangly build Lark could imagine someone creating them by snapping them off the uneven tops of the mountain-spires.

The Emergency Room front desk—a long, thin, square glass

box—floated over to Lark. The Revelonian clerk adjusted the camera mounted on the glass. "You brought in the three—car accidents, you said?" she asked.

"D-dunno about car accidents," Lark stuttered, slowing her normal lizard voice to give off the impression of stupidity. "I found them in Drachmore Park, in that ship I parked outside? Looks like some kind of defunct model Leech … ?"

"Are you Growen, ma'am? You are aware that this is an Undecided Zone, and no extraterrestrial military vehicles have permits to land here?"

"Growen?" Lark put her claws to her face in mock shock. "Gee golly, no, I'm just a tourist. Came on an interstellar bus to tour the park, got lost from my group, found these blokes in that ship … just in time, too!"

The Revelonian stared at her for a second, giant wet eyes glittering annoyance. Or maybe tiredness. Long night, perhaps?

"Are they going to be okay?" Lark asked, feminizing her voice as much as possible. People sympathized with femininity.

The Revelonian shook herself off with a sigh, shuffled some papers in front of her, and tapped a button on the back of the mounted camera. A red recording light lit the side, and words appeared backwards on the glass as the Revelonian spoke again: "Patients' names?"

"Eh, Juliet and Jordan Kim," Lark said. When she spoke, words appeared on the wall, but she couldn't read them. "Is what they told me …" She cocked her head to try to—read it—

"It's in hospital code to protect your confidentiality," said the Revelonian. "Go on?"

"They told me before passing out, I mean. Really seem to love each other." Buy sympathy. "The furry—"

The clerk's giant eyes narrowed. Er, yes, they were a bit more politically correct around here. "The *Biouk*'s their adopted brother, they said. Part of a vegetarian commune." That explained their nutty strangeness, right? "You have to put them in the same hospital room, they're blood-bound from birth, that's their religion." Make them easier to guard. "I don't have their insurance information, but when they wake up I'll make sure they'll provide it. I'll even chip in if they can't afford it." She intended, of course, to do no such thing. Doctors were like vultures, except worse because they fed off you while you still lived.

"That's all I know," Lark finished. "I'll just wait outside their room?"

"Absolutely, head right on over. I'm sure they'll be glad to see you when they wake up."

Lark didn't plan on being around when they woke up.

The windless sky above the hospital roof chilled Lark's skin, covering her in goosebumps. Reminded her she was a mammal. She didn't mind, though. Bloody welcome relief after dry Forge, and steamy Luna-Guctala, and that stuffy Maggot.

Lark held her compupad outstretched at arm's length, gazing for a moment at her reflection in the screen. Her lizard-faced silhouette against the starlight, leather jacket and all—she matched what she wanted to be. She'd done well.

Lark swiped the compupad screen and drew her hand up to project the holographic map of the hospital bedroom where her cargo slept. She'd dropped a video camera in the room on her way out to the roof—perhaps once she got paid she could ditch this clunky camera-set-up and install surveillance gear in her helmet like the Ebon Shadow's.

A brief wind fluttered around her, just a breath, and Lark sighed. She set the compupad down on the hospital roof beside her, trying to keep that smile. This was it. She checked and double-checked the ammunition in the chamber of Veradan's flayer rifle. Just guard the three musketeers 'til the Frelsi picked them up. They'd been down there with doctors buzzing around them for about three hours, and beans, would Rana return her call already? He'd missed several payments on her daily work expenses.

Eh, who was she fooling? She didn't even want the drachmas anymore. Well she did, but more than that she wanted to find out what happened to Benzaran's sister. Her knee jiggled; she chewed her lip. Surely the child was on Revelon. Perhaps Lark could find some computer technician to extract the tracking data from her broken wristband ... ?

Lark's compupad beeped.

Lark yanked it out of her jacket. Captain Rana! Blast it all, she almost *wanted* to hear him repeat everything a hundred times now —and when she swiped the screen to answer—it was merely a text.

"Your services will not be required by the Frelsi anymore."

What?! Lark pummeled the voice button like twelve times. He didn't pick up. *Fine, text, whatever.* Perhaps he was too embarrassed to talk after she'd insulted him for his repetitions. "I've acquired both targets!" Lark replied.

"Our intel indicates otherwise."

"Then your intel is false! I've got them both here with me: Santa Lucia Hospital in Telemore City, Revelon 15. Even throw in the furry free of charge!"

"I've received no ping of my Frelsi IDs or names checked in there."

Lark sucked in her breath. "Well, I gave them different names, for security," she texted. Beans, if a Frelsi person checked in to a civilian hospital it pinged their commanding officer? Damn totalitarians. She imagined they justified it with a "need" to know who to reimburse for healthcare. *Sheep will be sheep ...*

A large file download appeared in the transmission window.

"What is this?" she texted back.

"What happened to Bereens and Benzaran."

Wait, what wonkiness was this? She tapped to open the file.

And jumped almost off the roof as a guttural scream blew out the compupad's speakers. Video played. Blue and green lights flickered on the floor of a long glass room, and from the shadows charged a Banshee, teeth flashing, eyes glittering with a contagious horror as electricity sparked around her arms and shoulders and she flung herself at—

Lark shrunk back as if the thing might break out of the screen and eat her soul. Beans, that was Benzaran, attacking Bereens. Shots rang off-screen. The video feed cut off. Another file auto-opened on the screen.

Lark's stomach turned. She'd seen the burnt injuries, in real life, on Bereens's knees, femur, and lower-leg—probably from a neodymium mace—but the close-ups? She tilted her head in morbid fascination. A bit of bone protruding from that one, there. The next photograph showed blanched skin, claw marks on his neck, a knife in his shoulder-blade—and then his medical records attributed his death to asphyxiation and loss of blood. "Death?" Lark laughed aloud. "You're putting me on."

We somewhat regret the loss of this talented patient, said the note in the Growen medical records. *But we celebrate Benzaran's graduation as a Stygge candidate, after rescuing Captain Diebol from Bereens's assassination attempt and taking the patient's life when necessary. These people can be cured.*

So ends my notes on patient 339.

"Of all the nutty sick jokes," Lark gasped. The compupad told her the video and photographs came, unedited, from a Growen security cam, model some-number-Lark-didn't-care-about. The injuries did happen. The attack did happen. But she had Bereens alive!

"This is fake," she texted back. "Where did you get these?"

"Growen security breach opened up on several Revelonian-owned servers about four hours ago, giving our data-miners momentary access. The rest of the medical record includes a full typography of Bereens's genetic code, matching the code on file at his home base. These are real records."

Four hours ago? That was when Bereens sent that message from the Growen Commander's holo-pen! How had—so—? Lark's jaw dropped as Rana's messages kept coming. "I'm sorry I cannot give you more information on our decision. I have already told you more than I normally would, simply because meeting you, when you brought in the Frland boy, led me to believe perhaps you're someone who can be *reached*. Made to regret. I'm sorry."

Lark's stomach began to crawl up her throat in panic. Seriously, with the condescension, croaker? "At the very least," she texted. "You know Bereens was alive when he sent the emergency transmission to you, four hours ago. I was there when he did. I wouldn't know about that transmission otherwise, would I?"

"We did receive a vague warning, apparently sent minutes before his death. It was blasted out on multiple frequencies; almost anyone with a text radio could have picked it up."

"Look, I can send you a video right now of both targets, alive. Those records are fake."

"Fake like your employment history?"

Lark froze. "What the bloody hell do you mean?"

"We recently acquired this." Another file.

It was the list of bounty hunters sent out to assassinate key Frelsi figures, with the names of their targets beside them. Lark sucked in her breath—her name was on the list, yes, but—"I turned that job down, sir!"

"Maybe so." The lack of repetition was eerie now, in text. "But you also hid the truth from us. If we had had this list, we would have had evidence to accuse the Growen of violating the Spaces Treaties before the entire committee of Undecided planets, drastically changing the balance of the war. Now they've had time to clean up bank accounts and erase connections, so it looks like something we fabricated after the fact."

The text continued faster, a rant rage-scrolling across the screen. "More importantly, if we had known about this list when you knew about it, we could have protected and moved the people on it. Thirty lives would have been saved—to include, by the way, Lem Benzaran's *nine-year-old sister*. You let us fly in the dark while the Growen sent assassins after our *children*."

The last sentence thudded into Lark's chest, sharp against her sternum; the compupad slipped from her fingers.

She cursed; her hands stumbled over each other to catch it—she batted it in midair—

The compupad sailed back behind her onto the roof to land with a nasty crack.

She scrambled after it, picked it up undamaged, cursed it out anyway—her delay in response was as good an admission of guilt as any. She struggled for something to say, something better than *how the bloodseas did you know—*

"What would make you say that?" Blast, that was weak. They knew! They knew she'd lied to them, and now they didn't trust her when it counted!

"We're done here," Rana wrote. He seemed so different in writing, without his repetitions, so somber and dark, with nothing for Lark to mock. "We mourn the loss of our friends, and the Growen have already accepted paperwork from us requesting the return of Bereens's remains. I do not have the fortitude or time to appeal to your conscience, but at least I can appeal to your intelligence. I'm unsure how long you planned to continue milking the allowance we've been sending for your work expenses, but I'm sure you understand the charade had to stop sometime.

"It was my fault we hired you, and I take full responsibility for that. Our background check looked good at first. But I misread you: you were never merely a liar. You were always entirely a lie."

Lark slammed off a bitter response, struggling for some grain of truth, some proof of the moment, but the frequency returned with *you no longer have access to this channel.*

"No! No, open up!" Lark screamed at the screen. "You really think I'd be satisfied with putting you on to collect that piddling daily allowance? I don't risk my tail to earn pocket-change! I'm just a bit above stealing lunch money from grieving parents!"

You were always entirely a lie. Lark sucked in her breath, ducking her compupad back into her leather jacket. This had never happened before. She always wove them so well—she knew all the tricks. That was why she'd only falsified *half* her employment record. Everyone knows a lie sells better with a core of truth.

Damn, Commander Diebol was good. Mental note: when your enemy opens a security breach by sending messages from your holo-pen, take the opportunity to discredit him by altering his medical files so everyone thinks he's dead, or evil. *Bloody fantastic.* The trick bought the Growen time to hunt the escapees without Frelsi interference: three bodies languishing unconscious in a hospital couldn't run *or* defend their good names.

Speaking of wrapping a core of truth in a lie—that video, and that girl? Nutty. Freakish. Terrifying. *Something* went down in that center, and Lark didn't plan on leaving her back open to *that* lassie any time *ever*.

Lark tried to chuckle at the wry thought, but something thick and heavy drowned her heart and filled her up, choking its way past her throat, heating her face as it rose into her eyes until—no, were these tears? What was that? Lark took off her helmet and set it down beside her. Wipe that off. Next step, right?

Next step, though? Leave the three musketeers to get picked off by the next Growen agent to waltz in with a nurse's costume? Wait weeks or maybe even months for them to wake up to call the Frelsi and explain all this? But what about that little girl? What could Bricandor possibly want with a little girl like that? How long did she have?

Lark was in this to rescue kids. That was what she did. When you told a story to a kid, they understood it was a story, not a lie, and they loved you for it. They didn't disbelieve you, cut you out of a job, or leave you with dying people to—

One life versus three? Was that the calculation here? What if no one came to kill them—what if the Growen assumed the poison would do the trick? What if it did? Lark clutched her forehead in her claws. What if she waited here guarding these people, and because of that the girl died, and then they died, too, because of the poison? What if she came up Oh for Four?

And now Lark knew it truly, truly was her fault, even more than she'd thought.

Shyte, what was happening to that little girl?

CHAPTER THIRTY-SEVEN

Carl

A WEEK IS A LONG TIME.

Sandwiches go bad in that time, friendships can form in that time, and persistent anaerobic mold can get into your spaceship engine during that time. All bad things.

But Carl refused to deliver the little girl until he could get Bricandor on the phone, and apparently the man had gone into a coma. The sniveling spaniels he *could* get a hold of did their best to hide that fact, but he wasn't stupid.

Actually, he was stupid. Here he was on his hands and knees, struggling to rewire the compuscreen behind his seat so the little girl could play computer games while his ship drifted, destination-less and not earning money. What the actual hell.

Carl threw the screwdriver on the floor and cursed.

"Is it too hard for you?" asked Juju Benzaran.

He didn't look at her. He sat on his ass with his forearms draping over his knees and wondered how much a psychiatrist would cost. The compupanel he'd removed lay by her feet, reflecting her quizzical face as she tilted her head and folded her hands politely. Around her that presence hung as heavy as old lady perfume.

"Can I help?" she asked.

He grunted. It was kind of a laugh-grunt.

"Maybe it would be easier if you took your helmet off?"

"No," Carl grunted.

"Do you sleep in that helmet?"

He looked up at her. Why did she ask? Training, maybe, along with a photographic memory for a genius child the Frelsi could use as a spy. Perhaps she was an android. Maybe the whole job was a set up so his enemies could uncover his identity, using her. The Frelsi and the Growen working together, to find out who he was.

Delusional grandiose paranoia. Carl shook the psychosis out of his head and gripped the screwdriver, ignoring his eternal back pain to push himself forward on his hands and knees again. Procedural work, wires, colors, organization—he could hide from the fog-presence here. Hide from the crazy. Just a stupid kid asking stupid questions.

Or an android trying to out him.

"Are you really, really ugly?" she asked. "Is that why you hide your face?"

Carl shrugged. He actually didn't know if he was ugly or not. Didn't really care.

"Or maybe it's like when the mountain-man met Njande? Do you glow?"

"Mountain-man?"

"He had a really big family, like mine! And he rescued them from an evil king who made them work really hard, and he did it with Njande."

"And he glowed?"

"No, see, at first he didn't know Njande very well. He saw him in fire, or heard him when he was alone on the mountains. That's why I call him the mountain man. But on one mountain, after many sad things happened to his family, he asked to see Njande, and Njande said yes!" The little girl giggled.

"That's funny?"

"Because Njande only let him see his backside! Like his butt."

Carl *hmf*ed. He was familiar, of course, with the outlandishness of interdimensional mythology in general, but this story was just odd.

"Do you wanna know why he couldn't see the rest of Njande?"

Not really. Carl ripped out the audio-visual cable.

Well. Yes, actually. "Why?"

"Because Njande's like space. You can't just go into space without protection and stuff, you just like die!" She widened her eyes and wagged her finger, as if Carl possibly didn't know about space. "Njande's made of stuff like anti-matters, like how if anti-matters touches you it blows all up, you know? Even after only seeing a *bit* of Njande, the mountain-man's skin was spitting out radiation stuff! And his family were scared, so they made him wear a mask to hide his glowingness." She fidgeted on her heels, twisting her ankles here and there to spin her little white skirt. "I guess that's not you, though. You would know the story if you *were* glowy."

"But maybe I am," Carl sneered. "Maybe I spoke to a different interdimensional, so I don't know yours."

"Mmm, no, then you'd be crazy right now," she said. "Njande's friends woulda told you about him, and his enemies eat your brain." She took a step back, and crossed her arms across her flat chest. "You are evil. And Njande is going to kill you. But—" She squinted at him. "You don't have a ba-eater."

Carl rocked back on his heels, his fist on his utility belt. He opened his mouth to ask a question, and then realized he didn't want to ask anything—he wanted to argue with her, and why would he want to argue with a nine-year-old? No one was going to kill him, he wanted to say, and no one was driving him crazy. This, too, was paranoia—the fear of insanity itself, a kind of insanity.

Carl clicked the panel back in place and handed her the video game controller.

Ten days circling Revelon now. Carl compromised and took a call with Captain Diebol.

"I don't know what he wants with her anymore, or if he even wants her at all at this point. I know I don't," the Captain said. "Honestly, I'd recommend you drop her out your airlock and cut your losses—don't bother wasting a bullet—but Bricandor will call you tomorrow, I hope."

Carl cut the call and leaned back in his leather chair, crossing his hands over his stomach. Diebol really made more sense than anyone. Didn't divulge unnecessary information—still kept that coma-thing under wraps—but didn't give you the run-around either. Didn't try to lord it over you. Didn't take his boss's job. Considerate sense of economy, too: Carl couldn't believe he hadn't thought of the airlock himself.

"Mr. Hell-Spawn?"

Carl swiveled in his chair. The little wisp-girl smiled and stretched her hands towards him. One hand, palm-up, held a sandwich: two slices of bread with red goo between them.

For a moment he thought she'd broken free from her stasis field. He glanced down at her ankles and knees—nope, field still yellow, still functional. Back up at her face—wan, glistening with sweat. Hm. She'd put a lot of effort into getting into the galley and back.

"What's that?" he asked.

"It's a sandwich!"

"Is that my dehydrated lechichi?"

"Yeah but I put water innit to make jam."

"I was saving that."

"Oh."

She tilted her head to the side. She was a tiny mist-wraith, something from a fairytale, something from the quiet part of his nightmares, he thought. Maybe he'd invented her: blonde hair against dark skin was a rare mutation. Against the onyx background of his ship her short white skirt and scuffed ivory pants almost seemed to glow. Like the mountain-man.

"You never eat anything," she said.

"I keep nutri-tubes in my suit."

"But those are gross, and you have this yummy stuff."

"I was saving that."

"For what?"

He didn't know. He was just saving it.

Besides, eating was a waste of time. Much more efficient to start the IV drip in his suit: vitamins, protein, sugars, steroids, adrenaline-shots if need be, all there.

"Do you want this sandwich or not?" she asked. Her arm trembled with exertion just holding it up: that stasis field worked, anyway.

"Do your parents call all their enemies Hell-Spawn?" Carl asked.

"No. Just my dad, when he's mad. But he also calls my sister that."

"Why?"

"When she does something silly. It's for silly people, and bad people. Like you." Her eyes glittered like a wolf's. "If you don't tell me your name, you're gonna be Mr. Hell-Spawn forever."

"Whatever will I do."

"Maybe eat this sandwich?"

If she'd gone through that much trouble, it had to be poisoned. He took it from her with a half-formed smirk and tapped the inside wrist of his glove. The toxi-chemsensors in his palm charged up and sent their read-out to his helmet.

Negative. Not poisoned. Strange. A ruse to get him to remove his mask, then?

He set the sandwich on his dashboard. "Thank you. Now go play," he said.

"If you aren't gonna eat it, give me half," she pouted.

He gave her half.

"Also, it's boring playing against the computer," she said. "You come play with me!"

He wanted to say no, but he didn't have anything else to do. He'd spent most of last week tinkering with his engine, but it didn't need any improvements, and doing the same thing over and over reeked of craziness. He couldn't start researching a new case because of his policy—focus on one thing at a time—and suddenly changing policies in the face of stress also seemed crazy. So if he said no to the girl, he would only sit here for the next twenty-four hours like somebody's neglected wife waiting for a phone call. Stir-crazy.

Carl picked up the second video game controller.

Carl's eyes fluttered open like he'd shocked himself with norepinephrine. It wasn't a nightmare this time. Something real was wrong.

He turned his chair around, slowly, his hands poised on the twin flayer-guns at his hips. He rose in the darkness of his ship, his eyes flitting from the read-out inside his mask to the shadows around him. He watched under the table, in the corner by the video-game compuwall, his reflection in the hallway, the graph tracing the little girl's heartbeat on his right lens …

Her heartbeat was elevated.

He'd locked the polymerwalls so she couldn't leave the cockpit except to go into the galley. She wasn't in here, so he tapped the pattern on the side of his helmet to load the kitchen camera.

She was curled in the corner crying.

Her sounds ached at his core like he'd eaten rotten smung-worms. *Stop it.* How could he make her stop that? Dump her out the airlock? Not now, not with that call in a few hours. Also—that sounded horrible. Even returning her home for ransom would be more lucrative than that.

Maybe just inject her with sleeping serum? He had some hallu-cinogenics, too. Knock her right out.

That still sounds horrible. What is wrong with you?

What, indeed. These were just his normal thoughts. Why'd they exude *stench* now? What mental disease made everything about him feel so wrong?

The shadows in the corners wrinkled with presence, presence that threatened him, that heard his thoughts—and *despised* them.

Njande's going to kill you.

Carl listened to the little girl cry herself to sleep while he swiveled back and forth in his chair turning the video game controller over in his hands. He couldn't rest.

Right—left—X-button—no! Carl's space frog plopped into the candy abyss, and the compuwall lit up with ridiculous singing pink stars. *Game Over!*

"Ha! I win again!" Juju threw her hands in the air and danced, pointing her fingers everywhere like a performer at a laser show. Carl laughed out loud.

"You better not laugh, I'm gonna kick your butt again!" she said in a tone clearly learned from someone else.

"You'll win whether I laugh or not," he said.

She sat back down on the floor. Her lower lip dropped in a gentle frown. "Aw, I'm sorry, I didn't mean to make fun of you for losing. I'll win quieter next time." She paused. "Uh, I mean, maybe you can win one." Her little hand patted his shoulder. "Yeah, maybe you can. You just hafta practice. A lot. A lot, but I mean, you can do it. Probably!"

"Do you really think I care about winning this game?"

She didn't take her hand off his shoulder. "Don't be silly, Mr. Hell-Spawn. Why would you play if you didn't want to win?"

"You told me to."

"But I'm not the boss of you."

This was true. He chuckled. Her words made him feel more sane, and healthy. Crazy, though: she'd *caused* his temporary psychosis, and now here he was thankful for her giggles. Wasn't that called something? Stockholm Syndrome? Oh well.

The psychiatrist can fix it later, he thought as he stood up, one hand on his aching lower back as he made for the kitchen. Maybe it wasn't worth worrying or thinking too much right now. She kept things simple, and maybe he should, too. One thing at a time. Right now: sandwiches.

"I thought you were saving that!"

"I think I was saving it for today," Carl said.

She clapped her hands in excitement as he handed her the bread and jam. Carl opened the bottom panel of his mask to eat with her, grinning at the dainty way she picked crumbs off her white dress. "Hm, you know Mr. Hell-Spawn, it's funny, but I guess you shared a sandwich with Njande?" she said presently. Or asked.

"What?"

"Anything you do to someone who is friends with Njande, you do to Njande," Juju explained. "I've never talked to Njande, but they say he's friends with me, I guess."

Carl grunted. If that was the case, he sure was letting Njande win a lot of video games.

Carl hated Bricandor for waking up from his coma, and he hated Bricandor for calling on time, and he hated Bricandor for surviving past infancy. The only thing he didn't hate: Bricandor, like Carl, would take no less than delivery in person, even though now it meant they'd have to meet up on a freighter near Luna-Guetala, on route via vector 33956.

Carl drugged the kid to sleep and dropped her off without a word within the hour. Nothing else to report. He did his job. Minded his business. Collected his fee.

Escaped that damned presence at last.

CHAPTER THIRTY-EIGHT

Jei

I DIDN'T MAKE IT AWAKE PAST THE DOOR OF THE MAGGOT. THE blitzer rescuing us turned into a lizard, and then in my delirium and pain my nervous system shut back down, as if Bricandor hadn't quite let me go.

A purgatory writhed around me for some time. You always hope those drugs will put you out, but they never sent me into the black, only into some strange real/not-real painless dreamworld, punctuated by needles and agonized awakenings, bones in suspension and med-bot beeps and charts. I re-lived the reeducation center over and over in frenetic medical nightmares. The anesthetics forced me into strange recesses of my mind, and I found myself wandering out of it into the radio channel I kept with Diebol.

Usually, I would enter our mind channel through my own white hallway that ended in a dark void, and in the center of that void, I would find the cage where Diebol and I had shared captivity together, with sticks, and our carved game-board, on the floor. On the other side of the cage lay Diebol's void, and then his white hallway, leading to the door to his mind.

Now, as I came to Diebol's side of the cage, stepping over the twigs scattered across our small playing field, I found his cage-door was open. I didn't step through it—I knew I couldn't, because I'd tried before—but I gazed down Diebol's hallway to hear Bricandor screaming in a deep, unearthly voice:

"You thought you would rescue me? Arrogant fool, I rescue only myself! I am supreme, you were to guard the offensive! To kill the prisoners! You were attached to me, weren't you? Do you think I am attached to you in some way? I am *not*. And now—" A leaning in, a scent of rancid saliva. "—Now I will purge your attachments until there is *nothing* left."

A room number. 256. A blood-smeared door handle. Diebol entered, and his screams slipped from the darkness under the door with the smell of burning flesh.

When I finally awoke, I still was not awake. I was inside our radio-channel, in the hallway leading up to the wooden cage in my past, and the door to the rest of my mind was locked. For some reason I didn't care. Morphine was the reason, maybe … before me lay everything else as always: my white hallway leading to a black void, a cage in the middle of that void, and on the other side of the cage, Diebol's white hallway.

But something had changed. Pain echoed through that ancient chamber, dripping like blood mixed with mud over the distant cage. The lights in here flickered like a scene from a bad horror tale. Blood squicked under my boots as I drew closer to the cage; the acrid iron scent choked me into shallow breaths. I opened my cage door; sticks on the game-board caught fire as I crept towards Diebol's side of the cage.

Hm.

I'd never tried to steal information from him this way before. Sometimes when you're on a radio call you can hear background noises and other voices, things that maybe the person on the call with you doesn't want you to hear. Sometimes people leave radios on when they should turn them off. Perhaps our connection worked like that; perhaps I could overhear some background noise from his head, even though the walls separating the cage from his mind kept me from actually walking into his thoughts.

I had nothing else to do—I couldn't get out into the rest of my head, and anyway for some reason I had to know if Bricandor had really tortured him. I had to hear this. Did I want to gloat? Did I want to help him? No idea. I wanted to listen in on someone's real world, since I couldn't access mine, and now I was awake enough to handle it. Or more awake than I was when I first heard him screaming from Room 256.

I reached the cage door. My palms pressed rough wood as I leaned against it, peering down Diebol's hallway. At the end of his hallway, the bloody room 256 door had been replaced with a clean polymerwall. The blood on the hallway floor left a clean, semicircular swath, perfectly symmetrical, at the wall's foot.

I tried the iron latch on the cage door.

The door swung out with a long, loud creak.

I took a deep breath and wrapped the color green around me like an invisibility cloak, leaving the cage open behind me to cross over about a foot of darkness into Diebol's well-lit hallway. The clean, bloodless semi-circle on the floor seemed to spread towards me.

Oozing cracks criss-crossed his walls. My brow furrowed. What happened in here? We'd only used the channel twice in the interrogation center, and then we kept to our own sides, so *I* hadn't caused this damage. I half-expected to find Lem's name graffiti'd somewhere, or maybe her fist in the wall, but the cracks seemed to come from the other side, from inside Diebol's mind. Brain damage? Did almost losing Bricandor shake him up that much? Or did Bricandor *do* ...?

I crouched by the polymerwall, staying outside that suspicious clean semi-circle, and closed my eyes to listen.

Weapons firing, children crying, hushed voices in conference— my own voice, Lem screaming in Biouk, Bricandor laughing, hard officers' shoes clicking across metal floors—echoes of Diebol's thoughts filtered towards me. No words, though. Only a mess of subconsciousness. I glanced at the chronometer on my wristband, wondering how long I'd wait here.

My chronometer read 3:39, no AM and no PM, and not the normal military time it usually displayed. Huh. Was that a number important to me, or important to him?

I counted the cracks in the walls while I waited. Details, I needed to watch for details—little patterns his subconscious wove into the hall. 3:39, and fifty-six cracks.

Presently I got bored of hearing nothing, and returned, through the cage, to my own hallway. I don't know if I spent seconds or days there.

Presently, bored with that, I came back through my hallway, back to the void, back to the cage …

This time, on the way into Diebol's hallway, the lock on his cage-door stuck. *Bloodseas, did I miss my one chance?*

I shook the lock. The wood creaked.

What if I—

This was kind of messed-up, but maybe he deserved it.

I side-kicked one of the wooden bars out. It splintered, and I stepped through.

Funny, I'd never thought of that before. As a little boy I could never budge it, and once you get used to failing at something over and over you forget to keep trying.

I shivered in the light. The numbers on my wristband hadn't changed. But the clean semicircle had spread half-way down the hall. I stood at its edge, staring down at my toes. I didn't know what any of this was. I didn't even know how this worked, this radio, beyond a rudimentary understanding of cortical voltages. What would happen if I—

The clean semi-circle seeped under my feet, and I saw my reflection for a moment peering wide-eyed and nervous back at me before the floor became translucent and white without reflection. I shuddered. I hated my own reflection now, after that mind-room, and it had nothing to do with my self. I liked my self just fine. Just didn't want to see him all over the damn place.

I leaned close to Diebol's polymerwall, my heart pounding after the sudden hallway change. I didn't know what freaked me out about spying on him this way. It just wasn't something I did. This wasn't my head, my side of the field. That this could be done—

I could hear him talking in there now. Listening to debriefs, his boots up on the table and his arms crossed as he chewed on a tooth-pick with his eyes open and his eyebrows lowered. I don't know how I could *hear* his expressions, his stances, but I could. He was bored to death. He wanted out of this. He wanted to do it already, destroy us already, with this burning ache inside him like a lion's hunger. He snapped at someone. *Bricandor* reprimanded him. He growled back and settled further into his chair.

Holy shyte this was weird. I didn't like this at all. I didn't like my brain-signals anywhere near Bricandor—

"He's found the vector," Bricandor said. *I have?*

"I was unaware you could read minds at such a distance, father," Diebol muttered.

"Are you questioning me?"

"No. Simply ... stating a fact."

"You. You, I sense it on you, you are the leak somehow. Where is he? He's *close*."

I backed away from the polymerwall. Ooookay. Okay, no. Not doing this right now. I did *not* need Bricandor to know I could hear.

A roar froze me in my steps.

"This is the only way we can salvage the situation!" Diebol shouted. "And I don't care if you have to *explain* it or apologize or whatever to whatever sniveling press of whatever planet you want groveling before you, we *will* fly through the Undecided Zone, and we *will* carry out the Stygge attack from the air!"

His panting, his breathing, his hunger to start *now*, to slice something open—was he like this before? No. It was off. Something was off with him, like something was off with Lem when she charged his throat. It was a similar something. Like a panic, like a drug addict screaming at you for taking away his syringe.

"No, you cannot call off this attack!" He screamed. "Oh,

you'll put me back in 256, dear alpha wolf? Go ahead. I've already had the worst. There is *nothing* worse you can do to me— I'm empty!"

Diebol sunk into his chair, his head in his hands. My breath paused. Call off the attack? This would not be a bad thing. I couldn't hear Bricandor's response.

But I heard Diebol's restrained breath, breath that wanted to scream, but out of respect held still. "Yes, Bereens sent a warning, and now they know to keep their ground forces alert to their weak spots," he said. "But listen to me, please, Teacher—they're expecting our original plan, using the ground resources we already have on Guetala." He swallowed, gulped, begged. "But on the third of this month two planets in the Undecided Zone swing through Luna-Guetala's orbit, putting *this* area of space, right above Fort Jehu, inside the Undecided Zone."

My eyes widened. It was brilliant. The Spaces Treaties limited Growen or Frelsi conflict to specifically contested planets—any attacks in the Undecided Zone would cost financial and political support from the Independent Planets. Diebol went on: "We couldn't bombard the planet from orbit before because of their long-range missile capacity, but with this month's orbit—*now* they can't just fire a long-range missile into the Undecided Zone, can they? They have to wait until we're already close enough to lay down suppressive fire and deploy our Stygges."

He leapt to his feet. I felt his boots hit the floor, his hand—it was sore, stiff for some reason—clench as his fist slammed the table knuckles-first. "That's the entire point! They won't be expecting us to break the treaties!" And then: "So you can break it to transport goods and prisoners, but not soldiers? So the assassinations we paid for just didn't happen, then? Where does your moral compass *come* from? No! No, you listen to me! You know as well as I, and far better, that *this is our best shot*. This planetary alignment, this zone angle, it happens once in a *lifetime!*"

I leaned in. I couldn't help it. I leaned in against the door, my ear almost touching the ice crystals crackling across it.

"Very well," said Bricandor. "I will lead the troops into victory on the third. *You* will kill Bereens."

"For all you know he's already dead."

"For all I know?" That gentle laugh. I shivered. The gentler he sounded, the more trouble you were in. Something I'd learned a few years ago. "My son, let me tell you what I know."

The ice melted in a wave, and suddenly Bricandor's eyes shone through the door, as large as suns, staring into mine, into me, as blue as fire, and no, I wasn't going to play this game. Nope, nuh-uh. If Bricandor didn't know why I was "close," Diebol probably did, and he'd step in any second. I backed away from his messed-up hallway, slipping in the slick puddles on the floor, stumbling, turning to run—

I made it to the infinite darkness between the hallway and the cage. It was quiet, throbbing with heartbeat. My wristband glowed. Five numbers now: 33956.

"You know you're the only person to use my first name since I was ten?"

I whirled. My throat sealed in fright. Diebol's voice carried towards me, not from his polymerwall behind me—but from our cage! He was between me and my mind. *How did he get past me?*

I caught my breath. He kept talking: "When you called me Jared, back in the interrogation center. I do believe even my father's forgotten that name. It's a remnant of this place, really."

I saw him now, leaning on his cage door, waving his hand at "this place." He stood on the edge of the light, shadows cast about his wan face. His friendly tone darkened.

"Does my name have something to do with how you made it past me?" he asked. "How did you break my side?"

"I don't know," I said.

"Are our EEG signals similar enough that my channel took you for me?"

"I hope not."

Diebol laughed.

I didn't like this new laugh. It was suspiciously free, like a child's—like a child's in that strange, amoral way that a small boy might tear the legs off a squirming insect and laugh, cruelty and curiosity shimmering out of wide eyes that see no sin. There's a reason children make terrifying horror antagonists. It's not because children are safe.

"Are you—alright?" I asked. I started down the hallway towards him, my eye on his ashen hand resting on the lock to the cage. Was his skin normally that … light?

"Oh, I was quite angry with myself when I found you'd slipped past my door," he said. "You almost outed this place to Bricandor. You idiot. But otherwise … I've never been more alive." His teeth flashed in the shadows.

"We can't actually fight in here, you know," I said. "I know you want to. But it'd be like yelling at each other over a radio."

"I'm not sure about that. We've never tried. You know electricity can be used as a weapon, and we're shooting electrical signals to each other now. Why not up the frequency?"

"I think it's voltage, not frequency, you'd need to increase."

"No. It's current that hurts." Diebol laughed again. "I should know."

I narrowed my eyes. My twisting gut didn't know if I wanted to ask, but oh, my gloating hatred did. "How do you know?"

"I'm not going to satisfy your mockery," he sneered. "You would love it, wouldn't you, if I stepped into the light scarred, skin seared away by my father's work, my irises blood-lined and my muscles shuddering still from the electric impulses I've endured because of you. But you'll never see me broken. When we meet again, you'll see a man more clean and healthy and terrible than the doctors in your nightmares." He smiled as my fists clenched, and the lights in *my* hallway flashed red beyond the cage. "How's that PTSD treating you?"

I said nothing for a moment. The screams were real, then. "Why the galaxy did you let him do that to you?" I asked.

"Is that an actual question, or a subtle attempt to encourage me to assassinate him?"

"It's a real-ass question. Is he really still stronger than you?"

"Stronger by far, unfortunately." I was near enough now to hear him lower his voice. I could see his tired eyes blazing with a faith like Lem's, and it was eerie as hell. "But everything he does to me is geared to make me stronger. I believe he does, one day, want me to take his place, and the current price I pay under his hand is only the birth-pangs of my new self."

"That's all very poetic, but no one has the right to torture someone into becoming better."

"Except your Njandejara, apparently." He laughed again, and stepped back to open the cage door for me.

I stood still, struck by the thought. For a moment the parallels gripped me, and my resolve failed. "Is it like that?" I asked Njande in the shadows.

"The hand that holds the instrument, and the hand that does not stop it, to me are one and the same," Diebol shrugged.

"So what's the difference between a surgeon cutting out a cancer, and a serial killer slicing out your fingernails with a scalpel?" Njande dropped a question onto my lips. "There is a difference."

Diebol didn't like that question, and didn't answer it. He waited with the cage door open; I stepped past him, almost chest to chest; we paused for a second. He smirked, closed the door behind me, and locked us both into the cage again.

"It doesn't matter that you found the vectors you came for, really," he smiled, showing me all his teeth. "Because as long as you say hello to Lem for me, we're even."

The communication line cut off, and I woke up.

CHAPTER THIRTY-NINE

Jei

MY EYES OPENED WITH A FLUTTER. WHAT HAD AWAKENED ME?

A clear, blueish darkness welcomed me to a new world of crisp-smelling air-conditioning, stiff linen, and a soft machine hum. I jerked upright. Moonlight streamed through glass windows.

Good, I could break the glass to escape if I needed. That ventilation shaft was another escape route. Was the polymerwall locked? How fast could I get to it? My bed lay about four feet away from what I suspected was an entrance, but polymerwall's not always clearly delineated, and anyway two robots guarded that wall, their orb-shaped heads tilted down over plain, long, cylindrical bodies like men sleeping. My fists clenched against the sheets. I could take them. I didn't see any weapons on them—

Because they were med-bots. I was planning to fight med-bots. With tiny fragile arms. And programming that required verbal consent before they could even twitch *one* of the hundred or so medical tools in those tube-bodies. Really? *But you never know, these could be re-programmed to—*

No, self, no, shut up. No crazy for you. Not fighting any med-bots today.

I heard breathing, though, from the beds to my left, between me and the window. Could I defeat *that*?

"… Jei?"

My breath fell out of me like I'd dropped it. Lem, it was Lem. Bloodseas—my shoulders slumped forward as blood rushed back to my brain, and all the muscles I'd tensed relaxed in an avalanche. Wow, I hadn't taken a breath since waking up. Wow. Thank goodness. Lem.

"Hey," I grunted, lying back down. I didn't look at her yet.

"Where are we?"

My heartbeat slowed as the fear in her voice gave me control over my own. "It's okay, Lem, we're in a civilian hospital. We made it."

"Did we? Are you sure?"

I turned my head now to look at her. She lay on her side about six feet from me, tears sparkling across her nose in the moonlight and trickling across her clenched fist onto her pillow.

Oh man. I sat up to face her. I wanted to hug her, slide over next to her on her bed and cradle her and tell her nothing would ever go wrong again …

But I couldn't make her vulnerable like that. I didn't know everything Diebol did to her, or how she'd feel about physical contact with a guy now, or how much her soldier's pride hurt right now, crying in front of me. I held my hands out to her across the space.

"Yeah. We made it. High five."

She looked at my palms for a second with a sniffle.

"Don't leave me hanging here," I murmured with a smile.

"You're doing it wrong," she muttered.

What? "No … I'm pretty sure I haven't forgotten how a high five works."

"That's two hands, that's ten. Also you're holding them all down like I'm going to give you soup or something. I don't have any soup."

"Well I don't know that," I smirked. She had a weird way of refusing reassurance, the same way she'd called me an idiot for taking that knife for her back in the gym. She was afraid of some kind of closeness. I dropped my hands to my knees. "Soup wouldn't be the first surprise you pull out of nowhere," I said. "How are your hands?"

"I—sore. But—" She leaned off her side, kind of onto her back, and held her long dark fingertips up against the moon. "I look fine. That's kind of scary, actually." She ducked them under the thin sheet that covered her and spoke at the ceiling, her voice trembling. "You know that was the worst about it, when it happened. I didn't see it. I didn't know what he did to crack open my fingertips like that. They were fine when I went in there, and then holy shyte pain, and then when I came out they bent all whack, and on this I could see muscle—what the hell did he do?" She curled up tighter as her voice rose. "Shyte, Cinta, did Cinta—"

"He's in the bed on the other side of you," I said. "Asleep."

She rolled over and sat up. I stood and stepped to the foot of her bed, just in case she leapt at him or something. The poor guy had bandages the size of his face covering his chest and shoulder, and a huge clear respirator on his snout that fogged every time he wheezed. Four med-bots stood at the head of his bed, moving every now and then like trees over a cemetery to inject something into his IV or flash a readout on their visages. The sentinels showed no alarm in their vigil, swaying like ghosts over a grave with mournful hums and whirrs, pale denizens of the night between the Biouk's life and death. It didn't take a doctor to see he might not make it.

"That's a lot of med-bots," Lem choked. "I think—I think they have him in a coma?"

"We can ask the doctor in the morning."

"How'd he get so filked up? He was at least awake when I—did they—so they shot him? Where'd he go, how'd he—" She pressed her palms against her temples. "Holy shyte, what's even going on?"

I leaned on the foot of her bed, gripping the metal bar tighter and tighter as she freaked out. I didn't know. I didn't know how we'd gotten here, what the rogue blitzer wanted from us, how on earth he'd found us, or even … even if we'd really made it. I thought we had. My palms heated the aluminum bar, and I thought for a moment about trying to break it, to bend it under my weight, to prove I was stronger than something …

"Lem?" I swallowed, interrupting her. "Lem, can you look at me for a second?"

Her eyes met mine.

"I need you to help me, and I need you to let me help you. I don't have any answers right now, and it's messed up what happened—and—and I wanna just—" I thought about saying jump out the window, but best keep that to myself. "Look, right here, right now, I only have you, and Njande, and Njande's very invisible and very terrifying, so I need you. Stay with me, here. Don't go nuts on me. Please, please let's help each other stay calm, and figure this out, and—" I felt my shoulders weakening as I let go of the bar with one hand to reach out to her. "Can I please get a high five so I know you're real?"

Her lower lip quivered as her eyes glistened wet. She struggled for a second—and then she exhaled. With a brave throw-back of her shoulders she smiled under wet cheeks and wrapped her hand around mine to squeeze my wrist.

We'd made it.

"That really wasn't a high five," I said.

LEM

Lem's chest ached inside-out when Jei mentioned Njande. His eyes screamed at her past the hair falling over his face in the shadows as his knuckles whitened on her bed-post—shyte, Njande terrified him. Jei was as scared of the confusion and what-the-hells as she was, and on top of that his only comfort was a hurricane. She remembered the ba-eater and almost cried for him—what was that like, to have those tentacles boring through all the most private parts of your mind, seeping through your thoughts like liquefied corpse? Did that stench wash out?

Jei's fear took Lem out of herself, and they met somewhere in the middle as she clasped his wrist. "Jei, why were you fighting Njande?"

"Whew, I—" He withdrew his hand to run it through his hair, standing up straight as he exhaled and glanced nervously out the window. He tried to laugh. "Way to cut to the chase there, Lem."

"I don't want you to die like that," she said.

"What did it look like?" he asked, still looking away from her.

"Did you get a chance to see your throat before we got here? You were clawing at yourself. You're lucky you didn't bust an artery or some shyte like that."

"It can't have been that bad, it's not like I have claws."

"You were bleeding, though." Lem wrapped her sheet around herself and rose to stand next to the window. The hospital towered above a winding city of spires—well, maybe not a city. Town, really. She could see past the road wrapping around the outer circle of buildings into a coniferous forest, and beyond that into the mountains. And somewhere out there, beyond the sleepy colorful spindles, outside the reign of traffic lights controlling empty streets, outside the quiet normality of families and shops waiting to open, lurked Diebol.

"You know, he was right, in a way," Lem murmured. Jei's reflection glared in the window beside her, not at her, but out into the night sky. He leaned on the glass, one arm over his head, jaw clenched. "Don't punch me or anything for saying this," Lem added. "What he did sucked. But he's not like Bricandor. He doesn't just wanna win. He wants to end the messed-up part of—it's like, if it wasn't for Njande, we could be friends." Jei's silence unnerved her. "I'm not saying—not excusing anything. But he was trying to take this off the battlefield into the hospital. To fix war."

"If he wants to fix war he can start with himself," Jei growled.

"Yeah," Lem said. "Maybe that's his mistake, then. Trying to change his enemies first." A spark of inspiration grew inside her as she spoke, as if her ordinary words carried something of the Warrior-Queen again. "What if we could change ourselves first? I don't mean cure ourselves—I mean—" She paused, her ears ringing with the crack of broken knee, the memory of the supply woman she'd throttled back on the freighter, and the terror of not being able to control her own fingers reaching for Diebol's throat when he said she belonged to him. Her bitterness insisted only more cruelty, only more violence could protect her, but something else cried: "What if we could be so powerful, so persuasive, just *exuding* goodness, that we didn't have to kill to win wars? Can you imagine a soldier like that? So perfect, so in tune with nature and her body and physics that she could just *subdue* her enemies with her mind—"

Jei tilted his head to look at her. "Breaking their will to fight. Are you suggesting—learning to shut off minds like Bricandor can?"

"Gah, no. I mean like—Njande told me there's somewhere in some ancient records of his words, where he says that those reborn through his dimension are like wind," she said. "You don't know where they've gone, and you can't pin them down. Electromagnetic warriors so good they make their enemies like harmless kids. You don't have to hurt a kid to stop him, right, 'cuz you're so much bigger." Jei looked away, and Lem's words failed as embarrassment hit her. She couldn't read his face—was she just blabbing now? "I—don't know what I'm talking about," she said, shuffling back to her bed to lie down.

"That's not like you," Jei said.

"What?"

"You're basically the avatar of confidence, what's gotten into you?"

"I dunno. I sound stupid." She sighed. Imaginary warriors, saving the universe from heat death … "Yeah, maybe I got delusions of grandeur. Everything that's impossible seems possible to me."

"You just see another layer to the universe." Jei inhaled as he collapsed against the wall with his hands in his hair again. "It's actually pretty terrifying. I don't know what to do with it. It's like all my life I've had these rules about 'How It Works.' Big is big, small is small, weak is weak, and things stay in their labelled boxes. Sentients, sapients, and interdimensionals all have organized places.

"Now there's this whole other abyss of Meaning in front of me, and everything matters so much more and less, and wrapped up in all of it there's Njandejara …"

"What'd you mean everything matters more and less?"

"Well—if he's meddling with everything, then everything's going to turn out the way he wants in the end, so nothing anyone does matters. On the other hand, if he works through a million different bits and pieces behind the scenes, invisible, and he lives outside of time, and time is a place that touches many spaces, and if *we make decisions that touch him*, through time, into all those spaces—then on our level *every little thing you do* changes the universe. Everything matters, and nothing matters."

"You may have lost me there."

"I lost myself, too," Jei laughed softly. "It's—it's all paradoxes. Like—" He stopped himself, palms out and eyes closed as if asking for Lem's patience as he inhaled. "Okay, so when you fought the ba-eater at the Center. Maybe Njande was going to save me a different way, and it could have happened another way, but it *didn't*. I saw *you* and reached out for *you*. Everything depended on *you*. At the same time, everything depended on him. You were dying, fading around him, like a glove on a hand, while he fought the ba-eater. I saw it—you were yourself, but you were—in him, too.

"He just—he throws a wrench in everything that makes sense. You're yours only when you're his, everything matters and nothing matters—he bridges opposites."

"Quantum," Lem grinned. "Like the electron."

"What?"

"I'll explain it later. I wanna find better words." Lem paused. "You're not having some kind of existential crisis, are you? Like nothing's real, there's no truth, shyte like that?"

"No. No! The opposite. Reality's *more* real, breaking into the shadows where we live, trying to burst through these walls and your sheets and those stars—" He pushed the wall, gripped her blanket, pointed to the sky with his eyes shining—"Reality's bulging out into our universe, and truth is more binary than I thought, and evil more evil, and above all else Njande's suddenly incredibly important." Jei slid down the wall to sit on the floor, knees bent and head back. "I'm sorry. Thanks for listening to all this—this."

"I adore it," Lem laughed. "I could talk about Njande forever. I'd like to—I dunno, make this a thing we do. Study Paradoxes."

"A 'thing we do'?" Jei asked. "Like what, a weekly lunch or something?"

Lem almost punched him. She couldn't quite tell if he was making fun of her or not. "Yeah, if we get back or whatever," she chose to say nonchalantly, instead. "If you were down with that."

She messed with her hair and bit her lip, rocking a bit on her heels. He smiled. The moonlight threw tired shadows into the creases by his eyes, and she suddenly wanted to pester him about his name again, even though she knew it now.

"I think I am," he said. "I think I'd like that."

For some reason, his smile made her think of Diebol.

CHAPTER FORTY

Jei

I KEPT EXPECTING TO WAKE UP AGAIN—TO DISCOVER THIS WAS ALL Diebol's dream. But sunlight brought a clean, fresh look over the whole hospital room, and no one looked more awake and alive than Lem as she puttered around Cinta's bedside, out of the way of the med-bots but ready to jump in, to set them straight if, for some reason, she suddenly earned a medical degree in the next five minutes. Bright and alert and ridiculous.

"I see you're walking already, without my permission."

I whirled. A blue Bont lizard in a white coat stomped into the room, her thick tail dragging near the floor. *Without my permission*, she'd said.

"I don't like asking permission," I grunted.

"Oh, me neither. Pleased to meet you awake. I'm Doctor Francis —your caretaker the past two weeks," she said, her scales flickering a pleasant shade of sky-blue across her face. "The enhanced tissue repair factors fixed you right up, didn't they?" The light color rippled down her shoulders to her toes like a friendly smile as she extended her claw to offer me the back of her hand. I touched the back of my hand to the back of hers.

Lem offered no such politeness. "Tell me what's going on with him," she said, slipping between me and the doctor. "Not him, the human, him, the Biouk. Tell me if I can help. Blood, kidneys, whatever, you got it."

So the doctor began to explain gunshot wounds and shock, and organ damage and comas; apparently having gone into shock made Cinta's organs fight against the doctor's "tissue repair factors" with "necrotic fibrosis," and as the talk waned to bad news Lem stepped close to me and leaned her shoulder against mine. I realized it wasn't a sparkle in her eye, but a gleam, a glint, like desperation or vice, or light on a withheld tear.

"This can't be happening to him," she muttered.

"Do you feel like … maybe you're still asleep?" I whispered back. "As if we didn't escape?" She snapped her head around to give me a wide-eyed glare. I backpedaled. "I'm sorry, I'm just finding myself in a series of continual awakenings, each more real than the last, and I don't know—don't know for sure what—did we talk last night?"

"Yeah. Yeah we did."

"Any idea what day it is?"

"The clocks on the med-bots say—shyte." Her whisper died under a hiss. "How long were we in the—shyte, she said we've been out two weeks. Why hasn't Diebol come after us?"

I remembered the screams of torture from the mind-radio. "He was busy with some personal health issues."

"How would you kn—" She shook herself, eyes wide. "Wait, did the Stygge attack already … ?"

Blood pounded in my temples. "We need to call Rana, now."

"Yeah. Excuse me, ma'am?" The doctor looked up, her snout a curious turquoise as Lem asked: "Is there a public transmission station on this floor?"

"Of course! Down the hall to the right. Forgive me—" The turquoise became an awkward, shy aquamarine. "I would have offered as soon as you woke up, but I had thought most vegan communes don't allow technology, and I didn't want to—er, offend."

"Wait, what?" Lem stopped at the polymerwall. "Vegan what now?"

"Do you call it something else? I'm sorry, the woman who brought you in said … ?"

"You got the wrong room," Lem laughed. It wasn't a pleasant laugh. It was nervous.

"Jordan, Juliet, and Hratsch Kim?"

"No …" I looked at Lem. Her jaw clenched. I shoved my fists into the pockets of the grey hospital tunic to hide their almost—tremble. The doctor tilted her head, her scales a full, confused turquoise again as she checked the screens of the med-bots by our beds.

"Well, this is the right room," she murmured. "These are the names we were given at check-in."

Bloodseas, we both knew what happened next. This was where the doctor told us we had amnesia, and didn't know who we were, and then Diebol stepped in to tell us we were insane, and—no, no, just no!

Lem and I both plunged through the polymerwall, almost stumbling over each other into the crowded hallway of nurses and orderlies and floating gurneys.

"To the right!" Lem shouted, skidding on the tiled floor as she changed directions towards the glass box down the hall. "Transmission booth!"

"Careful, might be a trap!"

"On it!" She ripped a light fixture out of the wall, spinning it over her wrist like a mace, ready to clobber anything that leapt out. People began screaming as the hallway lights flickered and a green Bont in black leather jumped from the ceiling vent right in Lem's path.

We knew the drill by now. Lem charged the leathered Bont while I went for the transmission booth. Lem swung, electricity arcing across her fingers as the Bont yelled something and drew a blitzer's rifle—I threw up an em-pull, yanked the glass door off its hinges, hurled it between Lem and the inevitable gun-blast as I slid into the booth—

"I'm trying to help you, you piddle-sucking nincompoops!" screeched the lizard, stumbling to catch the door, to shield herself from Lem's electricity.

"I've heard that one before," I muttered. I dialed into a private Frelsi frequency, keeping a watchful eye on Lem's duel behind me as I entered my passcode.

The Frelsi server rejected me.

Invalid user.

My heart seized in my chest. I double-checked, triple-checked—

"What's taking you so long?" Lem shouted, hurling an electric blast at the lizard. It dodged, screaming something about helpful blitzers and Maggots and explanations.

Invalid user.

I sucked in my breath, gripping my hair with my hands. Bloodseas, I—

I didn't exist.

LEM

When timid orderlies in blue pajamas began firing tranquilizer sticks at her from behind desks, Lem began to suspect the blitzers weren't coming. When the Bont lizard in the leather jacket began screaming about a helpful rogue blitzer, Lem began to suspect it was time to drop the light fixture and come up with an apology.

"You know the blitzer who got us out?" she panted, backing off a few steps.

"Yes!" The lizard hissed, her skin still cool green, as if she didn't even register normal Bont emotion. "Lower your voice, imbecile, everyone here doesn't need to know everything! I'm the one who brought you in!"

"Lem, get in here," Jei interrupted. "You'll want to see this."

… It was one thing to find out their identities had been erased.

It was another completely, when they called Rana on a public civilian frequency, to find out why.

"You had a list of all the guys the Growen assassins were gonna hit, and you kept that shyte to yourself?!" Lem stormed out of the clear booth to get the torn-off door back from the stupid Bont mercenary. "Do you have any idea how bad you've screwed up?"

"Shhhh!" The lizard hissed. "So you didn't get home as early as you could have, boohoo, don't get your knickers in a—"

"No! That's not it! There are people in danger we were supposed to protect, a whole defense strategy we were supposed to explain, and now we're here, and not there, and—gah! *Why* would you lie to the good guys?"

"There are no good guys," the mercenary scoffed. She turned her head back to the orderlies, and the pale, almost white-blue doctor at the end of the hallway. "It's alright, mates, we're just having a little talk. She's got a wee bit of that PTS-mawhatchit, no worries!" To Lem, she hissed, "It's not my fault your bloke didn't put enough detail into his message back at the Growen tower-ma-whatchit, now is it?"

"Girl, you did not just—"

"Lem, can you bring the door over here?" Jei stuck his head outside the booth. "Don't waste your time on this *person*." His withering tone made person a filthy word, and Lem shuddered as she stepped back into the communications box with him, suddenly sorry for the lizard. Cadet Commander Bereens was back.

The booth's transparent walls faded to a private opaque as Rana's voice apologized for the second time. "I'm sorry, sorry, sorry, I believed the leak was genuine, real, real as my webbed toes! When she lied about her record, and the list …" He gulped. "Friends of mine, friends, died, you know. Forgive my emotion." He cut himself short, and didn't repeat the word; emotion wasn't important enough to repeat. "We fortified our ground forces in response to your warning. Good warning, thank you. Growen didn't attack, they were set back, must have seen the fortifications, good stuff. Well done."

"They didn't attack ..." Jei repeated, his eyes distant and dark. Lem and Rana both waited in silence as he trailed off. Suddenly he stiffened. "What day is it today?" He snapped. "I keep asking and no one's telling me! Come on, what day is it today?"

"Excuse me?" Rana seemed taken aback by Jei's tone.

"Maiesta Third," Lem said.

"Bloodseas!" Jei covered his face like he'd been socked in the eye. "It's today, the attack is today!"

"That isn't isn't *isn't* what you sent in your transmission? Not what you sent at all? Was that transmission wrong?"

"No, it was right at the time, but they've changed it since then!"

"When did you learn that? You said you *just now* woke up from two weeks under?" Rana without repetitions meant confusion or suspicion. Lem looked at Jei as he stood there, mouth open for a second, one hand in his hair.

He took a deep breath, looking first at her and then at the voice box in the wall. "Alright, I'm going to level with you both here," he said. "While I was unconscious I overheard Diebol and Bricandor, in my mind. Diebol and I have a mental connection. It's like a radio. He left his on by accident, and I overheard everything. They're flying in through the Undecided Zone to bombard you from orbit, and drop the Stygge warriors from the air. I even have their flight vector—33956!"

Rana's silence was not good. Lem bit her lip and looked at the floor. Yeah, she'd guessed Jei and Diebol had something weird going on. But a brain-radio? Yeah, it sounded bad. Should ... should she be angry at him? Was this a betrayal, or just ... just like her and Diebol in the hallway, or in room 256, or ... or anywhere else? Was this ... ?

"Do you know your Growen patient number, Jei—Jei?" Rana asked softly.

"It's 339. Why?"

"Do you know Benzaran's?"

"Uh—no, actually. 56 … 56 what?"

"567," Lem filled in for him, almost whispering.

"Your vector is just your patient numbers, just numbers you remember," Rana said. "It isn't … Jei—Jei, it isn't real."

"Captain, no, it's not *like* that, head-radio's no more unrealistic than an electric eel, for shyte's sake, it's—"

"Even if you were right!" Rana raised his voice. Jei shut up fast, and Lem found herself tightening to attention even though Rana couldn't see her. "I cannot ask Command to send Aversion Ships, or missiles, or anything-thing into the Undecided Zone based on your brain magicks. Mind doohickies. I can't put brain doodles in a report!"

"Sir, I believe him," Lem said. "If you've seen him and Diebol together it's—"

Jei held up his hand and shook his head. Lem closed her mouth.

"Lem-Lem, do you have a mental health evaluation from the doctor there, there, there-ish?" Rana asked.

"No …"

"See, I know *some* of the information in the leak is real. I know you aren't well. Every good lie …" Rana sighed. "Every good lie has a core of truth."

Lem cringed. Did he know, then, about her attacking Jei?

Before she could stammer Rana lowered his voice again, his gurgle kind, and careful. "Cadet Commander Bereens, based on your *previous* mental health diagnosis," he said. "And based on how you, and the leak, indicated Torture. And based on your *you* now. Based on everything. All the things. You will both rest. We will stay vigilant here. We will watch the skies. You will stand fast 'til we arrange permission from Revelon to transport you. Pick up. Ride home. I'm filling in the paperwork now. Right now. Now." He paused. "We care about you kids. We care. Rest up. Wish all the best to you. The good byes. All the good things."

"We wish you all the good things, too, Captain," Lem sighed, smiling at his terrible speech. She missed the old croaker. "See you soon."

JEN FINELLI, MD

"Over and out," Jei said. He whacked the red button under the voice box and collapsed onto the little booth's bench with his elbows on his knees and his head in his hands.

Lem opened her mouth—

"Before you say anything, yes, I have a mental health diagnosis, no, I don't want to talk about it, and yes, I understand why Rana won't believe me," Bereens muttered. "And it's not your fault. None of it's your fault."

"Shut up," she said. Her heart was drowning somewhere in her stomach, because she believed him, and didn't know what to do about it.

"For what it's worth, at least they're coming to pick us up," Jei said.

"Yeah, I'm not looking forward to getting a full psych eval, and questions, and all that other shyte." Lem choked. "Dammit, forget that though! The attack fleet's probably on their way right freaking now! How is it possible we went through *so much* to get that stupid transmission, and now it's all for nothing?"

"At least they know now." His voice was muffled through his hands.

"And you're—you're talking to him, in your head? How often *is* that?"

"About once a month. It's not—I don't share information with him."

"But you stole info from him! So why can't he do the same?"

"Because I don't leave the radio on. He only—he was tortured. That's why it was on."

"Tortured? Shyte, did you help him?"

Jei's face jerked up towards her. "What? Why would I do that?" he snarled.

"To win him over!"

"I'm sorry, you're going to have to drop this line of thinking right now." Jei rose to leave. "Me, right now I need sugar or gin, not sure which, I'll figure it out."

306

"What, you're just gonna give up?" Lem stepped between him and the door. The door fell down behind her, and finally shattered.

"We have orders," Jei said, looking past her at the broken glass.

A cruel phrase jumped to Lem's lips, and after only a moment's thought she let it out. She leaned forward to whisper in his ear: "And in the meantime Diebol wins Luna-Guetala."

Oh, she knew better than to push him like that. His eyes blazed, and he gripped the edge of his tunic into a wrinkled clot. He glared at her and said nothing.

"Oh, I'm sorry, I know he's one of your trigger words," she said.

His eyes narrowed. Lem shivered—too far? She enjoyed "too far." "I get it," she said. "I know they can't order us to do shyte while we're in Undecided territory. So. We do what they need, without orders."

They were chest to chest in the doorway. He looked away from her, down the hallway. "Go on."

"We're gonna hit the Stygge transport ship before it leaves Undecided territory." Lem straightened her tunic like she knew what she was talking about. "If it causes a political fiasco, we've got evidence already that we're unstable, went rogue, and disobeyed orders. Plausible deniability."

He stared at her for a moment, as if deciding whether or not she was joking. "We'd need interplanetary heat," he said.

"I hear Revelon has a missile defense system."

"We'll need a ride."

"I'll arrange that."

"Disguises?"

"On it."

"Security read-out and blueprints of the defense system we're infiltrating?"

"That's your specialty." Lem stepped out into the hallway. "Better hurry …

"… We don't have much time."

CHAPTER FORTY-ONE

Lark

L<small>ARK</small> <small>FOUND</small> <small>HERSELF</small> <small>LEFT</small> <small>ALONE</small> <small>TO</small> <small>AWKWARDLY</small> <small>EXPLAIN</small> everything to the doctor, and while she would have preferred to launch into her fallback amnesia lie, she realized there'd be no controlling the nutty Frelsi cadets unless she told the truth. So she did that.

She didn't intend to tell so much truth, though! The blasted doctor kept asking follow-up questions! The woman seemed itchy to report someone, whether Frelsi or Growen or whatever, and Lark figured of the two sides she'd rather the Growen came out the bad guys. She *tried* to explain to the doctor that reporting was useless— didn't the woman know all governments on all planets were connected, and war was just a conspiracy, and the Growen controlled all the Undecided Zone and the Frelsi, too?

Bloody sheep, the lot of them.

Mr. and Miss Frelsi Sheep still hadn't come back from their phone call when the doctor returned to muss with something over the furry's bed. Lark stood and leaned against the wall, pretending to watch, her neck ducked down into her leather collar and her face heated.

Presently a shadow and a warmth passed by Lark's left, and the doctor leaned up against the wall beside her. Lark tightened her arms around herself. Awkward, standing alone with someone who knew Lark'd almost conned her out of her pay. Even now, Doc couldn't get paid 'til she logged the patients *as* Frelsi in her system. And their Frelsi IDs had been deleted. Ergo, pay delay.

The doctor deserved it, though! Healthcare people made bank off everyone else's suffering, how did that make sense?

Still. Bloody awkward.

"You know, miss," said the doctor. *Oh beans, here we go.* "I'm not quite sure where you're from—I'm certain you didn't grow up on the Bont homeworld—but from where I'm from we've got a little saying."

Lark hugged herself tighter.

"'The kreekaw only crows when he's hurt.' I don't know if it's biologically true about the bird, but I believe it's true about you."

"How do you suppose?" Lark grunted.

"I know you're suspicious of every government and authority and essentially everyone who isn't you, not because you really believe logically that everyone's out to get you, but because something *has* got you already. I don't pretend to know what that is—whether you've got a bad employer after you, or you're trying to work off a traumatic experience—but perhaps you should tend to that before you continue this particular line of work."

"I like my job."

"Oh, I know, I like mine, too. I'm not saying quit, only—take a break. So you can heal, and stop cawing at everyone. Experience the good side of the universe for a bit."

"Not sure what good means."

The doctor shrugged. "For me it means seeing my children laugh all the colors of the rainbow, or that glow when a family tells me how *healthy* my patient's become. I suppose it's different for you."

Lark didn't huff, but she didn't answer, either. The doctor straightened to go and offered Lark the back of her claw—polite salutation. Lark touched the back of her claw in return. She should address the topic, really, she thought. Laugh it off, make it a joke. "Looks like neither of us is getting paid today," Lark said.

"Oh, that? It's no big deal, I like my job enough to do it free. I hope you feel the same way."

Lark's retort—"Eh, I gotta eat"—died in her throat as the doctor smiled a sky-blue and left. Lark wanted to feel the same way. Why didn't she?

Her compupad vibrated. It was Rana!

You're back on assignment. Guard Bereens and Benzaran until their transport arrives, and don't let them leave the hospital. Will pay your agreed-upon daily allowance, transport, and upon safe arrival on Luna-Guetala, your final reward.

Fantastic! Lark texted back an affirmative, and left it at that. But ha, she told him so! Told him they were alive!

It felt so hollow. She'd still gotten people killed. Blast, she'd felt so stupid, so insecure and *confused* these past two weeks, about her methods, about her outlook on people, about everything—she just wanted to return to what she knew: rescuing children from bad guys. When it came to adult politics it was all grey blends of evil and alright, complicated and ugly, but with kids it was easy, black and white and good. You don't hurt kids. They know the truth in fairytales.

Perhaps *that* was the good side of the universe.

A loud *plunk-kloop* sound startled Lark—Miss Sheep ran into the room so fast the polymerwall almost didn't have time to soften. "Lark Scrita, is it? I need to talk to you."

No thanks, nutter. And no thanks to Captain Rana for sharing my name.

"Outside? On the roof?" Lem Benzaran asked.

Well. That was classy. Lark liked that. "Alright," she said.

Once outside Lem Benzaran didn't skip a beat. She licked her lips and grinned, pointing both forefingers like pistols at Lark. "I get you."

"What?"

"Your colors don't change, and it's not because you're calm, it's 'cuz you're not Bont. You got the mannerisms down, the speech, everything, but there's just something missing. I know how it is, I play that game. Used to dress up and try to pass as Biouk, and still —I mean, I still try to talk as close as I can, you know?"

"Don't project your feelings on me," Lark growled, wrapping her jacket tighter around herself. "Is there a point here?"

"Well okay, grumpy-butt. I gotta borrow your disguise tech for a hit on the Growen."

Let Miss Sheep run amok and lose Rana's reward? No thank you! "Mate, you can't just mooch people's gear. I didn't save your britches to become your pack-mother."

"Well pack-mamma, I guess I can just beat you up and take it then." Benzaran grinned with all her teeth.

"You—ha!" Lark put extra effort into the scorn in that laugh. "You couldn't."

"With no one around to save you from this evil Stygge-magic?" Sparks flickered around Benzaran's wrists.

Lark's claws jerked to her utility belt as her heart jumped. Benzaran chuckled, and sighed, and sat down on the roof with a disheveled plop. "I'm joking. You kinda buy 'me-as-a-Stygge,' don't you? I'm surprised. You don't seem like a follower."

A follower? Like a sheep? Lark's heated face could have fried eggs.

"Here's the thing," Benzaran said. "No one's all business. I get that you don't like the Frelsi, but I *know* you don't like the Growen, all helping their prisoners escape. You like a little anarchy, a lil freedom, right? I can help you make some. Just need a ride to one of Revelon's remote missile centers, and lemme borrow whatever it is that makes your Bont disguise so good. That's it."

"I've got a temper on me, but that doesn't make me daft," Lark snapped. "I know bloody well what you're trying, with that follower comment, and the anarchy thing, and you can belt it all the way up. People don't manipulate me, and no one's using my tech for some pointless Frelsi operation. I don't throw my pearls to pigs."

Lem half-smiled. "Pearls to pigs, huh. That's an interdimensional expression. You Contaminated?"

"Bloody hell, no." Lark lowered her head to glare at the mountains in the distance. A long pause lowered her voice into a soft rasp. Eh, who cared who knew. "My parents were."

Benzaran's eyes widened. "And the Frelsi failed them somehow," she said.

"Yes." Benzaran was just guessing, Lark told herself. Just guessing, just lucky. This nutter didn't *get* her, they weren't two lonely angry girls thrown together by forces and fate and other superstitious piddly-winking, and Benzaran's bowed head didn't mean sympathy. No one sympathized with Lark Scrita. No one cared. The closest anyone ever came was pity. Arrogant, rich-person, guilt-driven pity.

"I'm sorry," Benzaran said.

"Fat lot of good your sorry does, six years after the fact," Lark sneered. "I know you just want something from me. Don't play nice. Spit out the cash or belt the hell up."

Lem's softness evaporated like dry ice in the desert. "Not everything outta everyone's mouth is a lie," she growled. "You really think I hafta play sympathetic with you to get what I want? You really think I can't *take* what I want, right now?"

"You keep loading that gun, mate, but I don't see you firing it," Lark jeered.

"Because I don't want to!" Lem threw her hands in the air. "Gah, what universe do you live in? Is it impossible to imagine that someone might actually be nice to you? That maybe you're not the only person in the damn galaxy who wants life to be different? Bloodseas, you're such a whiny brat!"

"Sure, mate, lecture me, that's going to get you into my pockets," Scrita muttered.

Lem rubbed her palms over her eyes. "Gah, Njande help me, I know," she groaned. "I know I'm messing this up. I know it's whack to try to threaten or force you or whatever. It's—it's a stupid habit, a weapon I fall back on, because that's what *works*. I don't talk my way out, I got my own crutches, and when I whack people with them they work. I'm sorry."

"Why are you telling me this? I'm not your psychologist," Lark grumbled. She squirmed; proximity to honesty might scald her scales.

"I'm saying there's a right way to do this thing, and I don't know what it is. I don't have time to play tact right now, and I know it's messed up for me to just thrash you—"

"—And besides you can't—"

"So I'm just *asking* you, girl to girl, hook me up with your disguise thingies. I'm not asking you to help the Frelsi. I'm asking you to help me."

"And what am I going to get out of that?"

"I'll owe you one."

Well look at the ovaries of steel on this one! With Rana's message still fresh on her compupad Lark had everything to gain by *stopping* Benzaran, and here the girl wanted help for *free*? The sheer class of it all, or perhaps the lack of class, blew her mind.

"I said some shyte back there about anarchy and blowing stuff up," Lem said. "I wasn't just puffing smoke. I'm going against orders. I'm putting myself out here because I don't want to repeat your story.

"And—" Lem paused. "I don't mean to talk outta turn or anything. But if you want revenge for your parents, this is a way to do it."

Opposing the Frelsi *and* whacking the Growen? Lark gripped her fists against her chest and blinked back angry tears, completely unable to pretend anymore. It was the most disgusting bait, and she wanted it more than the Frelsi nutter could even imagine. Here, she didn't have to side with the ghost, or somehow overcome her blasted inabilities and throw her whole life away in order to make someone pay. Here, the waitress came to her asking for the poison.

Lark knew full well that she wouldn't feel satisfied. Until she somehow atoned for her parents *herself* she would *still* hate herself for her cowardice. But she wanted this third way out. It was time for her to find the good things in the universe, like the doctor had said, to let her parents settle for this small sin offering: Lark desperately needed *rest*. Forget money, that little boy's glee when she brought him home, and that Benzaran child's hope when Lark mentioned Lem, *those* were the good side of the universe and yes, Lark needed a stint there like she needed oxygen.

In the two weeks she'd waited for the trouble twins to heal, Lark had gotten her wristband fixed. It was time to put that to good use.

Time to keep a promise to a little girl.

CARL

Bricandor probably wouldn't kill the little girl. She was a weapon, right? Maybe she'd even have a stable life now—kids under Frelsi care spent a lot of time getting bombed.

Even if Bricandor did kill her, that was his business.

Whatever you do to one of Njande's friends, you do to Njande.

This guilt thing, though.

Carl pinched his forefinger and glove together to check off the next item on his pre-flight checklist. The enormous, copper-colored hangar bay of the Growen spacecraft carrier buzzed around him with Stygges decking out their two-man fighters for the upcoming space battle over Fort Jehu. They all dressed in gray cargo cloth, with multiple pockets and zippers, and each one did his or her work in silence—none of this screaming orders like a normal blitzer unit. Carl approved. But he wasn't getting combat pay, so approval or not, he needed to leave before the fight started. The spacecraft carrier was already nearing Luna-Guetala.

Engines test go—Carl circled to check the landing gear of his ship now.

He had heard, and never understood, the metaphor about weights on people's chests: unless you had a psychosomatic disorder, mental relief did not manifest in your thorax. But today Carl *felt* that metaphorical weight lifted. The air seemed lighter, thinner, almost empty, even though he knew the fluid in his breathing mask hadn't changed: that heavy perfume-like presence was gone.

He kind of missed it.

What.

It was an accurate assessment of his emotional state, though.

Carl did another external weapons' check, still plowing through his preflight checklist. Was the girl a weapon in *this* battle? It took a lot of arrogance to have glass dolls delivered to your construction site. Bricandor was assuming he'd win, obviously.

Eh, and he probably would. That one there, the girl lifting her spaceship with one hand? That wasn't normal. She was electromagnetic for sure. Oh, and that guy. That guy standing by the window, blinking and pointing at meteors. He looked weird. But every time he pointed at a meteor it exploded. Carl didn't know what that guy was, but he would rather not fight someone whose warm-up routine involved winning staring contests against rocks. Carl liked rocks. They were quiet.

Carl's skin crawled a little. Just a little. He'd never liked that metaphor, either, because skin cannot physically crawl, but he felt his arm-hair twitch and that qualified. Really, now, what did Bricandor want with the girl? Carl made a point of respecting his clients' lifestyles. Even if that involved killing little girls with rare hair mutations. But he was definitely curious.

Carl sighed. "Computer, search for private psychiatrists on extremely remote, unpopulated planets," he whispered, stepping over his tool-trunk and checking off the next item from his checklist. Time to end this temporary insanity once and for all.

CHAPTER FORTY-TWO

Jei

THE BONT BOUNTY HUNTER'S STOLEN MAGGOT REEKED OF MILDEW. The warm metal floor hummed uncomfortably underneath me as I found the auxiliary safety straps and fastened myself behind Scrita's pilot seat. Lem squeezed in beside me, fumbling around for her straps as the ringed outside panel slid shut and oxygen began to hiss from the seams in the floor. This little spot was for prisoners and cargo, and maybe that reality, after spending so much time as an actual prisoner, accounted for the fluttering in my stomach.

"You sure he'll be safe here?" Lem asked me.

I studied her in silence. Her stealth-modified blitzer helmet—more of a pressurized jumpsuit for your face—still threw me off, and her familiar cadence in this new masculine voice sounded too perfect, too her and yet not her. She fit the persona Scrita gave her so well that to hear her ask about her Cinta seemed ... strange.

"Yeah," I said. "The doctor's transferring him to a more secure building right now. Diebol doesn't need any bad publicity from killing helpless civilians in sickbays; maybe on a less media-savvy planet, maybe for a more important target, but right now he can't take the extra attention while he's got a warship in Undecided territory." I leaned back against the inclined floor, inspecting the barrel of my new blitzer-issued rifle to avoid eye contact. "You're gonna hate me for saying this, but with no powers, and you free, Cinta isn't worth it like we are. Diebol probably doesn't even know he's alive." It crossed my mind Diebol wouldn't bother killing a civilian who was already good as dead, but I didn't tell Lem that. "Diebol wants *us*. Cinta's safer if we're farther away."

Lem opened her mouth, but Lark Scrita glanced back at us over her shoulder. "All set, mates? Aw, don't you two look quite the nasty blitzer couple, all cuddled up there. Prepare for takeoff and all that."

Lem grumbled and inched away from me a tad. *This girl.* She turned her head to stare out the window as we lifted off. The floor rumbled underneath us until we reached the tips of the long, thin trees that tangled like kelp through the world's low-grav upper atmosphere, and then, when space swallowed us, everything became quiet.

Lem yanked back the bolt of her rifle. "Hold up," she snapped. "Why are we going into space? The missile command center's on Revelon."

"Don't knot your knickers, it's harder for them to see you coming if we drop in from above," said Scrita, pushing against the grey-green control panel buttons to speed up the ship. "Come on, mate, you really think I'd give you guns if I planned to kidnap you?"

"Well, you didn't give them to us. We found 'em in the compartment back here."

"I knew they were there."

"You definitely didn't." Lem laughed. "I know you're a liar, remember?"

Scrita now grumbled something incoherent. They'd found each other's buttons pretty fast, these two girls.

The unease in my core wouldn't rest. This wasn't normal for me. My meditative state guaranteed I never felt anything more than a quiet caution before a mission, and even on my first space flight— everyone throws up their first time—my stomach stayed quiet. Now? It was like I'd swallowed a time bomb. I could feel it ticking.

Say hello to Lem for me.

What did Diebol know that I didn't?

I couldn't shake the feeling that we were too late. We were too late, and walking into another trap.

LEM

Wind smashed against Lem's face as the rings of the Maggot split open.

"We're over your drop-point in sixty secs, parachutes on!"

"We have parachutes?" yelled Jei.

"Strapped to the back wall!"

"This is not what we agreed on!" Lem shouted. She unstrapped herself from the floor and yanked the soft tab on the wall, dropping a parachute onto her lap.

"And I didn't agree to anything at all, so I suppose it's fair, then!" Scrita called over the wind. "Thirty seconds!"

Lem plunged her arms into the straps on the chute and stood, gaping wide-eyed back and forth from Jei to the ragged, pine-infested, spiked terrain below. Jei set his jaw, placed his hands on the ceiling, and planted himself, legs apart, in front of the open gap in the ship.

"There's a big field up ahead not far from your main gate! Jump there!" Scrita yelled.

Lem sucked in her breath and turned to Jei. "I haven't done airborne school yet," she gulped.

"I can't hear you!" He gripped her hand. "Ready?"

No, not really.

But that's what made this awesome, right? *Act it to be it.* "More ready than you'll ever be!" Lem shouted—and she jumped, yanking him out the ship with her.

The rushing shock of sky falling at her jolted her lungs as Jei yelped his surprise, tightening his grip on her wrist. "Spread your arms and legs!" he roared. She obeyed. Her chest heaved in drowned gasps; her eyes watered; her fingers dug into Jei's skin.

But her mind cleared, pressure-washed by blasting oxygen. A grassy field closed in on her. Parachute? Parachute, when was he going to say parachute? She drew in her arm to find the tab to pull—

"Not yet!" Jei yelled.

"Where is it?" she screamed back.

"Right shoulder, above the strap! Pull ... now!"

Her fingers closed around woven cord. This had to be it. She yanked. She yanked everything she found there.

It was like falling groin-first on a tightrope. Jei let her go as the parachute deployed with a whoosh, and the sudden slowing jerked the harness against Lem's body and damn it chafed. Lem instantly missed the rush.

"Man, this isn't half as fun," she said as they floated towards the lime-green turf. Patches of it gleamed turquoise in the mid-day sun.

Jei didn't answer.

"Dude, you mad at me already?" she asked. She gripped the harness, trying to lean forward to see him as he floated a few feet away from her.

"Next time, wait for me to count off," he called. "Or you can count off. I don't care. But somebody has to count."

"If I waited 'til you counted I'd have time to freak myself out," she shouted back.

"Maybe so, but I will punch you next time you pull a stunt like that!"

"You can try! Anything I should know about landing?"

"Don't land on me," he said. "And don't land on a tree."

"Great, thanks, I couldn't figure any of that out myself."

"You're welcome!"

The floating didn't last as long as she'd expected—the ground came up pretty fast. She could see individual blades of grass now. She was still moving forward, so—run, right? *That's what you're supposed to do, run.* She started running.

The ground and her legs met with a lurch. The impact stung for an instant—she managed six steps or so and fell forward with her chute on top of her.

She crawled out from under it to find a blitzer towering above her, legs planted apart and both hands on his flayer rifle. Grey armor cast tight shadows on his abs.

"You're really scary-looking in that uniform," she said.

"Was that your first jump?" Jei asked as she stood up and brushed herself off.

"Yeah, that's what I was trying to tell you. Haven't taken airborne school yet."

"That makes more sense, then. Because I mean, I was going to say …"

"Yeah, yeah, it was bad, I know. Forget you. I see two security guards at the front gate over there who wanna know why blitzers are jumping here, let's go steal their faces."

"Roger that."

They'd landed almost smack-dab in the middle of a field about an acre wide and long, with tall pines and jagged spires of rock surrounding them in the distance. At the end of the field a twelve-story-high domed cylinder stood sentinel over the wilderness, only the tip of a white missile silo that rested much deeper underground. The conifers growing around the dome stretched high over the silo dome, unimpeded by Revelon's low gravity field.

Lem and Jei swaggered down the field towards the nervous security guards at the iron gate. Tan stubble coated the exposed wrists, hands, and jaws of the thin, rock-looking humanoid Revelonians; they stood about twice Lem's height and half Lem's girth, like impressionist, living statues born of mountain and pine. Sun glinted off their reflective green uniforms and helmets with black visors.

The left guard shouted a challenge in Revelonian, one hand outstretched palm-forward and the other holding his rifle steady. A real blitzer helmet would have translated what he said, but Scrita's illusion did nothing. Lem glanced at Jei.

"Don't answer," he muttered. "Steady 'til we're close."

Four more marching steps. The other guard screamed a warning. He didn't like Growen blitzers marching on his missile silo, apparently. Sweat beaded on Lem's forehead. "Jei ..."

"Revelonian rules of engagement. One more warning shot before they're cleared to fire."

Lem held her swagger steady. She could see the two security cameras atop the iron gate now; almost read the name-tapes on the guards' uniforms. Her throat tightened.

"You better do it now or I will," Lem hissed.

"Count with me. Three beats."

Another screaming order. "One," Jei said.

"Two," Lem said, with two more steps, her fingers hungry for the rifle strapped on her back. The warning shot came.

"Three." The Revelonian rifles aimed.

Lem and Jei threw out their hands. The weapons flew into the air with Jei's surge; with Lem's the security cameras fizzled and popped as Lem and Jei rushed the guards under the up-pointed rifles, Jei right, Lem left. Lem yanked the chloroformed cloth from the pocket in her tunic. Her knuckles rasped against mineral-skin as she grabbed the front of her guard's uniform, stepped on his knee, heaved herself up into his high face—she jammed the wet cloth over his nose and held it there as he flailed, her teeth clenched, her breath held ... until finally, he fell.

"It's like climbing a tree," she said, jumping off him and stroking the transformation film Scrita had glued under her left collarbone. She heard a faint hum as the camera looped over her ear processed the guard's face. She stretched out her hands as they changed, rippling with rocky edges as tan mineral crawled up her arms like a fungus. She clenched her fists, satisfied, and looked over at Jei.

"Don't let anyone punch over your head," Jei laughed. "It looks real but—" The fake Revelonian wiped his long, thin fingers clean through his neck. "The physical part of the simulation software definitely doesn't know how to deal with this height difference."

"Noted. My head doesn't even make it to my dude's chest." Lem grinned and propped her guard up against the iron gate-posts. She leaned against the metal as she waved the guard's security pass against the lock—

And she fell through as the gate softened like polymerwall.

"Not iron," Jei said as he walked through after her, chuckling.

"Yeah, I got that," she grumbled, picking herself up.

They marched across another field and around the periphery to the second security checkpoint. Same drill. Swagger up without a word. Jei took out weapons while Lem took out cameras. Climb some giant people, chloroform some spikey faces. Borrow those faces for the next gate's security clearance. This inner perimeter had people in it—mostly Revelonian guards walking around or chatting up repair personnel, and a few private contractors in long blue robes —but only one or two recognized Lem's new Revelonian face, and she just smiled and nodded and kept on keeping on until she'd left their talking behind.

"This is almost too easy," Lem said as they approached their third gate.

"Don't ever say that. That's like saying you're too alive right now," Jei said. "I really hope none of those guys was telling you to get back to your post."

"Good thing I'm already back at my post—*twice*," she said. "That just blew your mind, didn't it? Pshh! Being three people in six minutes makes for crazy double-speak!"

"Good thing," Jei echoed absently. He glanced around them as they rounded the corner away from the crowded courtyard, towards the small white door in the side of the building that led to the missile silo's repair sector. Lem could sense his stiffness.

"Dude, chill," she said.

"We're running out of time," he said.

"How do you know?"

"My brain-magic says so," he said.

"Gotta love your brain-magic."

The guards tucked into the cranny by this side gate seemed more anal than everyone else. Lem saw the one guy's hand stretching towards the alarm before Lem and Jei even made it within ten meters; the other guy straight up started firing when he saw them.

But Jei kept the guards' hands down, and Lem fried the cameras. It really wasn't hard, not after the Stygge training center. They each stole a face and an ID card, passed the iris scan, and slipped out of the sunlight into the frigid innards of the missile silo's repair center.

Lem shivered, gripping her biceps and looking behind her as the fat little door shut behind them. Her soft boots made no sound on the honeycomb patterned metal grates lining the floors of the dim hallway.

"Holy shyte it's cold as my heart in here," Lem said.

"They live on a cool planet. It's a searing summer sun out there to them—this is probably refreshing," said Jei. "Also, new record for most ridiculous thing out of your mouth."

"How's this: Frelsi mess halls serve real food."

"Stop, you're breaking my brain."

"All part of my evil Stygge plan." Lem glanced around the corner and narrowed her eyes as she adjusted to the darkness. "Repair-dude coming this way."

"He's yours, we just need one identity to open the exhaust channel."

"Roger that," she said. She almost laughed—her mouth felt funny using Jei's planet-Alpino version of military speak. She usually just said "yes sir" at home.

The honeycomb-patterned metal lining the walls pulsed with soft red light; long shadows draped the rough contours of Lem's Revelonian skin as she stalked towards the poor repair-man and his bright orange suit. She didn't blame him for jumping when he saw the tall guard. Still, her intentions aside, she smiled and waved as she approached.

He shouted something, and whirled and ran.

"Dammit!" Lem bolted after him. Jei stepped out behind her and threw his hand out—Lem felt a soft rush of wind. The repairman's boot flew up in the air. He fell. Lem leapt, tackled him, and stuffed her cloth over his face.

"I think smiling means something different in their culture," Jei said.

"I think you should be careful about yankin' people's feet out from under them! You almost whacked his head on the metal!" She stiffened, waiting for Jei's retort as she photographed the man to borrow his face, but it never came. Fine, now wasn't the time. "Where we gonna stow him?"

"There's a janitor's closet down the next hallway."

"Dang, you memorized those blueprints like you built the place."

"It's what I do. Hurry up."

At last they knelt by the grate in the floor that led into the bowels of the silo. Lem unlocked the grate with her repair-man's privileged iris scan, heaved the metal bars out of the way, and gazed into the well.

Her head grew lighter. Below her a ladder led into the warm darkness of an abyss. This was where the fiery exhaust went when the missile fired. This was where you didn't want to be when explosions went off.

"Would you be angry at me if this is a trap, and we die in there?" Jei asked.

"No," Lem said. "We're not going to die, and I'm not going to be angry."

But the heat in the exhaust tunnel made her think of Fort Jehu burning.

CHAPTER FORTY-THREE

Carl

THE FLOOR SHUDDERED AS THE STYGGE SPACECRAFT CARRIER released its first volley of missiles.

Carl still felt he needed to review his pre-flight checklist another time, but he was already cutting this exit closer than he preferred. He slammed his toolbox shut and shoved it through the polymerwall under the *Huntress*'s pregnant beetle-belly. "Huntress, load equipment." She'd make sure it went where it belonged. "Computer, showcase download progress." He pushed the ladder up after the toolbox while the computer brought two download screens to his visor: one screen showed the ongoing psychiatrist search, and the other his new collection of Growen archives. While he was here, he might as well steal everything Bricandor knew.

About two percent complete on the psychiatrist, and eighty on the stolen goods. Carl pushed his arms through the polymerwall and heaved himself up into the belly of his ship.

The ladder was, of course, nowhere to be seen—the *Huntress* had cleaned it up—and Carl stood in a slick black tube just his size, embraced by 360 degrees of wall. "*Huntress*, load pilot." The floor rose, and Carl emerged in the ultra-reflective doorless black hallway that ran down the *Huntress*'s core like a spine. He counted paces—twelve point five—and entered the polymerwall that led into the cockpit. If you entered at eight paces, or at thirteen, the *Huntress* shot you.

Carl found those numbers comforting.

Crack.

Carl lifted his boot and groaned. Who'd left this video game controller here?

His ship seemed so quiet. And smell-less. That presence around the girl, was it addictive? Because he suddenly wanted it.

Was it in the galley?

What a strange question.

But Carl became quite convinced of a presence in his kitchen. He drew his top right flayer pistol and raised it as he crept to the polymerwall between the cockpit and the galley …

A glow-whip slashed through the wall, winding around his neck. He choked as the whip yanked him forward—he slammed against the floor. His weapon went off, burning a hole in the cabinet as a small person leapt atop his shoulders and pinned his arms behind his back. He rolled left, hard, and whacked the person against the galley wall. He was on his back now, its leg pinned under his body. Wrists next. He snatched its wrists with one hand, reaching for his gun with his other—a boot kicked his hand away. Wow, this creature was flexible.

His senses argued. He saw a blitzer, but felt softness flickering through the armor like it only existed sometimes—

Humanoid female. He'd guessed lizard before. He'd guessed wrong.

"Lark Scrita," Carl said, on top of her now. "How did you get in here?"

"You ran over your checklist four times, you obsessive oaf, how did I *not* get in here!" she snarled back. "A Stygge was looking at me funny so I had to hide somewhere!"

Four times on one checklist? Wow. This was ridiculous.

It was time to accept it. He cared. Clearly, these were symptoms of caring about that little girl, and her weird aura-person, and clearly, something had changed, and he could either remain in denial about that change and continue letting fools sneak onto his ship in his distraction, or he could deal with it, here and now.

"Why do you have the interdimensional around you?" Carl asked. "Where does he come from?"

"I don't know what the bloody hell you're talking about, you wonky bastard, and I don't have time to find out!" Scrita screamed. "They're going to kill the kid, so either shoot me now or let me go save her!"

"How do you know—"

"Bricandor has a history of buying kids from different suppliers, you nincompoop, he's into some freaky thingamasex, now shoot me or help me!"

Hm, no, he needed the waif in one piece if she was to explain this interdimensional business to him. Also, this was a very difficult lifestyle choice to accept.

"Turn off your pan-sense projector," Carl ordered. "It's annoying."

"What?!"

"The—thing—that changes—your—appearance!" Carl enunciated.

"I'm not daft! I won't do that!"

Carl leaned close to her face. That was what people did for emphasis. "If you want to save her you will turn it off. You will be my prisoner. I have Commander-level access to this spacecraft carrier's halls. I will bring you to Bricandor. You will bring the girl to my ship. You will not talk too much." Carl took a deep breath. This was so much talking. "Go."

Carl jumped to his feet, jerking Lark Scrita up with him. He released one of her hands—she reached into her shirt—

He pinned her hand against her chest. "No weapons," he said.

"I'm turning off the pan-sense thing, you imbecile!" she hissed. "Bloodseas!"

He released her. She turned into a lizard.

"No. Off."

"No one knows me as anything but this!"

"You don't *want* Bricandor to know your business-persona."

"Fine," she muttered. She turned into a human girl.

"You waste time."

Carl dragged her out of the cockpit, slapping shackles on her wrists along the way. Yes. This was fair. He would trade the annoying gullible wannabe to Bricandor for the girl.

CHAPTER FORTY-FOUR

Jei

I COUGHED, NARROWING MY AIRWAYS AGAINST THE SMELL OF ACID waste mixed with burnt organic *something* as we ran through the exhaust tunnel. The grime on the walls made abstract shapes under the light of the wristbands we'd borrowed from the mercenary's Maggot; the twisted details in the shadows reminded me of the arabesque tattoo art drawn by humans on my home planet.

Alpino. Temperatures like Revelon's over a gravity-field like Luna-Guetala's created a biome of fresh lime-green plains and volcanoes and spectacular roving rainstorms that covered almost the whole planet …

How was it possible that remembering home made the squirming in my stomach *worse*? It really felt like I'd forgotten something, like my keys or uniform cover or imminent death.

Say hello to Lem for me …

Up ahead we found the base of the missile—white, clean, shining and unused, its giant exhaust ports pointed at us like bus-sized rifle barrels. It was intimidating to imagine what would happen if those went off.

"Not a bad way to die," Lem said.

"You'd have at least five seconds of horrible incinerating pain," I said.

"That's still faster than a flayer cartridge to the gut."

I shrugged. If I wanted to go, I'd shoot myself in the head, not the gut, but I didn't plan on telling *her* that.

Not that I planned to go at all! Bloodseas, that was the second time I'd thought about self-inflicted death in the past eighteen hours. I'd never do anything like that—the thought really bothered me! *Yeah ... that psych eval, though.*

The floor and the walls became hole-filled metal mesh as we reached the ladder that led out of the exhaust ports into the control room above us. Reservoirs of acid gleamed below. It reeked like caustic apple juice—if apple juice could dissolve your flesh.

"What's that stuff for?" Lem asked.

"Clearing the debris out of these exhaust tunnels to prevent a fire before take-off," I said. "Or it's part of the fuel mixture. I don't know as much about Revelonian missile design. Either way it'll flood these hallways before the missile goes off."

"Ick." Lem gripped the ladder and raced up ahead of me. I followed, my stomach pounding now with my heart and my head. We were so close now. We just needed to steal the identity of the top-brass engineer who monitored the computer above us, unlock the computer with his DNA, enter vector 33956, and steer the missile as it neared the Growen spacecraft carrier. Lem opened the grate at the top of the ladder, and leapt out into the light.

Her strangled cry jolted my whole body.

I raced after her, my palms scraping the rough rungs in my haste. An ambush, a surprise, Diebol, what?

I broke into the room above and my terrified heart curled into a ball and hid in my throat.

Empty, wide and empty white floor stretched off into the distance, reflective walls echoing my gnarled form back at me—it was empty, why was the room so empty? Clean, completely clean, without a smudge or a spot, no tiles, no seams, just vast reflective ivory. The enormous side of the missile loomed twenty meters to my right like another white, spotless wall—

I needed to be sheltered, needed walls close to me, but I couldn't go *to* them—what if this was the interrogation center, and I'd walk, walk, run, but never reach a wall, always trapped on the infinite plane? *No door!* One of the walls was polymerwall, said my brain— but I didn't dare test to see which! What if I couldn't find it? Touched the wall, and couldn't get out?

"We know the layout," I gasped. My voice was tiny in the vast room. "We can get out any time."

No, screamed my insides. *No we can't, we tried and tried and couldn't! Couldn't even touch the wall, couldn't sit against it, couldn't lie down without rolling ...* Phantom electric shocks shuddered through me. My upper legs burned, bone smashed to mosaic by neodymium maces; my knee felt weak, my throat singed and the smell of blue poison suffocated me.

"Calm down," I said to us. "Calm down, it's just an empty room!"

You're afraid of empty rooms! Diebol's reflective mind-chambers with the moving walls—you didn't know they'd do this, did you? It's worse than PTSD. It's a phobia. You can't do this. Run. Squirm back into your little hole like a cockroach afraid of the light.

That voice. I didn't move. I hadn't moved since stepping into the room. I stood legs apart, hands stiff by my sides, fingers twitching and cold sweat seeping down my underarms to my elbows as I trembled, my tongue dry, a man incapacitated by emptiness. Beaten by nothing.

"I can't do this," I croaked. "I can't—"

Are empty rooms really empty? Or is emptiness how I got into you in the first place? Nature abhors a vacuum. Vacuums breed me*!*

The thing. The oil thing I could not beat. "Njande, help!"

I didn't get a magic surge, miraculous vision, wild Lem experience. I couldn't feel him in this panic, and I didn't see him fight besides me.

But my logical mind remembered my green thread.

I forced myself to turn my head.

Lem was curled up nearby, rocking, her eyes closed, singing to herself through paroxysms of panic, fighting it and snotting and choking and losing. "He's stronger, stronger, it's okay, it's okay! Gah—hth—it's okay!"

No one should see her like that. I didn't think anymore. I dropped on my knees, slid to her side. Wrapped my arms around her shoulders. She didn't shrink away.

She gripped my hand. She gulped. She kept her eyes closed, didn't look at me, as her singing grew softer and she pushed down the crying. I squeezed her hand tighter, fixed my eyes on her face, on my safety, our green thread, as I breathed too fast. *No emptiness, no.* If she was there, she was there, the room wasn't empty, and we could always leave. She was there, so Njande was there …

Our breathing slowed together. I held her still; she fought off the fear for both of us.

My heart rate returned to normal.

Lem opened her eyes.

She glanced at me and took a deep breath. Yup, that was a "let me go" face. I stood up and backed off, not even helping her to her feet, and she got up and followed me across the room, and we never, ever spoke of it again.

What would we have said, anyway? "Yup, Diebol sure ruined our lives." "I promise not to tell anyone you're afraid of open spaces now." "I bet you fifty drachmas they never let us run another mission again."

Because we still had one mission left.

LEM

Lem stretched out her shoulder as they crossed the large room, taking slow even breaths. Bloodseas. That was rough.

'S'not really an empty room anyhow—just a giant circle with a

332

second circle inside it. And a beautiful big missile inside that second circle.

If their wimping-out hadn't already alerted the technician, he'd have his computer set up behind the missile. Lem trotted along the left side of the cylindrical warhead behind Jei, tracing her hand against the six-foot-thick clear wall that separated her from the power within. She felt safe touching the wall. *It doesn't move, see? Not a centimeter.*

Jei froze. Lem peered over his shoulder—

Thick, shimmering blue blood seeped around the side of the warhead.

It flowed, creeping across the floor towards them. It was fresh. Lem pressed her back against the missile's wall. Jei did the same, weapon at the ready, as they rounded the bend.

A long body lay splayed on the floor, blood draining from the neck.

Blood dripped from the simple white desk protruding from the missile wall, and there on the desk under the compuwall lay the head of the lead engineer.

Solid black eyes stared wide open at them—behind them?

Jei whirled and threw out his hand. Heat whooshed past Lem's cheek as she turned; yellow light blinded her eyes for a moment as a flayer cartridge whizzed past her face. She blinked, and tripped backwards.

A red mace flew at her face.

Electricity blasted from her forehead, exploding the weapon away from her. Pain coursed through her temples. The adrenaline burst made time seem slow, and she had a moment to wonder, *Wait, is that mine?*

Jei was pouncing forward beside her, rifle blazing. Lem's head pounded with aftershock as she stumbled, but she saw the man in black leather crouched like a spider in the corner near the ceiling, a stark blotch glued against the white wall by em-static. One hand pinned his pistol against the wall as he stabilized himself after Jei's deflection; the other hand, outstretched, levitated two neodymium maces. The maces spun like turbines, generating two forcefields, repelling the cartridges from Jei's gun.

"Your radio's open, Bereens," Diebol said.

His green eyes burned.

CHAPTER FORTY-FIVE

Bricandor

HOW HE LOVED CHILDREN.

With the Flickerform pleased with his little human sacrifice, and the Awakener poised inside the Frelsi base, Bricandor, Master of the Galaxy, was fueled for victory. He stood at the head of his space-craft carrier, in the center of a room built of windows, space a panorama around him as he threw his fingers through the air like a conductor. The Frelsi had come out, drawn to the bait like cock-roaches, in fighters and missile interceptors and other little toys—as if the missiles were the problem, as if that were all.

They should have stayed in their safe little hole.

His Stygges flooded from underneath him, a wave of ships each with one pilot, and one destroyer. Poof, a Stygge ship flew by, and a Frelsi engine blew out. Oh, was that a Frelsi pilot, strangling to death for no apparent reason? There was a Stygge ship behind him.

Bricandor closed his eyes and searched for little minds. One— poof! He turned it off, held it for a few seconds, and it blinked away.

Oh, and another mind. This one called itself Rana. A Captain, a Captain given the option to lead from the rear, but oh, it appeared a true officer, like the generals of old, rode into battle from the front.

Pity. He would have lived to lose his bet to the Biouk.

Snap!

And the life was out.

JEI

Two spinning, floating forcefields of color protected Diebol as I pinned him in the corner with a steady stream of bullets. At least this answered that nagging feeling in me. It was good to see him. He'd drop a shield eventually. And then, before the Stygges took Fort Jehu, I was going to kill him.

"Holy shyte," Lem groaned, still gripping her head, apparently in pain from her electric explosion. "That's my mace—you killed that dude with my mace! What did that guy ever do to you?"

"Cautionary slaughter. I figured you might need him," Diebol smiled. "Are you upset you didn't get to strangle him first?"

Lem growled and threw her hand towards him. Her fingertips sparked—the charge fizzled uselessly into her palm—she grimaced.

"Screw this." She knelt and raised her gun, stabilizing herself against the outside wall while I leaned against the missile, both trying to angle a shot in around his dual shields. Diebol drifted his outstretched hand upward like a conductor starting a crescendo; the red mace rose from the floor again to swing at Lem.

"You can levitate three maces at once?" Lem whistled, rolling out of the way. "Hell, that's one way to get around the DNA-lock."

"He did that to impress you," I teased darkly.

"Well, I'm impressed!"

Something flickered in his eyes. Ha! Her approval distracted him. I threw an em-push from my right hand to knock one of his shields above his head; I slid forward under him, swung my rifle through the new gap towards his stomach, finger taut on the trigger—

Diebol gnashed his teeth. As I fired his em-push jerked my aim to the side towards Lem; I pulled back a second too late, and I shot her instead of him.

LEM

A burning flayer cartridge from Jei's rifle seared Lem's deltoids. A weird clarity penetrated the pain: she saw Jei's horrified face turned towards her, Diebol's bitten lip as he dropped one forcefield to level a pistol at Jei's unguarded temple …

Her mace floating mid-air …

Lem leapt, snatched her mace out of the air, and twirled it into a forcefield between the pistol and Jei. The shot bounced back into Diebol's shoulder. He fell—his head thwacked against the wall on his way to the floor. His mace and Jei's mace clattered down beside him.

"Now we're even," Lem said.

JEI

Lem ran to the missile, gripping her shoulder with clenched teeth as she dragged the headless Revelonian towards the compuwall; I trotted to the corner with my gun to make sure the unconscious Stygge stayed that way. Behind me the air popped as Lem shocked the dead man's chest to simulate heart-beat so the computer would interpret his fingerprint as living and unlock the missile controls.

I aimed the rifle at Diebol's head. Lined my eye up in the sight. Stroked the trigger. I couldn't believe it. Finally. Finally this was happening. Why did it freak me out? I began the squeeze as my breathing slowed and the moment froze.

The gun swerved to the side.

"Are you kidding me—" I yanked it back with every magnetic

cell in my body—it was like pushing against a wall. His hand shot out to grip the barrel—it burned him, I'd recently fired it and his palm sizzled, but he didn't care. He grimaced, grinned, rose as I pushed, and he pushed, and his other hand flew to my throat, and I elbowed it off and slammed my forehead against his face, and he softened my blow with another magnetic push.

"You can't shoot me," he whispered. "You can't give your all against me. You're trained, a trained monkey, and you'll always hold back just a little bit."

I growled, shoved my shoulder into his, and fired the gun. The impact forced him to let go as the shot hit the wall—I sensed a change in his magnetic field—glanced behind me to see two maces hurtling towards my head—

I ducked, grabbed my yellow mace out of the air, and spun to block the other one, his black-lit violet. I whirled away from him and fired one-handed with the rifle.

He deflected the gun and leapt at me, catching his own mace mid-air and slamming it down across my shoulder. I blocked; the impact crushed me onto the floor. I braced for his blow—

But he hurled his mace to the side, at Lem and the missile controls. His other hand drew back like an archer's pulling a bowstring: the rifle in Lem's hand lifted to point at me! My em-push whacked his mace out of the air to save her but I couldn't get a forcefield going with *my* mace, couldn't do two things at once, and she was going to shoot me and—

Nope. She yanked her gun off-course. The flayer cartridge hit Diebol in the thigh.

"Will you *stop* that?" He roared at her.

"Oh, does it suck to be shot? I wouldn't know." She slammed a button on the compuwall. The floor reverberated with a rush like a thousand rivers un-dammed at once, and the computer began to count down. The missile glowed orange.

I took advantage of Diebol's pain. I swiped his legs out from under him, leapt to my feet, forgot the stupid gun, and swung my mace at him with both hands. He fell—

And grinned?

I heard Lem scream behind me.

I whirled to see her fall into the closest manhole, into the exhaust tunnels, dragged in by Diebol's electromagnetic power. The grate locked over her.

"Oh dear," Diebol said. "It looks like starting the missile put the center on lockdown. No more opening anything with stolen retinal scans."

"Dammit," I cried, running for the vent. I slammed my mace against it. Again. Again! But every time the magnetically-sealed floor shut off the neodymium lasers on the mace's tip, turning it into a useless staff of faux-bamboo.

"I suppose you'll have to stop the missile or she'll be fried," Diebol said, picking himself up to lean against the wall. "My, if I'd known you two would come in through the exhaust tunnels, I'd have started the missile myself. Oh wait—" he cocked his head. "Is that screaming? I suppose the tunnels are filling with acid now."

"I am going to plaster your brains across the walls," I snarled.

"I wonder what dear Njande thinks about that," he laughed. "In the meantime, who else will you kill? Little Lem, or her entire home base?"

CHAPTER FORTY-SIX

Lark

L ARK COULD SEE HER REFLECTION IN THE BRONZE SURFACE OF every wall as the Ebon Shadow dragged her along, and it shocked her. Bully, she couldn't remember the last time she'd seen herself as a human—five years ago? Her once-chubby face had become gently moon-like, with almond eyes like her mother's, and her father's light-coffee skin had pimples now. Whose silky, ragged shoulder-length hair framed this accusation of the past staring at her?

"Stop looking at your face," said the Shadow. "It is fine. It is appropriately helpless and small. You need to match it."

Beans, what an ass. He was right, though. Lark began to pull back from him and cry, playing up the captured damsel bit. Men loved that shyte, she'd done it often right before bagging crime-lords for small lawless towns. Small lawless towns would empty their treasuries for you if you'd get rid of their crime-lords. Feed you pie, too.

The Ebon Shadow was running now—on legs twice her length, forcing her to trip and trot and race and oh bully did she want to choke his stupid neck, but in two shakes and a half they'd busted into the command-center where the compuwalls glowed a neglected blue behind Bricandor while the old man twitched, flicking his fingers at his reflection in the windows 180 degrees around him.

What the … ? Lark *thought* she'd lied about Bricandor being into wonky thingamashytes, to get the Shadow moving, but … but these were certainly some wonky thingamashytes. Behind Bricandor four humans in gray vests stood in a square, each holding a cup for—some kind of … ritual?

"He's much shorter in person," said Lark. "Beans, he's like my height."

No one moved to answer the intrusion. Oh goodness it was so odd! Someone do something!

The Ebon Shadow cleared his throat. "I found this Frelsi sympathizer attempting to sabotage your ships."

"I'm not a Frelsi sympathizer!" Lark hissed.

"You've tried twice to rescue my Frelsi target. You have interdimensional-aura around you. You hate the Growen. Therefore you are Frelsi."

"My gosh, you're so daft," Lark grumbled. "Everything isn't black and white, you sheep!"

Bricandor turned, revealing the little girl lying unconscious behind him, her outstretched limbs draped over a small table decorated with triangular symbols. The old man dropped his hands in frustration. "*Excuse* me?"

"We need to negotiate a price for this one. Right now," said the Ebon Shadow. "Alone."

Wow, this guy had no experience lying at all. That was what happened when you got everything handed to you on a shiny black four-gun billion-drachma platter—you got soft in the head.

"Excuse you? I happen to be busy!" Bricandor said.

So the Ebon Shadow shot him.

And it all went to hell. Lark heard herself screaming expletives as the entire right polymerwall bust open for a horde of blitzers to charge into the room. Bricandor stood calmly, with one hand raised as if in half-prayer, while the Ebon Shadow's bullet veered past his face.

"You imbecile, he can block bullets!" Lark screamed as

Bricandor picked up the girl and walked left, leaving the room with his four Stygges in formation around him.

"He didn't block it, he deflected the gun." The Ebon Shadow unhooked Lark's shackles, his back to the blitzers as shots ricocheted off his armor.

"He can do both of those things! You do not shoot a Stygge! You are not a better sharpshooter than a Stygge! I don't care if you *are* a Stygge you do not shoot a Stygge!"

"Go get the girl." The Ebon Shadow unfurled one of the large tubes from the pack on his back and leveled it towards the charging blitzer crowd.

"'Go get the girl?' What the blasted bean-sauce do you mean 'go get the girl?!'" Lark cringed behind the Shadow's armor, seriously wondering how much it cost. The Ebon Shadow flicked a button on the side of the tube. Lights and switches emerged from its surface—bloody hell, it was a rocket-launcher!

The Ebon Shadow fired. The recoil did nothing to him. The shot bowled over the first row of blitzers.

Everyone ceased fire for a moment.

"Aaalright, I'll get the girl," Lark squeaked. She made a break for it as the one-man tank resumed his battle behind her.

Lark somersaulted through the left polymerwall of the room as cartridges exploded behind her, missing her back by centimeters.

"Stygge Bricandor!" she cried from her appropriate kneel.

"Really now?" Bricandor turned, his knife in one hand and Juju's dainty wrist floating in the other. "Who *are* you, anyway?"

The four Stygges holding cups in the corner of the room didn't move. They awaited orders. The whole empty bronze room awaited Lark's answer.

"I am what you want. Whatever you need *her* for, I can do better. Please take me in exchange for her. I love her. Please."

Bricandor tilted his head that same strange way he'd done when they first charged in on him. "She isn't lying," he murmured in surprise. "She doesn't know this child at all. They have no ties. Yet somehow, Flickerform, she isn't lying? Why would you want this one?" He seemed to be trying to sneer, but a vague cloud of confusion over his face kept it from happening.

Lark's heart thundered in her chest; her fingers clenched as her breath grew hoarse. "Because I carry around this Interdimensional all the time, the one you hate, and sometimes I even talk to it," she said. "I bloody hate it, but unlike this lass I know what it is. You're into twisted things, you can twist that. You can use me."

Bricandor dropped the little girl and walked towards Lark, his steps slow and deliberate like a hunting cat's, his hand outstretched like a divining rod, trembling with old age. "It is true and untrue?" he muttered.

"Take me, kill me," Lark hated how small and tiny her voice sounded. She hated that the smallness wasn't on purpose. "Do whatever you want to me, but let her go."

His withered fingers touched her forehead.

Lark tackled him. The Ebon Shadow blasted through the polymerwall on rocket-boots and scooped Juju Benzaran off the floor. Lark wrapped her glow-whip around the old man's neck. The Ebon Shadow looped through the air back towards the exit.

"Nice stalling!" said the Shadow.

But she wasn't stalling. It was real! Lark let out her breath in a delighted gasp of utter relief because she'd done it! Whatever *it* was, she didn't know, but she'd done something good, said something right, as herself, the child of her parents, and—and—

And everything froze.

Lark could not move. She could not breathe. She saw the Ebon Shadow hurled to the ground as Bricandor closed his fists and the rocket-boots exploded. The Shadow curled around the girl, protecting her with his body as the four Stygges pounced, beating him with their maces. Lark would have gasped as his armor crumbled under the violet neodymium, but her lungs would not—not—

What? Think. What. No. Words.

Dead?

CHAPTER FORTY-SEVEN

Lem

LEM GRABBED THE LADDER AS SHE FELL INTO THE MISSILE'S exhaust tunnel. Her weight wrenched her arm—pain shot through her underarm and shoulder as she slammed against the metal rungs with a stunned cry. Light glittered on the surface of the acid below her like the eyes of a predator. It was rising.

"Hoookay," Lem scrambled up the ladder to the vent's door and slapped the retinal scan key.

It didn't activate. The little screen wouldn't even turn on to look at her.

Acrid fear rose into the base of Lem's throat. Oh no. Oh no no no.

Lem pushed against the grate. She couldn't angle herself right on the ladder—couldn't position herself for a good shove—she was stupid, stupid weak.

A sharp scent stung her nostrils like the air outside the leather-tanner's shop in Cinta's town. Lem glanced down to see acid licking her boots.

"Oh no. Come on!"

Lem panicked and leapt shoulder-first *up* at the vent, off the ladder. Impact—ringing clang—no dent, and as she fell back down to land her foot slipped on the slimed rung.

Shyte shyte shyte!

She tumbled into the acid.

Agony enveloped her. Every pore and nerve bathed in fire—her fingers gripped iron and she jolted out from under the surface of the liquid to shriek. Her eyes stung with fumes, and squint as she might her vision still blurred with painful tears. She scrambled up, coughing against the vile thirsty vinegar smell, curling herself up on the highest rungs of the ladder as her lungs blasted vitriol in Biouk. There weren't words strong enough to describe this. There just weren't.

Every neuron was firing. Electricity arced around her, jumping through the tunnel as she clenched her teeth. *Calm down, try to calm down.* Bloodseas, how was it possible for her belly, her breasts, her skin to burn *more* once she got out of the acid? Shyte, her jumpsuit was wet, and the liquid was seeping through that, held against her skin—!

"Njande, I'd love to do that goddess thing now if you don't mind," Lem snapped, her hands slipping on the ceiling above her as she pushed. "Come on now, any time."

Acid lapped her knees.

"Njande!" she screamed. "Njande, what the hell, how am I supposed to save the universe if I'm *dead*?"

Thighs. It burned at her thighs now. She curled tighter, trying to fit higher up in the tunnel, but she was too broad to double up all the way. Her body shuddered. She flailed.

"Come *on*!"

The agony rose to her belly. She couldn't. She was too angry and freaked out. She couldn't control her powers. She didn't have power! She was weak. She was going to die.

Holy shyte, then, what was even the point? Her chest heaved in a terrified, hacking hyperventilation. She didn't want to dissolve, alive, in acid. She had a knife in her belt. She could kill herself. No point in prolonging the suffering. This level wasn't designed with a way out.

Jei had said that.

Then he'd said that hope was overrated, and *we don't fight because we're guaranteed to win, we fight because it's the right thing to do.*

Shyte. Her fingers tightened on the ladder. She didn't reach for the knife.

Was it really that stupid and simple? So simple it didn't matter what Njande was doing? So simple she wasn't *allowed* to give up. Because it was wrong, and that was it.

"Man, screw you and right and wrong," Lem groaned.

But Jei was right. Maybe Njande wasn't going to rescue her. Maybe he was. Maybe he thought she could take it. Maybe he was off fighting thirty dragons. Maybe he was ready for her to die so he could port her into his dimension and she'd save the universe from there. Maybe this was the best of twelve possible terrible timelines he'd had to choose between.

And maybe screw what he did, in this moment *she* was here, and she wasn't going to let go.

If he's acid, I don't care.

The liquid lapped her throat, and she gasped, but her heart-rate slowed, and the electric light stopped bouncing throughout the tunnel, and a slow, peaceful strength began to drip through her muscles.

To love him was her decision, *no matter what he did*, because it was right—miracle or rescue or not.

JEI

These levels aren't designed with a way out.

But that's when I make one.

I dropped my staff as Diebol walked over to the compuwall to stop the countdown. "I almost want to let the missile fire," he laughed over Lem's cries. "If I alter the course just a little bit, it'll hit her home planet. Won't that start a lovely political game between Revelon and Luna-Guetala."

He wanted me to fight him. To step in his path, to struggle to keep the missile alive and Lem in torment, to make me the actor in her demise. To choose like a rat in a maze.

But I refused to choose.

I closed my eyes. I knew a way. I knew one impossible thing: Lem had busted the door down on the tanker ship because she believed she could *push through.* This one time, just this one time I needed to believe with all my soul, with every neuron in my being, that impossible things could happen.

I knelt and placed my fingertips against the vent, my breathing slow, my shoulders forced into relaxation. Then! My breathing faster, deeper, my shoulders heaving with pure energy, untamed fire, the stuff of the beast within rising with no room for anything here but impossible, wild, crazy hope, Lem's hope, in oceans and oceans of green!

Flood me, Njande.

I pulled. Lem pushed. Diebol reached his left hand towards the missile controls and raised a gun towards my forehead with his right. Njande screamed in my ears, in my mind, and the force of *Lem*'s nature in my muscles surged above the steady roaring ocean of *my* peace in her heart as she shoved from below, and for the first time in my life I knew without a doubt that he was *with* me.

We did it.

The vent cover ripped off and flew at Diebol; the flayer cartridge meant for me ricocheted off it as Lem scrambled out of her prison. The vent smashed Diebol's chest, knocked him stumbling backwards over the Revelonian's dead body into the puddle of blue blood—

The floor rumbled. Diebol's eyes widened. I grinned.

The room lit up with orange as the missile thundered; a column of flame shot out the open vent; heat radiated from the tiles under me.

The missile was airborne.

JEN FINELLI, MD

All three of us leapt for the controls at the same time. We became a tangle of limbs, elbows, dripping acid, claws, heat and bruises as Diebol tried to swerve the thing off course and we fought back. The screen on the wall lit up above us with soft, quiet beeps, a gentle antithesis to the brutality playing out on the bloody floor below it, and it wasn't long before the camera on the missile showed a Growen spacecraft carrier, large and pregnant with missile pods and small fighter ships.

"Change the missile's course!" Diebol screamed. "Your *sister* is on that ship!"

Lem froze.

I held Diebol back, rolling on the floor as Lem knelt, stretching for the controls—*no, Lem, no*, but could I blame her, it was her sister!

The light cast against Lem's face drew shadows like warpaint as she faced us to bare her teeth. She dropped her hand and set her jaw, soldier through and through. "I won't take the chance that you're lying," she said. "And if you're not lying, Njande's got her. Because this time, I can't. This time I'm too damn weak and tired and far away and small to rescue her. So Njande's got this one. Because my weakness is his strength."

The camera feed shook, fizzed with static, and then cut out as the missile exploded.

CHAPTER FORTY-EIGHT

Carl

HE DIDN'T REGRET THIS. THAT WAS THE WORST PART OF ALL OF this. He should regret this, right now. His armor seared his skin, heated by the laser'd maces; the blunt force pounded against his ribs, his spine, as the armor dented inward. The financial cost of this armor—

Forget the financial cost, you stiff idiot, hello, the pain!

But bathed in this presence around the girl, he didn't regret anything.

Carl tried to crawl to the door, keeping the girl safe under his shell. But he couldn't move. The electromagnetic field held him immobile while the Growen peeled him open, cracked the egg to get the girl out. No. He could close up. He was good at being closed.

The presence was a person.

A person he could—see.

"Excuse the interruption," said the person. "But I have to keep a promise to a friend."

A rift opened in the space right above Carl and the girl, like a womb in the air, and as the gap widened a being stepped through it. Carl didn't loosen his grip on the girl; he could see through the crack in the visor, past the blood trickling down his forehead, but he had to blink over and over to figure out what it was he was seeing.

It had the height and strength and life-force of a tree, but none of its stiffness; the brilliance of a star, but none of its dead heat; the raging mobility of a river but none of its coldness; the glory of a man but none of its baseness.

"It's just not your time yet, and for this timeline to work, you have to live a little longer," the being said as it lifted the four Stygges away from Carl. "And you and I don't know each other well enough to work together, which is my favorite work, so. My arm will work my own salvation."

The Stygges shrieked as the being threw them against the wall. "Sleep," he ordered.

He unwrapped Lark and Bricandor from each other. "Breathe," he ordered Lark.

"Run," he ordered Carl. "Or you will all die, and I will not save you."

Carl didn't need to look a gift-giant-thing-in the mouth. He scooped up the girl and stumbled out the polymerwall. *Make for the ship.* Blood flecked from his mouth onto his tongue; his whole body creaked and cried.

And yet, even as he left the room, it seemed like the thing stayed with him.

LARK

Lark scooted back against the wall, breathing like hot bellows, chest in and out as her grey ghost manifested into an enormous biped and clashed against the monster that peeled itself out of Bricandor like a worm emerging from a fruit.

What the actual blasted piddle-beans.

Bricandor screamed in pain as the thing tore out of him. Something like a hauntingly beautiful brown and purple butterfly emerged, its wings glittering with silver skulls; the ship shook when it stomped its six limbs.

"Flickerform," the Grey Ghost called it.

As the beings fought Lark suddenly realized Ghost was a name woefully misplaced. Ghosts were dead. If you murdered this energy-being twice it would still have more life in it than anyone Lark had ever seen before.

"What are you doing here, Njandejara?" The Flickerform roared. "This is my meal, none of your business!"

"Brain-child, come back!" screeched Bricandor.

"Shut up, old man," it hissed, kicking him aside like a rag as it charged the ghost.

"So you won't be helping him with this battle, I gather," said the Grey Ghost, sidestepping the attack and crossing his arms. "You know when it starts, yes?"

"Shut up! I'm hungry!" The Flickerform rose into the air and teleported, flashing like lightning towards the crack in the wall where Lark could see the Ebon Shadow staggering with Juju Benzaran. With a violent explosion the Ghost stepped in his path; the collision shook the ship.

Alright little bugger, time to stop gawking and get the filk out. Lark scrambled to her feet after the Ebon Shadow. A giant butterfly-claw crashed down beside her, as thick as a tree-trunk, spined like a rose-stem; she dashed around it, breathing hard. The Ghost pushed back the insect; as Lark left the room she saw the Ghost wink back at her over his shoulder.

Lark gripped both hands to her aching chest, stumbling over the forty or so blitzer bodies the Ebon Shadow had left behind, and ran for her life.

CARL

Even the overly-talky little bounty hunter sat in utter silence as the *Huntress* fled the spacecraft carrier's explosion. Carl glanced at the mirror on the left side of his compuscreen to look back at her. She sat by the black lacquer table in the middle of his cockpit, and the little girl slept strapped into the seat beside her.

The bounty hunter was crying.

Did every female he brought into his ship from now on plan on leaking salt-water? Because that was going to get old fast. Carl set the ship on auto-pilot to head for the Frelsi base on the planet below, and with a powerful wince rotated his chair to reach for the med-spider hanging on the wall. It disengaged from the wall; its eight legs whirred with sensors as it crawled over him, injected an anesthetic, and began to peel back his broken armor plates.

The anesthetic wasn't really strong enough.

"Oh, alright, we're just going to get undressed, right here," Lark Scrita grumbled, throwing her hands in the air. "I've got the hint, you loon, I'm going to another room. Which room won't shoot me?"

"That's unnecessary for the time being. I wear clothes under my armor," Carl smirked. Did she not? "Do you need a med-bot?"

"No, I don't. I'm breathing fine now. You check the girl?"

"Yes. Antidote delivered. She'll wake shortly." Carl bit his lip. This was a new thought. "Do you need psychological counseling? My ship can—"

"No I don't want to talk to your bloody ship," Lark snapped. "I was crying because I'm angry with that big glowy thing that saved us, and that's no affair of yours."

"It is not. But I'm considering forming a partnership with that— thing—so—data would be appreciated."

Lark dropped her cheek on her hand and laughed. "Beans, you're so stiff. Well. I do know a bit. Wild rescues aren't actually the rule of thumb with that thing. Usually it leaves your family to die." Her face contorted. She choked behind clenched teeth. "Because it's 'their time.' Never mind that *you're* not ready, out of a thousand possible universes, it chooses the one that leaves you an orphan."

Carl mused for a moment. "I'm not looking for rescues. I like the company." He almost regretted it the moment he said it. How impractical! He planned on rearranging his entire life—because he knew full well that Being would do that—for "the company"? He'd just now lost one of his most lucrative clients—

Oh shyte, he'd just lost his most lucrative clients.

Well. There really was no turning back now, was there?

LARK

Lark stood with the Ebon Shadow, watching as the groggy little girl began to mumble something and open her eyes. "What do you think he wanted with her?" Lark asked.

"You told me he wanted murder-sex."

"Yes, well. I actually have no idea what he wanted. It was creepy, it was."

Juju cuddled into the leather couch, eyes still shut, smacking her lips like a kitten. Lark elbowed the Shadow. "Ey, let me do the talking, alright, mate?" Lark said. "She'll be afraid of you."

Lark flipped the film on her shoulder back to Bont lizard and tapped Juju on the shoulder. "Hey," Lark whispered.

The girl's eyes shot open. She leapt to her feet and shoved past Lark to throw her arms around the Ebon Shadow's neck. "Mr. Hell-Spawn!" she cried. "You came back!"

Lark sat back against the black leather seat and rolled her eyes. Alright, then.

The little girl turned and pointed, one arm still around the Shadow's neck. "Hey, that lizard made me swallow a tracking device, you know."

Lark narrowed her eyes. "How'd you know that?"

"Any candy a stranger gives you is prolly a tracking device," the girl explained. "That's why you don't take candy from strangers."

"Oh." Lark scratched her head. That—made sense?

"Are we gonna play video games now?" the girl asked the Shadow.

"Well. You could tell me about Njandejara," he said.

"I don't really know a lot. I wanna play video games."

"Dammit," he muttered.

Lark whacked his shoulder. "Don't swear around kids, you blasted imbecile."

The girl whacked Lark's wrist. "You sweared," she giggled.

"Psh." Lark leaned back with her hands behind her head as the little girl climbed off the Shadow's lap to scoop up a video game controller and turn on the compuwall behind the pilot's seat. It was quiet now. Lark psyched herself up for a few, deep breaths, and got her story ready as she turned to the Shadow to ask—

"You could stay on my ship for a few months," he said. "You're the first person I've ever worked with who I haven't killed. That seems like a good sign."

Lark stiffened. Beans, she'd wanted to ask for exactly that, but when he put it that way, not so much. "I'll think about it," she said, feigning nonchalance. "If I don't have too many of my own jobs coming in."

"We would share jobs."

"Oh, right, because you just lost your cash-cow."

"Yes. You have some new contacts I could use." He didn't seem at all ashamed of that. Beans, this bloke was so bloody honest. This might be awkward.

"Warning. I'm five years older than you and terrible with women," he said.

What? "Ha! You've got nothing to worry about, mate, I don't go for masks," Lark snarked, eyeing the outline of his abs all the same. "How the blazes you know how old I am, anyway?"

"It's my job to know."

Definitely a phrase she'd be adopting. As a wise fellow once said, "great artists steal ..."

"We're not taking money for the little girl," Lark said suddenly. "Just so you know." A part of her wanted him to argue, but she was glad when he didn't. Juju's video game turned on, and other than that they flew in silence.

The grey ghost in her peripherals smiled. Lark reached out her hand into his space with a sigh, and for a moment just let him be there, comforting in his untamable presence. She didn't forgive him. Perhaps one day she would.

And as she quietly slipped a copy of her business card to the Ebon Shadow, finally, *finally* someone asked her where she'd gotten it made.

"I actually kidnapped a woman for these ..." she began.

CHAPTER FORTY-NINE

Cinta

THE AWAKENER ... HE HAD TO WARN THEM ABOUT THE AWAKENER ...

"I would say that baring his form to the flesh-bags like a disrobing whore was the last straw, but I've said it so many times it's becoming ludicrous. Njandejara has made a mockery of interdimensional pride."

"Never fear. His weakness is easy: the pain of his little ones hurts him more than it does them. We go through them. This Jerusha-Lem, first. Our researchers have determined she's slated to destroy the universe in every timeline but one—and that one requires the one thing Njandejara cannot do. It's unfortunate for him that he's fallen in love with her."

"What is unfortunate is that we can't travel to check the timelines ourselves."

"It doesn't matter. We are many. Keep the feeders sucking energy out of their dimension, and the rest of you continue infiltration. Flickerform, how is Bricandor?"

"He heals. I had to teleport him to safety, and that never goes well. I hate him dearly, but his power grows delicious. I begin to believe he'll live until the end of time."

"Accuser, you will take care of Jerusha-Lem, will you not?"

"From this day onward I will never leave her alone."

Cinta groaned. "Leave her alone," he whispered.

"Cinta?"

A different kind of voice reached his ears. He flicked them to the side; the dream-wraiths faded as a slow ache settled over his whole body and light tickled his eyelids.

"Cinta, did you say something?"

A naked, furless hand brushed against his forepaw. He opened his eyes.

"Jaika," he croaked. "Where am I?"

Jaika ran to the window as he blinked in the light. She wiped her hand across the window's surface, and it became transparent, blinding him with the welcome scene of Luna-Guetala jungle. A singing horned frog scampered along a branch, and in the distance a cluster of lechichi fruit called his name.

Jaika dashed back to the bedside and wrapped her arms around his neck, nuzzling his shoulder. Her dark skin seemed to gleam against the dull tan walls of the Biouk hospital; when she stood she almost reached the thatched roof. "You look so healthy," Cinta said. "How long did I sleep?"

"Almost a month!" Jaika cried. "Everyone said you weren't gonna make it. I wish you could meet the doctor who saved your life, but the Frelsi transferred you home before you woke up. How you feeling? Should I go get Mali?"

"No—wait," Cinta whispered. "I have time to see everyone later. Right now, I want to tell you something so important."

Jaika sat by the bed and leaned close to him, slipping her long hands around his small paws. The time when her hands fit inside his —he still remembered that. "I got something to tell you, too," she said. "I wanna become a pacifist."

Cinta's ears straightened atop his head. "Well. That is a bit strange. Because I want to join the Frelsi. I must tell your Captain."

Jaika's eyes grew heavy like ripe fruit. "He's dead, Cinta."

Cinta's breath stilled, hanging in his chest stunned, as if it feared the air.

Live by the sword, die by the sword ...

Some things are worth sword-dying for.

For many minutes, no one spoke. Maybe for Jaika people died all the time, or maybe, because words changed nothing, she changed the subject. It shocked Cinta that she did.

"I'm tired of death, Cinta, and I don't think pacifism and warfare have to be mutually exclusive anymore," she said. "Jei and I, we've got this idea about warriors who don't kill …"

Cinta sighed, and settled further into the soft featherbed, listening. *Her* ideas, he always loved, and he treasured the knowledge that she felt safe sharing with him, even when, at times, she sounded like a fish describing flight. He hoped joining the Frelsi would not mean putting his dreams for a clinic and a family on hold. He did so want—

A family? He did not have claws.

"Hey. Something wrong?" Jaika stopped talking.

"No. No, it is fine. Njande will make it worth it." But Cinta's ears drooped. The future looked terrifying and big already, twisting all three of his stomachs because people could be there one day and dead the next, and ba-eaters were whispering revenge, and all this without claws …

Jaika followed his gaze and sighed. She lifted his forepaws to her lips. "Oh, Cinta," she whispered. "Dear, dear Cinta. I'll be your claws."

He shook his head. "I must learn to adapt."

"I'll be your temporary claws, then."

A soft laugh breathed through his muzzle. She was so earnest … he would believe this fish could fly.

DIEBOL

Diebol walked by Bricandor's quarters for the fifth time today, twirling a knife in his fingers. So Bricandor didn't like Diebol's explanation for his failure to prevent the spacecraft carrier's explosion. Well, Diebol didn't like Bricandor's *lack* of explanation for how he'd magically survived it.

Nevertheless, Teacher, I'm always glad to see you well, Diebol thought.

But he knew. And perhaps he'd always known. His master spoke to an interdimensional.

Diebol wasn't pleased with himself. He'd had to kill thirty civilians or so to make his retreat out of the missile center, and after the whole fiasco—Diebol's hidden training center, Lem and Jei stealing that missile as fake blitzers, the flights through the Undecided Zone —Revelon wanted to join the Frelsi. But at least Diebol still believed they could beat Njandejara as *humans*, as *sapients*, without groveling before monsters. Was Bricandor even truly electromagnetic? What kind of deals did he make, and what hold did invisible creatures have over him, that they broke the laws of space to save him?

Diebol didn't bother hiding the thought. He knew Bricandor expected it. He'd obey. He'd bide his time.

But the alpha wolf should watch his throat.

JEI

Today was the day we began our secret order. Paradox Warriors. A bit dramatic, like Lem, but I liked it. The tree-frogs were singing at the top of their tiny lungs in the sun as we signed out an air-rider to take us into the forest.

We didn't say much until we left the fort. We kept near the trees, because we both still feared open spaces now. Heaven help me next time I went home: Alpino was *all* open spaces.

I parked the air-rider under a part of the tree where a little stream ran through its trunks, where the earth between its charcoal roots was soft to the step. Lem hopped off.

I looked after her for a moment. Her new secret "duty" to "Save the Universe from Heat Death" was hard to swallow and harder to believe, but I really didn't have any good questions; she didn't even seem to know much herself, and yet she was already planning on devoting all her energy to it. That was how she did things—all in, hard and fast. It was a great way to die. I was beginning to realize it wasn't a terrible way to live, either. It just wasn't my way.

We split up to look for stones. Was I even up for this? Maybe I didn't have the wildness it took to start a Warrior Order.

I wandered back to the air-rider, and followed Lem's boot-prints a few paces.

"Hey Lem?" I asked, leaning against a trunk behind her.

"Yeah?" She turned, crouching, cradling four stones in her arm and shielding her eyes with the other hand as stray drops of sun glittered through the leaves onto her face.

"You love Njande a lot, right," I said.

"Yeah. I hope so."

"How do you trust him?"

"What do you mean?"

"If we're most ourselves when we're with him—like how a fish is most itself when it's surrounded by water—that implies completeness. As if you can't go halfway."

"Uh, guess so? A fish half-in the water is kind of gonna die. So?"

"So that's a pretty big dive. How do you know he's water, and not boiling acid?"

"Because boiling acid sucks, and he doesn't."

I looked at her in silence for a moment as the smooth tree-bark hugged my side. I really hated that answer.

She noticed. "You know he's good, dude, he's proven it over and over again. But honestly? At some point I don't care if he's acid or water or whatever. He's my friend, and he gives all of himself, so I give all of myself, and if it's bad I don't care."

"You're an addict."

"I wish. You okay?"

I stuck my hands in my tunic pockets and sighed. "Yeah. I'm okay."

"No ba-eaters or anything?"

"No."

I wandered back off to do my part with these stones. I found an odd red one, and a soft mossy one, and a jagged triangular one shaped like the tooth of a Crajk-beast. The diversity was beautiful. They'd make a neat stone pile; a good way to commemorate today.

What a strange multiverse we lived in. Where did I fit into it?

"Njande, what do you want from me?" I whispered. I dipped my finger into the stream—a singing tree-frog sprung onto my hand from a wet root, resting for just an instant before hurling itself whole-heartedly into the water.

I just want you, dear one. You'll find giving that is hard enough.

Yes. I would.

CHAPTER FIFTY

The End

I AM A PARADOX WARRIOR.

I defend the weak, and my weakness is strength.

I train until I can subdue my enemy with the gentleness I would use to stop a child.

I have no attachments to anything in this world, and I am utterly attached to everything in it.

My best friend is a particle and a wave, like the electron, and like me. I treat others the way I would treat his child; I guard his heart by protecting those he loves.

I serve Njandejara, the Master of Paradoxes, and I study the opposites in the world around me, that I might know him—for that is the best thing of all.

INDEX OF TERMS AND CHARACTERS

Air-rider: Single or double-rider hovering transport vehicle, popular among civilians and the Frelsi forces for its low cost of construction and ease and safety of operation.

Alpino: Neighboring planetary system to Luna-Guetala. Various climate zones ranging from arctic to temperate zones, but due to extensive landmass and less than 50 percent oceans, much of the planet is covered in volcano-strewn prairie or cool deserts. Bereens's home planet.

Awakener: Someone who can cause another person to develop electromagnetic abilities without deadly cancerous mutation.

Ba-eater: A Biouk term for an interdimensional being that devours the human psyche. Used to describe gods and demons of multiple religions.

Bangla: A species of wide, many-trunked, vine'd tree common to Luna-Guetala jungles.

Bichank: The people group called "land-walruses" by many humans. Bear more similarity to a sentient bear with tusks. Populate Luna-Guetala jungles, but actually likely originated on the cooler planet of Alpino. Culturally similar to Biouk peoples, communicate verbally with a throaty, roaring language, and emotionally with eye movements like humans.

Biouk: See space-lemur.

Bricandor: Leader and supreme diplomat of the Growen Unification Forces. Possibly not human, but certainly human in appearance and appetites; rumored to have appeared or developed his Stygge powers after the Black Comet.

Cadet Commander: The highest rank available to a child in the Frelsi guard.

Captain Rana: Wonderfrog officer over the Eighth Combined Battalion in the refugee base at Fort Jehu, overseeing both children and adults in self and community defense. Commanding officer for Lem Benzaran, Jei Bereens, and Lem's siblings. Contaminated.

Carl and K'arl Hampt: Both alter egos of the Ebon Shadow bounty hunter, one silent and secretive, one talkative and flashy. The Ebon Shadow is the most feared mercenary in the galaxy, often hired by the Growen for jobs that would require breaking treaties with plausible deniability.

Cinta: Pacifist space-lemur from Luna-Guetala, 26 revolutions old, currently studying interspecies biomedical science to become either a researcher or a healer—he hasn't decided. Lem Benzaran grew up as his little sister for a few years, and since they have remained close.

Contaminated: A derogatory term for a matter-based, sentient being who speaks to interdimensional energy beings, usually specifically Njandejara.

Contested Zone: The areas not covered by the Spaces Treaty. On Contested planets, the Growen and the Frelsi fight for dominance. On Independent Planets in the Undecided Zone, neither is authorized outright displays of force. The Growen hold that all Frelsi allied-planets fall within the Contested Zone, but that Growen-occupied planets do not.

Dr. Patty Loylan: Physician assigned to the Eighth Combined Battalion at Fort Jehu. Also participates in interspecies research. Shy. Not contaminated.

Enforcer: The second-highest rank available to older children.

Fort Jehu: One of the larger Frelsi bases on Luna-Guetala, about an hour's journey by air-rider south of Retrack City.

Frelsi: Conglomerate of militarized special interest groups and refugee bases organized to protect people groups punished for refusing to join the Growen Unification Project.

Grenblenian: Common trade language throughout Luna-Guetala, adopted by most planets with a mammalian presence.

Gray: Frelsi slang for members of the Growen Incursion under the Growen Unification Forces.

Growen Unification Forces: Interplanetary social organization with primary goal of uniting all sentient beings under one centralized government. Spearheaded by interest groups claiming to defend the universe from interdimensional brain invasion by eliminating Contaminated people.

Jared Diebol: 21-year-old male soldier in the Growen Unification Forces, highly advanced to commander status given his Stygge training, electromagnetic abilities, and unusual voracity. Specialized knowledge of Frelsi electromagnetic pair due to his close mental relationship with Jei Bereens. Not contaminated; obsessed with curing contamination.

Jei Bereens: 17-year-old male freedom fighter, ward of the Frelsi refugee system. One of two known electromagnetic humans in the Frelsi forces. Highly trained, with specialized knowledge of Growen systems and technology due to his childhood in Growen captivity. Arch-enemy of Jared Diebol, opposite of Jerusha-Lem Benzaran. Contaminated, but resents it.

Jerusha-Lem Benzaran: 15-year-old female freedom fighter, ward of the Frelsi refugee system. One of two known electromagnetic humans in the Frelsi forces. Highly trained, with specialized knowledge of Biouk space-lemur society due to childhood living among the space-lemurs. Contaminated.

Juju Benzaran: 9-year-old female ward of the Frelsi refugee system, pre-fighting age. Quiet, with talents in early communication, unusual protection spell from Njandejara. Sister of Lem Benzaran. Possibly contaminated.

Lark Scrita: 16-year-old human living her life as a famed sixty-year-old Bont bounty hunter. Not contaminated, but the child of a contaminated couple killed by the Growen. Unallied.

Lechichi: A fruit common to Luna-Guetala jungles.

Lieutenant Seria: 20-year-old female freedom fighter, ward of the Frelsi refugee system, highly trained in communication and investigative skills. Not contaminated.

Luna-Guetala: The only known habitable binary or "double-planet" system, differentiated from a simple planet-moon system by the sheer size of the smaller celestial body. Luna, the smaller, more temperate twin, is often mistakenly called a moon by LG inhabitants. Neighbors the Alpino planetary system.

Officer Scritch: Local Biouk law enforcement officer in the civilian settlement near Fort Jehu on Luna-Guetala.

Njandejara: Interdimensional energy being interested in befriending matter creatures. Differentiated from other energy beings by being outside time, as well as outside space; rumored to be the ancient origin of all species. Considered a mental illness by Growen scientists, and a dangerous invasion force by Growen philosophers.

Meat-man: Frelsi slang for perpetrators of sentient trafficking, whether through slave trade, brothel ownership, or actual sale of sentient beings for edible consumption.

Retrack City: Large, cosmopolitan area occupied by the Growen forces during latter period of the Growen-Frelsi conflict for Luna-Guetala. Most populated and culturally celebrated spaceport on LG. About an hour's ride by air-rider north of Fort Jehu.

Revelon: Planet in the Uncontested Zone with fairly low gravity, mostly cool climates, and thin mountain ranges, inhabited by tall mammalians with keratinized, thick, rock-like skin.

Space-lemur: The human slang term for the Biouks, a sentient tree-dwelling race of omnivorous mammals characterized by small stature about half the height of an average human, enormous ears often as large as the head, powerful claws, a lack of tail, fangs that extend to the chest in adult specimens, and an extended lifespan often over a hundred Luna-Guetala revolutions. Divided into "moon" and "planetary" subspecies, with the "moon" species dwelling on the Luna twin of the Luna-Guetala twin planetary system. Language comprised of harsh, throaty sounds and snarls; emotions often communicated with ear movements.

Stygge: A person gifted with electromagnetic abilities who has allied themselves either with the Growen, or with another force bent on eliminating the Contaminated.

Undecided Zone: The areas covered by the Spaces Treaty. On Contested planets, the Growen and the Frelsi fight for dominance. On Independent Planets in the Undecided Zone, neither is authorized outright displays of force. The Growen hold that all Frelsi allied-planets fall within the Contested Zone, but that Growen-occupied planets do not.

Wonderfrog: The human slang term for the Bwangam people, a semi-amphibious sentient group with a body plan similar to a human-sized frog. Native to Luna-Guetala, but also population range includes the Burburan swamp systems. Language comprised of rounded, guttural sounds, with frequent repetition; emotions communicated with changes in skin color and aggressive, expressive body language.

ABOUT THE AUTHOR

Jen Finelli is a world-traveling sci-fi author who's ridden a motor-cycle in a monsoon, swum with sharks, crawled under barbed wire in the mud, and hiked everywhere from hidden coral deserts and island mountains to steaming underground urban tunnels littered with poetry. She was once locked inside a German nunnery, and recently had to find her way through swamp-filled Korean foothills dotted with graveyards on Friday the thirteenth under a full moon without a flashlight. On her quest to rescue stories often swallowed by the shadows, she's delivered babies, cradled the dying, and inter-viewed everyone from prostitutes to senators. If you want cancer-fighting zombie fiction, dinosaur picture books, scientists jumping into volcanoes, or talking cars and peyote legislation, you might like Jen. You're welcome to download some of her stories for free at byjenfinelli.com/you-want-heroes-and-fairies, or join her quest to build a clinic for the needy at patreon.com/becominghero. Jen's a practicing MD, FAWM candidate, and sexual assault medical forensic examiner—but when she grows up, she wants to be a superhero.

Byjenfinelli.com

IF YOU LIKED ...

If you liked Neodymium Exodus, you might also enjoy:

Alternitech
by Kevin J. Anderson

Taylor's Ark
by Jody Lynn Nye

Echo One: Tales from the Secret World Chronicles
by Mercedes Lackey & Others

OTHER WORDFIRE PRESS TITLES BY KEVIN O'DONNELL

Neodymium Betrayal

Our list of other WordFire Press authors and titles is always growing. To find out more and to shop our selection of titles, visit us at: wordfirepress.com

THE SECOND NOVEL OF THE NEODYMIUM, A SWEEPING SPACE OPERA SERIES BY JEN FINELLI, MD!

Across the solar systems...

On a normal day of mace-wielding duels and interplanetary sabotage, young Jei Bereens has things under control. He's plagued by night-terrors and an arch-enemy as slippery as the grime on his gun, but freedom fighters all around the galaxy look to him for help. He's got the favor of a mystical energy being and a best friend who'd die for him. On a normal day, Jei is legend.

Today is not a normal day.

Today, Jei broke an enemy soldier's mask and found his worst nightmare inside. Tomorrow, Jei's best friend will sell him out to his archenemy in the name of saving her Universe. And the next day, Jei will disobey orders and break promises to take his best friend down. **May the Fourth, 2022**

CPSIA information can be obtained
at www.ICGtesting.com
Printed in the USA
BVHW081325121021
618739BV00005B/104

9 781680 571851